Treaty of Versailles, The Power of Love

Treaty of Versailles, The Power of Love
By Michael Lachance

Skipper Pete Books
David City, NE

Skipper Pete Books
PO Box 283
David City, NE 68632

Paperback ISBN: 9781310893964

To the men with the upside pink triangle who were arrested, incarcerated, battered, and executed in Nazi concentration camps or by the Gestapo, God bless them and give them peace.

Prologue

Berlin, 1931, Erich joined the Brownshirt's when they were just another political party vying for power amongst many other parties in Germany.

The Brownshirt's power expanded and they often fought with other political parties. One night, Erich killed a communist sympathizer during a bar brawl. He fled and knew then he had to flee the Brownshirts or become a Storm Trooper under Hitler.

Erich and, his love, Nikki left for Canada.

Several months later, Nikki's mother demanded he return to Berlin to help her. Nikki returned, was arrested by the Gestapo, and sent to Dachau.

Despite the dangers, Erich would not let Nikki suffer or die a slave in a concentration camp. To save his love, he had to become what he hated most, a Nazi. He returned to Berlin with a plan to save Nikki.

Contents

CHAPTER 1: THE PSYCHIATRIST

Canada, 1954, it was warm outside for April and how the music had changed from 1931 when I was twenty and lived in Berlin; it was different, louder, and faster. Walter Jurmann had a great tune, "'Veronika, spring has come' from the 1920's that I liked." Nikki and I used to dance out of the sight of others at a club in Berlin. Now, the music of today upsets my stomach. Some tune played in this room to calm the patients I imagine, but I preferred the music from those days when we lived in Berlin.

Berlin was alive with such fun places, but soon after the Brownshirts and their agenda came into the lives of Germans, the fun was over. I was young and Nikki was young. We didn't care of such things or the Brownshirts. The terribleness of the first war, the Great War, was over and The Treaty of Versailles made sure Germany's guilt for the Great War would be known for years by debt and by destruction. We just wanted happiness and love again, but guilt is hard to overcome when your people are to blame.

The guilt I felt was heavy like the murky white haze in this waiting room from a smoker's pipe. Despite fresh flowers, there was a terrible feeling that this place mourned our souls and we all hoped for salvation. The secretary, a young woman with ugly hair, nodded at me as if to comfort me or flirt with me. I wondered if she had decorated this place as it was not what I expected from a Jew.

Surely, there would be some things of the Jewish faith,

trinkets perhaps like a Menorah. What I recalled of the Jews is they were kind people, busy people... so were we back then. Nikki was a student and I worked as a political liaison at the Reichstag. We always told people we were just friends, because it was safer for us.

Our friends thought of us as a cute couple, because Nikki was a boyish looking blond and I was dark and handsome. There was a darkness, but it was buried deep inside me and the darkness was not handsome, it was full of heartbreak.

For Nikki, the past haunted him too, but he managed better. As for me... when I closed my eyes to sleep, I wished for the daytime so my eyes were open and I'm not asleep. For me, sleep was when my thoughts terrorized me over things I did to other people, terrible things.

I unbuttoned my jacket as the warmth from my chest built up and it was hot. Damn Nikki to make me come for this, for my nightmares; they woke me in the night—not the middle, not the end, and not the beginning of the night, somewhere it was terrible to wake me, like when I was at my deepest and most peaceful moment in sleep.

Just then the door opened to the office, a door to an office within this one, "Mr. Smith?" Dr. Scherbit looked at the faces and I stood. He went back in his office and I followed. Just as I entered, he shut the door and had a pipe steadied in his mouth, his thick moustache covered half the distance of the pipe. "How are you feeling?"

How can he ask such nonsense to people who come to a psychiatrist? "Fine," the windows were open, curtains pulled back, and there was a chaise and a chair that faced a large clock; the chair and chaise had their backs to the door and there was a lamp by the window. Across from them was a bookcase with many medical books and a menorah. His desk was just to the right of the chaise.

Dr. Scherbit was shorter than me, perhaps five - five or five - six. He was stocky for a Jew and only a few years older. Would he know when he heard my words that I was a German? I can only say Erich one way as the "r" rolled off my tongue, "Err-ich" as a German would say a German name, a common German name. I nearly said, "ja" when he said my last name as this was a fake name, "Smith."

He motioned for me to sit in the chair, "for now."

"Yes," I barely got out without an accent, but how does he know anything. I could be Austrian or maybe Dutch. No, not Dutch, but Austrian.

"So, your name is Schmidt?"

My gaze must've widened, though I didn't feel it; it was wide. "No," before I said "ist," I licked my lips, "is it not spelled correctly? S, m, i, t, h? As you said it in the lobby?"

"Yes, but your numbers to your home, one-seven-eight," he grinned at me.

"So," what does it matter? He reads the numbers?

"People here do not put the cross through their sevens or mark their ones as you have. This is a European thing." He closed the file, "I thought your accent was German and so, is it Schmidt?"

My face warmed as I turned and looked at the door. I wanted to leave. "It *ist* Schmidt."

"The door has two sides Mr. Schmidt; on this side there is help and, on that side, there are reasons you came." He looked at his pencil, but did not pick it up. "I'm Dr. Scherbit. What can I help you with?"

I wiped my forehead. Could it be that hot in here? To say all this was for Nikki was selfish, but it was his thought to come here, his thought to see a Jew for this matter and his thought to see me well. "I'm here for... some problems to solve."

"Good," he drew his hand down his chin. "What type of problems?"

I was straight forward as there was little else to hide, "To save someone... a freund, I became an SS."

Dr. Scherbit's eyes did not widen, flinch, or blink. "You mean a... NAZI." He nodded at me.

"What is that nod!" My chest felt like an oven was pressed

against it.

He sat back calmly, "Es ist ein Kopfnicken, um fortzufahren," which roughly translated to "a nod to continue."

I was, now, soaked with my sweat and Nikki liked to see me sweat. When I thought quickly through some moments in the past of when I should have sweated like an animal, I didn't, because that was my training, not to let the enemy see me sweat.

"I'm... not comfortable with my back to the door." He stood and motioned for me to go to the chaise. He got one end of it, lifted and we turned it so that I would face the door. The windows were covered with a light curtain besides a heavier curtain. The noise from the street was riddled with people who talked, engines that roared, and birds who chirped. "May I close the window?"

"Bitte," he said.

I pulled the window down and the closed the curtains, then returned to the chaise. As I laid back, he sat in the chair with his back to the door. He did not pick up his pencil or pad. "Your first name is Erich?"

"Ja... yes," I said.

"Please begin," he said.

I thought for a moment and saw so many things that I didn't know where to start, but as my mutter would say, "to begin, start at the beginning." A chuckle pushed through my pursed lips for a moment before I felt sorrow for her.

"So, you found the beginning." He said.

My heart sank when I thought about it all. Yes, I found the beginning. "I was a young man in 1931 and Nikki was younger when we met." So, my pain flowed like a frozen lake and spring came to it ... a thaw began. I am lost in my mind amid all the thoughts, bad and horrible, but with some good things though I felt I could not speak a word of it.

I looked at the lamp in the corner of the room; its glow was luminescent and did not hurt my eyes. When I was young, I had a mysterious friend... a ghost, if there are such things. My ghost came to me in a faded white glow, much like the glow of the lamp. Her glow warmed me when I was sad and comforted me when I was scared. Because I am ridden with guilt about my story, she will tell it; she will be a guide, the white glow through that dark time in mine and Nikki's life.

Erich breathed in deeply and studied the lamp's luminescent glow. "I am here to remember, so... so I can forget these terrible things."

"You mean forgiveness." He dipped his head, "but you understand I am no priest."

Erich turned sharply, "I said, forget."

"No human being ever forgets, Erich," he took a toke from his pipe. The smoke rose over his head in a steady line and then dissipated into a soft white cloud across the ceiling, "so you must forgive yourself and then the bad energy of those emotions will subside... what you refer to as forget." Dr. Scherbit rubbed his hands together and put his pipe out.

Erich's face burned and he turned to face the door. He nearly got up to leave and then saw Nikki's face. He wouldn't betray him, so he sighed so heavy that his breath pushed the pipe smoke out and away. He laid back and looked at the lamp, his eye lids fell shut. "Indeed, Nikki was always in my eyes. I was quite comfortable and happy." His tense muscles relaxed, gravity pulled at his body, and the chaise welcomed him.

The white light faded away and he was back in Berlin, 1931 - spring. The park was quite nice and there among the trees was a handsome young man who held a book on socialism. He had dirty blond hair and a smooth face; surely, he would pass the test for Aryan purity.

Erich walked over and stood there, just close enough to disturb the young man. The leaves overshadowed the young man and Erich did not want to take his eyes from him. He sighed loud and the young man was compelled to say something.

"At the zoo, there are animals as loud." He pushed his wire framed round glasses up his nose. He wiggled them and Erich was, at first, offended, but then he realized he had been rude. The young man was not effeminate or grand; he behaved as any young man, stout and with a tough façade.

"I... sorry," Erich looked at him and grinned, "I mimicked a bear. Was it good?"

The young man set his book down. "My name is Nicholas VanEch. I'm at school in Berlin and am a lover of science and socialism."

"And one who loves to be frank and pointed so as to push away interest." Erich snapped at him.

Nicholas, caught off guard by this remark, stood and dusted himself off. He extended his hand and they shook. "I'm not here to look for friends. Truly, I'm here for my studies."

Erich looked at his watch, "but our picnic?"

"What?" Nicholas crossed his arms, "What picnic?"

"Here... you said you'd be by this tree and have a book on socialism." In the distance, two Brownshirts headed towards them.

"You're quite funny. No, I said no such thing." Nicholas saw the Brownshirts and he trembled.

Other people nearby rushed away to avoid unwanted questions by the Brownshirts.

"Forgive me, my name is Erich Schmidt." That's when Erich saw Nicholas's gaze fixed on the Brownshirts.

"We have some trouble." Nicholas said.

The Brownshirts stopped and stood right next to Erich. They were as young as Erich and Nicholas. In fact, one looked younger than Nicholas, a teenager. "Papers," he said.

Erich turned to face them and reached into his pocket. "Papers, as if you have the authority to ask?"

"We may ask whomever we want." The older of the two stepped towards Nicholas.

"Come now Erich, you have them." Nicholas hands trembled as he handed the man his identification.

Erich pulled wrapping papers from his pocket, "ah, here."

The younger Brownshirt took them and threw them down, "your papers!" He got in Erich's face.

"Erich," Nicholas pleaded.

"I'm a member of the Reichstag office. Schmidt, Erich Schmidt and here are my papers." He pulled his identification out, passed the young man and showed the older man.

"Schmidt, Erich?" He glanced at Erich's identification and then handed it back, "Kommen sie, Körbl." He eyed Erich and knew of him, nodded, and they left.

Nicholas fair skin was reddish around his cheeks and it wasn't from that cool spring day. As the Brownshirts got further away, he whispered, "Are you crazy!"

Erich turned to him and smiled. "No, not crazy... I will not be bullied."

Nicholas picked up his books and wiped the sweat from his forehead, "you... you are dangerous!" He dropped two of his books and Erich reached for them, "ah!"

They bumped their heads. As Nicholas stood, Erich picked up the books and held them. "Nikki, I am not dangerous."

"Nikki?" He reached for his books, but Erich kept them at his side, "my books Erich, please."

"Calm down, you'll draw attention to yourself." He smiled slyly.

"I will... I will draw attention!" He reached for the books again and then looked to see where the Brownshirts had gone; they were nowhere to be seen. Nikki, in a strong, but reserved tone, "give me my books and my name *is* Nicholas."

Erich handed them over, "You should know you are safe with me."

Nikki got the books tucked under his arm and walked off. Erich followed him as they headed out of the park and past the fountain where three statues of nude boys poured water into the pond from their vases. "Nikki, there's a café just there on Straße - 8."

"My name isn't Nikki!" He turned and faced Erich, "and what do I care about a café?"

"For me to make a proper apology I must get you dinner; our picnic was ruined by the SA." Erich motioned with his hand to the café across the street. "Wouldn't it be nice to eat?"

Nikki shook his head and then gave in, "don't know why I would agree, though I've just noticed your eyes and the blue is quite nice, even with dark hair." He shook his head, turned, and they walked across the street to the café.

The lights in the cafe glowed and then blinded Erich.

Dr. Scherbit tapped his pipe on a marble ash tray. The sound was nearly as bad as a hammer on a piece of brick! "Sorry, but the time," he said.

Erich sat up and looked at the clock to his side since he moved the chaise. "And this is how you calmly alert your patients?"

Dr. Scherbit thought for a moment, grinned, and then nodded, "Yes, you chose not to have the clock as your guide, so we are at the half hour." He got Erich's file and looked at the papers in it. "Thank you for completing the questionnaire." He closed it, "I will look it over and, now, have some idea of where we will go in our sessions." He got his pipe and lipped it. "So, you'll come after work, six-thirty?"

"Ja, six-thirty on Wednesday s," Erich stood, smoothed out his trousers and jacket.

"Good, then we will see each other next Wednesday for one hour." Dr. Scherbit got his notepad and pencil.

"Good day... Herr Scherbit." It was more appropriate to say doctor, but Erich wasn't pleased.

"Mr. Schmidt." Dr. Scherbit said as Erich grabbed the door knob, jerked the door open, and left!

He went onto the streets of Québec City and was distraught over the meeting; he didn't want to go anyways. He got to the corner street, waited a moment before he took out a cigarette and pushed up against the office building. The wind wasn't too terrible, so he lit up and smoked. People passed by and he thought to himself as he saw older men, had they been in the war? A puff of white smoke hung near him, "So, you are here to comfort me?" He walked off. The trail of smoke from his cigarette went over his shoulder and floated behind him, "not now."

Nikki made sweet and sour red cabbage with bean soup. He knew the smell of his bean soup would hang in the hallway as Erich came up. He thought it would help to soothe his nerves when he returned from the doctor's appointment.

Erich turned another street and headed back to the flat which was a mile or so from the doctor. He walked at a pace like a German foot soldier and drove his heels into the sidewalk. If other people around him weren't busy with their own thoughts and the noises of cars and buses, they'd have stopped and been terrified to hear his heels slam the ground!

Their flat was a nice place in east Quebec City that bordered the Fleuve - St. Laurent River and was along the Chemin St. Louis Street. Erich, despite the lingering bad feelings, felt better. "Nikki," he said aloud and was at their building. He threw his cigarette to the ground and stamped it out with his heel; Nikki hated the smell of cigarettes, because, like the past, the wretched odor lingered and upset him. Erich opened the door, exhaled hard, and then went upstairs.

He opened the door to their flat and went in. The smell of bean soup and red cabbage were so strong that Erich nearly dismissed the visit to Dr. Scherbit.

"Erich!" Nikki came into the hallway with his apron on and smiled, "so?"

"So," he didn't know what else to say, but did know Nikki would keep after him until he said what happened. They hugged and kissed. Nikki pressed his forehead to Erich's.

"So, that's it? Nothing more?" They kissed again, though Erich's pursed lips weren't as nice.

Erich did his best to keep his stomach calm, "I've done what you asked."

"Ah, then little was said or done," he drew his head away and dusted Erich's shoulder off. "And your next visit?" He turned and went to the kitchen. The hallway was quite long and the rooms went off of it like branches of a tree. The kitchen and dining room were on the left side while their bedroom, sitting room and bathroom were on the right and faced the river.

"My what?"

"Next visit," Nikki said from the kitchen as Erich hung his jacket.

"Perhaps," Erich said as Nikki set the rest of dinner out. They sat down to eat and just as Erich placed his serviette across his lap, Nikki bowed his head. "Ah, yes... our prayers to the Jew king."

Nikki's eyes said everything as he looked up and stared at Erich.

Erich sighed, but not as loudly as the day at the park, "I... am sorry." He bowed his head and Nikki followed.

"Thank you, dear Lord, we are grateful for this meal and for our lives here." Nikki looked up, "bean soup."

"And my favorite, sweet and sour red cabbage," Erich let his nose hang over the cabbage, "mmm."

"Seems so funny that we could not get such a thing when we first came here," he handed the spoon to Erich.

"Ich möchte alle davon essen," Erich scooped up some cabbage and smelled it.

"In English," Nikki said.

"I... would like to all of this..." Erich struggled for just a moment. Even after twenty years, there was no way for him to simply speak English or French.

"Eat all of it," Nikki said.

"Why do we bother?"

"Because, it was to be our ..." Nikki stopped and dipped his glasses.

"Way to America," Erich ate.

"Is to be our way from here to America," Nikki waited.

"So many years and so much here, I don't think we should leave." Erich chewed up his cabbage. "And I hear the Jews have a squad looking for ex-party members."

Nikki stopped, "if you want to be ugly, then I can eat in the sitting room."

Erich stopped chewing and looked at him, "no, you may get something on the floor." He smiled to ease the moment, but

Nikki wouldn't stop.

"We can have *our* supper or not." He set his fork down.

"Fine, I will… be peaceful." Erich knew not to push him further.

"At peace… please."

Erich, warm faced, "I'm doing all that you have asked me too. I'm… I went to the Jew and …" He sighed and then looked hurt.

Nikki got up, went to him and knelt. He touched his hand, "you have done so much to be good." As Erich swallowed some ego and pride, he looked at Nikki, "do not stop."

"I have done so much evil." He said.

"But only for good." Nikki kissed his hand.

"And is there such a thing meine freund?"

"Yes, I believe it." Nikki stood and touched Erich's cheek. "You have me and I know the truth of those things." He sat down.

They did as they had for each night and each day, a routine. Erich cleared the table and set the dishes and glasses in the kitchen. Nikki washed them and put them away while Erich tended to what little bit of left overs they had from supper. He watched Nikki work and smiled. His mind drifted as he thought on what it took to save Nikki, to save him from the Nazi's. Erich's smile slowly faded and Nikki caught him.

"Have you that stone?"

Erich rolled his eyes and then set a dish down with some schnitzel on it. "Would it not be better to rub schnitzel in my hand?"

"No," Nikki's cheeks tightened, his gaze fixed on Erich, and he lips pursed. "Where is it?"

"I…" Erich sighed, grinned, and looked up and away.

Nikki took the aventurine stone from his pocket, a greenish colored piece of quartz, "to help you feel better… and for love." He winked and held out the stone. Erich stepped over to him, glanced out the window and kissed him.

"My love is there without this piece of Irish rock." He got it from Nikki.

"Not if I find you without it again." Nikki nudged him and he nudged Nikki.

"Right, so then I keep it close to my heart." He got the dish of schnitzel and covered it.

"You were never a romantic, Erich Schmidt." Nikki finished the dishes and dried them off.

"But I was steadfast in my passion for you." He smiled.

"Ja… yes," he turned and looked at Erich who closed the cooler. "Should we walk this evening?"

Erich eyed him, "and our routine?"

"You worry as if the Gestapo was there on the river front!" He waved his hand toward the window. "It's been twenty years." There was no way for Erich to say no.

That evening, it was quiet along the Saint Laurent river as they made their way towards the main street and away from the river. Erich did his best to focus on the sound of the wind, the sound of the water over rocks, and the sound of crickets. The natural calmed him, but the unnatural picked his nerves.

Nikki tapped his arm, "your stone."

Erich stuck his hand in his pocket just as they went up the steps and into the lobby of the Hotel Frontenac. He rubbed the stone and thought, "it's cold… it's smooth… it's …" The goal was to keep his mind from thinking on the past.

"Ah!" Nikki was thrilled to see a small orchestra play in the lobby. After their visit, they wound their way back to their apartment and settled in for the night. Erich watched Nikki inhale deeply, so deeply that it was like a spell of medicine and he went into a deep sleep. Erich quietly slipped from the bed and took a book from the night stand. Then, he went from the bedroom to the sitting room. Once there, he turned on the table lamp and sat in an armchair that they found at a garage sale; it wasn't a handsome chair, but was very comfortable. He sat back and looked out at the St. Laurent river.

Nikki knew Erich had dreams filled with terrible images, and Erich often got up and went somewhere else, because the images were so intense that Erich had to keep his eyes open to stop the dream. So, he often sat and read until exhaustion took over and put him to sleep.

At Dr. Scherbit's office the following week, he laid on the chaise and looked at the lamp in the corner of the room. It was only a moment as he talked about Berlin and then his eyelids slowly lowered. The wood in Dr. Scherbit's fireplace burned quite nearly to cinders and all that was left were crackles of fire as they ate up the remaining bits of wood, "POP, POP... crack." His eye lids were so heavy, "POP" and then an ember floated up into the flute.

"POP!" Erich jumped and looked around, "POP! POP! POP!" He tried to sit up and saw he was in an apartment! He felt like a heavy blanket was on top of him and he couldn't move out of the chair! "HALT! HALT!" Then, there was the noise of people running down the alley and he had to get up, he had to see what was the commotion! He pushed up from the chair and made his way to the window where he knelt and tipped his head so that he could see out! There was a man and someone else, maybe a woman, running down the alley! "POP!" The man fell and the woman screamed so loud that her voice crashed through the windows and brick!

Three men surrounded her and Erich looked quickly for the phone, "Where is it?" He must call the polizei immediately, but then he looked at the alley and realized just then that there was no river! He turned back to his room and it was not the room in Quebec City! The men spoke German and the woman cried, "Why?"

"Juden!" The man said. "Jew."

Erich leaned over the window sill and looked at them, three Brownshirts. The light from the alley was dim and it made it hard to see the men. "It's not possible." He must alert the Canadian authorities. Then, it was clear that he was in his apartment in Berlin. "How?" He turned to the alley again, "POP!" They shot her, looked around, and then walked out from the alley and onto the main straße in front of his building. "Nikki," he went to the hallway. He stumbled as he made his way to the bedroom. "Nikki!" He yelled and got to the bed where he ran his hands all over, "Nikki!"

"Mr. Schmidt!" Dr. Scherbit grabbed his arm and shook him for a moment and then backed away.

Erich jumped up from the chaise with his fist balled and ready to punch the attacker, "DU!"

Dr. Scherbit eyed him, "You were in a state, Mr. Schmidt." Just then, the door burst opened and the secretary looked in, "Don't! It's fine." Dr. Scherbit showed his hands to Erich, showed him that they were empty and that he was not a threat. "We're fine, Lucy."

"Wer bist du?" Erich looked at the secretary as she closed the door and then turned to Dr. Scherbit. Heavy beads of sweat ran past his brow and along his cheeks.

"I'm Dr. Scherbit. You're in my office and you had a bad dream."

"Hilfe benotigen sie nicht, doctor," Erich shook his head and then took a huge breath.

"That's right," Dr. Scherbit moved to his desk and sat down. "It was Nikki who sent you to me." He kept his hands at his waist and then moved the to his desk.

"I... I was," he looked at the chaise, at the pipe and at the doctor. "Sheiße," he sat back down on the chaise. "It was so real."

"They are," Dr. Scherbit said. He got his pencil and pad.

Erich caught his breath and looked at the lamp; the glow from the lamp comforted him.

"You are alright to continue?" Dr. Scherbit got his chair turned to face Erich's side.

The light's soft glow brightened. "Ja, after those two were killed... it was then that I knew our troubles were so much worse. Hitler was in power, but not as Chancellor. We... we thought it was for certain that he would become this role. His influence with the National Socialist was profound."

"And that night?"

Erich studied the lamp's glow and everything turned a faded

white, "that night…"

He was in his apartment in Berlin, turned the light on and Nikki wasn't there. His heart sank and fear filled the void. He got dressed in a nice shirt, slacks and a tie. It was late, but he was sure to look sharp. He was employed at the Reichstag and could make his way around, carefully. He turned to the hallway and got his papers from the bureau by the front door. He looked at the mirror by the coat rack and his hair stood up in a few places, so he patted it down and tried to smile, "don't smile." His cheeks sunk and he was sullen. He looked at the newspaper on the bureau, "July 1932, National Socialist Win."

As he made his way onto the straße, there was a smell, "gun powder." He turned just enough to look at the lamp post and then at the alley next to his building. Were there really two bodies there? He looked around the neighborhood and it was quiet. He turned and then slowly walked to the lamp post. As he got closer, there was the sound of a small truck from down the straße. The brakes squealed for a moment, it turned, and he saw the lights shine past him. He saw the two lumps in the darkness and waited as the truck came to a stop behind him.

"Du!" A man yelled, "Polizei! Halt!"

"Erich Schmidt," he turned and held out his papers. The man eyed him as several storm troopers got out of the truck and went to the alley.

"Schmidt," he studied the papers and then eyed Erich. He handed them over without another word and waited for Erich to leave.

Erich knew to say nothing more, looked at nothing more, and walked away. He got to the next corner and hurried to get far away.

Dr. Scherbit tapped his pipe on the ash tray as their hour was up. "Erich, Erich?"

"Ja! What?" He sat up, turned and looked at Dr. Scherbit. "I… yes, it's time." He got up and went to the door.

"See you next Wednesday," Dr. Scherbit shook his head gently and watched Erich leave.

Without looking back, he went to the street. "What the hell is this I'm doing!" He shook his head, turned, and punched the brick siding! "For nothing." Blood oozed from his knuckles and the skin bruised. "Damn it."

After supper, they said barely a word to each other and Nikki knew not to push the matter. Erich was already disagreeable about going and, now, it was obvious that something had happened to upset him more. Erich didn't like that he started to talk about those times and then there was such a noise from the doctor 's pipe against the marble ash tray to stop him from his dream!

That night they laid in bed. Erich was not as mad as to be unaffectionate. He leaned over and kissed Nikki, "I'll be better once I've slept."

Nikki thought to say, *if you sleep*, but that would be a terrible thing to say, "gute nacht."

Erich did fall asleep and was asleep for a few hours before the first bad thoughts bled into his mind. The earlier meeting with Dr. Scherbit triggered the past to come to him in cold reality.

He dreamt that he was at Nikki's apartment in Berlin shortly after the man and woman were killed.

"Nikki!" Erich banged on the door.

A neighbor across from Nikki opened her door, Mrs. Damstrat, "Was ist das fur ein Gerausch?" She was mad, very mad and shook her finger at Erich. "Es ist drei Uhr morgens!"

Erich nodded as Nikki opened the door, "Entschuldigung Mrs. Damstrat, ja, ich weiß." Nikki had on his PJs and a colored shirt. Erich slipped past Nikki and got far from her.

Nikki shut the door even though Mrs. Damstrat kept shouting at them and another neighbor then began to shout at her! "Are you mad to come at such an hour!"

Erich turned on the living room light. "Pack your things."

"What?" Nikki adjusted his glasses.

"We're leaving. We can go to Canada and, from there, maybe we can cross into America." Erich said as they walked to the kitchen and only Nikki could stand in there.

"You've been drinking." Nikki got a pot of coffee ready.

Erich's face warmed and he grabbed Nikki by the arm. "I have not!"

Nikki pulled away, "Erich stop, you're hurting me!" He pulled again and looked hurt as Erich came to his senses. "What has happened to you?" Just then, He heard the last of the shouting in the hall and Erich let loose of his arm, "What's happened?"

"I…" Erich wiped his mouth, wiped away the sweat, the fear and the sickness, two lumps of sickness that weren't so easily wiped away. "I…" His face was flush.

The coffee pot was fast and whistled a moment before Nikki grabbed it and set it on a pad. He poured two cups of coffee and set one down, "ah, so you were drinking."

Erich spit in the basin, stood and pushed Nikki against the wall. The cup fell to the floor and broke! "They are dead… not from drink, but from bullets." A furor ran through him, heavy and dark like the coffee spilt all over the floor.

Nikki trembled and didn't know what to say or do and that is when Erich knew he'd man handled him. "Ich bin… entschuldigung." He stepped back and looked at Nikki whose eyes welled up and his soft skin was darker now. "I am sorry."

"You come to… come to my place at three in the morning and you, you wake my neighbors to come in here and hurt me!" He turned and walked away.

"Nikki," Erich followed him to the sitting room. There was a love seat from Nikki's parents, chipped and worn, a chair and two lamps.

Nikki stood near the corner of the room, perhaps like a child who's been wrongfully punished and would not turn to face his prosecutor. "Go, go back to your home." He turned to face Erich, "I want you to go."

"I can't."

"You can come here when you behave." Nikki looked at his arms where Erich grabbed him, though he wasn't bruised, the red marks of Erich's fingers were there. "You've left a mark on me."

"They killed two people in the alley."

Nikki eyed him, "What two people?"

"I don't know, but they shot them. Then, some Gestapo or SA came and got the bodies." Erich sat down in the chair, "Juden."

"You work at the Reichstag, you must tell them." He walked over to the love seat, turned on the other light and sat down.

"Reichstag, this is just a building now for nothing good." Erich put his face in his hands and thought, "We have a chance to leave for Canada and get to safety." He drew his hands down his face, "They are arresting people like us too."

"Leave for Canada? And my parents? And my things? What about my school and friends?" Nikki crossed his arms, "in the two years we have dated Erich, you don't ever say we must do this or that."

Erich sat up, took a deep breath, and looked at Nikki, calmly looked at him and then spoke in a soft and caring tone, "I say it now my love. For our future, we *must* leave."

Nikki felt it; Erich knew more than he did about the politics, about the dangers and the shifting minds in charge. "What about mama and papa?"

"We can see if they will go."

Nikki thought about it. "Mama loves the national socialist." He wrapped his hands around his stomach, "she... she will not go. She will..."

"Nikki?" Erich looked disheartened.

Nikki looked at Erich, "I can't leave."

Erich wiped his mouth again, "If we don't leave, we are dead or we will end up locked away." That note struck hard as Nikki contemplated his parents. "My father is old and needs care."

"We can just make that we... we are going for a trip for a few weeks." Erich looked hopeful now.

"What? And put him on the ship to Canada?" Nikki shook his head. "You're asking me to leave everything and who are you leaving?" He knew it was mean, but he felt that Erich was being unfair.

Erich's mouth hung open for a moment, "You know my mother died from influenza and my father …"

Nikki looked at Erich and tapped the spot next to him on the love seat. Erich stood and went to him, "Sorry, I should not have said such a thing." They hugged, "You are not alone."

"Not if you come with me." Erich and Nikki knew then that he had to go with him. His parents would be safe and looked out for by the new party. "Please come with me."

"Erich," Nikki said.

Erich studied Nikki's expression for hope.

"Erich!" Nikki shoved him; he jumped and opened his eyes!

"Was?" He sat up from the bed, wiped his brow and looked at Nikki.

They were in their flat in Quebec City. "You've had a bad dream." Nikki touched Erich's arm sighed. "It was a dream."

"Scheiße," Erich fell back on the bed, "damn these thoughts."

Nikki hugged him as he pulled the sheets off and sat on the edge of the bed, "sorry to wake you."

"There is never a need to be sorry." He touched Erich's back to comfort him. "We will be fine."

CHAPTER 2: TRANSATLANTIC VOYAGE

Erich was on time to Dr. Scherbit's office and it was then that the door opened and Dr. Scherbit motioned for Erich to come in. He did so and moved the chaise to face the door. Then, he pulled the curtains and the window closed.

"Are you well?" Dr. Scherbit asked and closed the door.

He eyed the doctor, "I'm here." He laid on the chaise.

"And problems this week or…" Dr. Scherbit went to his desk and sat down.

"I had a dream of …." He thought for a moment, "of people who were murdered and I rushed to Nikki to say that we must leave Germany."

"You were in danger." He pushed his pencil and notepad to the side.

"Like many others," he said, leaned up, and looked at Dr. Scherbit, "Just as the Juden." He laid back down and looked at the lamp. "We made arrangements to leave for Canada."

"Please," Dr. Scherbit toyed with his pencil.

Erich turned to the lamp and the soft white glow soaked into his eyes as he drifted back to Berlin, 1932.

Nikki was devastated; his mother said if he left, he'd be an enemy of the state. She begged him to stay and to help her take care of his father. When Nikki refused and said for them to come, it was like a switch for a bulb in that instant, she turned off to his idea; she was furious, threatened to report him, and yelled at him that he was always a selfish child and never thought of anyone else, "Go!" She screamed so loud that they heard her down on the straße. Brokenhearted over his mother's decision, he left with Erich.

Erich and Nikki made their way to the coast with cash and only a few things to start life over. Nikki got a book about the French Language and Quebec City. "We can have a place near the river, which would be nice."

"Better to find work and a cheap place first." They sat quietly on deck and watched passengers walk past.

"Nein, I have given enough up." Nikki eyed him and that was that.

Erich had money and changed a great deal of it out of Reichsmarks. He pondered the what they'd left behind and how would they make a new life.

The crossing was quiet, but eerie; Erich knew that the political parties were in the midst of a great deal of change. Hitler worked to ensure that Ernst Rohm's followers were "controlled" to the cause of the party's goals. What that meant just then, Erich didn't know, but it was enough to move him to get Nikki out, to get them out of Germany... for now. "If things don't go badly, we can return as easily."

"Sure, to my mother who says that I'm an enemy of the state, a disgusting child who puts his desires ahead of his parents." Nikki tapped Erich's leg.

"She..." Erich thought to make a joke, but knew it wasn't a good idea. "She worries and spoke only from the moment."

Nikki eyed him and then turned to their view of the ocean, "Seems so calm here. There is no upset, no anger, no Brownshirts forcing themselves on us."

Erich looked at clouds in the distance and butterflies swarmed in his stomach. He hated uncertainty and everything going forward was uncertain.

"No, it's oui," Nikki said to cheer them up.

"Oui, mon cher," Erich looked around and they had the deck

to themselves, so he put his hand over Nikki's.

"Do you love me?" Nikki smiled.

Erich swallowed hard, "What kind of thing is that to ask?"

"Do you?"

Erich sighed, "With all that there is in my soul and in my heart, I love you." He leaned over and kissed his cheek. Nikki turned and they kissed quietly for a few moments before a woman, by herself, cleared her throat. They didn't part so quickly, but Erich opened his eyes and looked at her. She grinned, nodded, and then walked away.

"We don't want to upset them." Erich said.

Nikki looked at her, "She can get her own deck." They returned to their room and settled in for the night.

Despite being out at sea, Erich had a friend who worked with the NSDAP who was deeply concealed about his personal life. This friend radioed information to the ship for Erich. There was an old code that they used at the Reichstag for simple communications and this was how Erich received news about the changes in Germany.

Erich stood outside the cabin, smoked, and read the message. The message stated "underlying air of militarization of Germany against the Treaty of Versailles".

Hitler sought to become Chancellor and then use Rohm as a tool to control the storm troopers. What wasn't obvious was what Hitler would do with Rohm. By 1932 mid-year, the Nazi's were the most powerful party and there were rumors, political rumors, that Hitler wanted a great deal more.

The next evening, Erich and Nikki had dinner in the main dining room aboard ship. Erich was sure he'd see someone he knew and have to lie about the trip, but Nikki insisted that they have a meal like everyone else. They had dress jackets, but did not have black tie and Erich was concerned about two men dining with each other.

Nikki and Erich stood at the host stand. The host nodded, "Gentlemen, follow me please."

Nikki asked without lowering his voice. "Are our freunds in

trouble then?"

"It seems many people are in trouble." He kept his gaze fixed on the path ahead of them, so he wouldn't catch the eye of anyone he might know.

They sat down and looked over the menus. Erich wiped his forehead again and looked at other guests, but never made eye contact. Normally, he was a very cool, calm man, but this business of being in the main dining room with another man and on a transatlantic voyage upset him.

"Do you think Brownshirts will come in the dining room and get us?" Nikki asked and looked over his wire frame glasses to chastise Erich.

They weren't the only Germans aboard and, certainly, they weren't the only people who talked about the changes. "You must not always be so loud."

Nikki rolled his eyes, "loud? This is what you do when you tell me I'm loud." He didn't like to be pushed around and fussed with Erich.

Erich spoke in a soft, but precise way, "You are cute when you are mad at me, but your boldness may come at a price to us."

Nikki moved his leg and touched Erich's leg, "I'm wonder..."

"It's I... I wonder."

"What it matters... I'm wonder, I wonder... scheiße, my mother and my father," His cheeks, normally fair skin, turned red. "What is... am I to do if they decide to leave?"

Erich sat up, sipped his wine and nodded at the waiter who came right over and refilled it. "We will take them in and make them at home."

"And the money?" Nikki huffed.

"We have enough," he held his glass up to Nikki who did not want to toast him, "To the future."

"Heil Erich," Nikki tapped Erich's glass. The clang rang for a few seconds before Erich got his composure.

"Not so nice," Erich sipped and then set his glass down.

"So, for tonight then I will rest on the deck and read my book while you discover the future." Nikki looked at the other people in the room to cool his temper.

Erich knew it was best to just leave him alone. So, they ate and drank and then they got up.

Nikki wasn't going to go back to the room, because he knew that Erich would scold him about the "heil" part. So, he stopped and sat on a lounge chair on deck. "I'll be back soon."

Erich nodded, got a cigarette from his coat pocket, and lit up.

Nikki shook his head, "disgusting."

Erich blew smoke up and away, no need to antagonize his love. He went to the radio room and waited a moment.

The radioman pulled his headset aside and looked at Erich, "Schmidt?" He took a card from a box. "Ja, es ist ein brief for sie," the radio man was quite handsome.

"Danke," Erich nodded and gave him a folded dollar. The radio man grinned. Erich took the communique and went to the deck where he found a quiet place, a private place to read. A Polish leader, Konrad Piecuch, was murdered by the SA, "CCE" was on the note, "continued consolidation by extermination." The elimination of political rivals to grow their power. It was a phrase that was used in secret circles and strictly among people you knew you trusted. "1933 will be the turning point" was there too and "a vacation to the alps." He knew that his freund, now, sought refuge with them.

Erich got to the rail and looked at the passing waves. He took a drag, the last one, from his cigarette and flicked it into the ocean. He crumpled the letter, dangled his hand over the side to ensure it did not blow back up on deck, and let the letter drop to the sea. He watched it for as long as it was visible and then it was swallowed whole by the darkness. The next few days were uneventful and they arrived in Quebec City.

"I've got us booked at a hotel nearby." He said as he got hold of a chest, two bags and his suitcase. He motioned for a driver to come help and then, finally, they were loaded up. He dreaded the thought when they packed because Nikki was the type of person who kept everything! Erich had one suitcase and a private bag.

Nikki had the chest, two bags, a private bag and his bag with his books. Their furniture was sold to add to money needed for the move.

The driver took them to the hotel and set their things out. They agreed to leave the majority of things downstairs and it was only a few days later when they found a nice flat just across from the St. Laurent River. Nikki was so happy to have a place by the water.

What Erich didn't tell him was that, despite the money he had so much of, there wasn't much left to speak of in hand; they had to get work. Erich's knowledge of the politic was helpful, but his real skill was in financial matters; he worked with budgets at the Reichstag and knew numbers.

It wasn't long before he got a job at a bank and thought about the future; if Hitler violated the Treaty of Versailles, they would have a lot of money going for war efforts; of course, that depended in total upon the allies and what they would tolerate. By now, his contact in Berlin sent word that, in fact, the National Socialist Party was in decline and had lost many seats in the November of 1932 election. Perhaps, his freund was completely mistaken; there was little chance of Hitler's continued success and Rohm would go with him, down and out.

Erich's job at the bank went well and Nikki went to school. To get their papers, Erich enlisted other Germans who lived there and quickly made friends at the bank.

Nikki's mother contacted him twice and, now, it was the first week of February 1933. The news of the National Socialist changed; they were in power and Hitler was appointed Chancellor. She wired messages to tell Nikki that his father's health was terrible and she needed help. Nikki was afraid to say something to Erich and wired her credit from their account. Erich would find out when he looked at the "books" as he called them. Nikki was tempted to change them, but lying makes matters worse.

After work, Erich got the communique from his freund that Hitler was Chancellor of Germany and that "CCE" was approved formally; Göring was responsible for the elimination of enemies of the state. The Reichstag fire of late February scared many of the political parties and the communist were blamed. Erich's freund told him that a new Law for the Protection of People and State was put in place, after the fire, with little opposition. He stood by the river with a cigarette and then looked at a street lamp; he thought that the light was far too bright, too loud, and tried to look away, but couldn't.

"Erich?" Dr. Scherbit tapped his pipe on the ash tray, "Mr. Schmidt!"

Erich snapped to and got up quickly, "What!"

"It's alright... your session." Dr. Scherbit stood up. "We've finished for today."

"I... ja, sorry," Erich stood and wiped the sleep from his eyes. He was in a daze, turned, and bumped the chaise, "sorry."

"No need, you did quite well and we are making progress." Dr. Scherbit walked over to the door, "next Wednesday then, six this time?"

"Ja, yes, of course," Erich got to the door, got his jacket, and was still in a daze.

He got home and looked for Nikki as he walked down the hall, "Nikki?" Then, he went to the kitchen and his sullen heart warmed up like flowers on a spring day. Nikki made red cabbage with dumplings. He knew not to touch things as Nikki would get irritated. He went to the fridge and got a bier, then turned back to the hallway and realized he hadn't removed his jacket. "Nikki?"

So much was on his mind after the doctor visit that he didn't think of it. He returned to the hall, hung his jacket, and then went to the sitting room. He sat quietly and did what he could to clear his head and that's when he saw the aventurine rock, "for love." He got the rock, held it in his hand and set his bier down. He held it tight and looked out the window. His knuckles turned a soft white as the blood pushed away from the top of them and his pressure on the stone built up. "Relax," he said, but it felt like the moment with the doctor was still with him, much like a lingering cold that made your throat sore days after the sneezes stopped. His eye lids fought to stay up, but gave in and slowly closed over his eyes. His mind, still dwelling on the meeting with Dr. Scherbit, found itself back in Berlin.

"Was?" He was in a bar with other Brownshirts and men from the communist party who yelled at each other! Erich wore a Brownshirt and was in a daze until a bottle flew past his head and hit a fellow Brownshirt in the face! The glass cut the young man's face and he threw his hands up to his face to stop the bleeding, but the blood came through his fingers!

The other Brownshirts pushed past him and a brawl ensued! A communist punched him and he recoiled; he turned and slugged the man! Then, he joined the melee and kicked another man, punched him and then grabbed a stein and slammed the man's head with it! The man whipped around, but did not fall. He pulled a knife from his side and thrust it at Erich!

Erich flung his body out of the way! He pulled his knife and swiped at the communist man! The man spat at Erich and kept swinging his knife at him as the other men fought around them! Erich looked for a way out and the Polizei whistles echoed outside on the straße, but there was no way past that man. The man charged Erich, swung his knife across Erich's chin and cut him! Erich felt his chin, saw the blood, and looked at the man who charged him again! Erich drew back and then thrust it into the man's chest!

"Ah!" The man screamed and then slumped onto Erich. Blood seeped onto the blade, and down to Erich's hand where it soaked into his pores. Another Brownshirt grabbed Erich!

"Gehen wir!" He shouted at Erich. "Gehen wir!"

Erich looked at this young communist man and saw the color in his eyes fade. It was then that his fellow Brownshirt jerked him from the dead man and they fled from the bar!

"Nicht mich!" Erich yelled!

Nikki grabbed him and screamed at him, "Erich! Stop it!"

Erich opened his eyes, swung his arms around, and gasped! "Nikki!"

"Erich!"

He blinked and dug his fingers into his eyes to get them to adjust. He stopped and looked at the room, but things were a blur; then, his focus returned and he'd knocked the table over, the bier was spilled all over the floor, and there was broken glass. His shirt was torn and he was soaked with sweat. "Damn this."

"You've had a nightmare." Nikki let loose of him. Erich sat up and pushed away from him.

"I ..." he saw the mess and heard the neighbor lady yell about the noise. "So... I'm sorry."

"My love, you are alright now." Nikki got his composure and his fair skin was pale, but slowly his skin warmed and his heart calmed.

"This is your fault!" Erich stood up.

"What?" Nikki's eyes widened.

"You... you had to have me go to that Jew! That damned Jew and look what he's done!" Erich pushed past and went to the hall where he grabbed his jacket.

"What are you talking about?" Nikki looked at the mess.

"These," he jabbed two fingers into his temple, "these filthy thoughts, they... they have been gone for so long and now you want me to remember!" He grabbed the door knob and yanked the door open.

The neighbor lady stood there. "All this noise, you should move!" She shouted.

Erich turned to her, "Halt den mund sie dumme frau!" Then, he pushed past her.

"What? What did you say to me!" She raised her hands to her mouth.

"Erich!" Nikki rushed to him and got between them.

Erich stood erect and looked her in the eye, "It translates, sorry to have disturbed you." He looked at Nikki, turned, and went down the steps to the street.

"And is that the truth?" She looked at Nikki.

"Yes, in his way... it is."

Erich mumbled to himself going down the steps, "shut your

mouth you stupid woman." He went through the lobby door, let it go, and "click," it was shut.

It was so late that Nikki wondered what a person does when someone is missing. In Berlin, he knew that you did not dare go to the polizei or the Gestapo. The Gestapo, as they called them, was a name some postal worker gave them instead of always, Geheime Staats Polizei which became, "ge-sta-po." He looked out the window and there was the smell of a cigarette! He smiled and knew that it was Erich who was there and smoked. He went to the kitchen, got the food warmed up, and set out some wine. That's when the door opened and Erich came in, set his coat on the rack, and looked up the hallway at Nikki whose eyes were red from crying.

"I'm so sorry," Erich went to him. Nikki wiped his eyes and was anxious to hug him, but afraid to move. "You... you know that I have made a mistake." They hugged tightly, "I love you and I... this whole thing is blowing up in my face."

"I'm here with you, no matter." Nikki smiled and did what he could to comfort his love.

"Ha, it will be no matter if I don't get this out of me." He regretted saying that, because he really did not want to discuss it any further, not with Nikki, not with the Jew or with himself. The images of the people he hurt and the feelings that those images caused hurt him so badly that he made himself sick over the matter.

"Come on, supper is ready," Nikki got his hand and they walked into the dining room. It was very nice with candles and jazz music played.

"I don't deserve such things." He looked at the chair that Nikki pulled out.

"We all deserve kindness." He waited.

Erich nodded and sat down.

They ate quietly and Erich's upset faded further and further away as the red cabbage and dumplings overcame his bad feeling with good flavor. "It's delicious," he said.

"Good," Nikki finished and then did not clean up. He sat back and just relaxed.

"I'll clean up the room." Though he knew Nikki had done it.

"No, you know that I've done it. You can relax and finish, then you can clean up this please." Nikki looked at the table.

"For you," Erich was happy to do so.

"For us," Nikki got up, came over to him, and they kissed.

"For us," Erich hugged him amd knew that "for us" wasn't just about clearing the table, washing the dishes or putting them away. It was about his meetings with Dr. Scherbit. He had to keep going, "for them."

CHAPTER 3: THE LETTER

Erich finished work early so he could make his appointment with Dr. Scherbit.

"Erich," Dr. Scherbit motioned for him to come into the office. He had his pipe, but it wasn't lit. "So, we've only got the half hour today then."

"Right," Erich didn't like the tobacco, because the scent was so heavy. He walked in and looked at the chaise. It was up to him now to move it, because the other patients faced the clock. To face the clock wasn't a matter of just sticking to the time they had with Dr. Scherbit; it was also to motivate them to dig deep and talk about their problems in that time. But not for Erich, it was about safety.

"How are you?" Dr. Scherbit asked and got his place by the desk.

Erich sighed and gripped the rock in his pocket. He went to the window and pulled it down. Then, he moved the chaise so that he would face the door.

"Agitated?" Dr. Scherbit studied Erich as he tried to get comfortable in the chaise.

"So easy for you, isn't it?" Erich huffed.

"What's that?" Dr. Scherbit mouthed the end of his pipe.

"To make such a diagnosis of me," Erich shook his head.

"It's not a diagnosis, just an observation," he tapped his pipe twice on his marble ash tray. "You are agitated and it is not merely at me."

"At home, I tried to relax and my mind went to places that

I've kept locked away." He rubbed his forehead and shook it. "I'm not a criminal."

"I did not say that you were anything of the sort." Dr. Scherbit got his pencil and notepad. "It's important to know that the more you talk about these things, the more painful it is." Dr. Scherbit got up and went to the chair on the other side of his desk. He sat down and looked at Erich. "Pandora's box."

"Ja, I understand pain." He pursed his lips and worried.

"In your case, there are the images and with each image, a meaning." He touched Erich's arm, "But, I'm here to help you."

Erich thought about what he said and hesitated, "Nikki's mother sent a letter."

"Oh?" He leaned forward, "When?"

He held the letter up. "I've had this letter since the time it came." The paper was discolored, a yellowish tinge with defined creases. "His mother sent it in late 1934."

"Quite a significant year," Dr. Scherbit looked over, "may I read it?"

"Be careful," Erich handed it over, "please."

"Of course," he got the letter, then opened it slowly. He perused the words and then thought on their meaning. "It seems she was a typical mother."

"She was a bitch for the mess she caused." His face reddened.

"She's alive?" He handed the letter back to him.

He got the letter and held it at his side. "No, she died some time ago. My Nikki was heartbroken over this matter, so that she has hurt us not once, but twice." He laid back on the chaise. "He didn't notify me of the letter when it arrived." He took a deep breath. "It was hidden and he made plans privately to return to Germany so that I couldn't stop him."

"Stop him?" Dr. Scherbit's brow rose.

"She made him lie." He put his hands across his chest. "She caused him to leave and then left me to figure it out... to stay here or go after him."

"I see." He said, returned to his desk, and made some notes.

"And you don't believe then in free will?" Dr. Scherbit set

his pencil down as Erich, disturbed by the question, sat up and turned to look at him.

"What?" He wiped the sweat from his forehead, "free will? This is not the case. Free, what is it to have this word, free?" He shook his head, "this is for fantasy, Doctor... for every action there is a re-action of equal, lesser, or greater force."

"I did not know that you were a scientist." He said, got his pipe, lipped the end of it, and then got it settled in his mouth.

Erich eyed him and then, slowly, he looked at the ceiling. "I'm no scientist. If you are a rat and I put cheese in this place, at this time, you will go to it or starve." He smiled, "this is the nature of free?"

"No, that is not nature... that is a controlled test to compel an outcome... to one end or another." He mouthed his piped again, "arbeit macht frei."

"I did not make that sign, Herr Doktor." He was agitated now and felt the urge to leave.

"No, but that was a control and compelled an outcome." Dr. Scherbit's pipe moved around when he spoke like a conductor for an orchestra.

"I see, so then his mother's letter was a control and the outcome was he lied."

Erich's emotions got the better of him and he wiped away a tear, but made it look like he was wiping away the sleep in his eyes. "He chose to lie and leave me."

"To help his mother," Dr. Scherbit's pipe dipped. "You would begrudge him that responsibility?"

"I begrudge him nothing. My bad feelings are that it was a ruse to get him to come back for nothing. She was selfish and led him to the wolves." Frustrated, Erich ground his teeth. "Before Hitler, we had such freedoms, such great places, and lived well." He covered his face with his hands, "Then, the SA came and places that we enjoyed were closed and some were destroyed." Erich kept his eyes closed, "many of our... freunds were taken away, but we were safe in Quebec City at that time." He turned uncomfortably, "I came home and found that letter. Nikki had prepared for a few weeks or so before hand. He returned to Berlin in January 1935." Erich pushed away the bad feelings by pressing his fingers against the bridge of his nose so hard that there was a 'crack' sound! "I was..."

"Heartbroken?" His pipe rose.

Erich choked for a moment to get his breath, "I was in a bad place and for the night I looked at his pictures. He was gone and what was I to do?" He got his composure, "I sent a coded wire to my freund, because he took a civilian job with the SS." Erich looked at the window for a way out. "He would help me. His response was that he would work on a plan, but for me to know that Dachau was open and that he feared for our freunds who had been taken there." He broke his concentration, "perhaps, I've said enough for this day."

Dr. Scherbit sat up, "you've only just begun." He cleared his throat, "are you afraid to continue?"

Erich sneered at the thought and for all that he did after the letter came, "I am afraid of nothing." He rested and then, "it took me some time to... to settle myself. I found that he made the voyage and was safe." He turned and looked at the doctor, "making notes?"

"No, not at this moment," he grinned.

"I spent several months of figuring out what to do if he was arrested... through 1935." Erich rubbed his stomach as it made him sick to remember these things. "He sent me letters and it appeared that he was fine." He bit at his lip, "he planned to come back soon, he wrote." He looked at the clock, there was a little time left. "Coming here before the change in power was much easier than to go back."

There were a few minutes left. "And what did you do?" He nodded as Erich turned his attention from the clock.

"I thought to act, to go and get him if necessary." Erich sat up. "The Night of the Long Knives came to mind when Rohm and party members were killed the year before." He looked at Dr. Scherbit, "I feared for Nikki."

"So, that was the worst of things?"

Erich looked at Dr. Scherbit, "You're a Jew."

Dr. Scherbit's expression came alive and his brows went up, "I am a Jew."

"Then, you know what would happen to him. So, you say the worst of things... you know it is so." He looked at the clock and their time was nearly over.

"I do." Dr. Scherbit sat up and pushed his hands down his shirt to smooth out the wrinkles, "I know that this is not NAZI Germany and that you are my patient. Make no mistake about my will though... as a Jew." He got up and looked at the clock.

"Indeed," Erich stood. "Are we done?"

"For today," he motioned for the door. "For the time when you see you are back in Berlin, if you're not here ... be sure to put something in your dream, so that when you are in your dream it will tell you to wake up."

"What?"

"In your dream, put a cat or a dog so that when you see the animal or whatever you choose, you know to wake up." He nodded and waved at the door with his pipe.

"I don't care for cats." Erich got himself together, went to the door, and left without another word.

The walk home was fairly quiet and the streets weren't so busy with people or cars. He turned down the one street that was similar to an alley to cut across to the river front. There were few windows and some clothe lines hung above him like colored canvasses. As he got about halfway down that narrow street, two men stepped out and one held a knife.

"Donnez-moi votre argent!" The man held the knife at Erich. The other man, shorter than Erich, got to his side and was nearly out of Erich's sight.

"Of course," Erich reached into his jacket for his wallet. He studied the man with the knife as he reached into his pocket. The man's hand trembled.

"German scum," the man said, "could do the world a favor."

Erich was calm and exhaled slowly, "German's are not scum, you mean Nazi's." he held his wallet out. Just then, the short man rushed up and tried to grab the wallet. Erich grabbed his arm, whipped him around, and then shoved him into the other man! Once he had him against the other man, he drove them back into the wall!

"Stop! I'll kill you!" The man with the knife shouted and swung the blade at Erich, but his companion was in the way!

Erich punched the short man so hard that his nose cracked! As the short man put his hands up to cover his nose, the man with the knife swung the blade at Erich! Erich grabbed his forearm, turned it and yanked the man out from behind the short man! He turned him around, locked his arm, grabbed his neck with his other hand and pushed the knife into the man's back!

"Ah!" The man screamed and then arched in such a way that he was nearly bent half way over as the blade dug into his back!

Erich turned the knife and looked at the short man who looked at him. Erich twisted the knife and then yanked it out. The man dropped backwards onto the pavement. The short man had blood all over his face and it ran down his mouth!

Erich looked at his hand and the blade. There was blood all over, sticky and wet. "Sheiße," he looked around and dropped the knife.

The police released him as there were two other robberies by the men on another street. Though the detective didn't like how Erich defended himself, he had little choice to say otherwise and let him go.

It was after Erich left the side street to the river front that his anxiety grew. His knuckles were red and there were some cuts on them. He had blood all over his sleeve and hand. He stopped at a fountain and tried to rinse it off, but it was dark now and Nikki would be very upset, "damned filth." He didn't wash his hands in a frantic way, but went palm over palm and rinsed them gently. His anxiety waned and he acted no differently than he had when he turned onto the side street. There were shadows on his hands and around his fingernails, dried blood that would take some time to get out. His sleeves had the same dark shadows. He pulled at his collar, ran his hands down his sleeve and got some of the wrinkles out. He stood, turned, and then went home.

He opened the door, "Nikki." It was after eight now, nearly two hours since he'd left the doctors. "Nikki," he said once more.

Nikki came from the sitting room, turned the light on, and his eyes blew up when he saw the blood, "What has happened?"

"Before you get upset…"

"Erich, you're… you are covered in blood!" Nikki went to him and hugged him.

"I was attacked and the men, well…" He hesitated.

Nikki looked at him and his bruised knuckles, "Are you hurt?"

"Nein, meir geht es gut und ich bin nicht verletzt." Erich looked at Nikki, "ja, in English. I'm…"

"Ich verstehe, English or German does not matter, okay you're fine." He looked him over, "come on."

They walked to the bathroom and Nikki ran the hot water. "We've been to this place before." He got a small brush and soap, and then he cleaned Erich's hands, "this jacket and… your sleeves." Nikki's hands trembled more and more until he couldn't manage the soap and brush. "I … I"

"Yes," he said.

Nikki dropped the soap and brush in the sink. He looked at Erich, "someone is dead?"

Erich didn't say a word, but his blood shot eyes eyes told Nikki all of it.

"So, the polizei?" Nikki hoped they came.

"Robbery on that side straße I like, they released me." He grinned, because he hoped it would ease the tension, the tight rope between them.

"We're not in Berlin!" He crossed his arms. "We don't have to use the darkness of a side street." He loosened his crossed arms. "I told you not to use that street."

Erich put his hands over Nikki's crossed arms. "It's alright." He warmed them and looked at Nikki, "I did nothing wrong."

"How can this help? You are already with the doctor." The tears weren't much, but enough to make his eyes glass over. "Erich," he broke down. "Can't do... I cannot do this again. I won't." Erich wrapped his arms around Nikki and after a few moments, Nikki eased back, "I must get supper ready." He turned and went to the kitchen.

They ate in silence and, afterwards, Erich listened to the news and Nikki read; that was the remainder of the night for them, because they knew anything more would lead to an argument.

The following week, Dr. Scherbit agreed and gave Erich additional time to talk about the death of the man. "It was justified, an armed robbery."

"Yes, it was." Erich was on the chaise and faced the door.

Dr. Scherbit mouthed his pipe, "Did you... enjoy it?"

Erich sat up, turned, and squinted at the doctor, "nein, Herr Doktor."

"When you're agitated with me, you enjoy saying *Herr* Doktor," he made a note.

After the moment passed, Erich talked about Nikki and when he left. "I knew there were bad things for Germany when Hitler defied the Treaty of Versailles in 1935." He tried to get comfortable, but the chaise was hot. "My freund tells me that Goering was ordered to make the Luftwaffe." He sat up for a moment to let the heat under him get out. "I believed that Hitler would start a war." He rubbed his hands together. "It was August of 1935 and Nikki sent a message that there was some minor trouble between his mutter and him, but for me to be patient, to let him help his parents was difficult." He sighed out of frustration. "I did not trust."

"Did you think he was still safe?" Dr. Scherbit studied Erich's expression.

Erich gritted his teeth, "Nein, I thought my plan must be used and arrangements made."

"So, you had documents forged?" He mouthed his pipe and sucked on the end.

"My freund knew a way to get to Finland and for me to just have a pack to carry on my back." Erich looked at the window, was there a way out? "He would help me."

"That was quite dangerous to go... you did go?" Dr. Scherbit leaned back in his chair.

Erich was cold and didn't speak for a few moments, but neither did Dr. Scherbit. He put his hands together and tightened his grip, "he wrote and insisted that he was fine. I believed the longer he waited, there would be no way for him to come back."

Erich shook his head to break the flood of horror of faces of dead people; their eyes hooked into him like a hook goes into a fish; the barb would not let him pull the hook out without tearing him apart! Young men begged with him for life and mercy and then there were images of Nikki bruised and battered. "His last message to me was September 1935... he was upset."

Dr. Scherbit set his pipe down, "how so?"

"His mother pressured him to marry, to find a good German woman, and make his allegiance to the party. He said he wouldn't and made arrangements to leave." He sat up and looked at the doctor, "I could take it no longer." He wiped the sweat from his forehead, "It was October when I wired him and his mother replied with her name on the message."

"That must've have been difficult." Dr. Scherbit was curious.

Erich's fists were clenched and a team of draft horses could not have pried them open, "She turned him over to the SS." He got his composure and breathed as Nikki taught him. "She wrote that he refused to find a woman and raise a good German family." The color from his knuckles faded from red to white, "She blamed me... that I made him queer and she did to queers what must be done." Beads of sweat slid past his brow, down his cheeks, and pooled at the sides of his mouth. "I hated her."

Dr. Scherbit got a mint and put it in his mouth, "She upset you."

"Upset? I was furious!" He punched the side of the chaise. "She was such a pig for the SS!"

Dr. Scherbit's eyes widened and coolness come over him. An upset patient posed an issue. He sought to manage a patient's emotions or if they could not or chose not to manage them, then the session ended. "So, then you were able to focus... to calm down and resolve the matter."

"Yes, I had to get him out." Erich sat up and looked for a way out!

Dr. Scherbit sat up, "It's alright Erich, just me and you here." He put his hands up on the desk and showed them to Erich, "Did you have training for this type of thing... to rescue someone?"

Erich dreaded to talk about it, "Sturmabteilung." He laid back on the chaise and ran his hands over his face to rub out the horror. "I was trained, but not to rescue." He took a deep breath, sighed, and then took another deep breath. "I dread to tell you the truth."

Dr. Scherbit looked at the clock, "We've a half hour or so and I love the truth." He cleared his throat, "You were a member of the Sturmabteilung... Storm Troopers?"

Erich chuckled. "I was with the original paramilitary wing of the Nazi Party ... to work for Hitler." He shook his head. "I was a young man then and thought I found my place among the public." He sighed, "I found brothers among the SA and... there were things we learned." Erich bit his lip to hold back. "I hurt people."

"I can only imagine." He took the box of mints and held it up, "You are the one with the memories."

Erich shook his head. "No, no candy will stop this." He looked away. "I went back for Nikki." He studied the lines in the curtains to distract him. "To save him, I had to become what I hated most ..."

"A Nazi." He set the mints down.

"My freund made it possible for me to assume the identity of a man, Brueder, Jan Brueder." He clinched his fist again, "I could not go back as his mutter wrote that she told the SS about me." He took a deep breath, "Brueder was the son of a party member and he was killed abroad. He was SS, but I didn't know to what extent. It... it was a chance for me to get back to Germany." He sat up and looked at the doctor, "You're sure about the rest of this Dr. Scherbit?"

Dr. Scherbit smiled and then nodded, "Yes... but someone would know Brueder then?"

"No, not many people; my freund said Brueder and his family were isolated in north western Germany near the border with Poland. He was, by chance, close to my age and appearance. His parents died the year before." Erich laid back down, "My papers got me to Finland... every dollar I had for us was going out of my pocket." He wiped his mouth. "It was the first part of 1936 when I arrived in Finland and it was bitterly cold."

"And the Nuremburg laws of the previous year?" Dr. Scherbit made a note.

Erich thought for a moment and grinned quite slyly, "for myself, all my family were German."

"You've said nothing about them." His brow rose.

"My mutter died and my vater... killed himself." Erich kept his composure, "for Brueder, his entire family was German. There was no question of his race or the papers his papers."

"The SS had records about Brueder?" Dr. Scherbit sat back and was deeply curious about this matter. He flipped his notepad to a blank page and waited to hear the rest before he made a note. What would his notes do to Erich if he was a former NAZI and a murderer of queers, Jews, and other people? He wanted to know the whole story before he passed judgment.

"Of course, but my freund had a new position with the SS HQ." He bit at his lip, "He destroyed the papers of Brueder's death and made it so there was little information in the record, only that he was a party member and with rank. The Gestapo was overwhelmed and the SS was in a state of change as Himmler took over." Erich pushed his bangs back and wiped his sweat covered brow.

"Your friend was quite helpful to you."

Erich thought for a moment and felt sick, "yes." He cleared his throat of the bad feeling and then, "I arrived in Helsinki and then made my way to Berlin." Erich coughed to clear his throat. "Through Gdansk; from there I got rides and stayed along the coast to Germany, to his home."

"And Nikki? Was there any word from him?" Dr. Scherbit got his pipe and sucked on the end of it.

"No, the communication and the letter were all that I had. He was taken by the SS and sent away." Erich's heart ached. "He was a lamb in a den of wolves. His mutter... she..."

"Perhaps, not to detract from her, but to focus on what you did to get to Nikki?" Dr. Scherbit looked at the clock and there was just fifteen minutes or so left now.

"The check points were a great risk to get through, so I got through by crossing farmland." He cleared his throat, "according to my freund, he made it so Brueder was at his home awaiting orders." He tried to get comfortable. The more he talked about the journey to save Nikki, the more he felt he laid on a bed of dull nails, not yet able to poke him.

"You mentioned this friend many times, but you don't give him a name?" Dr. Scherbit sat up and looked at Erich closely to see if there was a physical reaction.

Erich put his hands together to keep them from trembling. "This is what he was to me, a freund."

"Yes, but *what* is his name?" Dr. Scherbit persisted and moved his chair to agitate Erich, to provoke an answer or emotional response.

Erich sat up to see if the doctor got up, "What is the damn difference if his name is freund or whatever!"

"You don't want to remember him?" He edged back and they eyed each other for a moment. He tapped his pipe gently on the ash tray and sat back.

Anxiety crawled all over Erich like cockroaches and their little legs tapped his skin and they made their way into his stomach! "Ja... I think." He sat up, looked all over, and then stood up. His face paled as he thought about his freund, "Step... Stephan." Anguish, heartbreak, depression filled his mind.

"Erich?" Dr. Scherbit jumped up and nearly fell back over as his chair gave out.

"I feel sick." He looked for a trash can and then couldn't help it! He vomited on Dr. Scherbit's Afghan rug! He coughed and spat for a few moments as Dr. Scherbit's eyes widened!

Dr. Scherbit grabbed the waste basket, "one moment!" But it was too late; the deed was done, and the carpet was stained with Erich's feelings about Stephan.

"I… I am sorry." Erich looked at the mess, "I will clean it. Nikki will be unhappy for me to have done this to your rug." He looked around for a rag, but Dr. Scherbit already had a towel in hand and came over.

"I am unhappy too, Erich." They eyed each other for a moment and Dr. Scherbit forced a smile, "I will have it cleaned." He sat the waste basket down and tossed the towel over the mess. "What happened to your friend, Stephan?"

Erich's face turned ashen. "He…" He looked at the mess again and shook his head, "He gave himself … he went to Sachsenhausen … to protect us." He turned, went to the door, yanked it open, and stumbled out!

Dr. Scherbit was surprised and, now, more curious than ever about the whole story of what happened to Stephan. Why was Stephan taken away at all and how could he have protected them?

The secretary walked in and yelped when she saw the mess, "Good Lord!"

"It's fine, Lucy. Call Fritz and ask if he can come right away. I'll use the room across the hall for my other appointments." Dr. Scherbit stepped over the mess, went behind his desk and grabbed the most important things—his notepad, pencil, and pipe.

She shook her head and called Fritz.

Once Erich was on the street, he tried to get a cigarette out of the pack, but dropped them. A woman stopped and helped him to get them. He looked at her and was afraid, "Why have you helped me?"

She shook her head, "Quoi?"

"What do you want from me!" He asked and it was then he realized he wasn't being questioned. The woman just shook her head and was dismayed by him.

He got to the corner and headed to the river, images of his freund, bloodied, beaten, and hung from a tree flooded his mind. He looked for the cigarette, but it was already in his hand. He stopped on a quiet side street, got up against the wall of a building, and huddled there, "warum?" He saw the cigarette between his fingers, jammed his hand into his pocket, and got his lighter out. He lit up, took a deep drag, and just held it for a moment. When he exhaled, a cloud formed, a spirit in the form of his friend. "What!" He studied it. "Was? Was willst du?"

"I didn't ask him to go for me." Erich wiped his eyes. He took another long drag and then blew the smoke down. "You know I didn't. He... Stephan was arrested and I could do nothing!" He shook his head, "Stephan." He flicked the cigarette away and lit another one. "I... I wanted to get him out but, how could I?" He looked at the spirit. "He... when I saw him again... There was a note in Sachsenhausen's record book: STEPHAN FRIEDLANGER - BORN: 26 -05 -1910, Kleiststraße 1410, BERLIN, ID: Sch Para 175-DR, ARRIVED: 28 APRIL 1936, DIED 25 JULY 1936 - INFLUENZA."

Stephan's spirit was as tall as Erich with a broad build and smiled, "Don't smile at me, Stephan!" He took another drag and turned away. "Some angel," he looked at the cloud, "You see that this bothers me!" He turned back to Stephan and saw how his arms were inverted behind his body; his eyes were swollen and bruised and he nodded at Erich to say he made a choice.

Erich tried to put the cigarette to his mouth, "I did not ask you to lie for me, to protect me." He flicked the cigarette away and pressed his hands against his head, "Why didn't you run!"

He came over, brought his arms right, and took Erich's hand with his. "I saved you and that saved you both."

Erich, "I'm sorry to have kept your name to myself."

Stephan shook his hand gently, stepped back, and then faded into the darkness. "I have not forgotten you, Stephan... I, I keep you to myself."

A breeze came down the street and blew away what was left of the cloud and the cigarette butt. "Must I be condemned to these things as I live and they have died?" He spat and wiped the snot from his nose with his sleeve. "Nikki," he went down the side street to the river front where he turned and headed home.

As he headed up the river front to their apartment, it was warm out and it felt like he was burning, "Nikki." He blurted out, fumbled with the lobby door and then went in. He got to the stairs and hurried to their floor. "Damned woman," he said out loud and thought of their neighbor. He stopped for a moment so that his heels didn't hit the floor like some storm trooper on parade. He looked at the door, pushed his hair back and pulled at his collar, "okay."

He opened the door and went in. For this late in the evening, Nikki usually had supper on and would be near the door, but he wasn't near the door. Erich set his jacket on the hook and looked in the sitting room. "Nikki?"

"Ah, you're... what has happened?" Nikki had an apron on and walked up from the kitchen. "Erich?"

"I... got very sick." He dropped to the floor and covered his face.

"Erich," Nikki rushed up and knelt down with him, "what happened?"

"I... it just happened."

"What?" Nikki got his apron up to wipe Erich's tears away.

"You with this damned apron," They looked at each other. He got into a fetal position and laid down on Nikki's lap. "I saw Stephan."

Nikki thought for a moment, "Stephan?" He knew who he meant.

"Ja, auf der Straße in der Nähe der SS und er hat für mich gelogen." Erich cried and buried his head in Nikki's lap.

"Honey, when you get upset, you speak ..."

His face warmed. "German, Ja, I know. I'm a German!"

"Calm down, please... you must practice your breathing,"

and he carefully and nicely ran his hand across Erich's forehead, "breathe in and then out slowly."

"I, saw, him."

"You saw Stephan, yes. But, he's been dead for years. He's not haunting you." Nikki stretched his legs out and got comfortable.

"Why did he give himself for me?" Erich calmed down and his tears began to dry.

"He gave himself for us. He… honey, he did a great thing for us and so we must live a good life for what he sacrificed." Nikki hummed and pushed Erich's bangs back, "your bangs are nice."

"They are too long." Erich looked at Nikki and they kissed.

Nikki made a face as he tasted the vomit, "were you sick?"

"I… vomited on his carpet."

"Stephan? That's not possible." Nikki grinned.

"Ah, no… the Jew," Erich got comfortable as if he were going to go to bed right there.

"Don't say that name. It's Dr. Scherbit." Nikki held his love tightly, "and you're not to get comfortable here. You will get up, go to the wash room and clean up."

By now, Erich was in control and was grateful that Nikki was there for him, "yes, mutter."

"Ha, ha, get cleaned up." They eyed each other again and kissed, "move your ass."

Erich sat up and Nikki helped him, "that's not good English nor is it proper."

"Then, after supper you can punish me." Nikki smiled at him and it was such a warm smile that Erich, seeing it, could have just been better to look at Nikki. "You really threw up on his floor?"

"On a rug," Erich went to the wash room.

"Disgusting," Nikki got up and went to the kitchen.

CHAPTER 4: NIKKI, JAN 1936

The absolute horror of it all is that it was true; Nikki's mother, Elsa, turned him over to the SS and told them that he was queer, "Ruined, my son has ruined himself for das Vaterland!" Nikki had most of his things packed already and his arrangements made to leave. When he realized that the SS were coming, he panicked and fled onto the streets of Berlin.

An SS officer and guards stood at the house on Wilhelmstraße - 1436 and waited for someone to come to the door. She set her son's belongings near the sitting area where her husband sat; he suffered from Alzheimer's. She was overwhelmed by the disaster at hand. A dainty woman, she had a fierce personality to get what she wanted and her face had sharp chin creases from putting all her angst and anger about life into her expressions. If a neighbor saw her on the straße, they would say, "There, she comes with her dog on her face" and, most certainly, avoid her at all cost!

She opened the door and looked at the SD captain from head to toe. He was sharply dressed in his black uniform and there, behind him and in twos, four other SD guards stood with sticks.

"Bitte, guten abend Mrs. VanEch," he looked at her, "Captain Ehrlichmann, ist Nikki hier?" They waited a moment and one of the guards looked at the sides of the building to see that he wasn't at a window. Capt. Ehrlichmann was not blond; he had dark hair, short and tight. His demeanor was a commensurate professional soldier, but he was in the company of civilians and behaved accordingly as one German to another. He didn't need to pull his shoulders back for they were that way naturally as were his cheeks.

She shook her head, "Er lief durch die verzögerung!"

"Mrs. VanEch," he took his hat from his head, "state matters will always precede that of the individual. Your son, queer or not, is a German. So, we are not tardy... we are no longer occupied with other pressing matters."

She scoffed, "then, he is free to go, to run?" She turned and looked at his luggage, "there are his things."

"No, we will get him. We are curious about what he was doing in Canada." He turned back to two of the guards and nodded at them. He stepped aside so that they could go in. They dipped their hats at her, went in and got his luggage.

"It was another queer, Erich Schmidt." She thought for a moment and the hate that she had for Erich seethed from her and she wished he was dead. "He is the criminal."

Capt. Ehrlichmann took a notepad from his pocket, flipped through a few pages and then wrote the name, ERICH SCHMIDT-P.175. "Schmidt... and you know he is a queer?"

"My son spoke of him." She watched as they carried Nikki's two bags out. "He sent me a letter. I replied and told him that he brought this terribleness upon my family."

"He wrote... Erich?"

"Ja," she thought about the matter, "to be honest captain, I think he is a spy."

"Erich or your son?" He was puzzled.

"My son was a pawn in this fraud!" She looked at the other guards, "Erich Schmidt is the bad man."

"Why do you believe he is a spy?" Ehrlichmann studied her to see if she spoke from anger or truth.

"He worked at the Reichstag and fled with my son before the fire." She stood firm.

"That's not enough of a reason to say he is a spy." He made a note.

"He had a freund that my son said helped them to get away

and then helped my son to get back into Germany." She tapped the side of her nose to hint that Erich was clever and a threat. "Who has such power to do that?"

Capt. Ehrlichmann thought on the matter, "and this was in the letter?"

"No, only to call me an SS bitch." She covered her mouth and looked like she'd cry, "My son told me about the help."

"Did he give you a name of the other freund?" He looked past her at her husband.

"Nein," she said.

"The letter, you have it?" He looked at her hands and then her.

"Ja, I get it for you." She went to a bureau, got the letter from Erich and gave it to the captain.

He looked at his notes, "Unfortunately, there is little we can do to Erich Schmidt."

"But you can get my son?" She lowered her hand.

"Absolutely… but you understand," he fixed his hat so that it was precisely on his head straight, "he won't be back. That is why you offered to help him, correct?"

She nodded and then slowly closed the door.

He turned to his men. "We have his picture and he has left only a short time ago." He turned to his guard, a stout man with a grim face. "Johann, find out what you can about Erich Schmidt."

Johann nodded as they made their way back to their car.

Nikki stood still in an alley only three blocks away. He had his coat, mittens and heavy trousers on, so the cold wouldn't be too bad. He wiped his forehead and calmed his heavy breath, "what to do?" He thought about Stephan, but he'd have to go to his home and didn't want to get him in trouble too. He didn't need his clothes, but his papers. He searched his jacket and had them. He thought about a story that Erich told him:

> There was an African deer of some sort that was so very thirsty. This deer saw the lake and thought to get a drink, but there was a problem; crocodiles laid at the edge of the

water and were as hungry as the deer was thirsty. The deer saw his companion's edge up to the water, get attacked and jumped to any place to get free, but only to find themselves in the mouths of the crocs. The deer thought on this matter and figured that if they tried to bite, he must have a place where he can jump to that is safe, far from the mouths of crocs! Where was that place?

Nikki looked down the straße and thought about where to jump. He wondered if any of the queer bars were open as word from an acquaintance said that they met in private or underground. People walked along the straße and were not looking for him. They were on their way to eat or shop or to go home, not to get him. His face was like other young people and his glasses were like other glasses, so would it not be so easy for them to search him out, "nein." The straße, for the most part, was really not very busy. A street car passed and blew its horn and that's when Nikki walked onto the sidewalk and headed for the car! He figured that if he could get to the street car, he could get out of this area and over to somewhere less threatening. He had money and thought to contact Erich, but from where? He looked around and there were German polizei, but they were occupied with watching the people around them. He paid, got on the car and sat midway in the tram next to a grandma, "bitte." He muttered to himself, "far from the mouths of the crocs."

She nodded and he got comfortable. The car pulled away and went from the Spree River to the city's north. He looked a little disheveled, but was alright. Nikki's acquaintance told him that, due to the Olympics, there was pressure to relieve the city of its queers or the *filth*. There was also a rumor that Hitler would move to reoccupy the Rhineland and Nikki knew enough about history to know that this was another violation of the Treaty of Versailles, a chance for war. He was already too anxious to get back to Erich and this matter of possible war made him wish he'd never come home. The train's wheels made a clink and clank on the track and were a good distraction. He thought of his mutter and vater and then a horrible sense of guilt came over him as he thought of his vater, "papa."

The lady next to him looked his way, "hmm?"

Nikki sat low in the seat and shook his head. She turned her attention to the passing buildings. The car slowed to a stop and Nikki's anxiety climbed! Only a young man got on with a sack. The car took off again, "ding, ding!"

Nikki edged up some to see the coming streets and to decide where to get off. He saw other Gestapo as they talked with a couple of SS officers and he immediately sat low. The car slowed and he felt his heart beating out of his chest! Would they get on?

They slowed and then stopped just up from them so that the SS officers would have to walk a short distance to the door. Perhaps, the driver knew they did not want to get on. Nikki stayed low as a young woman got on with a baby, an older man with his newspaper and a mother and two young boys. The driver rung the bell, but someone yelled!

"HALT!" The SS ran to the tram. "HALT!"

The driver shook his head, because he hadn't even put the pedal down to go, "idiots," he said under his breath and opened the doors again.

Nikki thought that he could leave through the rear exit, but the other SS was there and waited. The SS men were strong and stout, so the thought of hitting him and then running away was not a good idea. The SS was like a city rat; you might see one or two as you go down the straße, but an SS blows their whistle or calls out and they come out of nowhere by the dozens. Nikki wiped his forehead and figured that it was dark enough that they would not bother with him.

The driver turned to look at the SS, "What is it?"

The SS officer seemed put off, "good that it is not you." He got to the top step and looked down the car, "is the light in here no brighter?"

The driver turned away, "No."

He walked a few steps in and looked over the faces of people who looked everywhere else. He took one more step and then looked at the driver, "and have you seen a young man, steel framed glasses, perhaps just short of one meter-fifty?"

"I have a schedule." The driver rung the bell. "Stay on and continue or get off and let me get back on schedule."

The SS sighed, "You will stay as long as is necessary. Did you see anyone that is like I've asked?"

From the outside of the car the other SS officer yelled, "Kristoff!"

"Ja!" He looked at the driver.

"Nein, I've not seen anyone." The driver rung the bell again and another street car was right behind him that blew their horn. "You see, there are now two of them behind me."

The SS officer stepped off the car and the driver closed the door so quickly that it nearly clipped the SS officer who sneered at him. "Damned animals," he blew the horn! He pushed the lever forward and they were down the straße in seconds.

Nikki exhaled so slowly that he might have passed out and the old woman held her hand out with a mint of some kind, "nein, danke."

She smiled and put it in her mouth.

The car stopped, let off the woman and two boys, and then took off! Nikki knew they'd be a mile away in minutes as the driver blew his horn several times to clear the straße.

Nikki sat back and thought, "The deer knew where to jump to... where will I jump?"

Capt. Ehrlichmann stood at the SS HQ main entrance on Prinz-Albrecht Straße-8 and admired the beautiful Nazi flags, "Capt. Ehrlichmann," a man said from the straße.

The Captain turned, "ah, Capt. Schaus?" He walked down to him with his hand extended, "so good to see you."

The man was Capt. Friedrich Schaus, "And you Conrad." He got out a cigarette and offered one to Conrad, "These are quite good, American."

"Nein, thank you Friedrich," Capt. Ehrlichmann looked at the passersby, "it's funny to me that as they go by, they seem so lost."

Capt. Schaus turned his attention to the people, "Perhaps, the hour has them in a rush to get home and they are mindful of nothing more." He lit his cigarette and took a drag off of it.

"Or they are terrified." Capt. Ehrlichmann smiled.

"Terrified?"

"Of us, this..." He turned and looked at the brilliant red flags, the propaganda posters and the SS officers around them. "This is home; this is naturliche... for us."

"Ah, of course," Capt. Schaus sighed. "So, you're working where?"

"At Dachau," he replied and felt quite good to have such an assignment, "There is a great mission to be done and the plans are in place."

"I've heard." Capt. Ehrlichmann got his notepad from his pocket. "A moment."

"Oh?" Capt. Schaus leaned over to look at the note.

"Nicholas VanEch." He showed his notepad to his friend.

Capt. Schaus read the note and then smiled, "We will keep a place for him."

"It sickens me to think that these... things live amongst us." He folded his notepad and replaced it in his pocket. "His mutter has turned him in to us."

"Good for her," Capt. Schaus nodded. "Himmler's plans along with the Fuhrer are our future." He grinned and his brow raised, "The Olympics are coming and my orders, as you've heard I'm sure... are to process new detainees as quickly as they come in." He looked at the passersby again, "and there among our German brethren are the enemies of the state."

Capt. Ehrlichmann looked at the people. Though it was late, there were still many people out and about. "Friedrich, I'm hopeful that there are not so many."

Friedrich grinned, "No matter, there are other camps soon to be operational." He looked at Conrad, "It's very good to see you. If I catch this Nicholas before you, there is a free dinner?"

Conrad laughed, "ja, of course." He extended his hand and they shook, "I must get back to my work. The queer is not the only filth on my list." He nodded, they saluted and parted ways.

"See you then," Friedrich said, turned and went down the steps to the straße. He was gone into the darkness in moments.

Capt. Ehrlichmann thought about VanEch and then turned to the offices. He trotted up the steps and into the building.

The street car slowed to a stop and the old woman got off. Nikki stood quietly as she made her way to the steps, then down and out. The driver looked back at Nikki and waited.

"This is the last stop?"

"No, but I want to know that you know *there* is a last stop." He turned back to his controls, moved the handle and they pulled away, "the last stop is coming next."

"Danke," Nikki looked at the straße and there were very few people.

"Perhaps, you should go to the U-Bahn?" He glanced at Nikki, "or do you need a train?"

Nikki knew that they'd be at the train station and, most likely, some of the U-Bahn stations. He would have to take a chance at some point or get a ride from someone. To do anything involved a chance and was a danger. He nodded, "I will need to go to the U-Bahn."

"Are you from Berlin?"

Nikki thought for a moment, "Nein, here to see a friend and… just going to places to see what Berlin is like."

"At this hour?" He asked and slowed to a stop, "you should be careful. The SS and local Gestapo are not likely to be nice if they stop you."

Nikki got up, straightened his coat and looked out. Some snow fell now and the cold chilled him. "Ja, thank you," he went to the back door.

The driver seemed offended that Nikki chose to go out the back and reluctantly opened the door, "tschus." He stopped, turned to the driver and they eyed each other for a moment. Then, Nikki stepped down and out of the car.

"Viel gluck," he shut the doors.

The lights went out inside the car and it disappeared down

the straße. Nikki tightened his jacket and pulled at his mittens, then turned up the straße to a U-Bahn entrance. He looked quickly and saw no polizei, no SS, "this far north." He wasn't anywhere close to out of Berlin, but he was far from the city center. He walked through the snow gathered around his feet and all over the ground. The crunch beneath his feet offered him some peace as there were no cars and few people. He looked down the straße and saw the U-Bahn sign. He thought to walk up and go past so that he could get a look inside the station. He made his way up to the station and then past the entrance. He did not pause, look to the side or take his gaze from the sidewalk in front of him. But, his peripheral vision told him that it was clear and he could go, get on and leave. He looked around one more time as he turned on a side straße, did a u-turn and then went back to the station. He went down to the platform. There were trains for another hour, but this one had just left, so he'd have to wait. The map was helpful and there were opportunities to go further north, pay for a way into Poland and do as he and Erich did before; he had to get to the coast and get on a ship to anywhere, even America if he could do it.

He looked down the station to see that no one was coming up, but there may be someone, SS or some person who is late to get home. Erich had taught him quite a lot of the way to keep low and, now, he was happy that he knew. "scheiße," he stomped his feet. It was colder in the station with all of the concrete. Then, there was the sound of metal on metal as the train approached. His heart lightened and the lights lit up a part of the track as it approached the station! He would go to Seestraße station. Then, he'd use his money to get a ride to a smaller town. He'd have to get a message to Erich soon and tell him what's happened.

The train pulled in and slowed to a stop. The driver opened his window and looked down the platform as the doors opened and only two people got out. Nikki boarded, looked around and, to his luck, there were no Gestapo. He went to the corner and sat right by a door. The conductor checked the platform and signaled the driver. It was only a moment and the doors closed.

Nikki bundled up as it was warmer in the car. The train sped off and it was a few stops before he'd get to Seestraße. So, he pulled up his collar and sat back. Then, something overwhelmed him… grief, "mutter, warum." He pressed his fingers into the bridge of his nose and sniffled, "warum?" A few tears made their way down his cheeks and soaked into his collar just as the train slowed to stop.

The conductor called out the stop, "Reinickendorfer!" The train stopped and the doors opened for a few moments. Nikki kept his eyes just above his collar and looked at the door, "bitte." There was such a silence that it made his stomach sour from the anxiety as he waited. Then, a bell and the doors closed. The train pulled away and went on to Bahnhof Wedding which was less than five minutes from here. He thought that he must be at the window to see if any of the Gestapo waited on the platform.

If they were there what could he do? He thought to get off at the stop before the last stop, Leopoldplatz. He thought about Erich and he'd have to apologize for all of the things he was so uptight about when they got ready to leave for Canada, "to check this and that" and "be careful to say nothing!" Erich was right to be wary of the Gestapo and, especially, of the system that was his worst enemy. "I will not go to Dachau, mama." He said under his breath and then stood to see the platform as the conductor announced, "Bahnhof Wedding." There were a couple of people, but his heart jumped when he thought about it, thought about the fact that there were two stations and no Gestapo. He felt a bit sickly and thought to get off, walk to the steps and get out quickly, but how to avoid them? The train pulled away and was gone from the station in seconds.

The train slowed and the conductor announced the station, "Leopoldplatz!" As the train came to a stop, there was a moment before the doors opened and he thought it was longer than necessary. He looked at the other doors and thought to force them open. He could run and go onto the tracks! The doors opened and he hesitated.

He stepped to the side of the door and waited, then looked

again. His heart pounded in his chest and he knew that he had to take a chance, out and up or out and down the tracks? The bell rung and he pushed his way through as the doors closed on him. He was out now and on the platform as the train pulled out of the station. The exit was just a hundred feet or so away. He studied the sign and listened. Then, he headed towards the exit just as a thought blasted into his mind that he should walk to the edge, jump down onto the tracks and walk through the tunnel; it was very dangerous. He eyed the edge of the platform for a moment and thought not to do it. The streets and a chance to get a ride were far more practical.

He walked to the stairs and went up. Just as he turned the corner, there was Capt. Ehrlichmann and he froze! They looked at each other and Ehrlichmann smiled. Nikki turned his head only slightly to look down the steps to run back and then down the tunnel.

"Have you a match?" Ehrlichmann asked and got a cigarette pack from his long coat. When he pushed his long coat apart, Nikki saw the Luger. He gently removed the cigarette and then returned the pack to his coat.

Nikki shook his head and his heart was about to burst from his chest.

"Ah," Ehrlichmann got a lighter from his trouser pocket, "There it is after all." He lit his cigarette and then nodded at Nikki, "no matter, then."

Nikki watched him descend the next two steps and then stop. He listened for other boots and there was just the noise of a car that passed by above. Colder air came down the steps and he felt like he rested on a block of ice.

"I'm a lucky man." He kept his gaze down the steps towards the platform.

Nikki had to say something and did so with a shaky voice, "you are?"

"My suspicion was that you'd take the train to begin, but you took the street car... didn't you?" He shook his head, "It was cold to wait here for so long, but you are to blame for the wait." He looked up the steps, "It occurred to me that you might head to the border with Poland, cross and then to Gdansk, perhaps to get to Canada." He turned and looked at Nikki. "My people reported no sign of you at the Berlin terminus and that is when the game changed, so I took a chance to come here."

Nikki felt the horror build in him that there was no way he was alone; there must be other SS with him on the straße. "I don't…"

"Don't know me? I am Capt. Ehrlichmann." He said, dipped his head and took off his gloves. "Your mother sends her regards."

A surge of anxiety and butterflies zipped through his veins and he felt faint!

Two SS came down and stood at the top of the steps.

"It's alright, just wait there." He took another drag from his cigarette. "Would you care for a cigarette?" He went up the two steps and got close to Nikki "to calm your nerves."

Nikki couldn't move. It was even colder now in the stairwell, but sweat dripped from his forehead.

Capt. Ehrlichmann held out the cigarette, "bitte."

Nikki carefully reached for it and got it from him. He put it to his mouth and it was backwards.

"Ah, you've got to use the other end," The men laughed.

Nikki was faint and his skin paled even whiter than normal, "my mutter ist…"

"Oh, she is fine," he got his lighter in hand. "We have your things and…" He lit the cigarette now that Nikki had it turned around. "I want more than you, Nicholas. As your mutter said that you have a freund, Erich Schmidt, and another freund who helped you to get into Germany."

Nikki took a drag and coughed.

They laughed to themselves, "You don't normally smoke?"

"Nein," he inhaled deeply only to cough harder.

"So, we have your things, but what we don't have is… Erich or the person who helped you." He put his lighter away. "You've wired him recently?"

Nikki felt the emotion well up inside him, but Erich made it clear to him that you don't cry, because it will insight them to do worse. He bit down and his cheek muscles burst out, "I don't know him."

Capt. Ehrlichmann smiled, looked at the other two officers and shook his head, "But he wrote your mutter, surely you must know him." He flicked his cigarette to the ground and stomped it out. Then, he knelt and picked it up. "It's disgusting to leave them on the ground." He held it tightly in his hand. "So much filth…," he looked at Nikki and their eyes were locked.

Nikki's hand trembled as he took another drag, but did not cough this time.

"I'm a citizen of Canada." Nikki held the cigarette close to his mouth.

"Nein, you are a German citizen who illegally fled to Canada with another queer." He got his notepad out, "and you are subject to the laws of Germany." He slowly flipped through the pages and stopped, then looked over his notes. "Nicholas VanEch, age twenty-three" and then he got right in Nikki's face, "for violations of the Reich code paragraph one hundred-seventy-five, you are under arrest." He grinned, but his cheek rose up on one side only. He flipped the notepad shut and put it back into his pocket.

Nikki looked at the other two officers and thought to run down the steps; he could make it to the platform and have the advantage of the flat surface to the tracks. He looked down the steps.

"There are men there." Capt. Ehrlichmann said, moved his long coat aside and touched his holster, "Nicholas, so you know, I will not chase you. I will draw and shoot before you get to that last step." He leaned in, nearly nose to nose. "I will not miss."

Nikki faced the overwhelming thought that he was finished and a tear ebbed out of his eye, slid down cheek, and stopped. He turned so that the captain would not see it and feigned a cough. As he covered his mouth, he wiped it away. "So," he put the cigarette out. "What's next then?" He knew it was over, for now.

Capt. Ehrlichmann pulled his gloves on and then smiled. He punched Nikki so horribly hard that Nikki doubled over and fell to the ground, "next!" Capt. Ehrlichmann kicked Nikki on the side of his chest. "That was next!"

"Owe!" Nikki screamed! There was no way to take that kick. He couldn't catch his breath, curled up, and looked like a dead man in a fetal position.

Capt. Ehrlichmann looked at the other two men and they came, got Nikki, and carried him up the steps. Capt. Ehrlichmann saw Nikki's cigarette, knelt, and looked at it, "must pick up the filth." He got the cigarette, whistled for his other men, and then he went up the steps too.

They put Nikki in handcuffs, then lifted him and tossed him into the back of a truck.

"Gehen!" Capt. Ehrlichmann yelled and got in a car behind the truck. The snow was covered everything. As the truck drove away, Capt. Ehrlichmann radioed to say that he had the one man in custody.

Nikki's lips trembled, tears slid down his cheeks, and his soft red complexion was ashen. He thought on his mother and then he thought on his love, Erich. He whispered, "I love you."

CHAPTER 5: THE QUIET TOWN OF GRAMZOW

Erich stood at the steps to the "Offices of Ibrahim R. Scherbit, Psy." and smoked. He looked at the sign and stared for a moment; no such sign would be displayed in 1936 Berlin or, for that matter, anywhere in Germany at that time. He thought the letters were very big and quite loud, but with what he knew and saw, he would have a sign too, "ERICH SCHMIDT, QUEER." The cigarette was nearly done as he exhaled.

He pressed the end of the cigarette against the bottom of his shoe to put it out and then rolled out the ash. The wind was a little strong as he went to toss it in the trash can by the street. A woman passed and smiled at him; he smiled back and then felt a surge of good feelings in him, but before they got strong enough to cloud his reason for this visit, his smiled faded and reality set in. He threw the cigarette in the trash, turned and went up the steps into the building.

Dr. Scherbit came out and nodded at him. Two people looked at Dr. Scherbit and then their hope faded when they realized he was there for Erich.

Erich got up, went in and then stepped to the side as Dr. Scherbit closed the door. "You've had that damned pipe going." He fanned his nose.

"And you've had a cigarette before you came in," he smiled and motioned for Erich to sit at the chaise.

Erich walked over, moved the chaise to see the door and window, and then sat down. "Yes," he sat down.

"Have you had any bad dreams?" Dr. Scherbit asked and tapped his pipe only once on the ash tray.

"New nightmares," he looked at the window and then the door to be sure that they were closed. The street noises often upset him and he was unable to concentrate. Then, he had to unbutton his jacket or remove it as it was too stuffy in the office with the window closed.

"Of faces?"

"Of things and faces, people that did not bother me before... they bother me now," Erich looked at the doctor to reassure himself of his place.

Dr. Scherbit had his notepad and pencil, but hadn't written anything, "As we get closer to the destination of this journey, it is possible that you will feel worse or... overwhelmed as the images gain more meaning."

Erich sighed, "and this will end when?" His face and chest warmed and he had to remove his jacket.

"It will never end." Dr. Scherbit said, "recall that I said, there is forgiveness; you do not forget."

"Yes, forgive and how will they forgive me?" He looked at Dr. Scherbit to see if his expression fit his answer.

"They cannot." He set his notepad and pencil down, "this is a subjective thing... that you must find it in yourself the opportunity to forgive." He leaned back. His eyes looked away from Erich at the ceiling as if he might be lost in thought or caught in a thought of what to say next.

"And if I can't?" Erich pressed his fingers against the bridge of his nose to push out the beginnings of a headache.

"It's likely," the doctor got his pipe and tapped out the used tobacco. "That the feelings about these things will eat at you and, over time, ruin your mental and physical health."

"I am there."

Dr. Scherbit put new tobacco in his pipe. "Internalizing is what this is and it's no good, no matter how terrible your actions were." He got something from his desk, a pill, went to a pitcher on a table on the other side of the office, "water?"

"No," Erich looked to see what he was doing and felt badly for him. "You are alright then?"

He swallowed the pill and choked for a moment, then swallowed and drank the water, "I'm the doctor here."

Erich turned and sat back on the chaise. "Yes, no doubt."

"I will add to your bill if you patronize me." He returned to his desk, sat down and got his notepad and pencil. "Where to begin today?"

"The house at Gramzow, Germany, I believe it was March of thirty-six," Erich said. He rested his head on a little pillow that was quite comfortable. He turned to the lamp by the window and stared at it; the faded white glow brightened again and he was blinded for a moment.

When the white glow dimmed, he was in Germany and rode in a truck with an old man, sixtyish and heavy set. The night was cold, but nice and clear. The old man mumbled German songs as he drove to keep his mind busy. Erich was across the border from Poland and managed to get to a highway where he hitched a ride with this old man who sang in broken words.

The driver asked, though not to be rude, a number of questions: Where was his town? Gramzow. Why was he gone from Germany? On holiday. What did his father do? Before he died, "He was a carpenter."

The old man laughed, "Like the Jew King, a carpenter."

Erich didn't find it funny, "Perhaps, he's not just their King."

The driver eyed him, "What does your mutter do?"

"She is dead." Erich said.

There was a moment where the old man paused and then apologized.

It went on for nearly a half an hour before Erich cleared his throat and asked how long to get to Gramzow. The driver said that as long as they didn't come to another check point, an hour or so.

Even if they had been stopped, Erich had papers that

Stephan sent and showed he was Jan Brueder. The driver found it odd about one other thing.

"And your bags from your trip?"

"I sent them ahead." Erich held his pack close.

"Gramzow is such a small town, a farm town I believe." The driver slowed to make a turn from the highway.

"Ja, it's a good place though." He knew that the man would try to drive him to the house and there was no way to allow it. Erich wondered about the neighbors too. According to Stephan, there were two families that may have known the Brueder's as their homes were nearby.

His biggest concern was the one he had the least to worry about; the Brueder's had met with Göring, Hermann Göring, and Mr. Brueder, Jan's father, knew him from the Great War when Göring was a pilot. Mr. Brueder was a mechanic and assigned to the Jagdstaffel 26 when Göring was reassigned there after a war wound to his hip. They were quite young and Göring only knew of his son, Jan, some years after the war, so it was likely he'd have no idea what Jan looked like other than similar to his father.

"It will be good for you to stop here." Erich motioned for him to pull over near the edge of town.

"Here?" He slowed down and shifted to stop. "This is nowhere."

"To you perhaps, but it's good for me." He got ready to get out by shouldering his pack and he put his hand around the door handle. "It would quite upset the neighbors if a truck showed up at this hour." He took some money from his pocket, "here."

"Nein, bitte," the old man waved his hand away, "I've enjoyed the company." He waited as Erich nodded.

"Danke," He opened the door, got out, and walked off into the darkness.

The driver shook his head and got the vehicle back in gear. He turned and drove back to the main road.

Erich walked down the dirt road until the driver's lights were gone from sight. He stopped, got a paper out and a flash light. He studied the small map and walked off to the Brueder's home. It wasn't that far, perhaps a mile or so. He had to hurry as it was nearly four in the morning and cold! Stephan said that the house was abandoned for the most part and that the records about the Brueder's house, as he had changed them, were confusing if anyone looked into the matter. Stephan told Erich that he'd been to the house and Jan lived upstairs. His uniform was in the closet along with all his belongings as no official had gone there.

Stephan made use of acquaintances, several of them, to further the fraud and create a web so that it would be difficult to trace the matter of Jan Brueder back to him. He pulled Jan Brueder's death notice and replaced it with orders that were already signed and slipped them into the distribution box; by doing this, the person who handled that box would send the papers out. Once the orders were in the hands of others, they'd be regarded as valid and without further review. Capt. Brueder was alive again and in the service of the Fuhrer. It was never easy to manipulate records, but documents were lost in the Reich fire, but those created by Stephan were valid. When the orders reached the commandant, he signed off on the position for Capt. Brueder and it was done. The acquaintances knew nothing about Erich and Stephan was sure they knew nothing about the real Jan Brueder. The funny thing was about Jan's body and what was done with it; according to Stephan's last message, he had to go to the port, miles away, to get him. The dock official said the name and Stephan told him there was a mistake. He forged documents and renamed the deceased, but a persistent official of the dock insisted that he see a copy of the papers. It was after the official read the notice that he released the body to Stephan, "no known next of kin."

Erich got to the house and there was a driveway made from cobblestone. He paused near the tree line at the end of the driveway and listened intently for any sound that wasn't natural. He looked at the trees and their shadows for things that didn't fit. Nikki had never really known this part of him, but he had more training, more experience than he ever let on. He took a five-inch knife from his pack, hooked the sheath to his belt and then looked around the house. The wind picked up and there were shadows all around, but nothing that prompted him to worry as he made his way up the side of the driveway. He turned sharply and went between the house and an outbuilding where some equipment was stored. He walked closely against the outbuilding so to keep his profile low and unseen. Then, he crept along and studied the windows of the house. He knew that there were other people who fled Berlin and that they might be in there. He knew that the Jews, political rivals and people of other ethnicities wanted out of Germany too. So, it was a good place to take refuge at this abandoned farm house in a town far from the main road. The back door looked like it was in place properly, not kicked in and the area beneath the door knob was unharmed.

He listened again for any unnatural sounds, someone kneeling and the floor boards would creak because of the change in weight or the sound of someone shuffling their feet to avoid a loud step or the click of a door that was closed as he stood there... nothing. He pulled his knife out, held the handle so that the blade was hidden against his forearm, reached for the door knob and turned it; the door opened. Why wasn't it locked? The door made a terrible squeak as it opened and he thought to yell, "Hello!" He knelt down so as not to make a big target and then studied the shadows ahead of him.

The wind caught some old branches and snapped one! He turned sharply, looked at the woods, and then leaned against the door frame. He waited a few minutes before he turned his attention back to the door and stood up partially. He got to his feet and went in; this was no indication that the house was empty and he knew that he had to search every room.

He was in the kitchen and saw the chairs, four of them; they were all neatly pushed to the table and untouched. He turned his flash light on and held the flashlight away from his body. He looked at the dust on the floor; it was undisturbed which eased his concerns as he walked from the kitchen into the living room. The wind played with the windows and wood siding of the house, but it wasn't such an old place or a bad place. He knew that they didn't have electricity here and got an oil lamp to work which was sufficient to light the living room. After a search of the rooms on the first floor, he went upstairs and checked the rooms; everything was fine. He went downstairs to the kitchen. He waited and then opened the basement door. "Damn," he said under his breath as it creaked as badly as the kitchen door. He knelt and edged his face just a bit from the door frame. There was no sound and no foot marks on the steps. He flashed his light, "hello?" He shook his head. "I'm the owner. So, you must come out and let me see you."

There was only the sound of the wind that blew hard against the house. He didn't like it and worked his way down the steps to the bottom. Just as he got there, the wind, the house and the creaks came to life! He held his knife tightly and then used his flashlight to see around the basement. As he looked at each corner, he focused on the things there: a side of beefed wrapped in wax, some canned goods and some other foods that were stored here.

"BAM!" The cellar door slammed shut! Erich jumped, turned and ran up the stairs! He felt his heart beat nearly out of his chest! He got to the top of the stairs and waited... a few minutes and there was a "BANG!" of another door! He opened the basement door with his knife ready and looked around. The kitchen door was across from him and it was open. Had someone been in here and fled? How could he have missed them? He kept his calm and breathed slowly to get his heart to quiet enough that he could focus on his surroundings.

The wind threw the kitchen door open and then "BANG!" The wind slammed the door against the kitchen counter. The breeze came in and caught the cellar door, but Erich was in the way and it could not close. In that moment, he realized the wind got the better of him, but stayed on his guard. He got up and closed the cellar door, then went and closed the kitchen back door. He turned the oil lamp up brighter so to see around the kitchen; he was hungry. There wasn't a thing to eat, but in the cellar, there was that meat and some canned food that was all good. He got a bucket of water from the well and brought it in. The pump at the sink, for some reason, didn't work at all, but it wasn't his home; it was a place to rest and then move on. He looked out the kitchen window and saw the outhouse which was some distance and by a larger out building; the cold kept him where he was… for now.

The next morning, he awoke and had slept in Jan's bed. Why not? He was to be Jan and this business of sleeping in his room would give him some idea of the man he played. Now, the morning day light crept in and he felt the cold all over him. He lit two fireplaces and knew that the smoke would dissipate by the time it was above the trees, so he warmed up and then studied Jan's pictures, his room, his clothes and some letters he wrote, but never mailed.

As he looked around Jan's room, there were things he missed about his life… a desk and chair, a bed and a window that looked out to the yard. His heart sank as he read from a diary of Jan's about his interest in the SS and that he felt proud to be a part of something that would return Germany to its glory. There was a picture of Jan and a nice young lady at some party, but it was hard to tell who she was as there were people there, but no posters or indications of the event. He looked at the closet doors and went over, then waited a moment. He opened them slowly and there were some shirts, a couple of jackets and a pair of work shoes. The uniform had to be there as it was not something he would take on a journey. He looked at the whole of the closet and then went to the hallway where another door was just up from this bedroom. He went and looked at it. It was a plain door, not as wide as a bedroom door and, most likely, a linen closet. He opened it and his eyes widened. There were no linens in this closet and no shelves as the closet held the black jacket, cap and slacks of the SS.

The epithets, the insignias, the rank and the material were nearly new; the Totenkopf on the cap stuck out as he lifted it from the shelf and removed the dust cover. He lowered the cap onto his head and pulled it down tightly. It was euphoric and sickening as he felt empowered and monstrous when he thought about the SS and then how Rohm was arrested and murdered. He removed the cap and got the jacket from the closet so he could get it all on and see if the fit was close to his frame.

The jacket was larger than he hoped and so was the shirt. Jan must've been barrel chested and the jacket was let out some to accommodate his frame. He knew some of the SS pins and rank, but the ribbons he did not know and the trousers were fine with a belt. Also, there was no way he could wear the boots. Jan's feet were a full size smaller. "Damned midget," he dropped them back in the closet, "where to get boots?" The uniform hung well and the shirt wasn't a problem. He'd tuck it in and no one would notice the larger fit. By the time he got to Berlin, he could get it all resolved, but afterwards, he'd have to meet with Stephan and find where Nikki was taken. He spent the rest of the day going over possible plans to get Nikki and leave. There was no question that he'd have to get Stephan to prepare one more set of fake documents. Stephan told him that with all the changes to immigration, such documents were available through other *sources*, but that meant dealing with too many unknowns.

He looked through the house now as it was daylight and went to Jan's parent's room downstairs and down the hall from the kitchen. It was plain and dusty with a bed, dresser and a sitting area with a window to the back and front. He looked at some pictures of Jan's parents, a nice couple. Then, he saw something in particular in a picture. He'd never seen the man in person, but he'd seen pictures of him at the Reichstag Offices, "Göring." There was no mistake that it was Herman Göring. And the man next to him who was shorter had to be Mr. Brueder, "Jagdstaffel 26." He studied the picture and noticed that Göring had a cane tucked neatly to his side and nearly out of sight. Mr. Brueder wore what looked like a mechanics uniform. He lifted the picture and looked at it. Göring was a hero, a fighting ace of World War I. Though he was tempted to take the picture, he knew it was wrong and, carefully, set it back down. His stomach growled and, as there was really nothing to see beyond that picture, he looked for some food.

The dried beef worked well for supper and he had a cigarette afterwards. Now, he felt comfortable enough to put a few more lamps on and sit outside on the front porch. If anyone came, he'd be Jan or a "freund" that heard the terrible news. Either way, he was ready. It wasn't nearly as cold that night and he enjoyed the smoke as he looked at the stars; there were so many of them, millions of stars scattered around the sky like white ink that spat itself on a black piece of paper. Some sadness crept into his heart, "Nikki" as he looked at the other chairs and was alone. The end of the cigarette flared as he pulled in a deep drag and then held it for a moment. For him, it was like numbness when he held the smoke in and then his mind cleared. The cigarette dangled in his mouth as he reached into his pocket and took out the money he had left, which was a mix of Canadian and German bills. There was no way he could let anyone see that money. He counted it, thought for a moment and pushed his bangs back. He must get a shave and haircut.

He thought about the SS and his knowledge of the rules, attire and structure; Stephan would have to tell him the rest when they met. Passage back was arranged already and Erich was sure to see that they had paid for their way as he felt the money would be nearly gone by the time he got Nikki and returned. Stephan mentioned that Erich, working as Jan, would get Jan's pay, but he felt this wasn't a good thing to take Jan's money.

The worst thing he felt was that he didn't know how long it would take, nor did he know if any of it would work. The SS was precise in most things and many of their men knew that there were Germans and other people who sought to get out of the country. If he was caught, he counted on life at a camp or they'd shoot him.

The ashes on the end of his cigarette were quite long now, so he flicked them off and the gray and black matter floated down and away near his shoes. He thought on some other matters such as where to stay and that the Olympics were going to be hosted in Berlin which he felt was an opportunity if needed.

A cool breeze came up and was enough to compel him to go inside and think what to do the next day; he had to contact Stephan. Though he didn't have a formal plan to get Nikki, he did have some idea to make it work. Nikki would have to have fake papers too, but fake in that the SS could verify them and not be suspect. Stephan was his only source and the most reliable. He got up, flicked the remaining ashes out into the wind and then went back into the house.

The next morning, he sat up and shook himself to get the cold off of him. Some snow fell, but he had to go. He managed to get the uniform into a small suitcase that he found and put some pieces of dried beef and canned tomatoes inside. From Gramzow to Berlin by car was nearly one hundred kilometers and could take a couple of hours or more. As he got to the door, he looked back at the sitting room and the hall to the kitchen to see that things were as they had been when he broke in. He thought, too, that his was a good place to stay when he and Nikki were headed back to Poland. Nikki would most likely try to clean it, "it's no matter if they're dead. We can't just leave it messy." He smiled and figured that would be the thing Nikki would say to him and then they'd clean. "So," he said, pulled the door closed behind him and went to the dirt road that would take him back to the main road to Berlin. As he stepped out, the sun's brightness hit him in the eyes and he squinted, "ah."

Dr. Scherbit cleared his throat as Erich studied the light's faded glow and then sat up. He looked at the doctor and felt the dryness in his mouth, "It's the time?"

"That and you've gone into so much detail about the Brueder home that I think a break is necessary." He tapped his pipe on the ash tray to empty the tobacco, put it in his mouth and lipped the end, "besides, I need a smoke." He smiled as Erich got to his feet.

"And me," Erich smiled at him.

"There's one thing I wish to know."

Erich looked at him and raised a brow.

"Why SS?" Dr. Scherbit asked.

Erich thought for a moment, "Nikki was in a camp at that time. The more I thought on the matter and communicated with Stephan, the more we realized that if there was an opportunity to be SS, it would fit better." He pursed his lips, "The Gestapo was far too involved with themselves and their ranks." He chuckled, "The Gestapo spent as much time spying on their own people as they did on German citizens." He cleared his throat, "Stephan worked at SS Headquarters and I had experience as SA, so it seemed a good fit to get access to Nikki's whereabouts, not be caught as myself and get him out."

Dr. Scherbit nodded, "such a great undertaking."

"Indeed, now for a cigarette," he brushed out his shirt, went to the stand and got his jacket. After he put his jacket on, he nodded at the doctor, "good day." He left and was on the street before Dr. Scherbit had a chance to get the tobacco into his pipe!

The walk home was quiet and he used that damn side street or as Nikki called it, "filthy alley where criminals lie," to get home. He enjoyed the warmer days as they went into late April; they loved the spring or that is that Nikki *loved* and Erich enjoyed.

He thought about the doctor and his willingness to see him, but in the back of his mind he pondered about the doctor's interest in that he was a German who lived in Canada and, now, stated that he had been a member of the Sturmstaffel. Would he inform his friends in Israel who had a group of their own to hunt down former members of the party and investigate them? Or would the good doctor wait to hear the whole of the story before he acted? Erich thought on the matter as he made his way home.

He looked at buildings, the people in cars as they passed and he looked ahead to see what might be coming. He had a funny take on people who looked down; he thought they looked down for one of two reasons, fear or guilt. He was trained to never look down, but to look straight ahead and in the eyes of other men so as to assert himself. He looked up the river path and thought more about the doctor; what did he really know about him? What did he know about this man who had listened to some of his secrets? Nikki held the details as he was the one to arrange it all.

CHAPTER 6: DR. IBRAHIM SCHERBIT, PH.D.

He held his pipe tight between his lips, drew in the heavy sweet smell smoke, and let the flavor soak into his senses. "Ah." Then, he got his pencil and wrote about Erich.

Patient: Erich Schmidt, 4/22/1954, suffers from a sort of post-trauma after incidents related to his return to Germany, 1936, where he masqueraded as an SS Officer, I believe. What's curious is that he does, at times, hold back things that, I believe, reflect the reality of what he did while in the position of an SS Officer, things that are malicious and a part of the Final Solution. However, it is important to note, that there is little evidence now to support in part or as a whole the aforementioned allegation. What it relates to is Erich's horror or guilt as he may have felt compelled to participate in activities that were egregious and, now, the activities can no longer be contained, so his thoughts of these activities are coming from his sub conscious to his consciousness in dreams; these dreams are only dreams in that they occur at night; in the moment he is awake, there is his realization that they have happened and he is guilty of what he did. Furthermore, Erich's friend, Nikki, believes that they are causing Erich's mental and physical health to deteriorate —agreed and acknowledged that such realities, psychological traumas, can and will cause substantive mental and physical health problems. With reference to Maslow's Motivation and Personality, Erich's psychological needs are met, but his safety needs are in question. Further consultation will continue for a period as necessary.

END NOTE.

The smoke floated around him in a heavy cloud. He wrote his initials on the note about Erich and then closed his pad.

Lucy knocked in a gentle way and then opened the door, "your last appointment, France Lachance, has cancelled and will come next week."

He smiled and did not make any other movement to indicate how he felt or thought of Mrs. Lachance. "That's fine, Lucy. Please close up and go home then."

She smiled wide and winked, "thank you." She loved to leave early and got her things before he thought to ask about the trash.

He got his brief case which had a flap over the top of it and a couple of small belt buckles. The walk home was quiet and he admired people he saw as they went about their business going home, selling things or making small talk along the sidewalk.

A young couple, with their eyes locked on each other, nudged their noses. He reached for her hand, but she resisted and looked at the passersby with concern.

Young people sat in the outdoor café and chatted like birds on a wire. Dr. Scherbit slowed his walk and admired them. Some were students from the university who had their books, but "not their brains" as he'd tell his wife, Klara, because they were there with girls.

Everything about the human condition excited him. It wasn't that people *were* people, they were conditioned and unconditioned and their parents and their family all had a hand in the making of themselves that intrigued him. Then, there were the people that, despite their upbringing, become so different and so far from their family's norm that they do not resemble any part of their being from that family. He smiled at an older man, most definitely in his seventies, as he picked up a schnauzer and carried it across the street.

He stopped and admired the man who, he thought, either lost his wife and this was his best friend now or had a wife and preferred the dog over her company or... "so the list goes on" he said aloud and a woman looked at him with wide eyes. He shook it off and pondered the idea that there is black and white in the world, yin and yang, but there is a great deal of gray. When he thought of that, he reflected on similar things that Erich knew and was involved in. "God help us."

He managed to keep his emotions to himself, but he had family in Germany before the second war. Two cousins, who he thought, fled to Italy and then planned to cross to Egypt or Libya, but they were arrested in 1938; they were taken to Buchenwald and the family did not hear from them again. When the war was over, they received a notice that his cousin had been found at Buchenwald; Matthew survived and when they saw him, they were shocked that their happiness turned to horror.

He thought about it all and stepped to the side of the walk and waited. His brother said that Matthew looked like paper; his skin was so thin that you could see through it to his bones. He shook his head and tried to smile, "smile Ibrahim". He told himself and he did. "Smile," he said again and looked around, but there were fewer people now and he felt alone. He turned and got back on his walk home, because his wife would have dinner ready and she was a wonderful cook. She was also certain to say something if he came late.

Ofer, his other cousin, was killed during some sort of experiment and they never did hear what experiment was performed on him. Matthew refused to discuss it. With all that had happened to the poor man, the family left it alone.

He dipped his head in prayer and said something under his breath, "God, filled with mercy" and then he whispered the rest of the prayer. He looked up and nodded as a man went by and tipped his hat, an unknown neighbor, "Shalom." Ibrahim saw him at the synagogue just a week ago.

He stopped at the steps and looked at the door to his house. This was his moment to shake off the job. As much as he enjoyed helping people be well in their minds, this was a time for him to let them go and be with his family in thought and in soul.

Klara opened the door and held her hands by her tummy, "You'll eat here Ibrahim, not down there." She was a beautiful woman, dark hair, deep brown eyes and, after three boys, she was still had a very nice womanly shape.

"No, I believe not." He got his pipe out and tapped it on the bannister; there were all sorts of gray and black marks from where he tapped his pipe over the years; they looked like spots of paint that splattered in thumb sized globules. He walked up, kissed her on the lips and then went in. As she pulled the door shut, she got his brief case and rubbed his shoulder.

"There now, the weight of your world is shared." The door clicked shut.

After dinner, they sat quietly and she hesitated, but then got up and cleared the table. She methodically went from the table to the kitchen and set things down. She came in and didn't look at him when she picked up the soup bowl, "you're thinking Ibrahim." She turned and went to the kitchen, set the soup bowl down, "what's bothering you?" She came back, put her hands on the back of the chair and looked at him, "hmm?"

He sighed, "Ah, after this time with you I don't want to trouble you."

"And with that, I'm supposed to go about finishing the dishes?" She said, pulled the chair back and sat down. "What is it?"

He smiled and got his pipe as he tried to get comfortable in the chair, "a patient."

"They take their problems to you; you take their problems to me and I pass them to ..." She smiled and looked up.

He chuckled, "well." He mouthed the end of the pipe, "Do I not pay you well?"

"If you did, there would be someone to pick up the dishes," she smiled.

"Ah..." He knew to get to the point, because she didn't care to leave things sit as the dishes sat on the counter, as the pipe sat in his mouth or that the table had crumbs and sat. "He's..."

"No, the patient," she said.

"The patient came to me suffering from nightmares." He sighed.

"Oh," she sat back.

"The nightmares were... are tied to real events of things the patient did years ago." He mouthed his pipe and wanted to light up, but not in the house.

She raised her brow.

"The patient may have committed some sort of crime..."

"And this was long ago?" She asked.

"Not long enough, but I do not have the certainty that he truly committed any crime." He got his tobacco pouch out.

"Then, why do you worry?" She moved the salt and pepper back to the stand and picked at some crumbs.

"For what he may tell me," he stuffed his pipe with the tobacco.

She stood and put her hands on the back of the chair, "Until the patient tells you something, you should not judge, Ibrahim."

"The patient may be a NAZI." He thumbed down the tobacco, put his pipe in his mouth and then sat back.

Her rosy cheeks faded to an almost pasty rose color and her grip on the chair tensed so much that her knuckles cracked. She cringed at the sound and then crossed her arms. "That patient would not have come to you."

"His friend sent him to me for... reasons I'm not quite clear on yet."

When Klara was nervous, she teased her bottom lip and he saw that she teased it. "Ah, I'm sorry to have said so much."

She smiled, turned, went to the kitchen and turned the water on. The clank and clang of dishes kept her busy so her mind did not go any further into what he said. Then, she shut the water off and there was silence. "My darling, this patient..." She came to the pass-through and stood there with a towel.

He looked up at her.

"You hear things, perhaps, you should..."

"No, I'm not ready to tell the police." He stood up, "besides, there's nothing for me to be concerned about yet."

She teased her lip, "and that's why you felt you should discuss it with me?" She asked, stayed for a moment and then turned and finished the dishes.

He looked at the table and then went outside to have his pipe. Under his breath he said, "That *is* why I discussed it with you my love, to see how you felt and confirm what I felt... not to judge, but to be cautious."

CHAPTER 7: BERLIN, RED CABBAGE AND SCHNITZEL

Erich arrived a few minutes before their session and admired the time he had to be with the "nut cases" he told Nikki. Nikki told him not to say those words, but Erich thought it was funny to be with them and wonder what was on their minds.

Dr. Scherbit did not say Erich's name, but nodded at him as he stood at the door. The room was empty now and Lucy got her things together, "good night." She pushed her chair to the desk and left.

"Here we are," Dr. Scherbit said as Erich hung his jacket and went about putting the room in order—moved the chaise to face the door, closed the curtains and the window (partially) and then got comfortable.

"Yes, here we are." Erich nodded at him and closed his eyes tightly to push out the dust and soreness.

Dr. Scherbit looked at his notes, "We left off that you were on the way to Berlin."

Erich opened his eyes and looked at Scherbit, "Ja, I did." He turned slowly and looked at the lamp in the corner. The white glow seemed so soothing that he stared at it only for a moment and he was there... in a car with a young man and on the road to Berlin.

Germany, winter, 1936, a young man drove to the U-bahn and he worked in a local factory. This was the way of things as Germany's output of military equipment leapt from the past year. Erich listened, but did not involve himself in the conversation so much that he would come to be known to the young man. "Ah, here is fine."

The young man slowed and then stopped, "alright then, veil gluck to you, Jan."

Erich didn't look at him, "ja, danke" and got out of the car with his suit case and pack. He shut the door without another word, turned and went to the U-bahn at Stettiner Bahnhoff which was a large station with many trains. This was a much safer place to go to as there would be many people and an opportunity to get a feel for his surroundings. There were more Gestapo than he thought he might see at the station and he didn't want to draw attention to himself by looking at a map, "know where you're going" he said to himself. He caught a quick glimpse of the platform and then got his ticket. After a few moments, he was at the train and gone... headed to downtown Berlin. Stephan would see him this evening.

As the train made its way south, Erich admired the peacefulness that the wheels made, "clickity - clackity" and so on. He rested his head against the seat back, took a deep breath and then sighed as the train slowed for the next stop.

He put his papers back and sat back as the train came to a stop at the next station. It wouldn't be much longer to get to Stephan's flat. The key was in the planter and there was no cause for further alarm, so he rested until the porter announced the stop for him, Belle-Alliance Straße.

Erich had some shopping to just get necessary things and he wanted to visit a store that he knew Nikki loved to go to... Warenhaus Jandorf which was the historical name, but now it was Hertie department store. After the SA blocked Jewish stores in 1933, the family owners, Tietz, were forced out of Germany and the store was given to new, Aryan, owners. Just then, the conductor announced, "BELLE-ALLIANCE STRAßE!"

Erich came out of the U-bahn and up the steps where he looked at the people who walked at a casual pace. There didn't seem to be quite the frantic commotion here as in other parts of Berlin. In fact, it felt quite normal even with the sight of a couple of SS officers who walked past and could care less about him.

There were elongated red banners with swastikas hung on a line across the straße and they were small triangles with the swastika in the middle of them. The sudden appearance of these banners disturbed Erich and the little bit of excitement he felt to be back home was short lived. He caught himself as he shook his head and then stopped. Someone might say something as to why he shook his head whilst looking up at the banners of the party. A cold gust of air pushed him and he walked off to Hertie with his small bag and backpack. Stephan lived a few blocks from here and he would go there shortly.

The newspapers were full of headlines about the Olympics of 1936 and the preparation for the games in August. Erich got a paper to see what all was going on as he must have information and a current knowledge of things. He went to Hertie and then to a local shop to get the coat sewn up; they said that a day was needed to hem it properly and were delighted to do their work for the SS! He didn't care and simply nodded, "danke." He left and went to a park near Stephan's flat and thought to wait for him until six in the evening. He felt awkward to get the key and go in the apartment without Stephan, so he waited by the small park.

Birds ruffled their feathers to fend off the cold weather, but the sun shined and there was a hint at spring and much warmer weather. A man, much older and tired looking, fed squirrels and pigeons. Some women walked by and Erich looked up at the sun which nearly blinded him, but it felt so good to warm his face.

"Erich?" Dr. Scherbit said, "Erich!"

Erich jumped and looked around the office, this business of going back to that time and delving into it so hard made him wonder which was the real place, "sorry." He felt cool and nearly cold as he didn't have his coat on, but it was late April in Canada and, though not spring yet, it wasn't winter either.

"Your accent... sometimes, comes on quite strong." Dr. Scherbit held his pipe above the ash tray ready to tap it if Erich hadn't snapped out of this journey through Berlin. "You did very well and... to tell you truthfully, I am surprised you made it into Germany under such circumstances all for a..."

"Freund," he sat up and said quickly, then wiped the sleep from his eyes. "He squinted to let his eyes adjust, "just a good freund, I mean friend."

"You know, it's alright to have such friends." He smiled.

"Thank you, doctor." He got up, straightened his slacks and got his jacket from the coat hook, "good evening."

Dr. Scherbit, "Practice your therapy!"

Erich nodded, opened the door and left. The steps passed by in a blur as did the street and the side street until he reached the river walk. He stopped and the sun warmed the back of his neck. He turned and looked at the sunset with its powerful orange glow; it was a great comfort to him.

Erich, normally, would have that time with Nikki, but now he had it all to himself and felt good about it; the sun was his to do with as he pleased. His eye lids dropped shut and he just stood there in silence while the rest of the world went on without him. It was then that something odd happened and unusual for him as the ends of his lips lifted upwards slightly so that he appeared to smile at the sun. The sun smiled back and they seemed to be good freunds; he thought about this word, freund, as it was considered a friend and not romantic. When he thought of Nikki, this was a romantic friendship and called for him to think "meine freund" when he saw Nikki in his mind. The sun was a freund... as a close friend with no romantic ties. "Freund," he said aloud and smiled wide. He opened his eyes enough to see his freund descend, so he winked, turned and went home. Nikki made red cabbage and pork schnitzel!

The smell of pork schnitzel crept out of their windows and down to the street where a few of the Canadians were jealous and inhaled the delicious smell. Erich got to the door and inhaled deeply, "ah." He went in and up the stairs. Just as he got to their flat, the door was cracked so that the apartment didn't smell so strong from the pork schnitzel. He looked at the door across from theirs as the neighbor lady often was so nosey that she once looked through the open door into their apartment. Erich caught her and said something in German to which she screamed and ran!

Happily, she wasn't outside her door, but Erich saw her shadow go past the base of the door. He smiled again and thought to himself, "none for you!" He went in, "Nikki!"

"Yes, I'm here." Nikki stuck his head into the hallway and blew a kiss to Erich. "Come now, it's nearly ready."

Erich went right to him where they kissed and hugged each other, "delicious... even from the straße, I could smell it."

"Yes, your jacket." Nikki winked at him, they kissed again and then Erich hung up his jacket. "Should I set the table?" Erich asked as he turned back up the hallway to the kitchen.

"When have you ever?" Nikki chuckled at the thought.

He smiled and, no, he had never set the table.

Erich sat patiently, because Nikki had to remove his apron, get to the table, look things over and then and only then would he sit; after he sat, he would turn to Erich for the "prayer" and then to eat. Nikki got his apron off and hung it. He peeked at Erich and then smiled, "yes, I'm coming." He sat down, looked at Erich and smiled, "thanks."

Nikki gave thanks, said "Amen" and they ate.

Erich dug into the red cabbage first, handed it off to Nikki and then got the schnitzel! He stopped and looked at his love, "Das ist wunderbar, meine liebe."

"Danke," Nikki got the bowl of red cabbage and took a portion for him, but not very much.

Despite Erich's love for food, especially this favorite dish of his, there was no way to miss that Nikki didn't take much from the bowl, "was?"

"English," Nikki got the schnitzel.

"What is wrong?"

Nikki took a slice of schnitzel and set the pan down. "Not a thing," he said.

The pork was so juicy that Erich let those juices float around his tongue and soak into his taste buds, "mmm." He swallowed and smiled, "so, all this delicious cooking and you eat so little."

Nikki sighed politely, but there was something wrong and Erich stopped chewing. "Nikki," he set his fork down.

"Ah, just a feeling of…" He watched Erich's happy expression fade and he knew to say no more, "home."

Erich chewed up the remaining food and took a drink, "We can leave for Berlin."

"Oh? So, to pack up with work and just leave, like you did to me when we left Germany?" Nikki asked, "no, I'm fine. We will go in the summer as planned."

Erich wasn't so easily fooled, "This is all that ails you?"

"Yes," he reached and touched Erich's arm, "yes, to see mama and papa's place and, perhaps, to look up old friends." He got his fork and ate.

Erich eyed him, "for the moment, I thought maybe there was some illness… physical illness."

Nikki knew to kill this matter before Erich worried too much, "it's nothing. I'm homesick." He moved the cabbage over to Erich, "How was the visit today?"

Erich smiled and knew when Nikki moved the food to him, he had to stop. "Good, we… it was Berlin of thirty-six."

"Ah, that March?" His brow rose.

"Ja, when I arrived to meet with…" he hesitated, "well, you know."

"And Hertie, you told me you shopped while I was in the camp?" Nikki rolled his eyes.

"Ha, only to…"

"Get your personal things, I know." He it was funny to tease Erich.

"So, it went well and he made his noise so as to stop me from going further about the uniform and the meeting." Erich got some more cabbage, wine and a half of what was left of the pork schnitzel. "I thought of those people."

"Nein," Nikki said abruptly, "Dies ist am besten für ihr treffen… mit Doktor Scherbit. Ich kenne die geschichte."

"In English," he moved the cabbage back to Nikki, "yes, it is best to wait to tell Herr doctor." He took a drink of wine, "you do know the story." They looked at each other and tried to smile, but it was hard to be happy as a shot of those horrible memories came to each of them.

Nikki's mind hung on a moment at Dachau where men were beaten. He got a drink of wine and looked out the window towards the street, "ah, well."

Erich's brief glimpse was, unfortunately, more gruesome and he felt his stomach turn, "The pork has settled." He smiled.

They knew to let the moment go or it would ruin their evening of pork schnitzel and red cabbage as if that was the worst damage it would do to them. "Can't let my stomach feel that this is over," he said happily. "You've gone to so much work for me."

"I have." Nikki said and they laughed, though it was not a hearty laugh; it broke the moment and they were going to be fine.

"You have and we will go to Berlin in the summer... we will go home." He said, leaned over, and kissed Nikki on the cheek.

"I will shop at Hertie." Nikki beamed.

Erich winked, "ja, you may shop as you please." He looked at the other half of the pork schnitzel and then at Nikki, "bitte."

"You eat it, for me I'm not so hungry." He winked.

Erich ate up the red cabbage and schnitzel. The evening turned into night, they cleared the table, and then went to the sitting room where Erich opened the window to have a smoke. Nikki sat and listened to a radio program. Erich knew his love well and knew he was homesick; it'd been close to seventeen years since they were in Berlin.

The glow of lamps along the river front showed through their curtains. After they turned in and were asleep for a couple of hours, Nikki got out of bed. He went to the closet, opened the door quietly, stepped in, and slowly pulled the door shut. He got between two packed moving boxes and pushed himself in deep so that his feet barely stuck out at the other end. The bottoms of the dress shirts covered his face. He brought his knees up to his chest, put his hands over his ears, and put his face into his knees.

Erich turned over and pulled what he thought was Nikki close to him, but it was the pillow. He woke and looked at the empty space, "Nikki." He sighed, looked at the closet door, and his heart sank. He pulled the covers from him and took a moment to get his bearings. He got up and made his way around the bed to the closet, but was careful not to bump or bang anything. He spoke softly, "Nikki, it's me."

He got next to the closet door, sat down, and listened; Nikki's breaths were labored. "My love, I'm here." He waited a moment and then heard the rustling of Nikki's arms against the boxes.

"Sie kommen," Nikki sniffled and whimpered like a puppy.

"Nein, there is no one coming." Erich leaned his head against the door.

"Ja, they are come for me." Nikki moved one box to block the closet door.

"Nein, you are mistaken. It is me; I am come for you." Erich reached for the door knob of the closet door, got his fingers around the knob, and turned it gently. "I am come for you, my Nikki." He pulled and the door popped open an inch or so.

Nikki sniffled, "Nein, sie kommen."

Erich heard the sound of the box as Nikki pushed it along the floor right against the closet door. "Nikki," he opened it a little more, then slid it out of the way. "My love, I am come for you."

"I... I am scared." He wiped his tears away and held up his hands.

Erich knew that was his moment; he opened the door and crawled into the closet. He moved the box slowly to the side and there was Nikki all balled up with his hands pushed out to defend himself. He spoke like a cat purred, low and rhythmic. "It's me, Nikki." He left the door partly open and the light from the river front showed his face, "It's me."

Erich moved the box so that he could slide up on the other

side of Nikki. Once he was next to him, he reached over and carefully put his hands-on top of Nikki's arms, "I'm here. They cannot hurt you." He gently eased Nikki's arms down.

"Will you stay with me?" Nikki asked and kept his head low.

"Ja, for my life, I stay with you." They looked at each other and Nikki slowly leaned over onto Erich. "Like our freund Stephan, he is always with us." He nudged his nose against Nikki's cheek. "For my life, Nikki ...." Erich kissed his head, wrapped his arms around him, and nudged his nose against Nikki's cheek. A memory of Stephan shocked him and a wave of sadness surged through him.

Erich held Nikki, but he thought about work to get his mind, his thoughts and his memories away from the past.

CHAPTER 8: STEPHAN, FREUND

After work, Erich enjoyed a nice conversation with the bank president and the success of Erich's work which included some extra funds; they had lunch and then he asked Erich to step into a bigger role that required more time at the bank and some travel. Mr. Jean Lachance, the bank president, was concerned with only one thing, "that some new interests of the industry are in New York and two of them are Jewish."

"This is not a problem for me, sir." Erich sat back and it wasn't a problem.

"My concern isn't for you only, it's a concern for them too... that you can manage yourself well among them and that they may say or ask something of your background." The desk in Mr. Lachance's office didn't appear that big until he finished what he said and then the desk seemed as big as Mont Blanc.

Erich sat up and took note, "I fled Germany because of Hitler and the actions they took against..." He hesitated to say what he thought, "the Jews; that should be enough to dissuade their concern."

"And it has dissuaded mine, Erich." He said happily and his desk shrunk back down and wasn't so large or as big as Mont Blanc. They stood and shook hands. "The account is yours."

Erich was in such good spirits that he didn't want to go to the doctor, but promised Nikki that he wouldn't miss; in fact, he stood before the mirror in his office and said that very thing, "I promise not to miss any appointments." So, with that in mind, he said "Bon nuit, Madge" to his secretary and she congratulated him too as he walked from there to the lobby and out onto the sidewalk. He thought about the trip to Berlin and smiled, because they would have extra money to do more than they had planned.

The weather was nice, but a bit cool even as they got closer to spring; it seemed odd that the weather wasn't warmer. He made his way past the shops and people to the offices of Dr. Scherbit, Ph.D. The office became *offices* when Dr. Scherbit acquired additional space in his building. As it was that day, he passed the park and the café; a wonderful espresso smell drifted from the windows and filled the air. It was tempting to stop and get an espresso, but he was close on his time and had to move along. One more block and he'd be there, but he didn't feel the desire to discuss things. He was on a high and a good one to be sure, so it was harder to imagine going there in happiness to discuss or relive unhappy things or moments from his past.

He stopped, got a cigarette out and stood there. The cigarette looked like it was held by someone else's hand! It looked detracted and distant as if it was a foot from him. The hand moved and a sensation of numbness came over him. The hand trembled now as it brought the cigarette up to his mouth and it was very much like someone else had to help him get the cigarette in his mouth. Just as it got close enough, the cigarette fell and blew out into the street. He watched it and did nothing, "damn you, Stephan." The words felt foreign, but they came from him or maybe from the person who had the cigarette. Guilt rode over him like a tank over the country side on its way to destroy the enemy, goodness. His face soured where his smile had been.

He gritted his teeth and made a terrible scraping sound as the top row of teeth gnashed at the bottom row, "scrape!" Nikki warned him not to do it, because it would damage his teeth, but the action was not in his control. It was under the control of something deep down within him and, now, it was out of control. He turned and punched the side of a shop to the surprise and shock of some people who passed by him, "Stephan!" His fists were so tightly balled that he could have smashed that wall down if he hit it again!

Another hand came up and touched his shoulder, "Monsieur, êtes-vous bein?" It was the shop keeper, a man in his sixties, short and stout. "Monsieur?"

Erich turned, came to his senses, and got the control of himself, "Zorry, sorry."

"Quoi?"

"Desole... Je suis desole!" He pushed the man away and marched off.

As he got to the next block, Dr. Scherbit's office was just at the corner, a few feet away. He turned the knob too quickly and the door got stuck, so he forced it open and something cracked! The door opened and closed, but it was broken. He went up the steps and got to the hallway where he had to take a minute to gather his thoughts. He could not possibly go in the office of the psychiatrist and act crazy! He leaned against the wall and then saw the sign for the wash room. He rushed in, turned on the water and splashed his face. It was then that he remembered his rock! The rock that Nikki insisted he keep with him for luck and to bring him back to a better place, the aventurine. He toweled his face, felt around his pocket and, yes, it was there. He got the rock out and held it tight, "soft," he rolled it around in his palm, "rigid, but not sharp." The stone's healing properties began to work their magic and he was calmer, more in this place than out on the street and punching things. Fresh air filled his lungs and calmed him even more as he pressed the stone to his forehead, "cool," and "soft."

He opened his eyes and there was someone with him in the bathroom! Startled, he turned and stared. Stephan smiled at him and shook his head as he pointed at the stone. Erich didn't say anything, but felt foolish now. He put the stone back in his pocket and closed his eyes, when he opened them, Stephan was gone. It was a few steps to the waiting area, but felt like a walk in a desert where his shoes weighed fifty kilos.

He sat down and wiped the sweat from his brow. "He'll be with you shortly, Mr. Schmidt."

Erich smiled as best he could and then it was time.

"Erich," Dr. Scherbit ran his hand along his moustache as a terrified man walked out of his office.

Erich went into the office and the window was opened to let the stench of his pipe smoke out. He went to the chaise as Dr. Scherbit closed the door, "you've been smoking your pipe."

"I was inclined to say that you smoked a cigarette, but you haven't... have you?" He went to his desk, got his pencil and pad ready, then sat down.

"No," he got the chaise turned and then moved the curtains some to block out the excess of light. He listened and noises from the street upset him, so he cranked the window closed.

"It's apparent to me that you have had some trouble." Dr. Scherbit put his pipe in his mouth.

He looked at the bookcase and didn't move, "ja." He took a breath and held it.

"Would you like a moment before we begin?" He asked, got some water, and took the glass to Erich.

"Dank... thank you." He drank, handed it back and then wiped his forehead. As the doctor went back to set the glass down, Erich took off his jacket and was covered in sweat.

Doctor Scherbit noticed and took his seat, "so, perhaps a few breaths to ease the tension and then when you are ready."

"Ja," was as much as he could get out. He wondered if Stephan would show up in the room and look at him while he talked. He mumbled, "Damn you, Stephan."

"What?" Dr. Scherbit lipped the end of his pipe and held his pencil.

"I..." He thought for a moment.

"You last talked about Berlin, that you arrived at Belle-Alliance Straße to meet with Stephan?" He got his notes back to a blank page and waited. "I understand that this will be very hard for you."

"Do you?" The chaise felt hot as if it were a restaurant stove during the supper rush!

"Erich?"

"I'm just, you know… this is a lot." He said and, finally, got comfortable as much as was possible.

"Yes, I know." Dr. Scherbit got his pipe and held it firmly in his mouth.

"It was at Belle-Alliance that I arrived," he turned his attention to the lamp in the corner of the room. The light, once again, glowed brightly and Erich found himself back in Berlin just down the straße on a bench. It was later now and the lights came on so that the streets were dimly lit. Snow fell, so he walked to warm his feet and to keep an eye around him of people.

"Erich!" Stephan shouted as he walked up. He was quite a handsome man, strong jaw and a modest-muscular build. His hair was short, military short, and dirty blond.

"Are you mad?" Erich asked, "To yell like that."

"Sorry… Jan," he said, but was so happy to see him after this many years had passed. They wanted to hug, but that was not possible nor in their interest. He motioned for Erich to follow him to the door and into the building. He grabbed the key from the planter, "as you're not inside." Erich looked around again to be sure that they weren't watched as often was the case with the Gestapo.

They went in and up the stairs to the third floor. Stephan loved it as it gave him a great view of the plaza and the small park across from his flat. He looked at Erich who smiled and opened the door.

Erich set his small bag down and put his backpack on the floor. He hung his coat and then he and Stephan listened for a moment, "its fine… is it?" Erich asked.

"Ja, it is fine!" They hugged and Erich felt awkward when Stephan kissed his cheek, fearful at first, but then he hugged Stephan back, "Ah, you've gotten skinny."

"And you've got quite strong, nearly as much as me." Erich said. They let loose and looked each other over, "without

Nikki…"

"Right, you don't cook." Stephan tapped his shoulder, "it's alright. C'mon!" They went in and to the kitchen. "Also, I want to practice mein English." The flat wasn't very big with one bedroom at the end of the hall. The kitchen and living room were one room with a small pantry. "So, make yourself comfortable."

"This is nice." Erich admired the flat; it was cozy with a couple plants and pictures.

"Thank you," he removed his coat and got settled on the couch. There was a "meow" and a calico cat ran in from the bedroom, leapt onto Stephan's lap and laid down, "guten abend Herr Felix."

"This is a calico?" Erich asked, reached over and when he tried to pet Felix, she swung a claw at him.

"Ja, but she's going to have a change and be a man instead of the bitch she is now." They looked at each other and then at Felix. A moment passed and they laughed aloud!

"What must I do about boots?" Erich happy expression waned.

"I took the liberty," Stephan moved and Felix jumped from him. He went to the closet and brought a pair of boots out. "There was no luck that you and Jan had the same foot."

Erich shook his head, "so, my past with you shows itself."

"Just in a good way," he sat the boots down next to Erich.

"Sehr gut," he tried them on.

Stephan tapped his lap and Felix jumped up on him, "such a good cat."

"This whole matter has me so tense, Stephan." Erich sat back. His whole body lost its muscle control and he melted into the chair. "In one hand, my excitement is there to be back, but in my other hand…" A bit of sadness filled him.

Stephan sat with him, "It will be alright. He's alive and he's…" Stephan stopped himself.

"Was?"

Stephan looked at Felix who was busy cleaning himself, "He's not on the list." He turned back to Erich.

"What list?" Erich's muscles got their control back and he sat up as Stephan was suddenly uncomfortable. He drew his hands down, along his cheeks.

"Dachau has a list of people." He bit at his lip and then turned to the window. "You were SA."

"How will you know if he gets on a list?" Erich sat up.

"The paperwork can be generated from either end right now." Stephan got up and looked out the window, "so beautiful out there."

"The list, Stephan," Erich got up and looked out the window too.

"He's at Dachau and they are somewhat new to this business of keeping inmates there." He tapped Erich's hand, "He's safe."

"And when will he no longer be safe?" Erich sat down on the couch and Felix, angry about the loss of his space, growled.

"For now, he's safe." He pondered, "And you've heard that Hitler ordered the Rhineland to be taken?"

"No, why?"

"Lebensraum for the German people... it was our land to begin Hitler announced." Stephan went to the kitchen. He got two glasses and poured some sweet red wine. "The Treaty of Versailles does not allow for this."

"The allies will act." Erich got up and went to the small bar that he set the wine on.

"No, they are still in the face of this matter. Hitler, they say, counts on their inaction." He took a drink. "We call it a need for resources to feed the over population."

Erich scoffed, "What population?"

"Precisely," he swirled the wine in the glass, "a nice flavor."

"For dessert," Erich said, "the wolf barks at the sheep."

Stephan raised his glass, "to the sheep that may one day defeat the wolf."

They tapped glasses and drank. "We hope," Erich said, "so, forgive me, but are things in place?"

"Ja," he finished the wine, "for now though, enjoy my home, supper in ten minutes just a block from here."

"Stephan, my…"

"There are no worries between us." He held out his arms. They hugged tightly, "I'm just happy, truly happy to have you here as so many of…" He pressed his fingers against the bridge of his nose, "many of our freunds are in the camps. You will help me to go with you?"

Erich nodded, "of course."

"Good, I am too queer for the Nazi's." They laughed as he wiped away the tears.

"You were too queer when there were no Nazi's." Erich said as they laughed, got their coats and headed to the door.

"No one is as butch as you." Stephan looked at Felix, "Felix perhaps." He shut the door.

It was nearly eleven when they returned. Stephan smiled, "sleep for me as I have to be up at six. Your orders, papers and story as we have discussed are all you'll need. Also, be wary of the SD." He pursed his lips. "They are everywhere with ears as big as elephants." He nodded, "once you have your uniform, come to the offices after tomorrow." He said while he removed his coat and then went to his room. "Erich," he said as he stood at his bedroom door.

"Ja?" Erich got the covers and blanket for the couch. Felix laid there and looked at him.

"You recall in the SA your demeanor?"

Erich's expression faded to a dull stare, but with strength underneath it, "of course."

"Take from Hitler where the allies are concerned. He believes they are afraid… they are unwilling to challenge him and he is a monster, because of this." He tapped the frame of the door, "You must be the same in the SS."

Erich thought for a moment and nodded, "gute nacht."

"Gute nacht," he closed the door and Erich finished with the blanket. Then, he shooed Felix off to the floor.

Stephan opened the door, "Felix," and he ran into the room.

The next morning, Stephan and Erich talked about the plan. Erich had to get his boots, trousers and uniform together today;

his duty day, as they called it, was tomorrow. Stephan told him that the orders were done, signed and on his desk. He had to act to avoid transfer of another SS officer with similar qualifications to Brueder. "And you are sure that no one knows Brueder?"

"No, of course not, but it's not likely." He smirked, "You've got to be the part of this man." Stephan said as he rushed to get his things and get to the station. "The new law is in effect too."

"New law?"

"Ja, February tenth," he removed a piece of paper from his pocket, "Neither the instructions nor the affairs of the Gestapo will be open to review by the administrative courts." He handed it to Erich.

"I'm ready." Erich said, looked it over and handed it back, "no judicial review… there is the criminal at work."

"There is an odd match with the SS and the Gestapo." Stephan said, "The Gestapo are vying for power too, but… I believe that Goring will continue to put them into or under the SS." He ate a piece of fruit quickly, "Himmler and Heydrich are names you want to know."

"So, the two are fighting for lebensraum." Erich said, "I read your notes and recall our supper conversation."

"Yes, lebensraum… their own living space," Stephan gathered some things to leave for work. "The Olympics are in preparation and there are some foreign workers present with more coming." He got his coat, looked out the window and saw the snow, "damn the cold."

"Breathe as Nikki says," he winked at Stephan who came up and hugged him, but Erich felt odd to hug him in a romantic way which was the hug Stephan gave him. "The Olympics are months away."

"Yes, but you can't just go to Dachau and take him; the Olympics can be a good cover." Stephan shook his head, "And I recall that you and I were so close at one time with much better hugs." He winked, turned and left while Felix meowed loudly, "and feed Felix bitte!" The door clicked closed.

Erich thought on it a moment, "We were very close." He

grinned and looked at Felix who stared at him, "I don't care for cats." He went to the kitchen and saw the bowl was empty, so he got the sack with cat food and put some in it. Felix came in and looked him over, "eat."

Felix didn't eat, sat there and licked himself.

Erich shook his head, went to the living room and cleaned up. He got his things and looked out the window at the snow. He dressed and had to get his uniform so that he would be ready.

The light was on in the living room and looked like just a faint fluorescent glow, but the glow was enough to catch Erich's attention and he walked over to turn it off. Why had Stephan left it on? The light grew brighter and it nearly blinded him, but it didn't hurt.

"Erich?" Dr. Scherbit said. "Hello," he tapped Erich's shoulder.

Erich jumped, sat up quickly and then looked at him. He cleared his throat. "I…"

"Get so deep into your story that you are not here." Dr. Scherbit sat down and made some final notes. "It's alright, because you are not the first to sit there and lose yourself in your thoughts."

"No, perhaps not," Erich got up, got his coat and walked to the door. He wiped the sleep from his eyes and looked at the doctor, "next week then?"

"How are you feeling?"

"Feeling?"

"Yes, Erich… how are you feeling at this moment?" He asked and set his notepad down.

"I…" He sighed. "I'm fine; I don't feel anything to be honest."

"Good."

"This is good?" Erich got the door knob in hand.

"Yes, because as you dig into those images, those moments that gave you grief, they will not upset you as much and… I hope that you will find peace with them." He got his pipe.

Erich thought on it, looked up and then looked at the doctor, "I hope so too as it pained me before I came in to talk about my freund." He opened the door and left for home.

He pondered about Prinz-Albrecht Strasse and gritted his teeth.

CHAPTER 9: SS, PRINZ-ALBRECHT STRASSE-8

Late March, 1936, the SS was located on Prinz-Albrecht Straße-8 in Berlin. Stephan made it clear that Erich must act the part. The building was part of a complex with a hotel at Straße-9.

"So, you went to the offices of the SS as this Jan Brueder?" Dr. Scherbit asked and made some notes and then set his pencil and notepad down.

"Ja, it was my goal to work as an aide to Major Fritz Gerheim and then I would go about trying to find Nikki." Erich moved the chaise to face the door.

"Please, for next time put the chaise back when you leave." Dr. Scherbit smiled and held his pipe up to signify a point.

"Ah, of course I forgot last time." Erich said, then turned the blinds some to take the brightness from the sunlight. The window was only opened an inch or so and not enough to let very many sounds disturb him. He removed his jacket, hung it up and then sat on the chaise, "so, I got my boots, trousers and was in uniform the next day."

"And, if I may Erich, how did you know where to go at the headquarters?" He lipped his pipe.

Erich took a deep breath, "Stephan, when we had dinner, told me about the place and what to expect." He grinned, "And I had some knowledge."

"I'm taken aback by so much that you did and were able to do." He tapped his pipe gently for a few moments and then got his pencil and notepad. It felt accusatory.

"With help... that was only possible with Stephan." Erich

felt a sick sensation build in his stomach, "you accuse me of something?" He laid back on the chaise and turned his head to look at the lamp.

"No, that you said this thing was possible with Stephan's help, yet you knew a great deal." He said.

"I was a SA, a storm trooper, and told you this. The SS is molded somewhat from the SA." Erich eyed the doctor.

"Then, I have misunderstood." He mouthed his pipe, "Let's get started."

Erich turned his gaze from the doctor to the glow of the lamp and he felt it saturate his pupils, then he was on Belle-Alliance Straße in Berlin. The U-Bahn was a short ride to Kochstraße station and he looked at the faces as he descended into the U-Bahn. No one eyed him or looked him over. The black uniform fitted perfectly and if he didn't stand straight, the uniform made him stand straight. He didn't have a long coat and it was cold, but he thought to get one once he settled in. It didn't occur to him to grab the long coat which was in the closet at the Brueders. His hat with the Totenkopf was squarely upon his head and he looked the part of an SS officer more than those who were genuine SS.

At Kochstraße station, there were a few Gestapo and he barely noticed them as he got to the steps. An SS officer, sharp in his uniform too, "Heil Hitler," and saluted.

Erich stopped for only a moment and then, "Heil Hitler." The officer was puzzled by the delay, but continued his decent as there were many other people behind him. Erich got to the top of the steps and made his way to Prinz-Albrecht Straße, SS HQ. There were SS and Gestapo everywhere he looked.

The sight of so many Nazi flags with bright red borders and swastikas overwhelmed Erich. Banners hung down buildings and small triangle emblems were draped across the straße with the swastika in the middle. People relished in the appearance of these emblems as if they would somehow be saved by the emblem or the swastika itself. Then, there were the standards on the building and the stone face of the eagle seemed sacred, but it terrified Erich. He recalled the Roman standard was the eagle and that it was supposed to be a messenger to the gods. As he came up Prinz-Albrecht Straße, there was a crowd of SS on their way up the steps. Gestapo went by in their plain clothes and silly hats as if they mattered. Erich despised them as much he despised the SS.

It was terrible that such a fine building was home to the SS and the Gestapo. Erich went up the steps, in the doors and stopped at the security table. He showed his papers and told himself not to answer to Erich, because as of the ride here he was Captain Jan Brueder.

"Jan Brueder, Captain?" The guard asked and looked him over.

"Ja," he knew to say as little as possible and removed his cover.

The guard made a call and then handed the paper back, "Department for Personnel, dritten stock." He pointed to the stairs.

Erich went to the stairs and made short work of the way up to the third floor. As he got to the hallway, an SS major passed him and nodded; he nodded back and went to the office where he would get his assignment. He passed another office where people typed on special machines with some sort of punch cards; there were hundreds of the cards and Erich was curious about them. He walked to the next office where there were several offices within it.

Stephan was there and waited for him. He opened the door and there were many people, not just SS, but secretaries and other personnel. Erich saw Stephan in a corner office.

"Wo ist Stephan Patz, bitte?" He focused on the secretary and waited as she finished her work. "Captain Jan Brueder."

"He is just there." She smiled nicely and then motioned for Erich to go to the office.

Erich, "danke," and walked to the office. Stephan stood and wiped his brow as the entire affair made him very nervous. "Captain Jan Brueder." He extended his hand to Stephan who shook it hard and vigorously.

"Capt. Brueder, nice to meet you," Stephan still had a firm grip on Erich's hand.

"My hand?"

"Oh!" Stephan let go and looked around, "the door bitte."

Erich closed the door and sat down, "you mustn't be…"

Stephan quickly put his finger up to stop him, "be so quick to rush you off." He got some papers from his desk, "Major Gerheim expects you and…" He looked Erich over, "your long coat?"

"It is in Gramzow." He shook his head so slightly that Stephan didn't really notice.

"I can get you an order to get another and some cold weather gear." Stephan finished up the papers, handed Erich the orders and the requisition form, then stood and motioned for him to leave. "Maj. Gerheim is on this floor, down that way and then to the right, office 343." He looked Erich over, "recall what I've said about the SD and Gerheim."

Erich smiled, "I do, danke." He said, got his things and stood, "Heil Hitler."

"Ja, Heil Hitler," Stephan was not himself over the whole matter now and it was never easy for him to lie.

Erich rolled his eyes and left. He looked at the door where an SS guard stood who looked right back at him. Erich knew to dismiss him and stand strong. He walked past the guard, into the hallway and down to Maj. Gerheim's office.

Erich bumped into an SD officer who came out of another office, "Pardon me."

The officer was nearly as tall and looked Erich over, "Captain Ehrlichmann." He held his hand out and held his gloves in his other hand. His long coat nearly touched the floor.

"Captain Brueder… Jan." He shook his hand and then stood for a moment, "I've got an appointment."

"Yes, and you're assigned to?"

"Concentration camps… and you?" Erich leaned in just a little as if to be in his face.

"Intelligence," Capt. Ehrlichmann kept his pleasant face,

"and I must be going too." He made a move to pass and Erich held out his hand as a courtesy.

"Good day," They parted. He got to Maj. Gerheim's office and there were ten to fifteen people who busied themselves on the phones or typed or worked on projects. The secretary glanced at him and then looked up.

"Yes?" She asked and saw his papers.

"Captain Brueder, Jan," Erich grinned.

She was quite attractive and had her hair pulled back so that her soft skin was visible to all; she was firmly in control and not a foolish woman. She held her hand out and he handed the order to her. "He's been asking for you all morning." She looked at it, stood and then motioned for him to follow, "I'm Zelma." They went past the staffers and to a much larger office than the one with the staff, "wait here, bitte." She tapped on the door and then went in.

"Bring him!" The Major announced.

She returned and waved for Erich to come in.

Major Gerheim stood and was an inch or so shorter than Erich; his shoulders were broad as if he'd been on a sculling crew or pulled nets in on a fishing boat. His hair was barely past the side of his head and looked much like Himmler's hair, short and tight, "Captain!" His office was adorned with books and two pieces of art—one of the Roman Emperor Hadrian and the other of a knight from the Crusades. There was a nice picture of him and his family that faced the doorway and sat on the corner of his desk. Erich thought the art was strange, but fitted a leader who believed he had divine purpose and power. There were two chairs and then a briefing table with a map of Europe that had a half white sheet rolled back, but meant to cover it all.

"Brueder, Jan Brueder," he said as Zelma closed the door. They shook hands and Gerheim motioned for Erich to sit.

"As I understand Captain, you have the skill of numbers?" He went to a small bar in the corner of the office, "and information catalogues," he said, "black or with cream and sugar?"

"Little cream and some sugar, bitte," Erich said. "Yes, all of those things," Maj. Gerheim brought the cup to him, "danke."

"Bitte schön," he returned to his chair and moved some notes on his desk to make it look orderly. "So, your duties are to assist with the census and to aide me with the development of information about certain non-Aryan people that live in Germany." He caught his breath, "then to move them to more appropriate places, the camps or out of Germany."

"It is an honor to do so." Erich drank some coffee, "quite good, sir."

"To the heart of the matter, Captain," he said, stood and went to the briefing table. "The SS and the Gestapo are at work, but often bang their heads into each other. Then, there is the SD lurking about for something to do." He coughed, "even with Himmler at the top, it's been difficult to work with them."

Erich approached the table with his coffee in hand, "I understand."

"I must know that you do." He moved his hand across the map. "There is the whole of Europe and with the Olympics coming in August; we must tend to our borders and our cities." He motioned for Erich to step closer, "We must remove the darkness that roams about our home land."

"Your goals sir, this is my duty." Erich clicked his heels.

"I didn't know your parents, but I heard that your father knew Göring." He turned to Erich and waited, "is it true?"

Erich smiled, "Ja, it is true. My father was a plane mechanic and met him during the Great War."

"You must be quite proud." He said as if to challenge Erich to the answer.

"I am proud, sir." Erich stood tall and firm.

"Ha, and me-too Jan... to have such a history of German service and the son of a man who served with Göring in my office," he sighed. "I'm glad that you are here." He tapped Erich's shoulder and that was it, "so, to work immediately!" He motioned for the door, "Your office is just across from mine, but we must share Zelma. She's quite nice when she's not busy, but she can be worse than an SS at Dachau if agitated." He smiled and waved his finger at Erich, "so, do not upset her." He looked at Erich's sides, "We do not normally keep side arms, but if you wish to check one out, I can do the order."

"Of course, sir, but not at the moment, danke," Erich took the coffee cup to the small bar, dumped out the contents and set his cup down. "And I will not upset Zelma."

"Go to your office, settle in and then we will go over your work in detail." He waited as Erich faced him.

"Heil Hitler," Erich said.

"Heil Hitler," Major Gerheim nodded and was happy that Erich was there to support him.

Erich had been in this game when he worked at the Reichstag offices. He left and crossed the small hall to his new office where it was half the size of Maj. Gerheim's, but quite nice with some chairs, two tables and his desk. There were some books and a good view out the back of the building. There was a fire escape for which he took specific notice and the window locks that were turned shut. He set his cap down and sat at the desk. There must be that time to get settled in and he realized that he must actually work. After a week or so, he would begin to figure out the matter where Nikki was concerned and how to accomplish his goal: rescue Nikki and get back home.

Zelma knocked and then came in, "here are the morning reports, the afternoon reports and two pages for…"

"This morning's report." He stood and extended his hand, "Major Gerheim has told me that you are responsible for many things here."

She shook his hand and was flattered, but not taken, "and to make sure that you get your work done so that I can get it to Gerheim."

"Absolutely," he sat back down so that she stood over him. "Secretaries are really the ones in charge."

"The Major might disagree." She smirked.

"I may look to your advice and experience if you permit me?" He leaned forward and they eyed each other.

"We'll see." She said, turned and went to the door. "Your boyhood charm would work better if you weren't such a man." She closed the door.

"Nikki would agree," he mumbled to himself and then looked at the reports. As he paged through them, he noticed the precise print of the writer. There were many names and movements of people from the cities to the Columbia House, a Gestapo facility that he knew a little about; it was used for interrogating prisoners and there were rumors of brutal beatings there too. "I hope you have not gone there." It was then he thought too, "Where are you, my Nikki?"

With a genuine job to do and the role to play as Jan, he worked diligently. So, from that moment, he read the policy manuals, memos from Himmler and other senior staff, the policies of the local offices, authority of the SS, chain of command and the authority of the Gestapo, which no longer answered to the courts. Days of reading and work, he had to keep at the job and never forget his mission or his role.

Days later, Zelma wanted to know when he would have the summation of detainees completed. He handed her the report and her brow rose, because she thought he would have an excuse and no report.

He drank expressos for most of the morning to keep his energy, but three cups before noon made him feel like he could run a thousand miles.

He was interested to read as it was, now, two volumes, *Mein Kampf*, by Adolph Hitler. Erich was no fool and had a history at the Reichstag Offices before the fire, so it was something of interest as Hitler wrote it while in prison. The book would give him a keen insight into something that he had no interest in before, but he believed in the phrase, "know thy enemy."

There was a knock and the door opened, "Captain." Maj. Gerheim stood there with his cap and long coat. "Let's lunch."

"Of course!" Erich got his things and his cap.

"Where's your coat?" Maj. Gerheim looked past him. "Jan?"

"I've misplaced it at our home in Gramzow." He said, "I'll be fine."

"No, this is not an option." He turned and they passed Zelma who bid them a good day as they went into the busy hallway. "We just order another."

"I have done so already." Erich was stunned to see and be around so many SS; it unsettled him to look into the faces of men who were on a mission to rid Germany of people like him, queers. A sudden surge of anger filled him as he thought about life before the Brownshirts. They were free to live and love.

"Capt. Brueder," Maj. Gerheim said and Erich nearly knocked him over as he had stopped to introduce him to another Major.

"Sorry," Erich got his composure back.

"Truly, I knew you were hungry, but we will eat soon." Maj. Gerheim chuckled.

"Yes, quite hungry." Erich shook the man's hand, "Capt. Brueder."

"Major Devstach," he was a short man, barely five foot-five whose neck was lost between his shoulders and chin.

"Major Devstach is in charge of the Racial Office." Maj. Gerheim nodded at another officer who passed by, "I work closely with him and you will work as close with his people, understood?"

"Yes, sir," he said.

"To lunch then," Maj. Gerheim nodded at Maj. Devstach, "guten abend."

"Nice to meet you sir," Erich said and it wasn't usual to say such things, but Gerheim thought about it for a moment and then turned his attention to his stomach.

They made their way down to the main lobby. Then, they went onto the straße and headed to a nice restaurant where many SS dined. It wasn't nearly as cold now, so Erich was fine in just his jacket. "You'll need the strength you have now to deal with some of these men."

"Sir?"

"There are many things coming and we must be flexible. I need you to be strong and to be flexible." He shook his head as they walked into the restaurant, a quaint place with an outdoor patio. "To be both at the same time is not possible, but..." He put his arm out to move Erich over and let some other people by them. Then, he spoke in a hushed tone. "With each person, how you talk to them, whether you are strong or if you need to be flexible, will determine your success and the success of my office." They removed their hats.

"I understand." He did understand that it was much like the politics at the Reichstag.

"Good," he turned and walked in, "zwei," he said as the host checked the tables.

"Sir," the host held two menus.

They followed him to a table and were seated, "So, you must be keen to the people we work with." With that said, Maj. Gerheim leaned over, "read the bios of each of our contacts. Find out what they like, don't like..." Erich took off his jacket and Gerheim removed his coat and then they sat down. The Major nodded at fellow members as the waiter got their jackets and hung them.

"You want me to send them things to gain favors." Erich listened intently.

"If it's required, but it must not be on our books." He half winked at Erich.

"I had some time at the Reichstag and know what you mean." Erich stopped and just realized that he'd made a mistake, "well, like..." There was nothing in Jan Brueder's history of work at the Reichstag.

"You worked at the Reichstag?" His eyebrow, particularly his right eyebrow, went up and he was surprised. His wife would say that both brows were tied to each other, but the right was unable to carry the weight of the left, so the left brow moved only partially.

"I misspoke myself." Erich's body cooled, tiny goosebumps bubbled up on his arms, and his jaw muscles tightened. "I know of the work there ... of the offices as a matter of consequence... before the fire."

Gerheim smiled.

He was not entirely convinced by the answer. "Well... such things happen." He got comfortable and it took a moment for his right eyebrow to calm down and then go back to normal, "the fire that is."

"Gentlemen, for the lunch special we do have red cabbage and..."

Maj. Gerheim, "No, I will take the eintoph and some bread."

Erich looked at the menu. "Eintoph, water and some bread too."

"Very well," the waiter turned and went to the kitchen.

"In my posts, there were opportunities for doing the things you mentioned." Erich hoped to allay any worries that now filled Maj. Gerheim's head.

"Ja, you were posted in München." It was a deliberate error, a test for Erich.

"Nein sir, I was stationed at Dusseldorf Special Unit for four months and then six months at a station near Stuttgart. Both positions were singular in nature due to the work." Erich spoke with the confidence.

Maj. Gerheim smiled, "be sure that you do not cause me to be curious again." The waiter set their water down and Erich took a drink. "Did you enjoy the Stuttgart assignment?"

Erich nodded as the waiter put the bread down and then left, "It was fulfilling, but there was a lack of social time."

Maj. Gerheim nodded and then he moved a piece of paper across the table to Erich, "Get to know the names on this list, know them well." He drank some water and cleared his throat, "The men on here enjoy certain things. Find out what and see that they get those needs fulfilled at the most appropriate times."

Erich took a bite of the bread, wiped his mouth with his napkin and then set it down over the note. "The bread is delicious." He felt the paper, picked it up and put it in his lap. "And the note to them will include your name?"

Maj. Gerheim took a bite of his bread, nodded and looked

around the room, "in a very discreet way."

Erich wiped his mouth once more and then put the note in his pocket. "I will show it to you first for approval."

He nodded at Erich as the waiter sat two bowls of stew down and then left.

Erich looked out the window at the straße and there was some glare from the sun light on the road. He felt that it was too bright and he was blinded by that light.

"Erich?" Dr. Scherbit looked over his desk at Erich who was in a daze.

Erich wiped drool from his mouth. He'd nearly gone to sleep while talking about all these things.

"I'm curious." Dr. Scherbit said, "Did you feel troubled to be in the company of these men who sought to punish Nikki or people like him?"

Erich rubbed the sleep from his eyes and the light from the lamp faded so that now the room was just shadows. "It sickened me," he said, sat up and looked for his jacket.

"Do you feel better after you've said these things aloud?" Dr. Scherbit wrote some notes.

"I feel nothing at the moment."

"It's after seven." He said, stood and put his notepad and pencil in his desk. Then, he got his pipe and locked the desk. "I will see you next Wednesday."

"Ja... yes." Erich got up and got his jacket. He fumbled a little with his jacket and then turned to look at Dr. Scherbit as he came for his own jacket. "He wasn't a bad man."

"Oh? Who wasn't a bad man?" He pulled his jacket on and got his bag.

"Major Gerheim," Erich looked at the window. He went over and put the chaise back to its regular place and then pulled the window shut.

"He was a Nazi officer charged with..."

"He didn't commit any crimes." Erich walked back and got the door open, "Understand that even as I was in uniform and became Jan Brueder, my soul was much more than those clothes and the same was true for Gerheim."

Dr. Scherbit smiled, "Perhaps you'll tell me why one day." He got the door from Erich and opened it fully. "We're both tired."

Erich agreed, "Good night then."

"Good night" and they went their own way once they were on the street. The doctor decided that it was better to go straight home this day as he was already late, no time to people watch.

Erich made his way quickly down the street, across the alley and onto the river front where he partially jogged and walked to get home faster. He trotted up the steps and into their flat where Nikki sat on the love seat with one of his books on social psychology.

"You're home," Nikki pulled at his apron.

"Ja, the... we went a little longer." He huffed. "You and the apron." He shook his head at the sight of Nikki dressed like a woman. "I don't ..." He stopped himself.

He got up and came over to Erich. They kissed and hugged, "good. I want you to be free of those things." He went to the kitchen, stopped, and turned back to Erich. "I am no woman."

Erich nodded. "He says I must forgive myself to be free." Erich hung his jacket and then went to the dining room. Nikki had everything ready for supper.

"Eintoph for tonight, there were some pieces of pork left and cabbage." He set the pot of stew out and some French bread.

"How funny," Erich smelled the stew, "you are the best chef!"

Nikki removed his apron, "funny?"

"Ja,"

"English darling," Nikki sat down, placed his napkin upon his lap and made cute eyes at Erich.

"Yes, for today I discussed my lunch with Maj. Gerheim."

Nikki sighed, "Ah, you remember him."

"How can I forget any of it?" He said as Nikki scooped some eintoph into a bowl for Erich. "Our first lunch was eintoph and bread."

"What a man to work for and that list of his..." Nikki handed Erich his bowl and then got some stew for him. "I think he should have fled as we did."

"Yes, he should have." Erich's heart ached. "He was a good man."

Nikki reached over and put his hand on top of Erich's, "You told him and he decided to stay."

Erich used his spoon to fan away the steam and then got a scoop of stew, "as I told herr..."

"That's not nice, Erich." Nikki dipped his chin.

"Doctor," Erich drank some wine, "his uniform was SS, but his soul was good."

"And so is yours," he got some bread for them, "fresh French bread."

"It will be... difficult when we return." Erich said, took the bread and took a bite.

"I know, but it's for the best." He pursed his lips and then smiled. He wanted to go home, to see his house, and remember his parents. After Erich saved him, he never saw his parents alive again.

"Even on the coldest days, your smile warms me." They kissed and let their foreheads rest against each other.

"I love you." Nikki smiled.

"I love you too."

CHAPTER 10: NIKKI & KONZENTRATIONSLA GER COLUMBIA

Erich got to Dr. Scherbit's on time, moved the chaise, closed the window and moved the curtains to block out the light. Now, it was dusk in the office and he saw that the lamp wasn't on. So, he turned it on and sat on the chaise. "I'm ready."

Dr. Scherbit smiled, "Yes, after all that." He sat down and shook his head. "Are you in a rush?"

"Perhaps, the matter upsets me so." Erich half rolled his eyes and laid back on the chaise.

"A deep breath to begin and then let it out slowly," Dr. Scherbit did it with him.

Erich exhaled and calmed himself as he thought on the images of Nikki beaten and bruised, but he pushed them out as he calmed down. "I'm ready."

"Good," Dr. Scherbit lipped his pipe.

"It was Nikki who went through these things that I tell you about now, but my heart was… for my freund, my heart hurt because he suffered so much."

Dr. Scherbit got his pencil and note pad, "I understand."

Erich turned and studied the lamps luminescent glow which grew up the curtain and then it filled his eyes.

Berlin, late winter, 1936: The first thing any person notices when they're forced from the dock onto the train is the stench. The smells were mild until you stood too close to someone and you were always close to everyone. When a person thinks of smells, they may think of a musty coat or body odor or a strong perfume, but in the case of these smells, they were far more potent. They were the odors that come from the sweet smell of old piss on clothes, rotten stains of blood from beatings, bad breath from bad food, body smells that were worse when they were too hot and bacteria that was a part of their sweat and grew on them. And it was never one person, it was always people shoved together with the entirety of odors that mixed together to form one disgusting smell similar to pig scheiße. Old urine and crap was enough to cause people to vomit and the stench from stagnant vomit was the worst.

Capt. Ehrlichmann knew the odors and loved to hate them. They were in a small room with gray walls and a desk between Nikki and Ehrlichmann. As he sat and looked at Nikki who was chained to the desk, he smelled the stench of old piss that saturated Nikki's trousers and his body odors filled the tiny room. He studied the bruises along Nikki's cheek, upper side of his face and his eye. "The filth in the air tells me that I am alive." He said, took a deep breath and looked at Nikki's bent glasses. "As a German citizen, have you heard of Konzentrationslager Columbia?"

Nikki glanced at Ehrlichmann and mumbled, "ja."

"I will tell you as you appear... distant." He looked at the walls and took a deep breath again. "This was the Gestapo's place of interrogation." He grinned at the thought of the terrible things went on here. "Columbia House, they tortured people and... some rumors were that you could hear screams out on the straße."

Nikki lifted his head and looked at Ehrlichmann.

"Your glasses," the frame on the right side was bent and Nikki wanted to put it back, but the metal was too fragile to bend them back, "they are damaged."

Nikki said nothing and lowered his head.

"I want to talk about Erich." Ehrlichmann said, "There is training for spies in Canada?"

Nikki let his head fall back down to where his chin rested on his chest.

The guard had been with Ehrlichmann at Nikki's home, Johann, and he stood next to Nikki. Ehrlichmann nodded. Then, Johann slapped the back of Nikki's head, "Who else is there!"

"Ah!" Nikki recoiled and struggled to hold back his tears. He didn't cry uncontrollably, but there was no way to stop his tears from sliding down the sides of his nose. Johann punched him again and the tears were knocked from his face! "I don't..." He mumbled and Johann raised his fist. "There's no one else, just me."

"Stop!" Capt. Ehrlichmann stood and waved his hand at Johann. "And you are a spy?" Johann laughed and Ehrlichmann laughed too, "I'm sure that you have a long way to go to be a spy." Ehrlichmann knelt next to him, "But Erich, he is a spy. He worked at the Reichstag before the fire and had a contact there too." He stood, "Who is that contact?"

"There is no one else." Drool hung from his mouth down to his chest. He tried to shake his head, "no one else."

"You can stop all this pain." He lifted Nikki's head up, "but I don't say it again until you have told me the truth." He looked him over, studied the bruises and then he let his head drop as he fanned his nose. "You have shit yourself?" He pinched his nose, "or this is the smell of queers." He looked him over, "You've been here for some months Nicholas and Erich Schmidt is here?" He looked at the officer, "Tell us the answer about your friends. You were in school and know the names of professors, idealist and others who seek to disrupt us." He was in Nikki's face, "You can go after you tell us." He let go of Nikki's head and sat down.

The guard noticed the stench; Nikki hadn't showered in a week. He let his head sag and the bruises throbbed.

"Where is Erich Schmidt?" Capt. Ehrlichmann stood and looked him over, "wasser." Johann poured some water into a small glass, then handed it to the captain. "Here," he held up Nikki's head and poured the water into his mouth.

Nikki gurgled and then spat some out; the water landed on

the desk and some on Capt. Ehrlichman's shirt.

"Sir?" Johann asked.

"No, it's fine." Capt. Ehrlichmann dusted the droplets from his uniform. It was then that he noticed the bits of blood on him, "take him to the station." He got a pen and wrote on some paper, then handed the paper to the officer. "I would like to keep you here, but this facility must be closed for Flughafen Tempelhof coming in August."

Johann summoned two more guards to carry Nikki out and to the train station. Capt. Ehrlichmann raised his hand before they could take him, "Nicholas." He looked at him. "Nicholas VanEch," he lifted Nikki's chin. "From here you go to the station where they will take you to Dachau... far, far away."

Nikki passed out, so the guards lifted him up.

"From Dachau you go to hell." Ehrlichmann waved the men off.

"Yes, sir," the guard nodded. They took him out of Columbia House, drug him to a car, tossed him inside and took him to the train station.

Nikki passed out and when he came to, he was on the ground at the foot of a ramp that went to a rail-car. There were a few hundred other men that stood in lines to go into the cars. Nikki looked up and tried to get an idea of what was going on.

"Get up!" The guard yelled at him and then shoved him. No one from the lines came to help him and, finally, the guard grabbed him! "Up!" The guard grabbed his glasses and held them.

Nikki tried to get to his feet, but his left eye was still swollen shut, "ja."

"Ja?" Another guard came over and grabbed Nikki.

"Was ist los mit du?" The guard looked at his friend, "shoot him."

"Nein, the order is to be sure that he lives." They moved him up the ramp and the men rushed out of their way.

"This is a fool's order!" They got him inside where there were another fifty or so men crammed into railcar. They dropped him and the guard put the glasses in Nikki's pocket. Nikki crawled to a corner, in-between the feet and legs of other men who stepped on him or jumped when he touched them. The guards left and yelled for the people to board! "Schnell!"

Nikki saw the legs, so many legs, and shoes around him. Shoes bumped him, kicked him, and moved him aside. He looked up, breathed in and nearly passed out. The air stunk with the stench of all those men who had gone without a shower, without a way to care for themselves and all jammed into the car. Nikki covered his nose. Between some of the legs and shoes, he saw a body... no, there were two bodies a few feet from him and intense grumbling about the stench as the doors were shut. Legs and shoes did what they could to get away from the two bodies, but it was not possible to move any further. The stench, now, with the doors closed was horrible and it was then Nikki realized that the two bodies were dead; for the dead cannot control their bowls.

Fear, loneliness and despair filled his thoughts and began to shut down the good feelings of home, Erich and his life. Those horrible feelings did more damage to his good nature than the beating Johann gave him. He turned and laid still so that he wouldn't get stepped on or kicked again.

A few moments passed and the car jerked! Some men let out a shriek as the train moved out of the station and then the chatter grew and grew like guinea hens cackling!

"You," a young man said, "You!" He touched Nikki's shoulder, "you are dead?"

"Nein," Nikki mumbled.

"Then, you must stand."

"Nein, I..." His jaw muscled tightened and he rubbed it tenderly to get the spasm to stop.

He got Nikki by his coat and dragged him to the corner, "MOVE!" He yelled even though there was little space to move.

"Let GO!" Nikki yelled at him and his hand flailed above his head, but he had no strength left to stop the young man. "What are you doing to me?"

"Helping you," He got Nikki to the corner after several other men cursed him for making such a fuss!

"No, let go of me." He had no idea what to think.

"You are badly beaten." He tore a piece of his shirt loose, went to the side of the car and wiped it on some snow to wet it. He brought it back to Nikki and set it on his cheek.

"Ah!" Nikki jerked his head away, "stop it!"

"Leave him!" An older man kicked at Nikki.

"And you are like them!" He touched Nikki's face again and held him in place, "It will help the swelling."

"Ah!" He jumped, "bitte."

"It will help you! Stop being such a baby." He got the cloth against Nikki's face and then he saw that an old man, crippled and slung over, had some snow.

He held it out to that young man, "bitte."

He got the snow from the old man, placed it in the material and put it to Nikki's bruise.

Nikki moaned.

The old man nodded at the young man, "when we don't care for each other, we are them."

"Danke, papa," he smiled at him and that was more than enough to cheer him up. "There, you see now. Don't be a baby."

He laid still and the young man held the cold cloth to his bruise as the train went faster on their way south to Dachau.

Nikki didn't notice a lot for the hour or so that they were on their way south. Then, he felt that his head was on a pillow and he came out of his injuries to look at what the pillow was; the young man had placed Nikki's head in his lap. When he looked up at him, the young man smiled and that made him feel better, "danke."

The car rocked back and forth as some of the other men looked for ways to sit and most of them didn't know where the train was headed.

Nikki knew, but his jaw was so painful that he couldn't say or even stand from where they kicked him on his legs. The train would take nearly seven or eight hours for them to make the journey. He rested and thought to regain his energy. His heart sank deep when he thought about Erich.

A soft hand touched his cheeks, wiped away the tears and then rubbed his head, "You mustn't cry."

Nikki turned and looked at him, "I am beaten."

The old man tried to listen to them and then sat down against the wall of the car, his legs pushed out between other legs and shoes, "ah."

Nikki said, "It's a long ride." Then, he closed his eyes.

"How would you know?" He asked and touched the snow to Nikki's jaw. "The guards said nothing."

"They told me." He turned to get comfortable.

"What? What did they tell you?" He leaned closer, "tell me!"

By now, some of the men that stood nearby heard him and wanted to know too. "So, say something young man," a man said.

"Dachau," he muttered.

"Dachau?" The young man looked at the people around him. When they heard that name, it spread through the train car in seconds. "Dachau," he and others said.

Slowly, the faint sounds of men arguing and angry about the way they were treated grew. Nikki looked between the cracks of wood at the passing landscape and the glow of sunlight warmed his face and filled his eyes.

Dr. Scherbit tapped his ash tray, "Erich?

"Yes," Erich jumped, looked at the lamp, but did not let the glow subdue him. He turned and sat up.

"Nikki told you about these things?"

"Yes," he rubbed his eyes.

"There's so much here, Erich." He wrote as he talked, "That these traumas affect you is a lot and, certainly, your poor friend." He turned and was uncomfortable, "forgive me for not being more precise, but to treat each trauma would take over a year."

Erich looked at him, "I understand."

"Now, this idea of Nikki beaten by Capt. Ehrl..."

"Ehrlichmann," Erich pushed his bangs back and studied the doctor as he wrote.

"What happened with him?"

Erich sighed, "For now doctor, I do not care to discuss it further."

Dr. Scherbit forced a grin; he wanted to know what happened, if anything, to the captain. "Perhaps, we should continue with Nikki on the train?"

Erich looked at the clock, "for twenty minutes?"

"If you can," he asked. He was ready with his pencil and pad.

Erich laid back down on the chaise, studied the lamp and thought about it. "They stopped on the way Nikki said. There was a check of the cars, the locks and the passengers."

Erich wasn't able to get as comfortable as he was when he arrived. "Nikki told me that they took the dead from his car and they were allowed to get off, but yelled at the guards about the conditions." He looked at the lamp again and closed his eyes. The faded white glow took him from here and back to the train and Nikki.

"No toilets, no chairs!" The man shouted at the guard who looked to his superior. The SS officer flagged more of his guards to the platform and they lined up in a formation about twenty feet or so apart from each other. The SS guards stood at attention and waited.

There were corrals around the ramps to the rail-cars that corralled the men as cattle to be boarded and hauled away.

"There are no toilets" the SS officer began, "and no chairs, because we do not have the resources to move you in those conditions."

"But we are human beings, not pigs!" The man was angry and shook his hand at them!

"And this business of a fence?" Another man said.

"You are prisoners."

"And is it true you are taking us to Dachau? To a concentration camp?" He was red faced more than ever. "I was told that I was being sent out of the country!"

"After Dachau, you will be processed out." The SS officer turned to his men.

A whistle blew! He turned to the man, "You complained, now get back on the train."

"What?" The man leaned onto the barrier and the SS officer looked at the guard, nodded and looked at him again.

The SS guard brought the butt of his gun up and knocked the man down! "Get back on that train, schnell!"

The man shook his head and was in daze. He tried to stand, but fell over.

"Get on that damned train!" The SS officer yelled and the men pushed into each other as quickly as they could move.

Nikki leaned up. He and the young man did not leave the car, but stayed with the old man and got comfortable in the corner. "What's going on?"

The young man looked between the boards as everyone pushed up the ramps and into the cars! "Seems that they are just boarding, that's all."

The SS officer yelled, "bereit!" The guards took off their rifles and held them in front of their chest.

"He has told them to be ready."

Nikki sat up and the swelling around his bruised eye was down, "They're going to shoot!" He tried to get up, but his leg was in so much pain, "AH!" He dropped back down against the old man, "HURRY!" He screamed at the people, "HURRY! NOW!"

"ZEIL!" The men lowered their guns at the backs of the men who, now fraught with fear, shoved others down to get into the cars!

"They are going to shoot!" One man yelled.

"They would not do that, we are just going out of the country!" Another man said, turned and saw the guards. "What threat are we!"

The man who was hit with the rifle stood and looked at the guards. "Why would they shoot? Someone must say something!"

Most of the men were in the cars and the SS officer seemed to calm down, but he panned each car to see that everyone was boarded. As he got midway, there was that injured man stumbled as he walked. The man turned and looked at the guards just as someone reached to pull him in.

"BANG!"

Many of the men yelled and the train cars appeared alive and in agony as the noises broke through the boards and into the air!

The bullet pierced his dress shirt just up from a very nice brown and cream button that was two buttons down from the top button, nearly the center of his chest. The cotton puffed out and the threads looked singed, a black color that showed through the bullet hole. His shoulders moved back and forth for a second or two and his face seemed so still and perfect until his mind caught up with what had just happened. He weighed only seventy-eight kilos and was quite a handsome man, but after the bullet pierced him, he was like a sack of potatoes. His knees buckled and he dropped to them.

For most people, their minds would feel the fall and say, "THROW OUT YOUR HANDS TO PROTECT YOURSELF!" But his hands didn't move and he fell, face first, onto the rough-hewn boards of the ramp. His face skidded a few inches as his body, driven by gravity and dead weight, pushed his face down the ramp. He skidded to a stop and trickle of blood flowed down the ramp.

"Klar!" He shouted, "Entfernen sie die mann!" Two guards ran to the corral, opened it, grabbed the dead man by his arms and drug him to a cart with other bodies. They lifted the sack of potatoes up and tossed it on the pile. Guards ran to the ramps, pushed them up and locked them.

The whistle blew again and then a bell rang; the train pulled out of the station.

The young man looked at Nikki, "How can they just shoot him?"

"They just shot him?" Another man let out, "My wife was to meet me and we... we are going to Spain."

Everyone was shocked and didn't know what to think now.

Nikki looked out the other side of the car and let the sunshine fill his eyes.

"Clunk," Erich though it was his mind that played a trick on him when he heard that sound, the sound of the train on the tracks, but it was Dr. Scherbit who tapped his pipe on his ash tray. "You are most annoying with that!" Erich wiped the sleep from his eyes.

"I know." Dr. Scherbit didn't do it again.

Erich sat up and then stood up.

"How do you feel?"

Erich looked at him as he moved the chaise back, "I feel like them, shocked."

"I am shocked too."

He opened the window a little more and went for his jacket, "We are all shocked at what happened." As he put his jacket on, he turned to Dr. Scherbit, "For Nikki, this took a part of his good nature."

"He'd never seen someone killed?" Dr. Scherbit asked as he got his things together and went to the door where Erich waited.

"Nein, how is anyone to look forward to seeing someone killed." Erich pulled at his jacket. "The whole thing was a horrible matter." He cleared his throat, "when killing becomes common place, the life of humans will not matter and more people will consider killing to be normal."

"Perhaps," Dr. Scherbit had his jacket on and his brief in hand, "Until next week then."

Erich nodded, went to the stairs, went down and then out to the sidewalk. His way home was, from the Offices of Dr. Scherbit, easier now. As he went along and passed people, he seemed a little more lighthearted. A smiled creased his face as he got to the side street, the one that Nikki didn't like, and he passed it. His gaze did not break from the way in front of him.

By the time he got home, different odors of different foods floated through the air and he went up the steps. Nikki's bratwursts were on the stove and he thought to make potato salad, though it normally goes with a cold dish. Erich stood at the door for a moment and just listened.

Nikki sometimes hummed or sang something when he was alone, so it was now that Erich would listen to him and let his words fill his senses like the food did, in a very good way.

Only a few moments passed before a man down the hall came out of his apartment; he made it a point to pass their door and take in the smells of Nikki's cooking. He was much older and worked at the train station all night, so he got his paper when he woke which was usually around seven or eight in the evening. He nodded at Erich as he passed and rubbed his belly.

Erich nodded back at him. He didn't care for the man to be in the hallway with just a t-shirt on and some very loose shorts; it wasn't appropriate he felt. He turned the knob and went in. His coat laid nicely on the hook and he got to the end of the hallway before Nikki realized he was there.

"Hello," he said.

"Ha, you're home and I didn't hear you!" They hugged and he returned to the stove, got the brats and set them out.

"You know that my body would be a stick if not for your food." He took a deep breath over the brats and then sat down.

"Your visit went well?" He got his apron off and set the potato salad down. Erich looked it over. "Yes, I know it's not normally with supper, but I thought to change it."

"It looks delicious." He smiled wide and it did look delicious!

Nikki bowed his head and Erich did his best not to sigh rudely. He dipped his head and Nikki said, "Dear Vater, we thank you for this food and that we are well here, amen."

Erich cleared his throat and then got a fork. He took the brats and looked at the juice as it dripped out! He chewed slowly and savored each flavor, "mmm."

"How was your visit?"

"It went well." He drank his wine. "We discussed your train trip."

"There was more than one," Nikki showed Erich his glasses. "You remember?"

"Ja, I remember." He swallowed, "You were so strong."

Nikki stopped, "ja."

"So," Erich spoke up to break the moment, "I did not go to the alley and walked passed."

Nikki wiped his eyes, "You listened for once in all these years."

"I do what you tell me often."

"Good, then you can clear the table."

"I do it with pleasure." He knew that Nikki thought about what happened to him. There was such an overwhelming emotion attached to what they did to him. "Come now, you don't let those thoughts beat you up now." Erich turned his chair, held out his hand and smiled, "We have come this far and they cannot touch us again."

Nikki fought to smile and held Erich's hand, "nein, nicht schon wieder."

"No, not again," they went back to their meal and it was a peaceful meal. Underlying the quiet were images of beatings, murders and horror that passed through their minds.

CHAPTER 11:
DACHAU, PASSION
& WHAT HUMANS
CAN DO

Erich was late, but only by a few minutes. Dr. Scherbit stood at the door and watched him as he came in. Lucy was already gone. "Just you and me then," he held his pipe.

"Yes, the time…"

"Ah, my wife is out. So, this evening you may speak for a while longer." He said as Erich passed him and went to the chaise, but Dr. Scherbit had moved it already.

"Thank you," Erich said as he took his jacket off and set it down rather than walk back and hang it.

"I was bored." He went to his desk, set his pipe down, got his notepad and pencil and got comfortable. "Lately, I've noticed that you are less upset… perhaps?"

"Yes, there… it's been a different feeling to me." Erich sat down on the chaise and then turned to look at the clock. When he first came to see Dr. Scherbit, he checked his watch, but it never kept the same time as Dr. Scherbit's clock. "The more that I say… there is a feeling that it's not so bad."

"Good," he made a note.

"But Nikki, when we talked last week." He turned to Dr. Scherbit, "He became upset at the memories of what was done to him." Erich tried to smile, "I feel as though I have cheated him in some way."

"Cheated him?"

"Ja, I mean yes. To have come here first... he," Erich cleared his throat.

"He has some very bad memories too, but you are the strong one and will help him." Dr. Scherbit smiled confidently, "and I welcome him as I welcomed you."

"To be quite honest herr..." Erich cleared his throat again, "Doctor Scherbit, Nikki has always been the strong one."

"Oh?"

"Yes, they beat him badly and then to take him to Dachau... it was very bad." He looked away and pondered the thoughts of it all. "I am here for what I did to get him home."

"Yes, you are..."

"Eine moment bitte," he sat back, "It's his story."

Dr. Scherbit sat up as Erich laid back and looked at the lamp, "So, do you blame yourself for what happened to him."

Erich thought for a moment, "yes."

"You blame yourself for the beatings, his time at Dachau?" Dr. Scherbit twisted his pipe around between his fingers and didn't notice that the ashes dumped out onto his desk; some partially dumped onto his lap too.

Erich couldn't move and felt numb all over. Then, he spoke in a whisper, "yes."

"You can blame yourself for things. But to blame yourself for what others did to Nikki *is* a fool's errand." He sighed, "The blame lies with those who did the act."

He let out a heavy sigh, "It's not so easy when you find out what I did, what I let happen."

"Let my words stay with you as a guide... a man with a conscience is his own judge and jury and feels when he's wrong, so he works to make those wrongs, right." Dr. Scherbit glanced at his desk, saw the ashes and fanned them away. "Look at all that was done, not only the things that were bad." He set the notepad and pencil down, "You cheat yourself, you cheat life and you most certainly cheat what you have with Nikki when you say you blame yourself." He got his pencil and note pad, then looked at Erich. "Now, shall we finish where you left off?"

Erich took a moment to get right in his mind. For him, it was a matter of blame and he blamed himself for what happened to Nikki and for what happened to Stephan, but he was not the one who did the act. There were many good things that he did too. "Yes, I'm ready." He laid back on the chaise and then looked at the soft white glow of the lamp; the white light soaked into his eyes and it blinded him.

Berlin, late winter - 1936, the train was close to Dachau and most of the men found a place to sit. Even with the body heat from everyone, it was still quite cold. Nikki sat up and was able to stand. He wanted to put some weight on his leg to get it to work, "ah."

The young man who had been a help to him stood too, "You should wait."

"No, they will yell for us to get off the train."

He smiled, "My name is Albert."

Nikki looked at him, "Nicholas." He nearly fell when the train cars jerked as the engine slowed.

"Not queer then?" Albert asked as he gripped the rail to hang on.

He leaned near to him and whispered, "No, I'm queer."

He laughed, "I'm Jewish, but…"

They smiled at each other and the old man stood. "I hope to have some food."

Nikki and Albert helped him up as the train crawled along. Everyone got up and pushed to get to a crack in the siding so that they could see for themselves; it was Dachau. The train stopped and some people fell into other people next to them.

It was at that moment when fear swept through the men. There were some noises outside and one man saw SS guards line up. They were just up from the side of a large house which was further down, but visible. The train did not go into the camp and it looked as though they were parked alongside the road that went to the gates, "Dachau."

Guards unlocked the ramps and lowered them. When everyone's eyes adjusted it was late in the evening and they were at a gravel road. Just a short distance from them, there was a fence with heavy barbed wire and guard towers.

There was an SS captain who had thin sharp cheeks that yelled at them, "SCHNELL!" He watched the crowd closely as they marched to the main road that would take them to the Jourhaus gates. From there, things were somewhat of a blur as they were put into lines and marched through the Jourhaus gates. There were twisted pieces of metal on the Jourhaus gates that formed letters and the letters made the words, "Arbeit Macht Frei" which translated to "work makes free."

Nikki looked ahead at the metal words and laughed to himself at the idea of those words, "Arbeit Macht Sklaven." He limped along with Albert and the old man. As they got closer, the camp was visible with short buildings and guards with machine guns. Other guards were lined up along each side and watched them as they walked to the camp.

The SS captain's eyes widened when he looked at Nikki as he limped along.

"Herkommen," he said to Nikki and the old man, "herkommen, bitte." As he walked over, another guard joined him.

The old man was between Nikki and Albert. They turned and Albert's face paled with fear.

"Come here... come on." The SS officer waited, now, just a few feet away. "So, you are injured?" He asked Nikki as they got within a couple feet of him.

The other men marched on through the Jourhaus gates and into the camp on the other side of the administration building.

"Nein, Ich... I'm fine." Nikki stood on his on, but his leg was weak.

"And papa, can you stand on your on?" He looked the old man over and nodded at a guard. The guard removed his shouldered machine gun and stood still.

"Ja, of course," Albert let loose of him, but he dipped to his side and then had to fight to keep his balance. "Ja, es geht mi gut."

"You're fine," he smiled at the old man. "And these two men, you are just their queer or... they were helping you?"

The old man thought on the matter as the captain got in his face.

"Queer or they helped you?"

He looked the captain in the eye, stood erect, the best that he could, and said, "To hell with you."

Albert closed his eyes and fought back any emotion that he felt, no grin or smile, no sadness, no hurt, no fear, not a thing, "he... he's my grosvater." Albert took a step and the guard aimed his gun at him. "He's just," he tapped his temple, "you know."

"Ah, he's your großvater and he has a mental problem." The captain tilted his head just slightly as he looked at Albert.

By now, most of the men were in the camp and it was Albert, Nikki, the old man, the SS captain and a couple of guards that stood there.

Albert realized that his help made it worse, "nein, he..."

The old man looked at Albert, "Do not pander to them."

The captain turned his attention to Nikki, "du." Nikki trembled from the pain in his leg and the SS captain, Capt. Schaus, looked at him, "your leg is bad?"

"Nein, just..." Nikki fought any feelings too.

"Bad," he turned and looked at the guard who walked over, grabbed Nikki by the collar and brought him a few feet away.

The SS guard pushed him down to his knees, stepped back and pointed the gun at his back.

Nikki screamed, "I, I AM FINE! I CAN STAND!" He jumped up and stood! "SEE!" He took a chance and stood on his bad leg, but if it gave out... "See captain! I am FINE!" He had his other leg bent at the knee and jumped twice, "you see... it's all fine!" He smiled wide and held his hands up as the guard kept his rifle on him.

From the administration building, Oberführer Hans Loritz stood at a large window and watched them.

Capt. Schaus looked at the old man, "You must be able to work and be fit... you must be healthy and strong!" He walked over, grabbed the old man by the arm and jerked him over to the side of the road where the old man fell down.

Albert fought back the tears and didn't want to look.

"This ist Dachau!" He pulled his pistol and looked at Albert, "as you said, he is not healthy." He aimed at the back of his head.

The old man scooted around and faced Capt. Schaus.

"BANG!" The bullet pierced the old man's forehead just above his eye. He fell back onto the grass and mud that was wet with melted snow.

Capt. Schaus holstered his pistol and looked at Oberführer Loritz who sipped on his coffee, turned and walked away from the window. A moment went by, "Move!"

Nikki knew not to look at the old man, but he did it to spate the captain, "Bis wir uns wiedersehen." He didn't look at the captain to provoke him further and ran with Albert into the camp. Nikki grabbed Albert by the arm, "Do not cry!"

Albert wiped his eyes, "what?"

Nikki jerked him hard, "Never cry! Never let them see you cry!" He looked around at the men and the guards who were busy with other men. "Wipe your eyes and don't let me see you do it again."

"Okay," Albert said as Nikki pulled on his forearm hard, "Okay!"

Nikki let Albert loose as they joined the rest of the men at the administration building; it was there that they had their heads shaved and were given uniforms with an upside down pink triangle. Albert's triangle was mixed another triangle so that he had a Star of David. Then, they were treated for lice with some sort of chemical. The guards took their remaining valuables such as watches, rings and bracelets and almost took Nikki's glasses, but gave them back after toying with him. Then, they took their shoes and gave them wood clogs which Nikki dreaded.

Nikki, unlike Albert, spoke German perfectly.

Much later, as they waited in the administration building, they got to a man who waved his hand for them to come in to a room that had a chair and desk. Albert was first, "count to twenty-five." Albert tried, but got as far as fourteen and did not know the rest.

"I, I don't know my numbers."

A guard came over with a stick that was about fourteen inches long and flexible. He raised it up and swung it down across Albert's back! "Idiot!"

"AH!" Albert yelled and fell to the floor.

Nikki looked at them, "No, wait! He..., Albert, you know your numbers!" Nikki tried to get close, but the guard pushed him back, "veirzehn, funfzehn!"

"Shut up!" The man yelled and looked at the guard who hit Nikki!

"Ah," Nikki let out, but kept counting and Albert counted with him, "sechzehn!" He counted off the rest of the numbers to twenty-five and they let them go to the next table. They were told what building to go to and then they went out to the yard. There were hundreds of other men with the Star of David, pink triangle, purple triangle and some had an "N" on their uniform. There was a mixture of symbols that the Nazi's put on the uniforms to identify what *type* of person they were in the camp.

Albert, "What do we do?"

It was dark now and the lights around the camp were a dull, dirty white glow that didn't have enough strength to make it to where that light might connect with the next light in the chain. So, there were dark spots around the camp where exchanges were made, deals were done and, sometimes, people were killed.

"We must find food and water." Nikki said took a whiff of the air, "what is that smell?" He looked at the faces of other prisoners who looked away from him; they had nothing for him or Albert. There were some men nearby with pink triangles too, so Nikki went to them.

He stopped near a man who was taller, rougher looking and rubbed his chin as Nikki looked up at him, "you don't need to bother."

"Bother, with what?" Nikki asked as Albert looked all over

the grounds.

"For now, there is food. I'm Duracht... your Kapo." He stood, showed his armband and looked Nikki and Albert over. "Go and get your soup bowls from that building." He pointed at the building across from them, "go!"

Nikki grabbed Albert and they hurried off, "c'mon!" As they passed the administration building, Capt. Schaus went inside.

Oberführer Loritz sat at his desk and nearly finished his coffee when his secretary opened the door. Capt. Schaus removed his headgear and walked in.

"Heil Hitler!"

"Indeed," Loritz said. He nodded at the chair and Capt. Schaus sat down. "We are under orders to treat the prisoners humanely."

"He was of no use to us... he was," Capt. Schaus fidgeted.

"Quiet!" Loritz got up and looked out the window at the empty area just outside the gate. "Now, there is no one at the gate. They are all inside." He looked at Schaus, "but this will change." He returned to his chair and stood over it. "In time, there will be hundreds of people, thousands of them. Then, the order will change."

"Sir?" Schaus sat up.

"For now, the orders are followed without waiver." He stood upright. "When the orders change, I feel that we will have to do what you did... alleviate pressure on the prisoner population by selective removal of those who cannot or will not be useful to the Reich."

"Yes, sir," Capt. Schaus said.

"Do not ever go outside your orders again." He walked over to Schaus and stood next to him. "Or you will be a prisoner too." He eyed the captain, "ist das klar?"

"Ja, Oberführer, das ist klar... perfekt klar."

Nikki and Albert had their soup bowls and walked back to Duracht. As they passed another Kapo, he grabbed Nikki.

"Come here," the Kapo was a disgusting man who smelled of pickled beef or fish.

"Stop it!" Nikki tried to pull loose, but wasn't able to get free. Albert, mistakenly, grabbed the man and pulled his arm!

The Kapo swung and knocked Albert to the ground, "you don't touch me!" He looked at Nikki, "you're going to be my boy."

"Thomas!" Duracht yelled at him.

"Ja, this is my boy now!" Thomas had Nikki by the collar.

Duracht pulled a make shift knife out and other men gathered around. "Nein, he is with me."

Thomas looked at the knife and Duracht. As he waited, many men gathered and watched as the two squared off over Nikki.

"Please, it is not necessary," Nikki held his hands up.

"Take him," Thomas looked at the men around him. "GO!" Most turned and walked away, but some stayed to mock his lack of authority at the hands of Duracht.

Nikki got Albert and they went to Duracht who kept his knife at his side. "You'd better pay attention from now on." He smacked Nikki on the side of the head.

"For what?"

"Other evil in this camp," he nodded for Nikki to follow him.

For the next few months, they were assigned a work detail under the command of Duracht. Nikki and Albert were protected, but Nikki had sex with Duracht to survive and have some protection. He would do what was necessary as he was incapable of a fight and knew he would most certainly be beaten, perhaps badly, and then end up having sex with a man who *was* a monster. Better to be under Duracht who was, despite his murderous nature, decent to him. Nikki looked at the night lights along the fence and thought about home. The whitish glow was bright and filled his eyes.

Dr. Scherbit's office, "How did you feel when Nikki told you about sex with... Duracht?"

Erich looked at the light as its glow faded and the room came into focus, "I wanted to kill him."

"To kill Nikki?" Dr. Scherbit's eyes widened.

"No, of course not," he turned to look at the doctor, "come

now doctor."

"Just to be sure," he lipped the end of his pipe.

"I wanted to kill Duracht. He was a political pig and I knew of him from my days at the Reichstag offices." Erich sat back, "I could have killed him when I was at Dachau."

"You went to Dachau?" Dr. Scherbit fiddled with his pipe.

"Ja, Stephan found the orders that he was sent there." Erich rubbed his jaw as he thought about it. "He made some notes for me and it was, I think, late May of 1936 when he found Nikki." He sat up and looked at the doctor, "Major Gerheim signed orders to let me see the camp as it was the first one to accommodate prisoners and an SS camp." He looked disheartened as he spoke, "but when I arrived and met Oberführer..."

"Loritz," Doctor Scherbit said.

Erich hesitated, "You seem to know more than a psychiatrist would know about such things."

"A Jew knows things just to know them; no one should ever be without their history." He laid his pencil and the notepad down. "Family of mine was at Dachau... much later though." He smiled and got his tobacco pouch.

"Stephan assured me that Nikki was alright as he was still in Ehrlichmann's custody." He rubbed his forehead as the matter upset him to say his friend's name again. "As for the commandant, Loritz was a pig looking to be fed." He looked at the clock.

"A pig?"

"He was at the camp as a matter of necessity to get promoted, that he made clear to me." Erich bit at his lip, "He knew I was at SS headquarters and that I may have some influence to put words into ears at there."

"Ah, so he was good to you." Dr. Scherbit put tobacco in his pipe.

"Ja, he profiled the camp as a perfect place where the prisoners were treated well. He showed me some rabbits in the back of the camp." Erich shook his head, "These rabbits were not for food though. They were to comfort the prisoners."

"Rabbits?"

"Yes, white with pink eyes. I think it was some sort of Aryan thing… that there were no other mixes of rabbits."

Doctor Scherbit made a curious face, wrote it down and then lipped his pipe again. He looked at the clock, but it would be another ten minutes before he could smoke. "So, did you find Nikki?"

"Nein… no, he was sent elsewhere just the week before I arrived." Erich ran his hands over his face, "this damned Captain Ehrlichmann gave the orders."

"He was the SS investigator?"

"He was SD or what they called the security service… intelligence of the SS." He thought for a moment to recall the details, "he believed there was some conspiracy of spies, but he didn't have enough information to put me as Capt. Brueder." Erich sighed.

"Ah, so this move…" Dr. Scherbit sniffed the tobacco pouch.

"Was just Ehrlichmann harassing Nikki," Erich turned to look at the clock and there were about three minutes left; Scherbit tapped his fingers on the desk. "You make some noise when you want to smoke."

Dr. Scherbit stopped tapping and had his pipe, "sorry." He set the pipe down, "as we have just a moment, how did you know about Nikki?"

"It was easy." Erich thought about the commandant, Loritz, "Loritz made it possible to satisfy my interest as to how records were kept. So, a simple review of the camp log and there was his name with the date he arrived, processed and then was transferred, which confirmed Stephan's work."

"So, where did they take him?"

"Ehrlichmann did not let them put that note." Erich stood and straightened up his shirt, "Instead he put that he was under the direct custody of the Kripo." He rubbed his face.

"Kripo?"

"Investigations which was with the Gestapo, but then put with the SD I believe," he yawned.

"Ehrlichmann made it harder to get to Nikki." He stood, got his pipe and his tobacco pouch.

"Yes," Erich laughed to himself, "but we had a lunch together and I thought to ask him."

"And on that, we must stop."

"Of course," Erich got his jacket and went to the door. He paused for a moment and looked at the floor, then he looked at the doctor who came from around his desk, anxious to smoke his pipe. "I believed nothing would come of this time with you."

Dr. Scherbit got his jacket and stood next to Erich, "and now?"

"That has changed." He said, opened the door and left, "good evening to you doctor."

Dr. Scherbit said nothing as Erich disappeared out the door and down the steps to the street where he quickly walked home.

Erich made great strides as he walked so quickly that cars, buildings and people passed by in colored impressions; if it were art, someone might say it was a Monet with spattered colors of people and nature that lived fully and freely.

He made the corner to the side street and avoided it; in fact, he seemed to forget it as he hadn't been down that street in sometime and even that thought faded from him as the images from his past began to fade; they bothered him less and less. He got to the river front and spoke French, which he rarely did, to a man, "bonsoir." The man nodded at him. He got to the door of their building, went in and trotted up the stairs to their hallway and then to their door. In all the excitement to get home, he missed the smell of brats and sauerkraut! His nose woke up in the hallway and he was overwhelmed with a desire to eat. But, his mind ran afoul when he realized he was here with nothing for Nikki. He quietly went down the steps back to the doorway and out to the river front. There was always a cart with magazines, newspapers and flowers.

He stopped at a cart with a small woman who nodded at him. "Je voudrais acheter des fleurs." She got a bouquet of flowers, some marigolds, fern and daises, but Erich grabbed a dozen red roses, looked them over and handed her the money. He hurried back to the door, up the stairs and to their door where he cleared his throat and tidied his hair by pushing his bangs back. He opened the door and the odor of the brats was so strong that the roses wilted a little, but held to their color, "Nikki!"

Nikki stirred the kraut, then set his ladle down and stepped to the hallway. "You're home," he looked at the roses. "AH!"

Erich didn't take his jacket off, but went right to Nikki, "Mon cher!" They hugged so tightly that Nikki's eyes nearly popped out of his head!

"Thank you! They are lovely." He smelled them, "such a good smell over my brats."

Erich pulled him close and kissed him hotly. He moved his lips over Nikki's lips so that some numbness came over Nikki and he let the flowers fall to the floor. He ran his hands down to Nikki's back side and pulled up.

"Ah" Nikki yelped, "easy or we'll have burned the food for supper." But he could not refuse and they kissed more with their hands gliding up and down each other, over each other's butts and groins. Nikki pulled back, "wait, wait!" He turned and wiped his mouth where some drool had formed and went to the kitchen. He turned off the burners, took off his apron and returned to Erich who had dropped his jacket to the floor next to the roses.

They embraced and kissed, mouth over mouth, lips pushing against each other and their hands gripping and pulling at each other until Erich got hold of Nikki's wrist with his one hand and his neck with his other hand. He forced him down the hall to the bedroom and then let him go.

Erich ripped his shirt off and pulled his undershirt off. Nikki put his hands-on Erich's firm chest and slid his hands down over the half curled black hairs and trail of hair that went down to just above his groin where they pooled, a puddle of black thin hairs. Then, he ran his tongue up the center of Erich's chest and back down again. He kissed his belly button and then his tongue glided all the way down to the top of his groin. Erich moaned and then grabbed Nikki's shirt and yanked it off!

He pushed Nikki onto the bed and then pulled Nikki's trousers off. His boxers were soaked where all his emotions had pooled. Erich looked at him and then at the wet that saturated Nikki's boxers. Nikki's strength wasn't just in his mind; it was there in front of Erich, long and thick, curved to the side and it throbbed, so he jerked Nikki's boxers off and flung them away!

Erich pulled off his trousers and boxers too. He slowly lowered himself on top of Nikki and they kissed passionately with their tongues darting in and out of each other's mouths. Their bodies were in one motion of love as two great ocean waves rose and fell, two different tastes and one mass of motion that built itself into an enormous rage! Erich slowly put himself into Nikki, "ah!" Nikki cried out and then wrapped his arms around Erich's back! He pulled Erich tightly against his body and ran his feet down Erich's legs and then back up to pull him in deeper.

"My love," Erich said.

"Take me," Nikki smiled as Erich buried his tongue in Nikki's mouth and the strong, but quiet moans drove them deeper into each other!

They turned over and Nikki was on top, so he sat down to have all of Erich. Erich's face twisted and turned into feelings of ecstasy as Nikki drew it out from him and made it part of his soul, "yes!" Nikki's fingers and Erich's fingers were intertwined as they embraced. Then, Erich grasped Nikki at his hips and forced him down as he thrust himself up! "AH!" Nikki tensed and trembled.

Erich reached up as Nikki looked down at him and he pulled Nikki's face to where he held his head just above Nikki's; they stared at each other with easy grins. Just then, Erich felt the surge of his love and all of it went from his soul to the soul of the man he loved, Nikki, "AH!"

Erich's mouth opened, "AH!" his body thrust forward and up! Nikki was lifted high and that pushed him to let it all out on top of Erich's chest in a heavy rain of his love.

"Hah! Hah, Erich!" Nikki wrapped himself around Erich so tightly that their bodies looked like one mass of sweaty, hot flesh that was joined midway by a deep energy that connected them for life.

As they breathed heavy and hearty, their love connected their souls and remnants of their orgasms slid down the sides of their bodies. They laid there for some time and it was Nikki who edged up and looked at his lover, "Ich liebe dich." He touched Erich's cheek and kissed him again.

"And I love you," Erich gently moved his hands up and down Nikki's back. "Je vous aime, my sweet Nikki."

They kissed gently and then he slid off of Erich to lie at his side. He rolled over and pressed his backside to Erich who wrapped his arms around him. They laid there quietly as their breaths calmed down and they cooled the heat that overtook them. Erich kissed the nape of Nikki's neck, held him close and slid back into him, "ah," so that their souls would stay connected in this physical way.

Nikki let his eyes fall shut and Erich bent his head so as to tuck his nose at the base of Nikki's head and take in the smells that drove some of his desire, "you smell so good."

Nikki let out a quiet growl and tucked himself into Erich so that he was nearly covered by him, "and you."

Erich felt a sense of guilt and dismissed it as quickly as it came up. It had been a few weeks since they loved each other. The nightmares overwhelmed him when he slept so he was rarely in the mood to love or be loved. Nikki was patient and though they had *encounters*, they were never as full and deep as what had just happened. Nikki relished in the thought that the nightmares might come to an end for Erich and that their lives would return to normal. Even the trip back to Berlin didn't bother him and, in fact, he looked forward to it as an opportunity to re-connect with old friends.

An hour passed and they remained with each other for that time. Nikki slid over and then rolled onto his side so he could look at his lover, "darling, my delicious supper is cold."

Erich smiled and touched Nikki's cheek, "it is no matter to me. I love your cooking." They kissed and Nikki couldn't stand the thought to leave it, "and you."

"I love you too." He ran his hand along Erich's cheek. "Come, let's have our supper." He said. They kissed again and got up.

The brats, cabbage and sauerkraut were delicious. Supper was over before they even knew they sat down and Erich was at his chair in the den with a cigarette. The window was open and he thought to just have a couple drags so as not to bother Nikki. Nikki was on the phone with a friend that they met in Quebec City. There was an underground gay community, but Erich was bothered by sneaking around and didn't enjoy it as much as those early days in Germany. He missed the few friends that they had and, especially, Stephan. He thought about Stephan and had a photo of him he kept in the desk. He smoked and looked at the photo.

The picture was kind and had good light for that day. Stephan was jovial and wanted to be remembered that way. Erich got up, went to the window and blew the cigarette smoke into the night air.

Nikki hung up and came to Erich. "So, you have Stephan with us." He hugged Erich.

"Ja, ich vermisse unser freund."

"I miss him too, my love." Nikki reached for the photo and Erich gave it to him, "I believe he watches over us to see that we have kept living."

"When he was arrested, that damned…"

Nikki rubbed Erich's shoulder. "Ehrlichmann," though Nikki did not normally have the desire to say his name, he felt some power over the captain for now.

"He was so close to me, so close to catching me." Erich looked a little sad. Nikki puckered his lips and turned Erich's head to his. They kissed and then touched their noses together, "I didn't want Stephan to do it."

"He wanted to do it." Nikki slowly rubbed his nose against Erich's shoulder, "he chose to save you."

"To save us," They hugged.

They touched their foreheads, then turned and looked at the river. Erich put his cigarette out and wiped at his mouth, "I hope to quit soon."

"You challenged the SS, searched Germany for me, but you can't stop this smoking." Nikki smiled at him.

"Even going to Dachau and the other camp for you," they laughed.

"He told me that after they took me from Dachau, he questioned me about you." He rested his head on Erich's shoulder, "you in a village or something." Nikki kissed Erich's cheek, "to get me to talk."

"Ha, I had lunch with that idiot the week after my visit to Dachau." Erich pursed his lips.

"And Albert?"

Erich was quiet for a moment, "He was there on the list and, as we know, he awaits us in Berlin."

"I miss him terribly." Nikki smiled.

"And he's learned to count in German?"

Nikki laughed, "I thought the guard would beat him to death." It was a hard smile and he let it go as it was too hard to keep when he thought about Albert and his German numbers. He felt some pride when he thought about the old man who faced off with Capt. Schaus at Dachau, "and Schaus?"

"You know what became of Schaus." Erich thought on it only for a moment. "Schaus was a monster and was arrested by the Seventh Army... they hung him for his crimes."

"The old man would be happy." They stood there quietly now and held each other as they watched people walk by on the river front. It seemed so long ago when Schaus did terrible things and he was a faded memory that seemed to come back up and remind them of what terrible deeds humans can do.

CHAPTER 12: EHRLICHMANN, FELIX & STEPHAN

Erich sat in the lobby of Dr. Scherbit's office and watched as two other men fiddled quietly with their fingers. He was dressed sharply and had a finance deal earlier with a large bonus; he was elated when his boss, Mr. Lachance, told him that he had his bonus check for the hard work and was very proud that he managed the deal so well with the Jewish men. Erich was glad it was over as there were some tense moments and a slight confrontation when one of the leaders, Mr. Bellow, pressed him on his background in Germany.

Erich managed the matter so well that Mr. Bellow shook his hand and thanked him for doing right when he saw the Nazi's purpose revealed. What bugged him was to come here after something good happened.

Dr. Scherbit opened his door and a young woman left; she wiped her eyes and seemed to be in mid terror as she tripped on the carpet! Erich went for her arm to help her and she yanked it loose!

"Ne touche' pas!" She sneered at him and then left.

Erich shook his head briefly.

"Mr. Schmidt," Dr. Scherbit had his pipe in hand.

Erich said nothing more and went into Scherbit's office where he would be safer. He went right to the chaise, moved it and then pulled the window so that it was nearly shut. He looked at the room and the clock, then went to the curtains and pulled them to where just a sliver was open. "She was quite upset," he took his jacket off.

Dr. Scherbit got to his desk, set his pipe down on the ash tray and sat down. "Yes, well, like you, she's been through some things."

"Like me," he said.

"Perhaps, not like you." Dr. Scherbit got his pencil and notepad.

"Ah," Erich got comfortable and sat down on the chaise. He looked at Scherbit, "You look as though you've put on some weight."

"My wife, when summer nears, is excited and cooks more."

"She likes the warm weather." Erich took a deep breath to get himself ready for the session.

"Yes, we hope to move to the United States of Florida for the warm weather." Dr. Scherbit looked happy about that future move.

"Oh?"

"It's always warm and there are opportunities there." He cleared his throat.

"To travel there will be costly," Erich laughed.

"How so?"

"My appointments with you," he looked the chaise over.

"My friend, by that time, you shall be happy and free from your troubles." He said, got his pipe and tapped his pipe on the ash tray.

"And for you I will have a present of a quiet bell," he looked at the ash tray.

"A bad habit," Dr. Scherbit put the pipe back on the ash tray, "So, we left off that you were to have lunch with a captain…"

"Ehrlichmann," he said, turned and laid back on the chaise.

"Erich," Dr. Scherbit said.

Erich sat back up and looked at him, "Ja, I mean yes."

"You do know that it's not just a matter of talking about

these things, but also that you take the bad energy from these images… from the past so that it can't hurt you anymore." He smiled and dipped his head so his glasses weren't in the way of his eyes as he looked at Erich. "You've practiced your skills?"

"Yes, to think on them and not let them have any emotion." He laid back down.

"Now, what was for lunch?" Dr. Scherbit got his pencil and notepad.

"I believe it was May, 1936." Erich turned his head to look at the lamp by the curtains. "Ehrlichmann had kept Nikki away for the last month and Stephan was unable to find him." The lamps faded white glow seemed to grow up the curtains and down to the floor. He studied the light and it was then that he was at a table in the café on Prinz-Albrecht Straße.

Erich sipped on an espresso and managed to look the room over which was filled with SS, SD, a few Gestapo and some civilians, most likely they were staff from HQ.

"Sir, are there others in your party?" The waiter asked.

"Nein," Erich felt his sixth sense turn his stomach.

"Guten tag, Capt. Brueder," Capt. Ehrlichmann stood nearby with his long coat draped over his arm. He had a Luger holstered and this was not appropriate for public places.

Erich stood and dipped his head, "and you, Capt. Ehrlichmann."

"May I join you?" He asked, but had his hand on the back of the chair already and had pulled it out.

"Of course," Erich sat back down.

Maj. Gerheim walked up and looked at them, "You two making plans to take over?"

Capt. Ehrlichmann, "Nein, sir."

"Ha, quite funny," he looked at Erich, "and you Jan?"

"No sir, I'm committed to my job with you." Erich nodded and smiled.

"Ah, you see, that's the polite way to say so! Not for me, but with me." He patted Erich's shoulder and went to a table with several other high-ranking men. It was just then that Erich recognized one of the men, Himmler.

The waiter stood patiently as the men talked.

"Ja, he enjoys this place too." Ehrlichmann said.

"Himmler?" Erich asked.

"Ja, Himmler." Capt. Ehrlichmann gave his coat to the waiter and then got comfortable. "How are you doing with your new role?" The waiter took the coat and hung it.

"Well," Erich took a drink of water. The waiter came back and they ordered, "No, no wine, thank you." Brats and soup was as much as he cared for, something simple and quick.

"It seems we missed each other a week or so ago." Ehrlichmann said with an air of curiosity. "I'll have a glass of red."

The waiter nodded and got the wine.

"Oh?" Erich asked.

"At Dachau," he eyed Erich who pulled a pack of cigarettes from his trouser pocket. The waiter came over quickly, sat an ash tray down and then left. He looked at Ehrlichmann, "Cigarette?"

"Ja," Ehrlichmann grinned, "So, you were there?" He took the cigarette and felt for his lighter.

"To look our first camp over and make myself knowledgeable of the operations," Erich said, lit up and then lit Ehrlichmann's cigarette. He took a slow toke from the cigarette and then blew it down to the ground.

"Did you find the plans worthwhile?" Ehrlichmann drank his wine.

The waiter set out the brats and soup for them, refilled Erich's water and then looked at them. Erich nodded as did Capt. Ehrlichmann at which point the waiter left.

"It's ambitious, but the German people are capable of great things." Erich laid his cigarette down and they enjoyed their meal.

"For the SS you mean," Ehrlichmann fanned his soup and got his serviette in place.

"The SS are not all of the people." Erich knew to tread lightly, "The people look to us to set the standard for our nation." He dipped his spoon in his soup and waited a moment, "to protect them and Dachau is an example of our ambitions to preserve our national strength."

Ehrlichmann clapped for a moment and then smiled wide as he sat back in his chair, "You are quite an officer, Jan." He took a sip of his soup and kept his smile. "And part politician?"

"I have no such ambitions." Erich was upset that he clapped and it was quite rude to do so in the restaurant especially with so many other people around, so many SS. "To clap at me is not appropriate," he sat straight; he set his spoon down and removed his napkin from his lap.

Capt. Ehrlichmann stopped smiling and got his composure back, "I apologize for my rude behavior. It's not often, in fact I doubt very many officers in here would say such a thing, but you, you have said what our Fuhrer believes and espouses to us."

Erich nodded and got his cigarette. He didn't wave it around like other people, but kept it quite still. Sometimes, a cigarette *was* a cat's tail.

"Truly, I apologize and have overreacted toward you." He held his hand out and waited.

Erich knew that there was a moment in a game when you had to decide if you were about to lose or win, what you did next mattered most. He looked at Ehrlichmann's hand and then he looked at the man, "I accept." They shook strongly and then Erich waited for Ehrlichmann to let loose first, which he did. Erich got his serviette over his lap and smiled, "How did you find Dachau on your trip? It's such a long way to that place." He dabbed his cigarette out.

"I had to manage a matter of prisoner affairs." He said, finished his soup and ate a brat.

"Oh?" Erich sipped his soup, "I thought you dealt with investigations only." He cut up a brat and as he sliced it deeply, he eyed Ehrlichmann.

"And other matters that involve security," he ate the last of his brats. "What did you think of the rabbits?"

"I found the matter humorous." Erich smiled.

"Humorous?" Ehrlichmann caught the eye of Himmler who nodded at him. He dipped his head at the commander and smiled.

"It seems to be a setting of Aryan perfection and it is unattainable for the likes of those who care for them." Erich sat back, "a sort of tease."

"That's true, but the animals are there to keep them at ease." He swished his wine around in his mouth gently, "idle hands you see."

"They have work." Erich said, drank his water and finished the brat.

"They have no women."

"I noticed." He raised his brow.

"Even lesser beings feel the need to... mate." He held his wine glass up. The waiter got it and poured him another glass. "Jan, if I may"

"Of course, but I don't know your first name, Captain."

"Conrad... Ehrlichmann," he had to catch his breath.

"Ah," Erich thought for a moment, "bold counsel?"

Conrad was surprised to hear the definition, "Ja, that's correct." He sipped his wine and felt more at ease with Erich, "as you said earlier about those people, the ones that must be controlled with rabbits, if necessary, are the ones who must also and eventually be removed, in total, from our lands."

Erich grinned and knew where this was going, "removed to where though? The camps will fill and then we have to feed them, cloth them..."

"Don't you see it as clearly, Jan?"

"I can see it as clearly as I see you." He eyed Conrad and his grip tightened around his knife.

"We were at the mercy of the allies, but Hitler," he lowered his voice, but spoke firmly, "has given us new life and new direction." He was elated and very excited as he spoke, "to think that our economy, our people were so beaten down that they looked as though to give up on life entirely while other... people came to Berlin, Frankfurt and other places and capitalized on our weakness." He took another drink of his wine, "Now, we are the power. We..." He sat up and set his wine down, "We will be the way of this world just as Alexander of Macedonia or Caesar... Caesar of Rome were... masters."

"The Romans did not come out so well, nor did Alexander." Just then, Erich stood up quickly as Himmler and Maj. Gerheim were at their table. Apparently, Conrad was louder than he thought. "Sir," Erich watched as Conrad had some trouble getting up, but got to his feet and stood still.

Himmler spoke softly first to Capt. Ehrlichmann, "It's good that such young officers of the SS are proud and committed to the beliefs of the SS." He turned to Erich, "such as our new arrival, Capt. Brueder who knows his history well." He nodded at Erich, "The history of Alexander taught us to challenge ourselves to be more than those we conquer and the Romans taught us the role of the conquered."

"My apologies, sir," Erich said, dipped his head and glanced at Maj. Gerheim to see if that was sufficient.

"There's no need to apologize, Capt. Brueder. Knowledge of history is what protects us from past failures." He nodded at them and then walked to the door.

Maj. Gerheim grasped Erich's arm, "You've made a new freund." He let him loose and followed Himmler to the door and out.

They sighed and sat back down, "I think I swallowed my tongue." Conrad said.

Erich cleared his throat and smiled, "The wine was the culprit."

Conrad laughed out loud, "We shall be good freunds Jan!"

Some other officers "shh'd" them.

They left and stood outside for a moment. Erich got his long coat on and looked at Conrad, "thank you for dinner."

"I enjoyed it." He patted Erich's shoulder. "We will work more closely as the number of detainees grows." He admired the red flags that were draped across the straße, "such a beautiful thing."

Erich looked up and down the straße, "Indeed."

"As for the camps that you mentioned before Himmler came to us, I believe there is a plan to deal with them so that there is no need to feed or cloth so many." He smiled and placed his hat squarely upon his head. Despite the wine, he was a professional soldier.

Erich had some idea of what he meant. "Some solution perhaps," they shook hands. "I look forward to our next meeting." They walked back to HQ.

"I don't like my next duty, but it's part of the day." He pulled at his holster.

"Oh?"

"Ja," he hesitated and then stopped.

"What?" Erich stopped and waited.

"When you processed in, did you process directly with Patz?"

"He had my orders." He didn't ever call Stephan by his last name.

"My people have found that he sent coded communications to a source overseas." Conrad studied Erich to note his expression. "It is connected with another matter I'm assigned."

Erich's face cooled as a swarm of butterflies filled his stomach, but he played the part of cool and collect well. "That's quite serious… if it was done as a crime.

Conrad turned and admired the red flags again that adorned Straße 8. "Spying is a crime…" he stopped himself. "Why send messages and then encode them if not to spy or conceal some action?"

"He is a spy?" Erich's mind went to work; how to get to Stephan before Conrad.

"We will find out and as to the person who received the communication." He turned and walked off with Erich in tow. "Come with me."

"To?"

"To see him arrested," Conrad laughed and shook his head.

Erich's heart missed a beat and he tried to hold back a

terrible cough.

"You alright, Jan?"

"The soup," he cleared his throat.

"It seems that this Patz did a similar type of code when he was at the political offices in the Reichstag before the fire. My sources have confirmed that." He pulled Erich close, "He is a queer too."

"Ah, so there are many charges, but I'm not an investigator." Erich moved so to loosen Conrad's hand.

"Nein, but you work with Major Gerheim in camp logistics." Conrad took pleasure in the thought. "We'll work more closely in the future."

"He'll be sent to Dachau, there is no other camp." Erich said.

"Ja, I know." He smiled, "come, let's see what this traitor says." Conrad looked at Erich as they walked, "I believe he has covered for another queer, Nicholas VanEch."

Erich's heart jumped, "Where is he?"

Conrad stopped, "*Why*?" He grinned and wondered.

"You gave his name." Erich eyed him, "a spy too?"

"He's in our custody." They were at the steps of HQ. "As for a spy, I'm not sure yet."

"You'll arrest Patz now?" Erich hesitated.

"Ja," he said just as a jeep pulled up with several guards who all looked at Conrad. They got out and came right to him. "They are here for his arrest." He flagged them to go into the building, "wait for me in the main hall!" They went in and Erich was dumbfounded; what could he do to save Stephan?

"I've been from my desk for a long time." He had to get away and warn Stephan!

"Maj. Gerheim knows that you are with me." He put his hand on Erich's back and they went up the steps to the doors and into the main hall.

Everything seemed to be orderly as if there was no worry in the place, but a few people took notice of the guards and knew that something was going to happen. As they went up the next set of stairs, Conrad had his men go up and wait in the hall. "He's in his office."

"Good, then no need to chase him." Dozens of thoughts raced through Erich's head as to what to do!

"Ah," he tapped his holster, "I chase no one."

They got to the corner of the hall and walked up to the offices where Stephan worked. "So, should I wait here?"

"Nein, I want you to see how this is done so that you are prepared." He smiled, "you may work with me more closely."

Erich was out of excuses and went in with Conrad. Stephan sat at his desk and the guards remained in the hallway. As they got to the door, Conrad moved Erich so that he was ahead of him as they went in.

Stephan looked up and was surprised. He smiled, but hid his smile as quickly as it appeared, "Captains at my door."

"Patz," Erich felt stricken with grief. He kept his emotions to himself, but felt the swarm of butterflies in his stomach.

"Stephan Patz," Capt. Ehrlichmann said.

"Capt. Ehrlichmann," he nodded, "Capt. Brueder... what can I help you with?"

Just then, the guards entered the office and blocked the doorway.

Stephan knew to keep cool and saw the men from the corner of his eyes, "So, this is not to go for coffee."

It was then that Capt. Ehrlichmann's manor changed for the worse, "You are charged with sending coded communications to sources outside of Germany and that those sources may be enemies of the state. You are charged under the Reich code one-seven-five and one-seven-five (a) as to engaging in sexual relations with men and a man in your office who is a subordinate."

Stephan got his composure and knew not to look at Erich, but he couldn't help himself; he looked at Erich and then back at Capt. Ehrlichmann, "You have witnesses and I have rights."

"Rights, not likely," Ehrlichmann said.

"We shall see." Stephan said.

"Patz, you will have your day." Erich was unable to do or say much else.

"As Capt. Brueder stated, you will have your day. For now, you are to step out and place your hands there." He pointed at the wall.

Stephan stepped around the desk and put his hands on the wall. Capt. Ehrlichmann nodded at his guard to come over. The guard walked up, handed the hand cuffs to him and he put them on Stephan.

"You can tell me the names of those you contacted and why you contacted them in coded messages, perhaps there will be some leniency." He got close to Stephan and breathed in his face, "For your queer crimes, I offer nothing."

Stephan did not look at Erich and turned away, "There is nothing for me to say."

"As you wish, we will see if a search of your apartment yields more information." He turned to the guard, "take him." The guard ushered Stephan to the door. "You should come with us to the apartment."

Erich thought there was no way he could go. "I must finish my work, though the matter at hand has been instrumental in its lesson."

"Some time at night when there are other opportunities?" Ehrlichmann asked and smiled.

"Of course, when the real animals are out," Erich mouth was pasty and dry.

"Jan, good day," he turned and went to the door where the guard held Stephan.

Erich had to beat them to the flat now! He watched as they left and made their way to Capt. Ehrlichmann's office. He hurriedly went downstairs, got a cab and left.

As he got to Stephan's flat, he had the taxi go to the corner and drop him. He wore his long coat and it was obvious that there were people who would see him. He pulled his hat low and stayed to the trees that lined the straße. It wasn't terribly busy as he made his way to the alley, up the fire escape and into the hallway. He ran to the flat, opened the door and made a mad rush to get his things! Every minute or so, he looked out the window to check for Capt. Ehrlichmann, other SS or the Gestapo. He knew that they would be here soon, maybe ten minutes or less or a minute more. It was nearly fourteen-eleven now and it was thirteen-thirty when they took Stephan.

He saw that he had his things, a case and his pack. He put the blanket away, made the couch up and then checked once more, but did it slowly and methodically. He sighed to calm himself and felt he cannot miss a thing. It was then he went to the window again and looked out. They were here! Two guards got out with Ehrlichmann! He went to the door, held it open and stepped out, but then there was a meow!

"Damned cat!" He listened intently and heard them down stairs. He reached for Felix, but he shot down the hall to the fire exit! He walked to the fire escape as quietly as he could with his boots, put his case out, grabbed Felix and shut the window! He slowly made his way down the fire escape and nearly fell as Felix clawed his way up his jacket, "you're tearing the leather... damn cat!" He got to the last ladder and looked up. The steps swung down and "clang!" He knew if they heard it, they'd come, but the window was closed. If his heart beat any louder, they would hear it too! Maybe it would be alright. He held the case in one hand and his pack in the other hand with Felix clinging on to him for dear life!

"Captain, the door is unlocked." The guard said, aimed his pistol and opened the door slowly.

The landlady stood there, "There's been no one."

"But you saw a man visit?" Ehrlichmann asked.

"Ja, but it was a few weeks ago. He had some luggage." She could care less and thought about the rent, "and if you've taken him, what about the rent?"

Ehrlichmann balked at her, "You will touch nothing."

"He came and that was it." She looked in the apartment. "Then who will pay?"

"If there is anything disturbed by you or anyone else, we will come for you too." He looked her over, "do not touch a thing."

She nodded, "Heil Hitler." She went back down the steps and shook her head.

"Check all of it, every room and be sure to look if there's evidence of this second person." He panned the room, "anything that has a different name or an address in Germany or beyond our borders," he thought, "Check addresses with names."

"Yes, sir," the men moved the sofa, pulled the carpet up, moved the table and went through everything.

Erich made his way to another alley by going down the inside alley that ran behind all the flats. His boots were filthy! He got to the corner and walked to the next straße where he hailed a cab. Felix's claws were dug firmly into his long coat. He raised his hand and a cab came to stop.

"You've got quite a bit to carry captain." The driver was a bit disheveled, dirty.

"Please take me," Erich pushed his case in and Felix tried to go up over his shoulder, "this filthy cat!" He yanked him down and let him loose in the car.

The driver turned and drove off, "You can tell me in a moment." They eyed each other in the rear-view mirror and he felt the driver knew that he was fleeing something or someone.

"Danke," Erich looked at Felix.

"Nice cat," the driver smirked.

"He is a bitch." He said as Felix climbed to the back window and laid down. He turned to look back at the flat and wondered now about Stephan; could he get him *and* Nikki? And what would he do when, not if, Capt. Ehrlichmann questioned him at Prinz-Albrecht Straße 8. When there's too much to think about, think only on one thing, so he thought on the changing landscape. The people that they passed were colored images or impressions and that eased his stress. The images became so bright that he had to close his eyes.

When he opened them, his gaze was on the ceiling in Dr. Scherbit's office, "scheiße" He sat up and swallowed hard, but there was little to swallow. The swarm of butterflies must have stayed with him all the way from Berlin; he felt sickly.

"Are you alright?" Dr. Scherbit asked.

"I... it's a lot to go over such things." He licked his lips.

"It is," Dr. Scherbit sat up and set his notepad down. "In going over such things, I must ask you if you feel that you are able to handle these matters well?"

"No, that's why I'm here." He laughed to himself at the question, "You're the doctor."

"I am." He got up. He walked around his desk to Erich who faced him. "With such strong memories, it's important that you know which ones are *then* and which ones are *now*."

Erich thought for a moment, "So I do not go crazy."

"So, that those things do not *cause* you to go crazy." Dr. Scherbit thought about schizophrenia and wanted to say something, but that would plant a seed in a very fertile garden. "You can make the distinction that you are here... now. That this is not 1936 and you are not in Berlin."

"And I'm not with the SS, right Herr Doktor?" Erich stood, straightened himself out and went to the coat rack.

"I really do not like it when you say that." Dr. Scherbit went to the door and got hold of the door knob to slow or stop Erich from leaving until he was sure about him.

Erich sighed and got his jacket on. He thought about it and was wrong to say it, "I apologize, sincerely."

"Danke," Dr. Scherbit said, but did not open the door.

Erich looked at him and shook his head. "It's Quebec City, 1954 and it's the second of May. Your wife has fattened you as she believes in cooking more during the spring and summer."

Dr. Scherbit turned the knob, "and I'm glad that you came to me Erich Schmidt." He opened the door and waited.

Erich walked past, stopped and turned to him as he stood there looking back at him, "me too." He turned away and was on the street before Dr. Scherbit turned off the lights to his office. He felt lighthearted and the butterflies were all but gone now. He didn't want to think about Stephan and was happy that Dr. Scherbit said nothing about their next meeting, but knew it would come up, "AH!" He yelled as he walked to push the bad thoughts from his mind, "not this evening!" Some people looked at him and moved away.

He got home and Nikki was there in the sitting room with a magazine. "I've subscribed to Der Spiegel." He got up and was dressed very nicely in trousers, a dress shirt and tie.

Erich held the ends of his jacket, but realized it was their time to go out for supper, "the British paper." He took his jacket off. "You look quite nice."

"And you," Nikki said, came over and they kissed. He held Nikki tightly. "It's not British."

"They had to approve it first after the war." Erich kissed Nikki. "So, it's your supper tonight." He loosened his grip, "and another jacket as this one is…"

"Smelly" Nikki said, took it from him and went down the hall.

"Ja, I thought you enjoyed my smell." Erich sniffed himself and made a face about the odor.

Nikki scoffed, "Erich Schmidt." He leaned out from the bedroom door, "you are a dirty…"

"I am no old man." He smiled.

"Ja, but you are dirty… and I like it." He smelled the jacket and tossed it onto the bed. "So, your appointment was fine?" He came back to the door and had another jacket.

Erich put it on and they went into the hall, closed the door and down the steps. "It was all good, but don't ruin our supper."

"No, of course not," Nikki bumped his shoulder into Erich's.

"Where shall we go?" Erich laughed.

"Chinese?"

"They have Felix."

"Erich!" Nikki smacked him, "I miss Felix, but he could not live for so long."

"That filthy cat." Erich saw that Nikki was a little upset, "A joke."

"For Stephan's sake," Nikki said as they made their way up the river front to the town square.

"I'm sorry." He hugged Nikki and some people looked, but

said nothing. "We brought him back."

"Ja, we did." Nikki said as they went up some steps to the main street.

"To Felix, we miss you." Erich raised his hand as if he had a drink, "and to our freund, Stephan."

They stopped and looked at each other. Erich was sad now, but not nearly as much as he would have been before seeing Dr. Scherbit. "Stephan," Nikki held up his hand too.

CHAPTER 13: STEPHAN, NEVER FORGET

Berlin, first week of June, 1936... Stephan had a cut up piece of potato sack over his head and his hands were cuffed. There was a single light that hung from the ceiling in this room that was only about ten by ten or so with a metal desk in the middle. Stephan was on one side of it with his hands cuffed to a chain that was anchored to the center of the table.

Capt. Ehrlichmann opened the door, "Stephan Patz." He did not have his gun with him. He studied Stephan for a moment as the sack turned to his voice. "How terribly rude," he pulled the sack off of Stephan's head.

Stephan's face was bruised, his side ached and the dark circles under his eyes were black from punches. He squinted to get his eyes to adjust and then looked around the room.

"You seem surprised to be here?" Ehrlichmann sat down and looked at Stephan's face. "My men, they have an abundance of disdain for people like you."

"I'm," he had to swallow to get some spat in his mouth. "I am innocent."

"Nein, you are guilty of engaging in queer acts. This is a violation of the Reich code, paragraph one hundred seventy-five." Just then, the door opened and Johann, his guard, walked in, handed him a file that was fairly thin and left. "My men are mind readers apparently."

Stephan looked at the door and then looked at the file, "more fraudulent charges?"

Capt. Ehrlichmann looked at him and opened the file. He read the first page and then looked at Stephan, "Have you ever forged any documents?"

Stephan coughed to clear his throat, "forged, what forged?" He licked his sore lips, "I have forged nothing."

"I told you that I could help you, but you must be honest." He turned the file around to face Stephan, "You sent coded messages to someone in Canada. Unfortunately, that nation is reluctant to reply to our requests to investigate the matter."

"I've sent nothing."

"Who are Nicholas VanEch and Erich Schmidt to you?" He tapped the paper and the file.

Stephan paused, "I don't know those names."

"More lies." He said, stood, walked over and knelt so that his mouth was at Stephan's ear. "We know that you know these other queers or... spies." His mouth was so close to Stephan's ear that he might have kissed him, "We know that Nicholas and Erich fled to Canada, but that Nicholas returned to help his mutter, supposedly." He exhaled into Stephan's ear, "I know you helped these men." He sighed, "Nicholas had your name in his belongings." He stood and touched Stephan's shoulder.

"I don't know them." Stephan said, "I work at SS Headquarters and am charged with processing of personnel and records." He coughed and some blood came out and onto the file. "My duties are checked by Lieutenant Herbstrase."

Ehrlichmann's face reddened and he picked up the file. He folded the file shut, rolled it up in his hand and smacked Stephan over the head with it, "LIAR!" He walked back around to the other side of the desk, "Lt. Herbstrase has indicated that you were left to your own devices on several occasions and that paperwork was not required to be checked by him unless it was for SS officers' captain and above."

Stephan had trouble to keep his right eye open; the swelling was worse. "My records are in line with my duties."

"You know Erich and Nicholas!" He sat down. "You know I have Nicholas." He knocked on the table twice. "Erich worked at the Reichstag just as you did, Stephan." He tapped Stephan's cheek, "you know him, don't you?"

Johann entered and had beaten Stephan, "Sir."

"You know my assistant, Mr. Patz."

"I know he has hit me for no reason." Stephan fought to keep his head up and his arms bent to take the pressure off of them.

"You insult me!" He shook his head, "he has never hit anyone who did not deserve to be hit." Ehrlichmann stood, "I need you to solve this puzzle, though I would prefer to avoid injuring you further."

Johann handed Ehrlichmann a pair of leather gloves with small square metal pieces where the knuckles would slide under. Ehrlichmann put them on and looked at Stephan, "As you refuse to tell me the truth, I will take responsibility for questioning you further." Another guard came in with an ugly white plastic cover and handed it to Ehrlichmann. "Normally, you would just be left at the camp, but I believe that you are impeding me in a purposeful manner." He got the plastic cover on and it covered his jacket down to his trousers, "nothing for my shoes?"

The guard shook his head.

"How unfortunate," he walked around the desk and Johann walked the other way. Johann grabbed Stephan by his hair and pulled him back from the desk. The chair made a terrible screech as its legs dragged against the concrete floor and Stephan's arms were stretched out from the desk!

"AH!" Stephan yelled and choked on his spat.

"Have you noticed the drains in the floor?" Ehrlichmann asked.

"What do I care about the drains?" He coughed and spat up on his mouth. The spat, so dry already, lapped onto the side of his mouth and clung there with the dried blood.

"What remains of you will go there." Ehrlichmann nodded at Johann who got a firm grip on Stephan. Ehrlichmann raised his hand and punched Stephan on the right side of his chest.

Stephan screamed! "AH!"

"That is likely to have cracked or broken a rib." He looked at the glove as Stephan tried to bend forward because of the pain, but Johann held him back. "A cracked rib can cause other injuries to you internally as the bone may fragment, but I must hit one lower." He aimed his fist and drew back.

"Please…" Stephan shouted.

"You have something to tell me?" Ehrlichmann studied Stephan's chest and then ran his hand down Stephan's rib cage to the lowest rib bone, "ah." He punched Stephan and the force of the metal in the glove cracked his rib!

"AH!" Stephan doubled over and Johann let him stay there, "AH!"

"Johann has let you go so that the cracked rib will deform by your own doing." Ehrlichmann looked as Stephan spat blood on the plastic cover. "That's it." He tapped Stephan's back as a mother would pat the back of a crying baby, "there you are."

"I… I don't." He coughed and a blood clot dripped from his mouth to the floor.

"You do know them." He nodded at Johann who grabbed Stephan again and pulled his head back.

"AH!" Stephan coughed which cast blood globules to pop out of his mouth, into the air and they landed on the desk, on him and on the floor. "No!"

"Ja, Stephan!" Ehrlichmann nodded at Johann who let him keel over to get his breath. "It can stop right now, but you have to let the truth come!" He looked at the guard by the door, "Sachsenhausen isn't complete, but you can be their first queer!" Johann smiled, "I truly hate to say it, but if I cannot get an answer from you, then I must bring your vater in." He stood and looked Stephan over, "time will run out for you."

Stephan's eyes welled up and he fought his tears. "He, he has not a thing to do with me." His words carried spat and blood with them out and onto the table. "Ah," he cringed!

"He said so as you declared you're a queer to him." Ehrlichmann got his mouth right up to Stephan's ear, "but I must use those means available to me."

Some blood dripped from Stephan's mouth and his skin looked pasty white. The light in the room was bright enough for him to stare at and leave his body if they hit him again. "What do you want to know?"

Ehrlichmann looked at the guards, "You see... he is a reasonable man."

Stephan coughed. "I need a doktor."

"What about Erich Schmidt and Nicholas VanEch?"

Stephan swallowed the mixture of blood and spat, then choked, "Nicholas... I, he was an acquaintance from some years ago." Stephan tried to get a breath, "AH!" When he inhaled, the cracked ribs poked him, "DAMN THIS!"

Ehrlichmann got next to him, "and Erich Schmidt?"

"Only," he coughed again, "only Nicholas... to help him to get to his parents."

Ehrlichmann grinned and looked at the two guards, "you sent coded messages to Schmidt?"

"I don't know him." He coughed and grimaced from the pain.

Ehrlichmann was calm and rubbed his hand on his chin, "I want to know about Erich Schmidt, Stephan." He looked at his gloves and then pulled them off. He shook his head, "The Weimar Republic got the Olympic bid, but we know that there are political factions... former Reichstag members... *spies* that wish to embarrass the Führer, to disrupt the Olympics!" He looked at his men and then Stephan, "You worked at the Reichstag with Schmidt. Before he worked with you, he was an SA member under Ernst Röhm!" He slapped Stephan! "So, do not say you don't know him!"

"I ... don't know what you are talking about."

"But you do know that Röhm Pütsch got rid of some of the members and Schmidt fled." He raised his hand and Stephan closed his eyes, "you helped Schmidt to flee, but kept in contact with him. If the matter wasn't important, why did you encode your messages?" He slapped him again!

"I … it was not for him, for Nikki."

"Coded messages for VanEch to come and help his father? His mother?" He slapped him again! "You are a liar!" He shook his head, "is there a plan to disrupt the Olympics?"

"I know of no plan." Stephan couldn't hold his head up anymore as blood oozed out from his wounds.

"Then, we must keep VanEch and wait to see if Schmidt comes." He looked at Johan and then patted Stephan on the cheek, "is Schmidt coming?"

Stephan didn't look up, but he did shake his head a little.

"So, the truth," he smiled at Stephan, "you do know him and that means that VanEch knows more." He nodded at Johann.

Johann looked at the guard by the door.

"Ja," Ehrlichmann smiled, "These are the moments that help us prepare for the future, Stephan." Another guard came in. "Take him," he watched as Johann untied him; they lifted him up and took him outside. "We will get Schmidt and your plans will fail."

It was just after noon and the sun shone through the woods. "Sachsenhausen," he looked around as they drug him past the side of the commandant's home and to the woods nearby. There was a lot of construction and prisoners that worked there looked away from them.

Spat and blood dripped from Stephan's mouth and he was barely aware of anything they did. The pain was so much now that his body began to shut down parts that hurt too much unless they moved that part, "AH!"

They dragged him into the woods, a hundred feet or so from the commandant's home, and nearly out of sight. "There," Capt. Ehrlichmann pointed at a tree with some ropes that hung from it. They brought Stephan to that tree and brought his hands behind him where they tied them to the ropes.

"This will be the last chance for you, for your vater." Ehrlichmann watched as his men pulled at Stephan's arm so that they were tight behind his back. They lifted his arms up by his elbows so that his arms were straight and up. "It will be most nearly a crucifixion that is backwards and without the cost of nails."

"Ah!" Stephan screamed as his arms strained to hold his weight up.

The ropes that bound Stephan's hands were looped through a ring and hung down from the tree. The guards went to the other end of the rope and pulled up so that Stephan's arms were bent backwards; he was up and against the tree, but partially stood on his own.

"This is wrong!" He spat. "I have done nothing."

"Talk to the Jew king and see if he believes you." Ehrlichmann put his hands against Stephan's chest to hold him in place. He nodded at the guards who pulled the ropes and lifted Stephan from the ground.

Stephan screamed! "AH!" His buttocks were pressed against the trunk and his arms were outstretched behind him. His shoulders stopped his arms from going up. "AH!"

They pulled him up another foot!

"AH!" Stephan tried to use his feet to push up so that he could lessen the pain, but his shoes slipped on the bark and he fell back down, "DAMN YOU!" His eyes were swollen so badly that he saw a little bit of the men, of Ehrlichmann.

The guards knotted off the ends and Stephan hung there, about two feet from the ground. "AH!" He screamed and his tears mixed with dried blood, wet blood and snot so that it looked like red sand and mud that dripped down past his lips where a thin string of spat formed and hung. "AH!"

Johann walked over to Ehrlichmann, "What of his vater?"

Ehrlichmann shook his head, "He died in the truck on the way here."

"I wondered why you didn't bring him." Johann looked at Stephan.

"Ah, it's not a problem." He studied Stephan, "If this Schmidt is stupid enough to try to get VanEch, we will have him." He ripped the plastic from his body, "damn!" He looked at his boots and there were specks of spat and blood on them "look at this scheiße."

"AH!" Stephan yelled. The muscles in his shoulders and arms weren't able to keep him in that position.

The other guard looked at the ropes, "For Schmidt to come, it's not possible?"

Ehrlichmann turned to the guard, "It is possible." He looked behind him at the woods, "He was a Brownshirt and my sources tell me he has some skill."

"What?" The guard was surprised.

"I have seen the record." He looked Stephan over and shook his head, "Stephan, tell me if Schmidt is here and I will kill you quickly."

Stephan turned his head slightly and gasped. He had something to say, "if... if he comes." He choked, "he will kill you for what you've done to me."

Ehrlichmann's grin faded, "you can go now and know that he will not kill anyone."

Stephan tried to raise his head to look at Ehrlichmann, but wasn't able to.

"I believe he went to train as a spy." Ehrlichmann and the Johann eyed each other. "VanEch had books on socialism and communism. He was at university and then left to Canada with Schmidt." He shook his head, "If they intended to flee for good, VanEch took quite a chance to come back and for what? His mutter?" He put his hand on the guard's shoulder, "He came back to set the stage for their return with the Olympics coming and the growth of our party, this is a good time to attack us."

"Ah!" Stephan's life began to fade from his body. The energy that kept him going until this moment slowly drained away and began to make the transition to that other place.

Johann looked at Stephan. "How long do you think?"

"Perhaps an hour, maybe less," Ehrlichmann looked Stephan over. "I'm hungry."

Stephan stopped crying and lifted his head as much as he could to see Ehrlichmann. "Never forget," he would say nothing else to him, but he wanted to look at Ehrlichmann, eye to eye.

"He's trying to look at me." Ehrlichmann reached for his pistol, "damn... I have left it inside."

Johann got his pistol and held it up. Ehrlichmann took it, checked the chamber and aimed at Stephan's face. "You wish to challenge me, Stephan?"

Stephan saw him now and closed his mouth, held his head up as high as he could and then spat at him. The spat didn't get anywhere near Ehrlichmann.

Ehrlichmann's face warmed, "Even now, you dare to spat at me." He cocked the hammer and took a shooters stance.

Stephan fought to keep his head up.

"BANG!" Ehrlichmann shot him in the eye. "I never did like that eye of his."

The guards chuckled and went to lower him.

"Nein!" Ehrlichmann yelled, "Leave him there."

They nodded and then they went back to the camp administration office. Ehrlichmann returned the pistol to Johann. "Get your contact at the Gestapo and see what they can find about VanEch and Schmidt. They must have more information."

"They will not do it without something in return." Johann smiled.

"Tell them it is for me," Ehrlichmann said. "The Olympics are soon, so we must get to him before he gets to us."

CHAPTER 14: SACHSENHAUSEN, HE'S THERE IN THE WOODS

Dr. Scherbit's office, Erich arrived for his appointment and was able to go right in. He got the chaise turned, the curtains pulled and his jacket hung. The noise from the street wasn't bad, so he left the window alone.

"Please remember to return the chaise when you're done." He grinned at Erich.

"Ah, yes I forgot last time." He nodded.

"Your friend, Stephan," Dr. Scherbit sat down and looked at his notes. "You mentioned that he was taken by Ehrlichmann?"

Erich felt sadness slowly climb onto his back, a two-hundred-pound slug that inched its way up his spine. "Yes, it was the next evening when I finally got word that Stephan was at Sachsenhouseen." He pinched the bridge of his nose to relieve some pressure, "Maj. Gerheim agreed that I should see the newest camp too."

"You went then," Dr. Scherbit held his pipe tightly.

"Ja," Erich got a tissue, blew his nose and then laid still.

"Erich, this is a very sensitive issue and I wonder if you're ready?" He set his pipe down and ran his fingers over his moustache'.

Erich pushed his fingers into the bridge of his nose again.

"Yes, I must," he looked at the lamps glow. A moment passed and he was at Prinz-Albrecht Straße-8, Berlin.

Erich took a car and left for the camp that was just north of Berlin. He wondered why Ehrlichmann went there as the camp was under construction in June of 1936 and had only a few buildings. He kept his hopes high that Stephan was alive and got to the commandant's house, Lt. Col. Lippert. Now, in the back of his mind, he wondered to about Nikki; where was he?

It was the evening when he arrived and he looked around to be sure of the place—woods to the south west of the commandant's home, main gate to the north, fence was partially up and there were a few guards, but it seemed quite lax as there were only prisoners to build the place. Col. Lippert greeted him and they had a late coffee. Erich hoped to see that Stephan was alright, talk to him and figure out how to get him out of there.

"So, you've come at such an odd hour." He sipped is coffee, "I was prepared to turn in."

"I apologize, Colonel, but I was going to my family home in Gramzow and thought to make the visit." Erich said.

They went to a small library with a sitting area. "Oh, there's no need to apologize." He sipped on his coffee, "the plan is that the camp will be an integral part of the system and with its proximity to Berlin, there will be an opportunity to process prisoners here rather than to Dachau so far south."

"That's good news." Erich set his coffee down as a servant came in with a fresh pot.

Col. Lippert shook his head and the servant set the pot down, then left.

"Ah, we had such a turn of events at our offices a couple of days ago." Erich shook his head. "We had an arrest there."

Col. Lippert nodded, "Capt. Ehrlichmann brought a man here from SS HQ." He sat up, "I was surprised that he brought him, because there's no place to hold him to be quite honest."

"Oh? I didn't know he was brought here." Erich eyes widened. "Dachau was my first thought."

"And mine, but no. They brought him here." Col. Lippert

sipped what was left of his coffee.

"But you mentioned that you don't have a place for..." Erich caught his breath.

Col. Lippert smiled, "No, there's no place as I said. He's there, in the woods." He motioned at his window.

Erich did what he could to keep his temper, "in the woods?" He forced a laugh, "in an outhouse or something?" He picked up his coffee and drank what was left.

Col. Lippert laughed, "Nein, they've hung him from a tree."

A wave of sickness and cold came down from the top of his head to his stomach where the butterflies no longer fluttered; they died. He set his coffee down, "from a tree, really?"

"Ja, this is a punishment used... if you've got the stomach for it." He got up. "I must get some things finished." He picked up his coffee and set it on the tray. "Lt. Klein can show you the camp."

Erich got up and nodded, "danke." He turned and the servant had the door open. "Best to you and your work here," he wanted to kill him, but that's not why he was here.

"Danke, Capt. Brueder and you," he looked at the servant and Erich left.

He went out to the grounds and Lt. Klein stood there. "You wish to see the camp, Capt. Brueder?"

"Ja, but there was a man arrested from my office" Erich looked Lt. Klein over, "I understand he's here, Stephan Patz, I believe." Erich looked towards the woods.

"He's been dead for hours." Lt. Klein pinched his nose.

His skin suddenly cooled and he fought the mix of feelings that jockeyed for his attention—fear, sadness and anger. "I see. Perhaps to indulge me, I have not seen this punishment your commandant described."

"I will point the way." Lt. Klein walked with Erich to the edge of the woods and raised his finger at the darkness and shadows. There were lights around for the construction and it was possible to see through the trees. "He's there," Lt. Klein wasn't going.

He nodded at Lt. Klein and walked into the trees; there were many of them that were quite tall. He looked at the trunks and then followed them up to the branches, but no sign of Stephan. Had they hung him by the neck? He wondered as he walked further and then saw an odd shape on the side of a trunk. It looked like a lump with a "V" that was sideways as though a branch came out at the top and angled down to the trunk. He got closer and saw that it was a man, so he looked back to check that Lt. Klein hadn't followed him. Then, the smell hit him and he knew that smell; it was when the human body crapped itself and the fluids were drawn down as there was nothing to stop the decay of human tissue or gravity.

He thought to just stop there, so as not to see Stephan in such a state. As a few minutes passed, he took another step and saw the figure more closely, "damn." He took another step and, now, saw the bloated face of his freund. He looked back again and the lieutenant was not there. "Why didn't you just run?" He asked in a hushed tone. "Just run," his eyes welled up.

"Captain!" Lt. Klein was at the edge of the woods and headed to him.

Erich quickly wiped his eyes and turned, "Ja, ich kommen!" He looked at his freund once more and bit at his lip, "The Jew King will look after you, freund; that is what I asked him to do." He looked up at the night sky that was riddled with stars, "and there you are." He turned and walked back slowly to give his eyes time to adjust.

After a walk with Lt. Klein around just a couple of buildings, Erich was at his car and left. When he got to SS HQ, he turned the car in and went to his flat. Felix was on the couch and meowed loudly; it was past three hours from his supper time. "Ja, I am hungry too." He took off his long coat and then sat down with Felix who rubbed on him. "I'm sorry to tell you that..." He began to cry and slid off the couch to the floor. Felix leapt down, sat and looked at him. "Damned cat," he looked at Felix and was overcome with grief and fury, "You left me with this damned cat!" The tears, the sadness consumed him entirely, "you left me." He curled up and cried.

Felix came around to his face and laid down. Erich looked at the lamp across from him; the glow grew brighter and he heard tapping as he brought his hands up to his face.

"Erich," Dr. Scherbit held his pipe over the ash tray, "Erich?"

Erich sat up and looked around. He saw Dr. Scherbit, shook his head and then realized his eyes were full of tears.

Dr. Scherbit was somber, "Are you alright?"

Erich got his senses and saw the tissue box by him. He wiped away Stephan, "ja." He cleared his throat and stood, "My time is over."

"Erich," Dr. Scherbit stood and walked over to him. He held out his hand and looked at him, "I'm so sorry about your friend... Stephan."

Erich looked at him and then looked at his hand. He shook and then left quietly. The way home was longer than usual as he took the side street for some privacy. He smoked and just stayed there so that he was away from people, people who had no idea of the horrors. He flicked the cigarette ashes and tried to smile, "Danke Stephan." He looked up, "you know Felix was with us till he went to see you... that damned cat." He ran the cigarette on the pavement to put it out, "he never let me forget, Stephan." As he stood back up and looked at the night sky, "thank you for what you did for us."

CHAPTER 15: PURSUIT, PUNCH CARDS & A GRAND OPENING

1954-May, Erich kissed Nikki and went to the bank. It was near the end of May now and he was excited that they had plans to return to Berlin in a month. It would be their first flight but Nikki preferred to go by ship. Erich was reluctant to spend so much time on board when they could be in Berlin in two days or so.

Erich enjoyed the job at the bank and Mr. Lachance was very good to include him in new financial projects with other opportunities. The only real problems arose when Erich was compelled to work with their British counterparts. He felt that the "Empire" exerted control through capital and relegated other people to "class" based on that capital. He admired the worker who sacrificed a great deal to have something for their family and felt a bit Marxist when he thought about the amount of control that so few people brought to the table when they dealt with the bank finances and how the money was managed.

The British bank executives came over and were at odds when they heard Erich speak. On two occasions, one man in particular, a Veteran of WWII, asked that Erich excuse himself from a meeting with them. Since he was a ranking member, a

Lord from the Empire, Mr. Lachance honored the request and tasked Erich with the paperwork side of it all instead of the meeting and negotiation of bank affairs. Erich took it on the chin and, though put off by it, he made no never mind of the matter.

That's what today was like for him as that same Lord arrived at the bank and wouldn't look at him. Erich wanted to stand and tell him that he was a German, not a NAZI! But, he kept his mind and eyes focused on his paperwork and the clock. In just two hours he'd go to Dr. Scherbit's for his meeting and work on his wellness; that's what Dr. Scherbit called it.

His secretary came in, "He wants to see you." She grinned politely and held the door.

Erich smiled and went to Mr. Lachance's office. He closed the door behind him and sat down.

"They've gone and are happy." He handed Erich some papers, "your numbers worked and have proven viable to keep us in the black."

"Thank you," Erich got the papers and thought about how he had pursued this matter in detail.

"So, you have your appointment today?"

"Yes," he got up.

"Erich, Lord Alexander was in the war and taken prisoner." He stood and forced a grin, "I know that you are not the man who captured him, but he has thoughts that upset him and when he heard you talk…"

"My accent is hard to miss." Erich smiled, "I understand."

"Good." He sat down, "There's a check in there."

Erich's eyes widened, "We've done well?"

"The pursuit of capital," he said.

Erich left and thought about it as he got his brief and the check. He tidied up his desk and then left for Dr. Scherbit's office. "The pursuit of capital" he said as he made his way to the street car and got on. He thought too hard on the matter "the pursuit of queers," "the pursuit of Jews," and "the pursuit of Poles." Then he caught himself doing it. "Stop it," he uttered under his breath.

He got off the street car and went to the doctors, a half block away. The day was nice, warm and clear. He went up the steps and thought he smelled tobacco from Dr. Scherbit's pipe through the windows upstairs. He shook his head and got to the waiting room; it was nearly empty. A man waited as Erich walked in and Lucy nodded at him. She no longer looked at him or asked him anything.

Erich sat down with his brief and was warm with his jacket on. Just then, Dr. Scherbit opened the door and a nicely dressed woman, mid thirty's and quite tall, walked out and looked at her husband. Dr. Scherbit took his glasses off and wiped them clean as she went to her husband.

"Ah, there is the man who tells me what to eat, what to do, what to wear... well, no more!" She grabbed the man, dainty and five-four at his best.

Dr. Scherbit had his hand with his pipe near his mouth and dropped it to his waist, "that's not what I said."

She pulled him along and led the poor soul out of the office.

Dr. Scherbit looked at Lucy, "close up for the night." She quickly got her things as Erich stood and went to Dr. Scherbit.

"Another successful case," he laughed and went past Dr. Scherbit. He took his jacket off and hung it up. Then, he went and rearranged things: moved the chaise to face the door, pulled the window nearly closed, shut the curtains and wiped the remnants of the last patient off of the chaise, "not a very pleasant smell she left."

"You see, my pipe smoke is good for that too." Dr. Scherbit left the door cracked and went to his desk. "How are you feeling?"

Erich sat down and got comfortable, but did not lay back, "better." He rubbed his palms across his face, "Nikki and I are well."

"Good," Dr. Scherbit sat down. "So, the British came? Is that what Paul Revere said?"

"Ha, I don't know this person." He thought on it a moment, "Yes, they came and left me at my desk." He saw the tissue box on the small table near the chaise and thought to move it away.

"An American who yelled to the American Colonials that the British were coming," he smiled. "Perhaps, the British man has memories that afflict him too," Dr. Scherbit got his notepad and pencil.

Erich saw the pencil, "I've wanted to ask you for some time why you use a pencil and not a pen?"

Dr. Scherbit held the pencil up, "with a pencil there can be change. With a pen, change is not possible."

Erich nodded, "I had a problem with the Lord that there is this notion of the pursuit of capital."

"And?"

"It was a sort of trigger for me." He pushed his bangs back, "I thought of the pursuit by Nazi's of queers, of Jews, of poles and of political opponents... that they took their possessions."

"For them, the pursuit of capital is a life necessity, but they do not pursue people." He set his pencil and pad down.

"No, but this matter of pursuing things just sat badly with me. I pursued Nikki and Ehrlichmann pursued me." He bit at his lip.

"You've put too much into it." He dipped his head so that his eyes were over his glasses.

"Perhaps, but..."

"It must be where you begin today."

"Yes," Erich laid down on the chaise. He turned his head and looked at the lamp. The days were longer and the sun tried to get through the curtains. The lamp lit up the sides of the darkness on the curtains and blurred his vision. "After Stephan, I was lost. There was no one I could trust to help me find Nikki and Ehrlichmann... he had put him some place that was hidden."

"And the man who helped Stephan?"

"Alex? He was an acquaintance and not to be trusted." Erich turned his head from the light and looked at the door. "Ehrlichmann met with me the following week for dinner. My face was so hot when I saw him that I could have set a house on fire."

"Go on," Dr. Scherbit said.

"I wanted to kill him, to kill him right there." Erich got his composure, "I didn't know if he killed Stephan." He turned his attention to the lamp again and this time he focused on the glow that emanated up and down the curtains; his angst and anger fanned out too and cooled near the ends of the light.

Berlin, July-1936, Erich was dressed nicely in his uniform and went to his office. Maj. Gerheim waited for him.

"Jan!" Maj. Gerheim waved him to come to his office.

Erich came in and was somewhat in a fog, "Sir."

"Are you alright?"

"Sorry sir, I was late to sleep." He walked over to the desk.

"No worries… we've got a big day today." It was then that Erich saw that he was in his dress uniform and had his ropes and ribbons in place.

"Sir?"

"Sachsenhausen opens today!" He got his small leather flap brief case and came around his desk. "We're going for the ceremony." He looked over Erich's uniform and was pleased, "for no sleep you look good."

"Danke," Erich turned and followed him to the door, "I have some papers to get."

"Nein, leave them." He ushered Erich to the door. "We have a car waiting."

They were on the straße where flags had been added and some markers of the Reich. It was warm and somewhat humid, but not enough to make him sweat badly. They got into a car and waited a moment. Erich watched Ehrlichmann come down the steps and his stomach turned.

"Jan!" He got in the car with them and patted Erich on the shoulder, "such a great day for us."

"Ja, a great day," Erich was sullen.

Conrad noticed it immediately and Maj. Gerheim spoke up, "He's had no sleep."

"What was her name?" Ehrlichmann laughed and seemed to be in very high spirits about the camp opening. The car pulled away and they headed north.

"Nein, just a lot of... work."

"Ah, he makes me sound like a tyrant." Maj. Gerheim opened his case. He got some papers out and read them.

"No, sir," Erich knew he had to snap out of the mood or risk questions that he didn't need or want to answer. "Ha, I'm fine. I should have had some of that coffee you drink Conrad."

Conrad smiled, "Ja, better than this mood you've acquired." He looked at the passing buildings.

"Nein, I'm fine and apologize for my moments in that mood." He thought to pat Conrad, but didn't and asked about the camp. "Do they have prisoners ready to go in?"

"Ja, there were fifty or so for construction and there are a thousand that will be there by the end of the week." Ehrlichmann seemed brighter now that Erich came out of his mood.

"Good," Erich could not make another mistake. "I've got a number of papers on my desk of transfers, but the tyrant wouldn't let me get them."

"Ha!" Conrad laughed and Gerheim eyed Erich.

"I make the jokes." Maj. Gerheim elbowed Erich.

They laughed and cut up now as they made their way along the country roads to Sachsenhausen and the party that was there.

After they arrived, Erich saw the cars, trucks and the guards and Officers of the SS. Himmler was there with other dignitaries too. Erich visited with Col. Lippert and Himmler.

"Captain Brueder." They shook hands.

Erich would have rather spat in his face; instead, he spoke to him appropriately, "Congratulations on your position as Chef der Deutschen Polizei." It was an awkward thing to say, but Himmler took it as it was meant, though a couple of his colleagues chuckled at this fresh captain.

Himmler made sure that his colleagues saw his distaste for their laughter and that they stopped. "You have caught my eye before Capt. Brueder."

"I believe in a leader whose actions aren't in words alone."

Erich had been around enough politicians and knew how to stroke their ego; it worked.

Himmler nodded at him and said nothing more. He went on to some other members of the SS, turned and looked at Erich one more time to let him know that he would not forget him. Then, he greeted the other SS officials.

Ehrlichmann walked up and stood by Erich's side, "That's got to be the greatest moment in the history of kissing the hand that feeds us." He gently pushed Erich.

Erich turned to him and, now, was in his right mind. "You worry that he'll make me your boss." He nudged him back and thought to beat him to death.

"If that's so, then it's good that I've made friends with you first." They laughed and walked around the barracks. Erich saw that some group of prisoners stood at attention and stared at nothingness. He looked for Nikki and there was a glimmer of terror in the eyes of the men when one mistakenly looked at Ehrlichmann.

"Did you just look at me?" Ehrlichmann stopped, eyed him and then looked up and down the line of prisoners.

The prisoner trembled, "Nein, Captain!"

Ehrlichmann looked at the group of officers with him and now was not the time. "No, you didn't." He walked away with Erich, "I've shot one man for this business of challenging me with a look."

Erich felt a surge of anger build in him. "I would," he said as he and Conrad looked at each other.

Ehrlichmann patted Erich's back, "thank you." He was quite serious and felt that they did have a sincere friendship.

After the dinner and a few more conversations, the men returned to SS Headquarters later that day and got to their paperwork.

The end of the day came and Erich got to his flat, fed Felix and then worked on his plans to get Nikki. He thought to falsify orders that would release Nikki to him, but he had to find him first and Ehrlichmann made it nearly impossible.

Two weeks had passed since the opening of Sachsenhausen, July 12th, and Erich went to the Inspectorate Office for the camps and had an opportunity to go over the new card system that worked with a type of punch card. This facilitated the information gathered on races in Germany and it was an opportunity for him to toy with a search.

"So, I give you any name and you can find it immediately?" Erich stood over the woman, sharp in her appearance and attractive with a hair lip, who had a box filled with punch cards. She showed him the cards with numbers, letters and a series of other numbers at the bottom of the card. At the top, there was the standard for the Reich. "Your name is Helga?"

"Ja," she smiled at him. "It may take some time." She hesitated and figured that he would give her a name. "Do you wish to give me a name?"

"What about a record of the search?"

"How do you mean?" She looked puzzled.

"Of who asked?"

"Normally, we make a note of the query. Some SD do it so regularly that we don't make the note of the name, just SD and the office." She looked impatient now. "You understand that this type of information is for a census of people in Germany currently?"

"Ja, I understand." He pondered, "Patz, Stephan."

Her eyes widened and then she wrote the name down and went to a file of smaller cards. She looked through them and there were many of these file cabinets throughout the office. She pulled the card and came back to him, "Patz, Stephan." She showed him the card.

Erich looked it over, "cause of death: Influenza" He looked at her and handed it back. "How often are they updated?"

"As often as is possible," she said. "You understand, Captain, that there are hundreds of these cards filled out daily."

"I'm looking for a prisoner that was taken to Dachau and is missing." She handed him the paper and he wrote, "Nicholas

VanEch."

She looked at it, went to another set of file cabinets and looked through them. She had a card.

Erich looked at the door and watched as some SS and some Gestapo passed by.

"Here," she handed him the card, but held the piece of paper with the names.

He looked it over and saw that Nicholas was transferred from SS HQ to Dachau and then location with "?? Ref: EHRLICHMAN-SD" and, finally, he was sent to Sachsenhausen on 18 July 1936! Erich handed her the card back and nodded. Then, he held out his hand.

She looked at his hand and then put the note with the names into it.

"Danke, Helga," he bent his head slightly and smiled with great charm.

She was somewhat amused and went back to her station.

Erich returned to his office and had to verify that Nikki was there. He had to pursue it immediately and to get them out of Germany and then to Canada. It seemed impossible without Stephan and he wondered if there was a chance at all that they would be free. The worst-case scenario he imagined is that they would be caught and executed together, but they would be with each other.

He got his papers and thought to make an excuse to go to Sachsenhausen the next day to check the "camps progression" and operations; it was well within his duties.

He went to Maj. Gerheim and waited. "Captain," Zelma showed him in. He smiled and she shook her head to let him know that no amount of his charm would work.

"Jan," Maj. Gerheim was on the phone. He finished and motioned for him to sit down. "So, you've been busy this day." He hung up.

Erich wondered now about the phone call, "Sir?"

"How did you find our new technology?" He poured some coffee and brought Erich some.

"Ah, it was an amazing thing to see so much information put together so quickly." He sipped the coffee, "danke." He knew then that the records clerk, Helga, had phoned Gerheim. "Bitch," he said under his breath.

He sat down and looked Erich over, "What brings you to me today?"

"I wish to go to Sachsenhausen to see how their operation has done after the prisoners arrived." He set the coffee down.

Maj. Gerheim thought about it and eyed Erich, "I like your initiative, but we were there only a week or so ago."

"Yes sir, but a great deal has happened in that time. They've acquired a few hundred new prisoners." Erich felt that Gerheim was more than just curious.

Maj. Gerheim thought on it for a moment, "I will join you." He said, took a drink of his coffee and then set it on his desk, "As this is Friday, we will go on Monday. Afterwards, I will go to my sisters further north."

"Very good," Erich wondered how he could talk with Nikki now. "Then, I will go to Gramzow to check on my family home."

He returned to his office to think on the matter of how to get Nikki out. Could he forge orders or just convince them to turn Nikki over, no. There was no way they would release a prisoner on his word. If he could get him out with just a couple of weeks before the Olympics, then the time would pass before anyone had any idea of what happened. Nikki and he would be in Poland the following week, then they'd be on a ship to Denmark and then home! He looked out his window and the sunlight seemed so bright that he felt blinded by it.

"Erich?" Dr. Scherbit held his pipe and was ready to tap his ash tray.

Erich rubbed the sleep from his eyes as he came back from his dream state.

"Are you alright?" He set his pipe down gently.

"Yes," he meant to sit up, but was better to lie still for a moment.

"You went back to Sachsenhausen and found Nikki?"

Erich turned on his side and looked at the doctor, "in some manner of speaking."

He looked at the clock and they had about ten minutes, "It seems there may not be enough time for that part."

Erich looked at the clock, "No, it will take a while to explain. Maj. Gerheim took the place of Stephan."

Dr. Scherbit's eyes widened, even in the darkness. "Is that so?" He sat up, "Now, you've piqued my interest."

"Ah, but Nikki has supper waiting." Erich chewed a bit to get the dry taste from his mouth. "I... I feel better to talk about what happened." He sat up, "Will this truly help me later on?"

"Yes," Dr. Scherbit said, got his pipe and set his pad and pencil down. "The more you discuss it, the more the bad energy is taken from it as you process those negative feelings."

"I did not tell Nikki what they did to Stephan." Erich pursed his lips.

"What Ehrlichmann did... that is what you mean?"

Erich looked at him and tried to smile, "ja."

"Ehrlichmann killed him or at least you thought so," Dr. Scherbit walked around to Erich. "That is all there is to know." He smiled and motioned to the door, "My wife has supper waiting too."

"Danke," Erich got to his feet and returned things back to their place.

CHAPTER 16: AN AFFAIR, A DEAL AND A WAY OUT

Late May-1954, it was a very nice afternoon in Quebec City. Erich left work early to take some time at the park and have dinner with Nikki. They didn't cause alarm by being together, though Erich would disagree. They were dressed in slacks, nice shirts and jackets.

"So, you have told him things about me, about what happened that you will not tell me?" Nikki asked.

They visited their favorite place, Mus'ee National des art du Quebec just on the west end of Battlefield Park. They enjoyed the collection of art and it was their time to go when most people were at work. They had the museum to themselves in some sense. "There are always things that we have seen and you know quite well that some things seen are not to be talked of." Erich stopped to admire a painting by Simone Hudon.

"She's amazing." Erich studied a print of the city.

Nikki didn't care for her work, "It seems dark and... lonely."

"There are people." Erich motioned with his hand at a few people who worked on a street. "I enjoy that it is plain and without complexity."

"It seems to be quite complex, La Halle Montcalm by Simone Hudon." Nikki looked at the work again, "no color."

Erich shook his head, "an etching."

"And no color," Nikki walked away. He didn't care for life

devoid of color, etching or not.

Erich made his way over to him as he admired a renaissance painting full of colors, nature and people. "You see this one is alive."

"Why don't you care for..." Erich asked.

He looked at Erich, "You know why."

"Sorry," Erich admired the work too.

"The etching reminds me of them, dark and devoid of life." Nikki studied the painting in detail, "I would like to learn."

"You're far too old now." Erich said to break the mood.

Nikki turned to him, wrapped him on his arm and scoffed. "A cold thing to say and a cold bed tonight." He moved over to another renaissance painting.

Erich smiled and made a quiet laugh, "Do not take away my night time privileges."

"Then, behave Erich Schmidt." He stopped and looked at Erich, "They took the color from us, the diversity of what we were as a people."

Erich knew he had kicked a nest of hornets now and had to quiet them. He leaned over as if to kiss Nikki which, even with Nikki's open personality, would have made him move on. "Ah!" He pushed him away, "not here!" He looked around and shook his head.

"You like the challenge to do it in public." He walked over and some people moved past them to admire a painting. No one saw the missed kiss and he knew Erich did it to toy with him.

"Not when you do it to be funny." Nikki raised a brow at him and then moved on.

Erich walked up to him, turned him and kissed him. There was a moment when they were alone and in that second Nikki pulled back. They eyed each other and Nikki smiled. "Alright, I forgive you." He shook his head at Erich.

"I recall that I looked at you when I was at Sachsenhausen and you didn't kiss me." Erich raised his eyebrows a few times, turned and walked off.

"Ah, that was quite a different time and place," he followed him out to the parc where they would have their picnic.

After their picnic and a leisurely walk through the parc, they made their way to Dr. Scherbit's office. Erich would go to his appointment and Nikki would go home to ready supper, do some chores and plan for the rest of the week.

"I love you." Nikki left him at the steps to Dr. Scherbit's office.

Erich wanted a smoke, but dismissed it and went inside.

Lucy nodded at him as he came in and there was no one else in the waiting area. Erich made himself comfortable and Lucy polished her nails.

The door to the hallway opened and Dr. Scherbit came in, "Lucy." He walked past Erich, "Erich come in." Lucy quickly got her nail polish put away, got her purse and left.

Erich got up and went into the office where the chaise already faced the door. "Did I forget from last week?"

Dr. Scherbit looked at the chaise and sat down at his desk, "no, the angry woman from a few weeks ago insisted that she face the door too."

"You're not supposed to talk about your patients to other patients." Erich took his jacket off and hung it up.

"Did I?" Dr. Scherbit looked tired.

"Would you like the chaise?" Erich asked and stood there for a moment.

"Ah, no," he got his pipe and put it in his mouth; it wasn't lit. "I'm trying to quit."

Erich sat on the chaise, "me too."

"We left off with…" He looked at his notepad, "Gerheim."

"That Monday, yes," Erich laid back on the chaise, but he realized then that the curtains were wide open and the room was bright. "Forgive me, but…"

"The light?"

"Just the world outside," he said, got up and pulled the curtains to where they nearly shut out the sunlight. He pulled at the window too until it there was just an inch between it and the sill. Then, he returned to the chaise and laid down, "thank you."

"It's you who must be comfortable." He sat back, "besides, it's nearly sunset." He got his notepad and pencil, "Major Gerheim."

"He wanted to go because he suspected something. That woman from records called him and spoke about my search." Erich stared at the tiled ceiling.

"You know she did?"

"Ja, I believed it." He waited before he turned to the light. "It's what happened after the call that convinced me he was suspicious."

"But you mentioned that he became like Stephan? A Friend?" Dr. Scherbit put his feet on his desk, a first for him with a patient, but he was comfortable with Erich and why not relax too.

"He did." Erich turned and the lamp, to his surprise, was off! "Is the lamp broke?"

"No, the woman, I mean patient before you… she turned it off."

Erich sighed heavily in annoyance, got up and turned the lamp on. The white glow climbed up and down the curtain's rippled fabric. "She is a dark soul; it suits her to have the lamp off."

"And Gerheim?"

"He was not such a dark soul after all." His eyes followed the furthest edge of the lamps light where it faded at the top of the curtain and followed it down to just above the lamp itself where the glow was bright. The glow comforted him and he felt his heart warm and calm. "We left in the afternoon for Sachsenhausen to be there after the prisoners had their dinner." His eyes were heavy and slowly fell shut.

Berlin, late July 1936-Monday, Erich and Major Gerheim got to the car. Erich packed things at the flat and fought with Felix over what to do with him. He planned, to that point, that they would go to the camp, conduct their visit and then leave. Maj. Gerheim's driver would drop Erich at the train station so that he could go to Gramzow. Erich's plan then was to go back into

Berlin, get his things, Felix and then go back to Sachsenhausen with forged orders to release Nikki to him for questioning. He knew that they would try to check, but no one would be at the office.

He did feel some confidence that Col. Lippert would not call, because he and Lippert got along well. He believed too that Himmler liked him and Lippert knew it. He had to use all these things to his advantage.

Monday morning, Erich stood by the car at SS HQ, "Jan, where's your bags?" Major Gerheim gave an overnight bag to the driver who put it in the trunk.

"I've got clothes there for the night."

"Very well," he nodded at the car and they left for Sachsenhausen.

It was busier than they expected. There were trucks at the gate, additional guards, some civilians that made deliveries and the camp had a few hundred new faces. Erich knew more about weapons than he cared to ever tell Nikki. He saw what he thought was an MG 34, a large machine gun, with its nose over the end of the guard tower just across from them and the guards carried machine-guns and the Mauser Luger.

"It seems that a great deal has changed in those two weeks." Erich said.

"Ja, even I am surprised." They walked into the administration building and then visited with Col. Lippert who took them out to the grounds.

Col. Lippert pointed up between the prisoner camps, "You see the design that our triangle puts the buildings so and the main area for the prisoners is centered here." He pointed at a common area in front of them. "The towers have a clear line of sight along the fence line." He pointed to the towers. "The fence is electrified."

"There is no chance of escape." Erich said.

"There is always a chance." Col. Lippert said, "These men are rats. They will scour the place, make thoughts of our defenses and if they are desperate or foolish, they will try to escape."

He had some of the men line up and they walked past them. Erich was in tow behind Gerheim and the Colonel. He hoped to see Nikki, but there were many men lined up with their striped uniforms and symbols. He tried to focus on the triangles that were on the uniforms, but it was a second for each step that they took and nearly impossible to make out a face. The pink triangles were quite large and the numbers beneath them were as large, so he must find out what number was on Nikki; the thought sickened him.

"Quite a sight, isn't it Capt. Brueder?" Col. Lippert stopped and looked at him.

Erich was preoccupied with the mass of men, "Sorry, ja, it is a sight."

"We foresee many more prisoners in the future." Col. Lippert turned and they walked away from the prisoners who were ordered to return to their chores.

"With the Olympics so close, it seems there would be more." Erich looked over the grounds and the barracks.

"There will be many more." Col. Lippert said, "Coffee gentlemen?"

"Pardon me Colonel, but are the registrations similar to the punch card system used at our offices?" Erich asked.

Col. Lippert seemed surprised, "punch cards? The ones used for the census?"

"Capt. Brueder has been absorbed by this system of identification." Maj. Gerheim gave him a look of impertinence.

"My apologies Col. Lippert, I *would* enjoy some coffee." Erich dipped his head at Col. Lippert first, out of respect, and then at Maj. Gerheim.

"His curiosity is no different than when I was a young officer." Col. Lippert said, "No, we use no such cards here… yet." He pointed at the administration office, "They have registration cards that are filled out by the prisoners first and, if possible, compared to records or their papers. If they are transferred, the card is put in our file and then given a registration number instead of a name." He chuckled, "as if the name mattered anyway with these people." They walked to the administration building. "The number corresponds to a name, the camp and their location within the camp." They went in and stopped in the small lobby, "and the symbols you already know of."

"Of course, thank you sir."

"Now, for that coffee," they went upstairs and to his office where the servant had some small snacks and fresh coffee.

They talked about things and matters unrelated to their jobs. Maj. Gerheim was most interested in the Olympics and that he had tickets already to several events. Col. Lippert said that he looked forward to time away and that there was mention he would be transferred in October. They discussed some politics, but that seemed to end in nothing good, so they talked about their families. Erich didn't say much, because Gerheim and the Lippert were old friends.

"Jan, you seemed to be there on your own." Maj. Gerheim said.

"With your permission Colonel, I wish to walk the grounds in their entirety." Erich knew it was not appropriate at this moment, but he had to look.

"Captain, you are too caught up in the matter, but as you wish." Col. Lippert was disappointed, but declined to say no.

Maj. Gerheim seemed interested too, "Michael, I will go with him."

"You've ruined my visit, Fritz!" Col. Lippert said, but was joking and laughed about it. "In fact, I have a great deal of work to do, but this was enjoyable."

Erich had to get downstairs before them to search for Nikki's registration! "Perhaps, a visit to the washroom?"

Col. Lippert pointed out at the hallway, "there, on the right."

The servant interrupted, "Sir, the room is under service."

Erich was elated.

The servant nodded, "down the stairs and on the left."

Erich got up, but Maj. Gerheim stayed and drank his coffee, "I'll be down shortly."

"Col. Lippert, thank you for your time and hospitality." Erich clicked his heels and dipped his head.

"You're welcome," Col. Lippert seemed caught up with Maj. Gerheim. "So, this Versheim was such a fool to pass up Himmler on his visit. We all know…"

Erich quickly made his way downstairs, past the washroom and to the offices. There were many people in there, but the sign was clear, "REGISTRATION." He walked up and the woman was quick to come to him, "Captain?"

"There was a prisoner transferred here." Erich sighed to calm his anxiety.

"Ja, there were nearly a thousand or so." She laughed.

Erich kept a stern look, "Just one I'm interested in."

She got her composure back, "the name or race?"

"Nicholas VanEch," Erich looked at the doorway and listened for the boots on the steps.

She took a piece of paper and looked at Erich, "to spell it please."

"V,A,N,E,C,H," he looked at the doorway and caught himself searching. He had to calm down.

"Danke, einen moment bitte." She went to a large file cabinet and then had to show the paper to another woman and they went to a file cabinet across the room.

She got a card out that was about the size of a half sheet of regular paper. She held it up and brought it to him.

Erich didn't like that she held it up, but he was still by himself. He glanced at the doorway and thought he heard Maj. Gerheim in the hallway. "You're very good."

She smiled and blushed, "danke." She showed him the card, "He is at the middle of the camp… just there." She pointed through the window at the barracks across the yard, "zweiundzwanzig."

He got her hand, kissed it and winked. "I'm sure that you'll keep this matter to yourself as I was supposed to know this already."

She was overwhelmed and the other women didn't seem to care, "ja." She smiled and fanned her face.

He smiled, turned and walked to the lobby and then out the door. It was near supper time and he knew that after they walked, Maj. Gerheim would insist to take him to the station so that he could go to his sisters and Erich would go to Gramzow.

"You're ready?" Maj. Gerheim stood just behind him while Erich looked at the camp.

Lt. Klein walked up and past, "Capt. Brueder."

"Lieutenant," Erich nodded.

"You met him last time we were here?" Maj. Gerheim looked at the sun setting.

Erich waited till Klein was further away and out of earshot. "Ja," he waited for Maj. Gerheim to take the lead.

"Oh no Jan, you wanted to make this tour." He motioned for Erich to lead.

"Very well, sir."

"You must use discretion when you are anxious." He patted Erich's shoulder.

"Sir?"

"Take time to listen, spend time with senior officers." He looked at the finished barracks and the ones in the distance that were under construction.

"Yes, sir," Erich fought the urge to ignore him and look for Nikki. "I was hasty."

"Yes, you were." He said, but admired the motivation in his young captain, "but your motivation has its benefits." He patted Erich on the back, "So, where to first?"

"Just to look the barracks condition over and then along the fence line to see the description is a model camp as mentioned by Himmler." Erich said as they approached the first barracks.

A Kapo yelled for the men to stand at attention. There were only forty or so of them at this barracks.

Erich did not let them go at ease, because that would be too hard to make out Nikki. He wondered if Nikki would know not to approach him. Then, he realized that Nikki wouldn't recognize him in an SS uniform and, certainly, would not come near him. He wondered what he could tolerate if he saw Nikki badly beaten and his heart jumped.

"They seem to be orderly." Maj. Gerheim looked at them as the Kapo stood at attention and was a gruff looking man with an afternoon shadow on his face. Erich didn't walk as quickly. "Let them be at ease," he said to Erich.

"Yes, they appear in good health too." Erich was disappointed that Nikki wasn't there and they got to the end of the line of men. "Tell them at ease."

The Kapo yelled at them to go to at ease and the men slowly broke up.

Erich looked in the distance to the end of the yard. There were barracks under construction and some brick buildings, "Seems there is more land than buildings."

"Now, yes. But, this is the future of things where there will be more of these buildings than land." Maj. Gerheim put his hand on Erich's shoulder. "We should go."

"ECK!" The Kapo yelled at a young man who stood some twenty feet or so from them and faced the SS officers.

Erich and Maj. Gerheim turned quickly! It was in that second that Erich knew; his heart nearly blasted out of his chest. He had to get himself back in his mindset as an SS. "What is it you're yelling at?"

There, between them and the Kapo, was Nikki. He was battered in his striped uniform with a large upside down pink triangle and the numbers, "0034" on his uniform. His eyes were sullen and the darkness under them looked like a dull black charcoal. His shoulders were forward, his hair was shaved off and his skull was scraped from the razor; there were lines or bumps on top of his head. He wore wooden clogs and looked so small and insignificant to the Kapo who walked up to him. "Halt!" Erich yelled.

"Captain!" The Kapo got right behind Nikki. "This man... sir, we are not permitted to approach any member of the camp without permission, sir!"

It was then that two guards headed towards them. He knew to put the matter to rest immediately, "Then, escort him back."

Erich did his best not to make eyes with Nikki.

Maj. Gerheim wasn't pleased and wanted to leave, "Jan, we're leaving."

"Sir," but it was then that Nikki looked at Erich and they locked eyes for a mere second! Maj. Gerheim saw it and squinted, but did not stop.

Erich walked on and did not look at him again. He stayed at an even pace with Maj. Gerheim all the way to the car. As they got in, he had to settle the matter. Then, he realized that if he said anything what would Gerheim think? "To look at me, I should have shot him."

The car pulled away and Maj. Gerheim chuckled, "with what gun?"

Erich looked out the window, closed his eyes and pressed his teeth together so hard that his jaw muscles bloated like a balloon!

"It's happened to me." He took off his hat. "These men are lost souls, so they see authority or power in us." He sighed, "They see a way to connect by approaching us, perhaps to save them."

"It's my first time to have it happen." Erich said, removed his hat and didn't break his gaze.

"It is unsettling, but don't let it continue to upset you." He nodded at the driver, "the train station."

The driver pulled away and drove to the station. They arrived at the station and Erich got his things, "see you tomorrow, sir."

Maj. Gerheim leaned to the window and used his finger to say, "Come here." Erich got to the window and listened. "Don't let it trouble you, Jan. I feel that it has burdened you in some way."

"It has," Erich tried to smile.

"Go to your family home; get yourself some time to forget this place... for now." He smiled, "see you in the morning." He motioned for the driver to leave and they were gone in seconds.

Erich stood there and watched as people passed him. There were flags everywhere and party symbols with the swastika emblazoned on them. He felt sick to his stomach and had to wipe his eyes when he saw Nikki's beaten face again. He turned and took the train back to Berlin. There was no chance he could get him out of there at this hour; it would be deeply suspicious.

Erich got in the main terminal and stopped to look at trains to Berlin. He saw the lamps overhead and studied one that gave his eyes some time to relax.

"Erich?" Dr. Scherbit said, "Erich?"

Erich opened his eyes, but wasn't so quick to rise up. He turned to be on his side and looked at Dr. Scherbit who had a glass of water.

"Here," he handed it to him.

Erich took a drink, "My mouth is so dry, danke."

"Bitte schön," Dr. Scherbit went to his desk and sat down. "We've got some time left." He looked at the clock and they had nearly thirty minutes to go. "I feel that Gerheim figured it out."

Erich sat up and looked at him, "He did." He set the glass down.

Dr. Scherbit gently nodded at Erich. "So, do you wish to continue?"

Erich shook his head and then wiped a little bit of sleep from his eyes, "I don't feel that I'm sleeping, but there it is." He got a tissue and blew his nose.

"You're in a type of day dream." Dr. Scherbit said, and then pushed his notepad and pencil aside.

Erich looked at him, the clock and then back at him. "You will bill for the hour no matter."

He nodded and had a sly grin.

"Then, I will tell you the rest of this part that there was a deal to have a way out." Erich tapped the chaise, "I'll have to buy this chaise from you when we're done."

"There have been many people who have been upon it." Dr. Scherbit smiled, "But I will give you a good deal."

"Ha, that's a Jewish thing to have a good deal or get one." Erich laughed.

"No, Erich. That is for any person who has investments." He shook his head.

Erich thought on it, "Nikki would have hit me by now. I... apologize. It was just a joke."

"I know." He picked up his notepad and pencil.

He laid back on the chaise, looked at the lamp and closed his eyes.

Tuesday, end of July - 1936, Erich came into the main hallway and was in good spirits. He had an idea to use the same plan the first week of August when the Olympics would be in full operation. He'd forge the orders to release Nikki to him. He made notes to have a change of clothes for him, to clean him up, to see that his mental state was in order for the trip and that they stuck to their story no matter. He felt, now, even without Stephan that it could work. He thought it through just as he got to the third floor.

"JAN!" Ehrlichmann was behind him and trotted up the stairs.

Erich stopped and turned, "Good morning, Conrad." He appeared delighted, but felt the urge to shove him back down the stairs and fought to keep the images of his love out of his mind and heart for now.

They shook vigorously. "You look well from your short trip."

"Ja, very short," he smiled.

Conrad touched Erich's shoulder to motion him up the stairs, "It appears that some tickets came my way for the Olympics. I've been a fan of the diving challenge."

Erich had to play along or risk being questioned, "And you're going to give them all to me!"

Conrad eyed him, "Ha! I wish only to see that you join me."

"What will it cost me?" They walked down the hall and Erich thought to ask him to lunch, so he could dig into where he'd be and what he'd be doing during the week, "dinner?"

"Ja, dinner and some drinks!" Conrad patted Erich on the shoulder.

"I can't." Erich said.

Conrad's happy expression quickly faded, "wh ..."

"Refuse," Erich smiled very wide and then laughed.

"You... you are a bastard." Conrad pushed him. "You know that wasn't funny!"

"Ha, it was and you will have to get even." Erich pushed him back and they went to their offices, "see you at noon?"

"Ja, you are right! I will get even." He stopped at his door, smiled at Erich, "noon" and then went to work.

Erich went in his office and found Zelma there, "you waiting for me?"

"Nein, he does though and I'm to get you as soon as you arrive." She walked up to him and tapped his chest, "Your charm is waning."

Erich's heart sank a little, but there were so many other matters at hand that he figured it must be something about work. "For now," he said, set his things down and went to Gerheim's office. The door was open, so he walked in, "Sir?"

"Jan," he was at the door and on the other side, "have a seat." He shut the door and quietly locked it.

Erich sat down and waited while he got two cups of coffee. He took one to Erich, "here you are... cream and some sugar."

"You remembered, though I'm not surprised." Erich took the coffee and smelled it, "very nice, danke." He turned to go to his desk and Erich saw that he had a gun holstered to his side. "How was your visit?"

Maj. Gerheim sat down and adjusted himself, because the Luger's holster was bulky and caught on his chair. "Very good, my sister and I had a nice visit." He took a sip of his coffee, "and your stay?"

"Quiet," Erich was careful not to read into anything, but it disturbed him that Gerheim was armed. For the moment, he felt that there was a game of chess being played. His face cooled and felt flush, so he was sure to sit up and took another drink of his coffee.

"It's such a busy place with so much going on here that some things are missed." He sipped his coffee too. "Even by the SD," he cleared his throat.

"Sir?"

"My duties include the punch card system, so I stopped by there early this morning." He smiled and looked at the morning sunlight that balanced between the buildings and the trees to shine in the office. "It was Helga who helped you."

Erich thought on it, "in the census office, ja."

He leaned over, unsnapped the holster and pulled the Luger out. He set it on the desk with the barrel pointed at Erich.

"Sir, what are you doing?" Erich fought to keep his composure.

"Jan, in this business there must be trust." He set his coffee down. "There must be absolute trust or we cannot function." He sat back a little, "I cannot function." He looked at the Luger. "It's a man's worth and Himmler believes that it is essential to the SS survival as we grow."

"And you believe there is an issue of trust with me," Erich hadn't moved. Sweat formed on his forehead and he felt wet under his arms. He fought to swallow, but he had never had a gun, whether on the desk or in someone's hand, pointed at him. He pondered for a split second to take it, but then what?

"I'm going to find out right now." He sat up, got the Luger and held it. "I didn't put it together until I recalled the men you asked about." He pushed back from his desk and held the pistol in his lap. "Stephan Patz... Nicholas VanEch."

"Patz was the man who..."

"Ehrlichmann arrested with you," he looked at his coffee, "VanEch?"

Erich swallowed hard, "I believe that Ehrlichmann told me about him. He was investigating him or someone close to him." He sat up and looked at the barrel of the gun. "I was merely curious."

"Eck," Maj. Gerheim said, got up and stood there with the pistol in his hand.

"Eck?" Erich didn't get it and set his coffee on the desk.

"Nicholas Van... *Eck*." He walked to the side of his desk and sat on the edge. "That Kapo yelled at the man, *Eck*." He shook his head, "I realized this was the man you sought and who came to you on Monday."

"Sir, I..." Erich fiddled for a moment and had to get a grip on the matter before it blew up in his face. He pulled on the arms of the chair to get up.

"No, Captain." Maj. Gerheim pointed the Luger at him. "Stay seated." He let the barrel slowly take its aim off Erich and go to the floor. "Trust, Jan... that's all there is, trust."

"I believe you are leading to conclusions that..." he bit at his lip and took slow, deep breaths to calm himself. He ran ideas through his head of how to get downstairs to the U-Bahn or to the flat.

"Are far-fetched?" He smiled slyly, "no." He looked at the window, "Some of us are not who we seem." He turned back to Erich, "Right Erich?"

Erich felt that it was nearly check mate, "Sir?"

"Don't," he stood up. "Erich Schmidt, that is who Ehrlichmann looks for. Erich come back as Jan Brueder and Patz helped you." He grinned, "Patz worked with Erich Schmidt at the Reichstag."

Erich felt that there was the queen and he was in the corner, "I don't know what you mean. I am Captain Jan..."

"Stop it!" He pointed the Luger at Erich, "Trust Erich, I must have a way to trust you." He walked closer and kept the pistol pointed at Erich. "Are you here for VanEch or are you a spy as Capt. Ehrlichmann believes?"

Erich got his composure and sat up, "I am no spy." His lower back felt like there was a furnace inches from it.

Maj. Gerheim looked him over and lowered the pistol. "It takes great courage to do what I *think* you plan to do or you are a complete and utter fool." The entire matter unsettled him so that he couldn't sit still.

Erich was baffled as Gerheim put the pistol in the holster and shook his head at him. "Sir, I..."

"Don't understand?" He walked back around his desk and sat down. He got his coffee and drank some, "You *are* Erich Schmidt."

Anxiety screamed at him to say nothing, so he gently nodded.

"And you swear you are not here as a spy, because if you are..." he touched the holster.

"I am no spy." Erich said firmly and was resolute.

"Ehrlichmann has not put it together, but he is only somewhat stupid." Maj. Gerheim got up and walked over to Erich, "get up."

Erich stood and they were face to face, "Sir, what do you plan to do?"

They eyed each other and Erich's anxiety surged through him like a team of wild horses! Maj. Gerheim looked at a picture of his wife and two children on the desk that faced the doorway. He stepped over to it, turned it away from them and then got in Erich's face. "We are not who we seem."

Erich hadn't noticed, but Gerheim's face was smooth with little black dots of his whiskers and he had fuller lips than he recalled. His hair was much thinner and it was hotter now with him so close. "What do you want from me?"

Maj. Gerheim exhaled and his breath smelled like whiskey. He tried to kiss Erich!

Erich backed away and then it all hit him. "You want me?"

Maj. Gerheim eyed him and waited. Slowly, Erich studied his eyes, his face and then his lips. He turned quickly when he heard a noise by the door. "It's locked." Maj. Gerheim grabbed Erich by his lapels and pulled him in! They kissed and Erich would tell Nikki that he was taken by the kiss as it was sensuous, warm and his body responded to it. Their lips were pressed against each other in a soft way and some tiny bit of spat or drool came out the side of Maj. Gerheim's mouth. His firm grip loosened and he leaned away. They looked at each other for a moment, "So, now I know." He lowered his hands and waited for Erich to say something.

Erich opened his eyes and looked the man over, "Yes, sir; we are not who we seem." He drew his hand across his wet lips.

Maj. Gerheim touched Erich's face and smiled, "We are not."

He went to his desk and turned the picture back. "I wish people to see my family when they come in, so there is no question that I am happy and proud of them." He nodded at Erich who wiped the sweat from his forehead.

Erich was taken aback by the whole experience and had to catch his breath, "This has been quite a moment for me."

Maj. Gerheim smiled, "and me." His momentary happiness faded and he looked at the door, "It will be tough for you, for VanEch." He went to the door and quietly unlocked it. "She hears everything."

"Ja, she does." Erich didn't know whether to sit down or run. "What, sir, will happen now?"

He walked past Erich, then turned to face him. "If and when Ehrlichmann finds out, you'll be finished and he will most certainly execute you and your freund." He rubbed his brow, "however, he believes in his friendship with you."

"I've seen that." Erich's pale complexion warmed.

Maj. Gerheim wiped the spat and sweat from his mouth, "I'm sorry about Patz." He got his coffee and took a sip, "ah, it's cold." He went to the counter and poured another.

"Danke," Erich looked at the door as his secretary knocked. "Come!"

She opened the door slowly and had a file in hand. "Col. Lippert called and said to call him about the Olympics." She stepped in, "Here is the file you asked about."

She didn't dare to look at Erich and felt uncomfortable about them. She sat the file down and left quickly.

"Danke, I'll call him shortly." Maj. Gerheim watched her leave.

The door clicked shut. "Will you help?" Erich took a leap of faith, something he knew little about.

"To get him from Sachsenhausen, this is not an easy task." He sat down and Erich sat too.

"I have a plan." He had nothing more to hide. Maj. Gerheim knew and there was no way to go back.

"Do you love him?" Major Gerheim asked and smiled.

Erich was surprised and didn't want to answer, "I…"

"I want to know if there *is* love between queers." He turned and got the holster from his side.

Erich looked at him sternly, "I love him."

"Then, the plan should be to get him from Sachsenhausen, get to a border and leave Germany." He took the holster off and set it on his desk. "You'll need an order to release him to you."

"Ehrlichmann will find out, but I thought to do it the day before the Olympics begins." Erich felt hopeful now and sat on the edge of his chair like a giddy schoolboy, "he has tickets for me."

"You're to go with Ehrlichmann then?" He looked through his desk and then got a note.

"Ja, but I will make it so that I go on my own and not ride there with him." He felt some nervous tension, but dismissed it as he thought about Nikki.

"It's not as though the Olympics are in München." He sipped on his coffee, then blew off the steam. "He won't be that far away."

"No sir, but I believe it will be far enough that by the time he has come to any conclusion, we will be gone." Erich felt some anxiousness in his heart that all this madness was going to end well.

"I have one more question for you… Erich." He sat up, "Did you kill Jan?"

Erich felt cool for just a second, "No, absolutely not. He died and…"

"Patz changed the papers of his death." Maj. Gerheim looked at him now, "that worried me." He pursed his lips, "You've taken quite a chance to say so much."

Erich sat back in the chair, "I am no murderer and, ja, I have taken a chance."

"You've got this week to get your affairs in order." He got some papers ready, "I will make the order and talk with Col. Lippert to confirm it, so he won't feel compelled to call."

Erich stood up, "Sir, but you will put yourself at risk."

"Ja, but I can say I was fooled by you too." He eyed Erich, "though, I'm not." He smiled and waved his hand at Erich, "go, get your work done so I'm not left with it when you do this." He looked over the file she left him.

"I'm grateful for your help." Erich pushed his uniform back into place and got up. "I did not imagine this as a way out." He clicked his heels out of habit and nodded.

"Stop that noise," he then looked up from the file. "Good luck to you both." He got his pen and wrote some things out. "The order will be ready by Friday."

"Danke, sir," he turned and went to his office. He shut the door and stood there for a moment and then the anxiety ate him up alive! He inhaled a gulp of air that sounded like a whale sucking in its last breath and then he fell to the floor! His labored breathing had to stop or he'd have to ask for help, so he put his hands over his mouth and slowed his breaths. He sat back against the wall and wiped the sweat from his forehead, "Nikki, I need you." Tears welled up in his eyes and his face was flush white. For a few minutes, he sat there against the door and let his body and mind get back to normal. He closed his eyes hard and then opened them. There was a great deal of paperwork to do and he had to get up, "Get up Erich Schmidt." He shook his head, "Get yourself up!" He pushed against the wall and stood up, straightened his uniform out and looked at his desk. "I can do this." He wiped his eyes.

The day went well and he had his dinner with Conrad at the local cafe. Conrad was clear that he would be at work for the week and one day to follow up on a case; Erich felt that the case was about Nikki, but Conrad said nothing more. So, they went back to SS HQ.

When he finally made it home, he drank three glasses of schnapps! Felix got a treat of fresh fish and he admired the life of a cat. He threw his feet up, boots on, onto the table. His jacket was unbuttoned and his cap and long coat were hung. "For a bitch you have it easy... cats." He watched Felix eat up all the fish, "better you enjoy that fish than me." He thought for a moment and poured another glass of schnapps. "To success," he drank it all and then plopped back on the couch. He studied the lamp in the kitchen and his eyelids fell shut.

"ERICH!" Dr. Scherbit said firmly and tapped his pipe hard on the ash tray.

"JA!" He got up quickly and looked around the room! Some drool came from his mouth. "Damn you and that pipe!" He stood and nearly lost his balance.

"We went much longer."

"Then you should rouse me!" He looked for his jacket, "Now, I have to pay for that too."

"No, I was caught up with what happened. I can't believe Gerheim!" He got his leather flap case, jacket and then turned off his desk lamp.

"It's true, every word of it." Erich shook his head to get his bearings.

"I'm... quite literally shocked." He went to the door while Erich put the chaise back, opened the curtain and turned off the lamp.

"I was so overwhelmed by all of it. After the schnapps, I woke the next morning there on the couch and that filthy cat was on my lap." He got his jacket and walked into the waiting room.

Dr. Scherbit closed and locked his door. "But you rescued him too?"

"Ja, Nikki made me bring him." They walked into the hallway and Dr. Scherbit locked that door too and then they walked to the street, "thank you."

"You're welcome," Dr. Scherbit shook his hand. "It's good that he gave you a way out."

"He did." Erich nodded as the doctor got a cab. He fast walked home so that Nikki wouldn't worry for long. "Queers do love, Major," he got some flowers at a magazine stand and then half jogged and half walked to their flat.

CHAPTER 17: EHRLICHMANN, PART I—A SPY IS HERE

June 1954, Erich was dressed in jeans and nice shirt. Sunday morning was sunny and cool, so he sat in his favorite chair in the sitting room and read the local rag. He felt more and more relaxed. The nightmares seemed to have become dreams now with some effect on him. He was happier that their sex life was better and smiled at the thought that only a few months ago, they were at a point where there was little romance. For years, he was constantly on some high alert; sounds and shadows were maddening. If he heard a noise, perhaps in the hallway, he'd be up! He'd get a knife from the nightstand, go to the area of the noise and then prepare to attack.

Nikki had similar problems, but his was the fear of insecurity; with all that Ehrlichmann did to him and then life at the camp with lice, the sexual abuse and the times he was taken by force and beaten, he would wake up and would go into the closet, shut the door and bury himself between the boxes.

"So, you feel good?" Nikki asked and stood at the door with his apron on.

"Yes, and you slept quite nicely last night." Erich set the paper down, got up and went to the love seat. "Come here, my love." He tapped the seat.

Nikki untied the apron and took it off.

"That's all?" Erich asked.

"Sunday is a day of rest." Nikki came to him, sat down and curled up at his side.

Erich wrapped his arm around him and kissed him. "It will be your turn soon."

"I'm not sure that I will go."

Erich turned and touched Nikki's face, "what?" He put his head to Nikki's, "why?"

"When…" He cleared his throat and sat up, "we were sick with the things that happened; it made it worse and harder to heal." He closed his eyes, "We waited too long and the things that we did became so common to us that we didn't stop to say this *is* wrong." He opened them and forced a grin.

Erich nodded, "No, we didn't."

"When we got back, it was as though we didn't believe it." Nikki sighed, "We returned to life here and acted as though that was it." He took his glasses off, "like these glasses."

Erich studied them. "What's wrong with your glasses?"

"Erich, they are the same type glasses from that time." He put them back on.

"So, in the base of ourselves, we hadn't changed and…"

"And we must, to live our lives." They kissed.

"But I've gone to the Jew and it's all going well." He hugged Nikki, "You will go and we will be good."

"Don't call him that anymore," Nikki smacked Erich's forearm, "change."

"Dr. Scherbit was impressed by Gerheim." Erich bumped Nikki.

Nikki laid down on Erich's lap and stretched his legs out. "Even now I find it hard to say his name."

"Gerheim?"

"Ah, no," he said.

Erich didn't need to say another name; he knew the name that Nikki didn't like to say and hoped to never hear again, "it's alright."

"In my nightmares, I see him coming for me." Nikki crossed

his arms.

"But you know this is not possible anymore." Erich held him tightly.

"But I still see him or sometimes when I go to the washroom at night, I..." He wiped away the tear, "he's there waiting for me." He got his breath and sighed, "He will be with me forever, I think."

"Dr. Scherbit has said, you do not forget, but you forgive and take the negative energy from the thing that upsets you." Erich looked at Nikki who made a face at him.

"So, you have learned a great deal from the Jew." Nikki smiled.

"Don't ever say that again, it's not nice." Erich eyed him, "His name is Dr. Scherbit." He tapped Nikki's shoulder, "To be honest, I like him."

"When it's over, we will invite him over to have supper with us." Nikki sat up, "that would be nice."

"What will the neighbors think?" Erich laughed.

"Not a thing." Nikki got up, "it's a nice day for a walk."

"Always a walk with you," Erich set his rag down and got up.

Nikki took the apron to the kitchen and then got his shoes, "We should get some fresh flowers."

"Yes, darling," Erich went to the front door.

"Ha, you've never said darling to me," Nikki went to him.

"I've never felt as good as I do now." He opened the door.

"To say so is good. That's why I don't believe I will go. Now that you are well, it's helped me to be well too." He waited as Erich got his hat.

"But you still see him and can't say his name," Erich eased the door shut, "Nikki... my darling."

Nikki looked emotional and didn't look at Erich, "no, I can't."

"I will go with you."

Nikki looked at him and they hugged, "He terrifies me."

"Then, we shall face him together and you will confront this fear once and for all." Erich let him loose and they stood apart now. "You are a man too."

Nikki eyed him, "Yes, I suppose." He opened the door again, "You will do it with me?"

"Yes," Erich walked past him into the hallway.

"Then, I will go."

They went down the steps and out to the street where the sun hit them. They walked along the river walk west to the parc and their favorite museum. Nikki was so close to Erich that they bumped each other as they made their way past other people and enjoyed their Sunday.

The next day, Erich sat quietly at his desk and thought about Sunday. He smiled and his secretary looked at him. "What?"

"It's not often to see you smile." She said.

He straightened his face out, then smiled wide, "better?"

"I may keep working for you if it's a habit." She winked.

Wednesday of that week, he left for his appointment and felt a little sad as he knew that they were going to stop at some point. The walk over was nice and the sun shined. He got to the office and waited a moment by the door. Then, he turned and went in.

Dr. Scherbit's office, "So, he will come see me." He set his pipe down and drank a glass of water. "The warmer air makes me thirsty."

"Yes, he will come see you. He believes that as I have gotten better, the stress is less now." He moved the chaise to face the door, went to the curtains and pulled them shut and then sighed over the whole of the matter to arrange the room for his session.

"It's true that if a couple has suffered traumas, then the one who is better will lift the spirits, the health of the other." He sat down and got his notepad and pencil.

"Couple?" Erich didn't touch the window as it was closed and the fan was on.

"Nikki has never been just a friend... we know that." He dipped his head so that his eyes were above his glasses.

"I suppose." He sat on the chaise and didn't look at the doctor.

Dr. Scherbit set his pencil and notepad aside, "These

distinctions did not matter until the Nazi's made them matter."

"So, you have no concern for queers?" Erich asked.

"No, I believe that, though I do not like the word queer, you have a right to life and to love as you wish." He smiled, got his pipe and set it far on the other side of the desk, away from his ashtray, "recall that queers, Jews, gypsies and other people were in the camps... together."

"You are one man." Erich laid back on the chaise.

"Hitler was one man; evil as he was, he did monumental things." Dr. Scherbit sighed, "One man can do as much good too."

Erich got comfortable and took a few deep breaths.

"So, the name Nikki cannot say?"

"Ehrlichmann," Erich turned to the lamp in the corner; its luminescent glow seemed constant like a star's glow at night. The glow sank into his eyes and put him at ease as if he were in a warm bubble bath.

Wednesday, July twenty-ninth, 1936-Berlin, Erich got to work that morning and went right to his paperwork. He did what he could to avoid Conrad, so he told Zelma that he was not to be disturbed. Though, he knew Conrad would push his way in and ignore her. At least, Conrad would have it from another source that he was, in fact, busy.

Germany had many guests, many dignitaries, and the straße's were filled with flags and swastikas and the standard of the Reich. The sea of red and black banners went on forever down the main straße of Berlin to Olympic rings that adorned the city. Erich couldn't help but wonder if Germany had focused on something more than one Aryan Germany and one German, how much better the German people would have come into the future.

"Ha!" Ehrlichmann shouted when she tried to stop him, "he sees his freunds!" He burst through the door and had his long coat on, his cap at his side.

Zelma shouted at him, "Captain!"

Erich stood and smiled, "It's alright and I will apologize now for him."

Her face, despite a natural soft white skin, was flaming red. She stopped, turned and went back to her desk.

"I should bring her to my squad!" Conrad was in exceptional spirits. "Jan!" He came around the desk and they hugged; it was awkward and Erich fought thoughts that tried to drive him to smash Conrad's head into the desk when he thought of Nikki's bruises.

"Conrad, it's good to see you!" Erich patted him on the back and went to the coffee stand, "coffee?"

"Nein, I bring great news!" He panted for a moment, caught his breath and took his long coat off, "so hot." He sat down and fanned himself.

Erich set the coffee down for himself, "wasser?"

"Ja, perfekt," he looked at the windows, "on such a nice day, your windows are closed?" He got up, opened them and fanned himself. "So, I have tickets, believe it or not!"

"Ja, I know and am very excited to go, danke!" He brought him a glass of wasser and they looked at each other. "You are a good freund."

"More so, we... have tickets to the opening ceremony!" Conrad grabbed Erich's shoulders and shook him, "Can you believe it!"

"No, I... how did you manage?" Erich smiled as best he could and then felt the surge of sadness and fury when he saw images of Stephan, "well?"

Conrad took out the tickets and showed him, "Himmler!" He held them up over his head, "the greatest event in Germany and we have seats!"

"Wow, this is wonderful!" Erich clapped and shook his head, "So, you will be over me then as he gave the tickets to you I see."

Conrad lowered the tickets and smiled, "Nein, I was at a meeting over the matter of the Olympics. Himmler was there to discuss some future operations of the SS and the SD." He tapped the tickets on his palm.

"Always a meeting and I never see my invitation." Erich got his coffee.

"He asked if I was going. Of course, I mentioned that you were going with me." Conrad looked barely disheartened. "He said, I've something for Jan."

Erich felt he knew what was going to come next.

"He handed me the tickets and said to give them to you." He lowered his hand to Erich.

"But you have tickets you said." Erich meant to hurt his feelings.

"I do, but they are not mine." He looked down for a single moment.

Erich set his coffee on his desk, walked over and looked at Conrad who looked hurt by the matter. He wanted to punch him and at that moment his face warmed, "I..." he had to think about the larger picture, the overall goal. "You were not mistaken to say *we* have tickets."

He forced a somewhat genuine smile and thought of politics, egos and his goal. He pushed Conrad's hand away. "Himmler trusted you to bring them to me. I trust you to keep *our* tickets and we shall have a great time."

Conrad was taken by what Erich said and it showed as he smiled warmly. "Jan," he lowered his hand and put the tickets in his pocket. "It has been a long time since I've had a freund. Truly, you honor me with your trust."

They eyed each other for a moment. Erich did not want to touch him again, so he nodded, turned and went to back to his chair. "You honor me to have invited me to begin. I look forward to the events, but do not try to fatten me up if you chose to eat all the food there."

"Ha, there will be food and lots of women!" He sat down and set his glass on the desk. "Himmler did say that we are to treat all people appropriately till the Olympics have passed and the foreigners are gone." He didn't like the restriction of his power to arrest or batter. "And have you read about this African... what do they call him?" He thought on it for a moment.

"I don't know, but I have read that he is fast." Erich sat down and waited for Conrad to jump at the chance to speak about

Aryan superiority.

"Fast, but that is the nature of his people." Conrad shook his head, "They live in the wilderness and must run fast or be eaten by a cheetah!" He laughed.

Erich eyed him for a moment and thought about what Maj. Gerheim said, "He *is* stupid." He laughed to go along and then looked at the work on his desk. "So, as much as I enjoy our time," he held up some papers.

"You sound more and more like an SS Oberführer with your diplomacy." Conrad got up, got his long coat and tapped his pocket, "to the Olympics!"

"Be sure to practice that you say sir, so it will be easier when I am Oberführer." Erich laughed and shook his head.

"Ha, you wish for that day." Conrad went to the door, stopped and turned back to him. "I don't see that the car would be practical, but the train to go."

"Ja, that's for the best." He nodded as Conrad left.

Zelma came in with a stack of files, "He is a rude man." She set the files down and waited.

"I apologize and, yes, he is rude." Erich got the files and set them close by him.

Conrad went to his office where the guards who'd hung up Stephan waited, "ah, my loyal men."

The larger of the two, Johann, said "loyal and hungry."

"We go to dinner and then to Sachsenhausen for a visit with my favorite queer." He got some notes from his desk, turned and waved at them to go. They all left and went down the hall, down the stairs and into the main hall.

Maj. Gerheim came in and looked at Erich, but he didn't leave the space near the door. "Those files, you'll have time to clear them up?"

"Absolutely," Erich stood.

He smiled and it was a sullen smile, because he would miss Erich. He looked for the secretaries, but they'd gone to dinner, "You do such a good job, Er... Jan. I will miss you."

"You... could come," Erich didn't finish the sentence before

Maj. Gerheim interrupted.

"No, Jan, don't ever say it again." He turned and stopped, then looked back, "its dinner time, come on."

Erich looked at the work on his desk and the calendar. The Olympics are on August first, three days away from today. He got his jacket and they went to dinner.

That night in the flat, he put together his plans and sought to close some matters that troubled him. He would not add to anything going on. As much as he wanted to avenge Stephan's murder, he knew that it meant going after Conrad and Conrad would be missed. Maj. Gerheim made it clear that he wanted no part in going with them, so that matter was put to rest too. The order was not done and Maj. Gerheim, during dinner, assured him that he would call Col. Lippert on a "social matter" and then say that Capt. Brueder would be by to pick up and interrogate VanEch on Friday. Lastly, Erich had to verify their transportation and border crossing. To get to Gramzow was no problem and very few people knew about the home of Jan Brueder. The border crossing was his biggest concern. Though there were many foreigners in Germany and many who crossed the border, it was still no small task to go to the crossing, show papers and get to the Polish guards who then checked the papers again and, finally, get into Poland. He knew that the Polish were not friendly with the Germans and the papers he had were for two Danes.

Their voyage was a ship from Copenhagen, Denmark on the second of August to Nova Scotia. It was a tight schedule, but possible. He knew that there was never a case of nothing happening and they had a period of hours to work with. Szczecin, Poland was just west and north of the border crossing and easy enough to get to which would put them at the dock on August first. The ship from Szczecin left the evening of the first and so he thought to get Nikki on Friday, July thirty-first. They would go to Gramzow, clean up, have some time for Nikki to rest and then leave early in the morning on Saturday, August first. Erich had money from the pay as Capt. Brueder and though he did not want to use it, he had to; he would return the money to some charity or something to ease his conscious for using Jan that way. Then, there was Felix.

Felix sat on the end of the couch and licked himself. Erich shook his head at this silly animal and thought that there was no way he could leave Stephan's cat on the straße in Berlin. "Cats," He got up, poured some wine and sat down again. He ran the matter of escape over and over in his head, paused at certain moments to see if there was a problem and then went on to the next part of his plan. "Things packed and into the car, to Sachsenhausen, to Gramzow, to... shieße!" He sat back and drew his hands over and down his face, "Nikki, Nikki." He thought about when he got Nikki, "will he know to keep his mouth shut?" He was overwhelmed for a moment and the thought that Nikki would be terrified of an SS taking him somewhere or for him to realize that it was Erich and then yell with happiness and relief? The entire plan would be done for. He shook his head, "Nikki." He got up and looked at the straße below. There were flags and banners all over. "I've got to have some supper." He stood, changed into civilian clothes, got his identification and went out.

Thursday, thirtieth of July - 1936, Erich got to work, greeted Zelma and went to his files. He didn't see Maj. Gerheim for most of the day and knew that Conrad expected him the morning of the first, Saturday, to go to the stadium. Erich's plan was to get the ticket from him and tell him that he will meet him there.

Maj. Gerheim agreed to cover for him on Friday in the event anyone looked for him. It seemed nearly fool proof, but Erich knew that after the fire at the Reichstag and the elimination of the political parties by Hitler, nothing was foolproof. He had a backup plan and another way out.

As for Nikki, he believed that a stern look or a mean one would keep Nikki from acting as if they knew each other, at least he hoped for it. Perhaps, better to avoid a look at all he thought.

Erich got back from dinner, sat at his desk and got a large number of files stacked up.

"Jan," Maj. Gerheim walked in and had the orders. He walked up and looked the desk over, "You've done quite a bit."

Erich stood, "By tomorrow sir, I'll have it all done and caught up."

Maj. Gerheim smiled, "good work." He handed him the order, "Col. Lippert enjoys your company. Remember what I said about senior officers."

"Yes, sir," it took Erich a moment, "listen to them and be sure that they feel they are heard."

Maj. Gerheim winked, "good." He looked the office over, turned and went to the door. "I may move in here." He said, "It's got a cozy feel, not so big." He left and closed the door.

"It does." Erich said. He looked the order over to ensure its accuracy, "NICHOLAS VANECH," "Purpose of transfer: INVESTIGATORY." It was signed and dated with Gerheim's stamp. "The plan is in the works." A burst of happiness overcame him.

At Sachsenhausen, Capt. Ehrlichmann stood over Nikki whose eye and the side of his face were bruised. His hands were cuffed to a wood post in the center of the table. "Patz is dead, Nicholas." He smacked his forehead, "What's left of him hangs from a tree in those woods!" He pointed to the window. "And you will be next if you don't tell me where Erich Schmidt is!"

Nikki's tears could barely get through his one eye, because of the swelling. "I..." he choked and some bits of blood came from his lips; they were terribly chap. "He's in Canada."

"He is a spy!" Capt. Ehrlichmann put on the gloves that he used to beat Stephan. He looked at the little squares of metal over the knuckles. "These are the same gloves that I used for Patz."

Nikki looked up and saw them, "Please, I have told you every..."

"Have you?" Johann walked over and pulled Nikki's head back!

"AH!"

"Stephan was his friend." Nikki gasped for air as Johann stretched his neck!

"Ja, but Stephan is dead." Ehrlichmann drew his hand back. "Now, it's your turn."

Nikki was in agony with his head stretched back and his hands cuffed to the table, "Ah!"

"One chance Nicholas," Ehrlichmann hovered over him. "Patz made false papers for you. Did he make papers for Erich!"

"Stephan got us papers to go to Canada." Nikki choked on his words and felt horrible to have said that about Stephan.

Johann looked at Ehrlichmann who nodded and Johann let Nikki go. Ehrlichmann lowered his fist. "Have you planned something for the Olympics, an attack or to spy?" He smacked Nikki, "Is there a plan to do something at the Olympics!"

Nikki coughed and spat. "Nein, I know of no plan!"

Ehrlichmann sighed and knelt next to Nikki who looked at him from under his outstretched arms, "Stephan could have made papers for Erich, ja?" He slapped Nikki, "papers for Erich to come to Germany?" Drool hung from Nikki's mouth and blood mixed with it to form a string that dangled from his mouth, "Nicholas."

He did not want to get hit again. "It's possible."

"Would he come for you?"

Nikki spat, "I..."

"Would he come?" Ehrlichmann balled his fist and thought to hit Nikki's jaw from between Nikki's arms, "hmm?"

"If he thought he could do it." Nikki closed his eyes, "perhaps."

"He comes for you or to spy?" Ehrlichmann smiled and moved his head slowly from left to right a couple of times as if to say, I'm waiting.

Nikki didn't know what to say and felt better to say nothing.

Ehrlichmann smacked his head, "I know he worked at the Reichstag and that you and he fled before the fire." He smacked Nikki again, "Erich could do it; with Patz help, he could get to Germany just as you did."

Nikki felt the tears, "I don't know." He coughed, "maybe."

Ehrlichmann stood, nodded at his men who followed him

into the hall.

Johann looked at Ehrlichmann. "So, it is likely that he's here, but he's not got to VanEch yet."

"Patz made documents for him, detailed documents, sent coded communications and for them to say so little after interrogations." Ehrlichmann thought for a moment, "I want a check of all work that Patz did and get the names so we can do their histories." He thought hard, "a spy is here."

"What about him," Johann dipped his head at Nikki.

Ehrlichmann thought for a moment as he pulled off the gloves, "let him go to the infirmary." Two guards came in, unhooked Nikki from the post and dragged him out and down the hall to the infirmary. "He is to be kept alive."

They got to their car and it was nearly three that afternoon. Ehrlichmann looked at his men, "take the day. I'm going back to the office."

CHAPTER 18: EHRLICHMANN, PART II - DISCOVERY & DESTINY

Ehrlichmann took the car back to SS HQ and went right to his office. It was just after four on Thursday and he thought to visit with Jan, but there was a lot of work to do before Saturday. Just then, Helga, from the records office, stopped by and knocked on his door.

"Helga, what's this?" He sat back and tossed his Mont Blanc pen onto the desk.

"Your inquiries will take some time to run." She had only one paper, "but I thought you might like to know that there was an inquiry for VanEch."

He sat up and his happy expression faded. "Oh?"

She nodded.

"And who made the inquiry?"

"Capt. Brueder," she fidgeted nervously.

A sudden warmth came over him, "Jan Brueder?"

"Ja, he asked about VanEch, to search for him." She said.

Capt. Ehrlichmann stood up and got his holster from his drawer. "What did you tell him?"

"Just that he was at Dachau, then transferred, on your orders, to Sachsenhausen." She brought her hands together and felt like she couldn't move.

"Was he surprised?" He got the belt around him and tightened it so that his Mauser was against his hip.

"Nein... he asked about Patz too."

Ehrlichmann's eyes widened, "I see." He bent at the waist and put his hands on his desk. "Does he know you've told me?"

"Nein..." She hesitated, "but I told Maj. Gerheim."

"Why?" He adjusted his gun belt.

"It's his superior officer and in our protocol to notify superior officers of inquiries." She looked like she might cry and her hands trembled.

Ehrlichmann saw her hands and took a moment to focus, "You've done a good job Helga, danke."

"May I go?" She couldn't move.

"Of course, my dear," he got the phone and looked at her. "Go," he said.

She turned and nearly fell over her own feet as she hurried out of his office.

"Operator, give me 3665." He waited.

It was just before five and Erich set some files aside when Conrad walked in, long coat on and it covered his gun. "Jan," he walked up to the chairs in front of Erich's desk.

"Conrad, I didn't expect to see you."

He looked at the windows that were open, "no, it's late. But, do you recall that you agreed to go with me some night to... what was you said, to see the real animals."

Erich grinned and set the last file to his side, "Ja, but tonight I've got..."

Ehrlichmann spoke strongly, "Nein, nein, nein!" and moved the chairs apart; "We will go out tonight and assist with some last-minute arrests." He eyed Erich who got his coffee and sipped it. "We need everyone this evening." He smiled, "and I need my freund."

"Very well, I did say I would go." Erich thought on the matter quickly and knew that something was amiss.

"Danke, I knew I could count on you." Conrad smiled in a

somewhat genuine way, but didn't like what he thought about Jan. "I'll see you at the car around neun."

"That will be good." He thought about Felix and would have to leave to feed him.

Erich got home, fed Felix, had supper and thought about leaving tonight. But, that would be the worst as Conrad would be alarmed and, if Conrad knew anything, it would confirm his suspicions. Erich would have to go along and make the best of it.

He dressed in SS fatigues for such a duty and left his apartment.

There were two trucks and a car on Prinz-Albrecht Straße with several SS guards armed with machine guns. Conrad came down the steps. "Ah!" he looked at Erich, "Jan!" He waved him over to the car and got in.

"Hello Conrad," Erich got in.

"You've dressed well for this evening."

"Danke," Erich got comfortable while Conrad spoke with the driver.

"We're going to a part of Berlin where… some of the people are to be picked up."

"Good, I look forward to it." Erich pulled at his jacket.

"Ja, with the Olympics just in a day, there's outsiders who have come into the country to do bad things." Conrad said as the driver headed south.

"Then we must stop them." Erich eyed Conrad.

"We must." Conrad opened a case and took out a Mauser Luger. "Here, this is for you." The Mauser was new and not loaded. He got two clips, a belt and the holster. "I didn't have time to put it together." He handed it to Erich.

Erich smiled, "I'm fine with it." He got it and loaded the bullets into the clips, put the clip in the Luger, charged it and then withdrew the clip.

"You've got to leave the clip in my freund to shoot more than once." Conrad laughed.

"I've charged one round, so there is one round less in the clip. The safest way to get the first round into the chamber,

Conrad, is this method." He pushed another bullet into the clip and slapped it into the Luger.

"Good," Conrad felt put off by that and looked out the window.

Erich smiled and thought to say, shut up you idiot. He got the Luger holstered and sat the belt and gun on the seat. "I'll put it on when we stop."

"That will be fine." Ehrlichmann thought on the matter of Jan and why he sought VanEch.

"Ah, there's another matter to discuss."

He looked at Erich, "ja?"

"I'll need my ticket for the opening ceremonies. Maj. Gerheim asked me to handle some matters that morning." He smiled and looked stern.

Conrad grinned, "Of course, as it happens I have the tickets with me." He took them out, separated them and gave one to Erich. "We will have a great time."

"We will." He tucked the ticket into his jacket pocket.

"Be sure not to lose it as I would hate to miss you." He put his ticket away.

"You won't miss me." Erich saw that Conrad had his hand just over his holster.

Conrad smiled, "We're only minutes away." It was nearly eleven and Erich's anxiety began to rise while he wondered what Conrad might do to him.

"So, who are we going to pick up?"

As the driver slowed, it was obvious that people saw them and fled into their homes whereas other people fled into the shadows and darkness of ally's and down the straße away from them. "Roma's, Jew's and queers," Conrad did not look at Erich.

Erich let it lie and knew that this was normal for the SD to be out for arrests.

The driver slowed and then stopped the car against the curb. The trucks pulled up behind them and the men got out. "Jan," Conrad opened his door.

Erich got out and got his gun belt around his waist. He

thought about Felix for a moment, damned cat wandering the flat and looking for him. Then, he thought about Nikki at Sachsenhausen and how horribly alone he must feel. He stood, took in a deep breath and thought, "you will not beat us." He turned and looked at the trucks, the men and, finally, Conrad who pulled his cap down tight.

"Come on, Jan!"

"Ja, okay, I'm coming. This is my first time!" He got his belt locked and came around to Conrad.

"They made us take down the signs for the Jews." Conrad put on some gloves and pushed the leather down between his fingers. "Signs make no difference, we know where they are." He then pulled a single punch card from his pocket, "You've seen these?" He got his flashlight and held the card so that Erich saw the name, "PATZ, STEPHAN."

Erich looked at it, "I looked at them and got some information about their use."

"Ah, good," Conrad ripped it up and threw it in the air, "Patz, filthy traitor."

Erich was, he would tell Dr. Scherbit, surprised and the matter caught him off his guard that he brought the card. He felt rage purse through his veins, his face warmed and he thought to shoot Conrad there and then. He and Conrad looked at each other as each thought about what might happen next.

"You are alright?" Conrad asked.

"Ja, of course though I believe records won't be happy." Erich shook his head, "You are, sometimes, strange to me Conrad."

"Foreign, perhaps," Conrad watched as his men stormed several buildings and began to bring people out, families dressed for bed and some children.

"We're here to work." Erich walked to the sidewalk.

"We are," Conrad said, "Put them there!" He pointed at some small fence or gate that was at the opening to an apartment building. His men were rough and careless as they shoved men and women along.

An older woman, a großmutter, shouted at them, "This is

wrong to do this to us!" The guard smacked her and she fell. Her daughter grabbed her and quickly got her to the fence, "mama, bitte."

Conrad turned to Erich, "Jan, do you hear her? This is wrong."

"She doesn't know the laws." Erich clasped his hands behind him and walked down the line of people.

"How many?" Conrad asked a guard, "Sgt. Richter, how many?"

"Dreiundzwanzig!" Sgt. Richter shouted.

There were two young men near the end of that line up and Erich was closer to them. They looked at the guards and Erich muttered under his breath, "Don't, bitte." He turned and looked at Conrad who was busy with the sergeant.

"I had fünfundzwanzig. Why are we short two?" Conrad looked around and saw the two young men push back just a few inches from the fence, "perfekt."

Sgt. Richter, "Was, Captain?" He looked too and squinted to make out the people lined up.

"Jan!" Conrad yelled.

"Ja," Erich didn't turn to look at Conrad and told himself already that he would not murder them.

The young men saw Erich turn away from them, pushed up from the fence and ran!

"JAN!" Conrad pointed at them as they ran towards the side straße a hundred feet away!

Erich turned, unsnapped his holster and drew! He aimed at the back of the boy that was in the lead, centered on him, then dropped his aim by a couple of millimeters and, "BANG!" The boy dropped and screamed wildly! He squirmed on the ground in agony as his mutter got up, but the guard jerked his charging handle back and then aimed at her, "NEIN!"

Conrad shouted at Sgt. Richter, "No one moves!" He ran to Erich.

The other boy skidded to a stop and turned back to see his brother's face contorted in pain! He looked up and two guards had their machine guns pointed at him; they were just to the side of Erich.

"Nein!" Erich shouted and then aimed at the boy's chest; the shot would have killed him in a few seconds. Erich muttered, "I'm sorry," and dipped his barrel, "BANG!" The boy dropped to the ground and held the side of his upper leg. "Sheiße," Erich lowered his Luger. "Ah, I was never very good."

The guards looked at him and shook their heads.

Conrad got to him and looked him over, "You just shoot him after you wait?"

Erich, now, felt he had some credibility as Brueder... as an SS. He turned and looked at Conrad, "The terror comes from the unknown. Will I kill or will I let live. Those few moments put the fear of the SS into him for his life." He holstered his pistol and smiled, "but my aim has never been the best."

Conrad holstered his gun, "Uberprüfen sie!" The men got clipboards from Sgt. Richter and checked each person. He eyed Erich, "Why did you ask about VanEch and Patz at records?"

Erich shook his head and then sighed, "So, that's what you are bothered about." He laughed and then laughed harder for a moment longer, "Conrad, you... you are the one to have pressed the point that you were investigating VanEch and I was there when you arrested Patz... as you said to me, we'll have future time together!" He shook his head, "Is that why you were so serious about this night?" He laughed again and looked at the two young men, "get them!" He said to the guards. Conrad who was stuck in thought now. "I looked them up as a matter of consequence to our past conversation."

Conrad exhaled hard, "Damn," he turned away. "I..."

"Ja, ja, you *are* sorry." Erich wrapped his arm around Conrad, "now, you do owe me dinner *and* supper." He took his arm from Conrad, "of my choice!" He walked up to the people on the line.

"Captain," Sgt. Richter said.

"Brueder!"

"Sorry sirs, there are only zwölf who came from the list." He looked at Ehrlichmann and waited.

"Capt. Ehrlichmann, this is your raid. We have only zwölf of the names on the list here and it's midnight." Erich smiled, "If there is nothing more, we should get breakfast… after we finish our arrest."

Ehrlichmann was still stuck in thought about whether he actually said anything to Jan about VanEch. He was with him when he arrested Patz. "Ja, fine… get them in the trucks and get those stupid boys injuries seen." Then, he realized that he had told him about VanEch.

Sgt. Richter yelled, "Gehen wir!" The guards got the zwölf people and loaded them onto one truck. The two boys were loaded into the other truck and both trucks left while Erich, Conrad and their driver waited. The rest of the people were released and went back to their homes.

Conrad and Erich walked to the car. He looked at Erich, then shook his head. "I feel…"

"Don't, it's done." Erich was wet with sweat.

They got in the car and Erich looked at the papers, "We should go out tomorrow night, but…"

Conrad spoke up, "Nein, with the next day at the opening, nein."

Erich was satisfied that the matter was over, though he felt the sickness in his stomach building again. In fact, it grew more than it had when they were on their way to that neighborhood. He took his gun belt off and sat it on the seat.

"That's yours to keep." Conrad said, "I was surprised you didn't have a weapon issued."

"Didn't occur to me as I sit at a desk," Erich grinned.

"I'm anxious to go to the opening and let work get off my mind." He looked at smiled. "There is so much expected from me."

"I believe there is too much." They were back at SS HQ after a short drive.

Erich, finally, got home at two in the morning and was exhausted. Felix was asleep on the couch and jumped when Erich dropped the gun belt with the gun on the couch next to him. "The part with Ehrlichmann is over." He told Felix who shook his head hard and then meowed. "Ja, I'm happy too." He was so tired that he didn't set an alarm and looked at the light in the kitchen. He was too tired to turn it off and stared at it for a moment, then fell asleep.

"Erich?" Dr. Scherbit touched his shoulder, "Erich."

"Ja," Erich slowly sat up and wiped the drool from his mouth. "Yes," he said.

"You are alright and we are at our time." Dr. Scherbit had his jacket on, his leather flap case and his pipe in hand.

"Just go, I wait here till next time." Erich got to his feet. "I don't understand how I can get so where I am asleep."

"You're not; it's a drifting moment for you in time... in the past." Dr. Scherbit went to the door and waited.

Erich went to move the chaise and nearly fell over it.

"Leave it, it's fine."

Erich got his composure and his jacket, then walked out. They went to the street and Erich looked up, "but the light is on."

"Go home and rest," they parted and Erich was home in no time.

He and Nikki had supper. Usually, they spent time together afterwards, but Erich was so out of it, he went to bed.

CHAPTER 19: SCHEISSE HOUSE, PART I — FELIX, NIKKI & EHRLICHMANN

Summer, 1954, Erich finished his work at the bank, went to the sidewalk and debated a moment whether to take a cab or walk. He had his briefcase and thought, better to walk. He figured to use the time to go over the final events of that return to Berlin in 1936. Some images, even now, still upset him and he thought for just a second that he saw Ehrlichmann at the light waiting to cross the street. His heart filled with anxiety, but then he looked again and it was, obviously, not him.

He went down the sidewalk and put his mind on the buildings and people as a distraction. Is it ever over? He asked himself and wondered if Dr. Scherbit's first words of advice were true, "You must forgive." Most of the real pain was that he blamed himself entirely for what happened to Nikki and Stephan, so he must forgive himself.

Thoughts overwhelmed him; he turned and ducked into an alley where he had an anxiety attack. The air pushed and pulled out of his lungs like a bellows for a monstrous fire! His chest and his heart beat so hard that it showed through his shirt as some large tumor that grew and crushed his lungs! "AH!" He shouted, but no one heard him over the cars, over the shoes that beat the concrete, over the voices of people who cried out in horror, "STOP!" He collapsed and crumpled up into what Nikki described as the cradle with his knees pulled up to his chin and his hands over his head.

He knew how many times, over the years, that Nikki was in the cradle and hid between two boxes in the closet. He balled uncontrollably and his briefcase fell over onto its side, "warum?" He felt the horror build up in his stomach and it was far worse than when you've eaten bad food and its trapped in your intestines, in your gut with no way up and a slow way down, "why?" He whispered and dropped his hands to his stomach and hugged himself tightly. "Why wasn't I punished?" What Nikki and Dr. Scherbit knew was that Erich was in the SA and quit them before he took the job at the Reichstag Office.

Erich did not bring himself to tell either of them that before he met Nikki, he destroyed property of other political opponents, beat members of rival political parties and, worse, he was in a bar brawl that led to the death of two men from the German communist party. He pressed down on his head to push out the thoughts, but no amount of physical force would force them out of his head. It didn't matter that other men, Von Helldorf or Röhm, had murdered many other people. It was March of 1931 when he himself was beaten badly and crawled away with his life; it was his call, he felt, to change or become a horrible man or be killed in the melees between the SA and the rival political factions.

By the end of April 1931, he found work at the Reichstag office as a political liaison where he met and befriended Stephan Patz. He was fortunate that, with his background and after the Prussian government crackdown on the SA, they let him have a job. From May of 1931, he kept to himself and worked at being a peaceful man. It was a stroll through the park where he met Nikki and fell in love; love drove his peacefulness.

The anxiety seemed to lessen and his pounding tumor wasn't so obvious, but he was caught up in the "why it wasn't him that was punished." He got some control of his emotions and wiped his tears away. If it had been him and not Nikki, then Nikki would have been safe, he wouldn't have been brutalized and Stephan would be alive.

He couldn't come to terms with the self-blame, because he didn't protect the man that he loved so much. He shook off the tears now and looked at his briefcase in the puddle, "sheiße." He reached over and picked it up; water dripped from the front of it and the sides, "damn this filth." The case was, frankly, fine and the contents, a contract and some other papers, were fine too. He pushed himself up and looked at his watch. He was ten minutes late to Dr. Scherbit, so he took a deep breath, got up and dusted himself off. His backside was filthy from the wall he was up against and his trousers were wet at the bottom of the legs. He pushed his bangs back and laughed as he had begged Nikki to cut them, but Nikki thought that he was cute. "I am not cute," he looked at the street ahead. He walked out, turned and went to Dr. Scherbit's office.

"Hello," Dr. Scherbit closed the door as Erich made his way to the chaise. The woman had moved it for him. "You're quite dirty, have you been robbed again?"

"Hello, doctor." He took his jacket off, but kept it with him. "No, this is an... the moment of the end has caused me to have an attack."

Dr. Scherbit shook his head and went to his desk. "Are you alright now?" He sat down.

"Ja, I'm alright." He took a breath in, held it and then let it out.

"Erich, before we begin, I... I must ask you something." Dr. Scherbit seemed to fidget.

"Of course," Erich turned and looked at him.

"Not to add to your anxiety, but you shot those two boys," He said.

"Yes, but I did not kill them." Erich brushed his shirt out.

"You *chose* not to kill them?" Dr. Scherbit steadied his pipe in his mouth.

"Doctor, I am not a murderer. I trained as a sharpshooter

when I was SA." He smiled, "no, my conscious could not bear such a thing." An image of Stephan flashed in his mind, hung from the tree.

"I wondered," he then got his notepad and pencil. "Did you ever hear if they survived?"

"No, I did not, but the shots were to non-vital places, the upper leg and the buttocks." He nodded.

"Oh, okay," he chuckled for a moment, "when you are ready."

Erich looked at the curtains, but they were closed along with the window. "So, this is it then."

"Oh, we are at the end of this story?" He asked.

"We'll have to see what I see… and say."

"And you're feeling better now, perhaps a little?" Dr. Scherbit got comfortable.

"Yes, besides my attack earlier, we are feeling much better, though I believe Nikki will still need to… work some things out." He turned to sit down on the chaise.

"Good," Dr. Scherbit sat back and listened. "One moment please!" He got a blanket from the closet and put it on the chaise. "I've paid one cleaning bill."

Erich smiled, "bill me." He put the blanket over the chaise and then laid down. The lamps glow was rich and warm as it saturated his eyes. He was back in Berlin, Friday, July thirty-first, 1936. It was the day before the Olympics and the opening ceremonies.

He rubbed the sleep from his eyes and looked at his watch, "NO!" It was ten that morning. He jumped up, got showered and got his things together. He was so concerned about being precise, but if they found anything, what would it matter, he'd be gone. He had a carrier for Felix and it was a nightmare to get him in the cage, but Erich shoved him in there and shut the door. His hand was scratched up and bled along the claw lines, "filthy damn cat." He licked the blood off, got his long coat and set his things at the door. The gun was on the couch and he was tempted to leave it, but walked over and picked it up.

He stopped at the door, closed his eyes and focused. "I am

ready." He had a car and loaded his things into it while Felix meowed and meowed, "quiet!" He shook his head, "Stephan, this cat of yours," then he calmed himself. "It's alright kitty." He checked that he had everything and then got in. The drive to Prinz-Albrecht was easy and Felix would have to stay in the car so he put the window down for him.

He checked in with Maj. Gerheim who figured that he'd slept in with all that was about to happen. Erich would wait till later in the day when the staff was gone to leave for Sachsenhausen.

"You've finished with those as well?" Zelma asked and took the files, "You are in a rush to leave for the weekend."

"Ah, not really," he smiled at her as she passed his doorway and went to her desk. It was just after four now and the drive to Sachsenhausen would take forty to fifty minutes. In another thirty minutes or so, the staff would leave; he knew that some senior officers had left, but Maj. Gerheim was still here.

Erich got up and made a pass of the halls to check for who remained. Most of the staff was gone now and there were many closed doors. He sighed some when he saw that Conrad's main office doors were closed and there was just a light in the back of the office, mostly likely left for the weekend. He wandered the hall and his boot heels made a precise hit when he walked to the stairs. He got to the main hall and admired just how nice it was and must've been before the SS took over. There were two guards that were on duty no matter the hour and he spoke with them briefly. Then, he returned upstairs and went to his office.

He looked out the windows and admired the view, but to stay and admire that view, he'd have to have a reason to be here, in that office, and that reason was worthless to him. He pulled the windows closed, took his time to walk around the office and set his files neatly at the corner of his desk so that Zelma would have them. He made sure that they were done for Gerheim's sake too.

"Jan?" Erich nearly jumped when he heard that name and turned so quickly, that his bangs slid across his face.

Maj. Gerheim stood there and laughed to himself, "Didn't

mean to surprise you." He had his coffee and held it up to Erich. "Thought that I would not see you again… so, viel gluck."

"And you sir," they nodded at each other and Major Gerheim went back to his office. Erich thought to take the files to him, but it was Friday and there was no need to do it. He got his long coat, his flat leather brief and his hat. He looked the desk over once more, the chair once more and the office once more to be sure that it all was in order. Everything was precisely put back. The desk was clear, the chair was pushed just near the desk and the lights were off. He walked to the door, pulled it shut and left for the stairs. There was some tension in the air as his heels tapped the floor. Would someone say, "hello" or "you're still here?" He got to the second floor and then the first floor to where one of the guards remained while the other walked the halls.

"Guten abend, Captain."

"Und sie," Erich said, smiled politely and then left for his car.

Felix meowed so loudly and heavy that his voice carried far from the car. Erich got to the straße and shook his head, "damn cat." The walk to the car was short and he threw his things in the back seat, then took a snack of fish from his brief for Felix. "Here, for my crime to leave you in the car."

Felix sniffed it and then went to the back of his cage, sat down and did nothing.

"Ah, so you're in defiance." He pulled away and then stopped. He shook his head, got his brief from the back seat and looked through it. "Ah," he pulled the "ORDER FOR RELASE OF CUSTODY/TRANSFER" from his brief and looked it over one more time. "I'm coming, Nikki."

The drive from Prinz-Albrecht gave him time to go over his plan again. There had to be time to think on the matter, to think again and be firm in who he was, SS Captain Jan Brueder. It was a very quiet drive north. He wondered if it would be as quiet when he got to the border to cross with Nikki. Stephan made the papers to use for that time, but with his arrest and murder, Erich didn't know if Ehrlichmann knew enough to look deeper and notify the border guards; all of it was a chance to take.

It was just past six when he pulled down the road that led to Sachsenhausen and some anxiety rose in him quite like acid from your stomach rises up your throat; he swallowed hard to push it down and to keep his wits with him. There were no mistakes to be made now. He thought to put Felix in the trunk, but how loud would that damned cat meow then! He pulled off the road, just a mile from the camp, stopped and took Felix out. It was warm and he'd be fine, "You must wait here for me." Then, he looked at the lock and thought about Stephan who was killed not far from here. He looked at Felix who looked at him and the two seemed to be locked in thought about what might come next.

Felix got up, licked the fish and then ate.

Erich nodded, lifted the cage out and set it just a few feet into the brush. He looked around to make sure he knew where he left him, "Be good, Felix." Felix ignored him and chewed the fish as Erich stood, got back to the car and left.

He pulled up to the camp parking lot and there was one staff car, but Col. Lippert's staff car was gone, "Olympics." He parked, got out and went to the trunk, "protocols." He opened the trunk, got his gun and put it on. Then, he checked his uniform in the reflection of the window; he looked himself over and got his long coat on; it was warm, but he wanted it on to cover his gun. He put his cap squarely on his head, reached into the car, got his brief with the order and stood. The moment was here and he sighed, then took a deep breath and held it for a moment as he studied his reflection on the window.

He shut the door and went to the administration office. When he entered, there was one guard there with a machine gun. He nodded at Erich and stood at attention. Erich dipped his head and walked into the building, to the back offices where the officer in charge was stationed.

Several guards and Lt. Klein sat by a radio and listened to Walter Jurmann; it was a much older song, but fun, "Veronkia, der lenz ist da." The men enjoyed the music and sung in broken words as they listened. Lt. Klein was at ease and they had no idea that Erich stood there.

Erich smiled and closed his eyes for a moment. He recalled when he and Nikki danced at a club in Berlin and felt something he hadn't felt in, quite frankly, a couple of years; he felt good. The song slowly came to a close and then there was silence. The silence lasted longer than he thought it should, so he opened his eyes and the men looked at him.

"Achtung!" Lt. Klein said. The men jumped to attention and a couple of them quickly got their jackets buttoned. They were very surprised by Capt. Brueder.

"Capt. Brueder," Lt. Klein said, "What is it I can do for you?"

Erich was taken aback by them, "Easy, easy men. I'm SS, but not without culture." He nodded at them as they all sat back down, "Walter Jurmann?"

A guard at the back of the table spoke up, "Ja, Veronika, der lenz is da."

His buddy pushed him, "Tobin!"

"Sehr gut, danke," Erich nodded at Lt. Klein to go with him outside. They went out the door and stood.

"Captain?"

Erich took the order from his brief and gave it to Lt. Klein. "Where is he?"

Lt. Klein was younger and new, but not foolish. He looked the order over completely, the dates, the signatures, the name of who was to be released and why.

Erich was concerned that Col. Lippert wasn't here, because it was Lippert who knew about the order, not Klein.

"I must call." Lt. Klein said.

"And hasn't Col. Lippert already alerted you to this order?" Erich sighed.

Lt. Klein thought for a moment, then shook his head, "I'm sorry, ja. He has told me." He looked at the office, "Tobin! Körbl!" There was no mistake about the noises the men made as they got their guns and gear!

Erich knew that it was necessary and if he sought to go without guards, there would be too many questions.

"And you don't have guards?"

"Nein, he is to be handcuffed and secured to the seat." Erich said sternly.

"Captain," Lt. Klein kept the order as the men came out. He told them to go with Capt. Brueder and get, "Nicholas VanEch." He got a roster from the wall where two clipboards were hung and looked the papers over. "Er ist 0034, house-zweiundzwanzig." He put the roster back on the wall and nodded at Capt. Brueder, "If there's nothing else, they will go with you."

Erich nodded at Lt. Klein and waited for the guards.

The men took the lead and walked with Erich behind them. There were a couple of Kapo's that saw them and turned away. At this hour, they steered clear of anyone that wasn't a prisoner. Erich thought as they made the short walk to the second barracks and figured that it was better to make a scene; if they made it traumatic, though he hated to do any more to Nikki, it would make it harder for him or any of them to figure out what was going on.

"Be sure to rouse them." Erich felt for his gun under his long coat.

"Sir," Tobin brought his machine gun around.

As they got near the barracks, there were some prisoners who stood by the door and smoked. The moment they saw the guards, a couple went inside and the others stood close, up against the building.

"ACHTUNG!" "ACHTUNG!" Tobin yelled and jerked the door open! Things bumped, fell or hit the floor as Tobin held the door for Capt. Brueder. Körbl stood to the side and waited.

Erich looked at the dimly lit barracks. There were bunks three levels high, a furnace in the center of the room -down from them and several men all at the ends of the bunks. "Nicholas VanEch!" Tobin yelled.

The Kapo, Richter, pushed Nikki out and he had his hands at his side. They were some twenty feet away and the light wasn't enough for Erich to make out Nikki's face, but his height looked right. "VANECH!" Tobin yelled again, "zero, zero, drei, vier!"

"Ja, er ist heir!" Richter yelled and then grabbed Nikki by the collar; he forced him along the wall, between the end of the beds and men, to Capt. Brueder. The guards stood behind Erich. "Heir ist VanEch!" Richter shook Nikki.

Erich's eyes adjusted to the limited light and he looked at Nikki. "VanEch, Nicholas?" He pulled his cap down just a little.

Richter smacked Nikki on the back of the head and Nikki through his hands up, then dropped to the floor and yelled! "BITTE! BITTE!" He curled up into the cradle, his hands over his head to protect himself.

Erich moved his long coat to the side and lowered his hand just over his Luger; his emotions got the better of him. He felt no compunction about shooting Richter, "HALT!" He yelled and stepped up to Nikki, then took a deep breath and got his emotions back, "halt."

Nikki was silent now and Richter made eyes at the Captain, then glanced down at Nikki.

"What are you looking at?"

Richter jumped to attention, "Nothing, Captain!"

Erich stepped up to Nikki, took him by the collar and moved him to the side with one hand. He left his hand just over his Luger and slowly stepped up to Richter. The guards watched and were hopeful that Capt. Brueder might do something. Tobin nudged Körbl who shook his head at him to stop.

Erich stood, literally, in Richter's face and stared at his eyes. Richter looked down and dared not to move his gaze to challenge Erich. Erich exhaled on Richter and looked him over, "are you an SS?"

"Sir?" Richter asked.

"Are you with the SS?"

"Nein, Captain," Richter made a look of curiosity and awkwardness as it was obvious that he was not an SS.

"You're not." Erich turned and looked at Nikki, "but you strike my prisoner as if you were an SS officer."

"I apologize, sir!" He trembled.

Erich thought on the matter and wanted to beat him, but

it was then a sense of coolness came over him and he saw a bit of white smoke or mist float in through the window. The mist seemed to hang just to the side of Richter and Erich got his senses back, turned away from Richter and nodded at Tobin and Körbl to get Nikki. He walked past them and they grabbed Nikki.

"BITTE!" "BITTE!" Nikki screamed and they drug him along the floor to the door, then out onto the dirt. "BITTE!" He held up his hands and kept his head down.

"Quiet!" Erich shouted and Nikki didn't say anything else. He glanced at the mesh window screen that separated him from Richter and saw that he looked in Erich's direction. Had this been a different time, he would have grabbed Richter by the throat, dragged him onto the dirt and beat him.

The guards handcuffed Nikki to the front and then walked back to the administration building.

Richter looked at one of his cronies, a short man with a nose like a witch. "That captain has been here before."

"That Nikki went to?" The witch then touched the side of his nose.

Richter saw the gesture and knew to be careful, because if he was mistaken they would kill him. Was it worth it to speak about it? Richter shook his head and turned away from them. The rest of the men went back to their games and cigarettes.

Erich knew to never look back. He stayed ahead of them and glanced at his watch. It was after seven already and he was concerned to get out of there. They got inside and, fortunately, Lt. Klein had the papers to sign for the release.

"Sign," Lt. Klein looked at Nikki.

Nikki was terrified and still bruised from where Capt. Ehrlichmann had beaten him.

Lt. Klein reached over, grabbed Nikki's hand and jerked it over, "SIGN!" The guards held Nikki's body as his hands were cuffed.

Erich fought every emotional fabric he had not to beat them all to death and looked away; this was a way to say to Lt. Klein, do what you have to, but get it done.

Nikki scribbled his name and they let him loose, "He's yours Capt. Brueder."

"Good," Erich said, "keys?" The guard took the keys for the cuffs and gave them to him. He nodded at the guard.

Nikki kept his head down and Erich got him by the arm, "danke, Lieutenant." He looked at Tobin and Körbl, "enjoy the music." They nodded and set their guns down as he walked out.

Lt. Klein, "gute nacht, Captain." He shook his head after Erich passed the hall and was out of sight, "SS" he rolled his eyes and the guards chuckled. "Get back to work!"

Erich did not look back and felt Nikki's arm; he was so thin. He had food and wasser in the car, but could not give him any at the moment. He opened the back door and set Nikki inside. Nikki was in a daze as he got the car started, put it in gear and they were on the road. He got half way from the camp and slammed the brakes! Nikki nearly doubled over into the front seat, "damn!" He looked at the tree line to get his bearings and it was dark enough now that it made nearly impossible to figure out where Felix was left!

"Are you going to kill me?" Nikki asked and lifted his head only a little. "My freund was killed in those woods."

"Nein!" He got out, walked to the back of the car and jerked the door open. He looked at Nikki, "stay still." He shut the door and looked down the road. "Felix," he walked away from the car. "Felix," he walked further away. Then, there was a meow, but it was from ahead of the car. He turned and ran up, "Felix!" Felix cried! He stopped and walked into the brush, "Damn it cat!" He saw the metal reflect and grabbed the cage, then hurried back to the car where he put Felix in the back with Nikki. He thought to un-cuff Nikki now, but what if he went crazy? Better for now to just leave things as they are until they got to Gramzow.

He pulled out and they were gone in seconds, onto the main road and then they headed to Gramzow which was over an hour away. He looked in the rearview mirror and saw Nikki looking at him.

"I did not mean to look at you! I apologize!" He bent his head down, "BITTE!"

"Stop it, Nikki!" He felt sick to hear Nikki like that and see that he was terrified. He took his hat off and shook his bangs out. They were quite long since he had last cut them in June. "Stop, you are safe Nikki." The roadway had some lights, but it was mostly dark in the car.

Nicholas slowly brought his head up and paused. Then, he lifted it a little more and paused.

"Meow," Felix cried out and had enough of this mess! "Meow!"

"My freund had a cat." Nikki looked at the back of Erich's head. "Do you know him?"

Erich felt that his stomach filled with butterflies and they swarmed so fast that he could throw up right there! "Ja, I know him." He turned the dome light on and Nikki squinted. Erich looked up the road to be sure it was clear and then looked at Nikki in the rearview mirror, "Ja, Nikki." He pushed his bangs back, "It is me." He smiled and Nikki looked at him from the shadows.

"Erich," Tears went down to his mouth where they went around his lips and trailed down to his collar, "Erich!" He couldn't move to wipe the wet from his glasses and the bruises made it tough for him to widen his gaze.

"Nikki," Erich turned his attention back to the road.

"It's a trick." He looked back at the floor.

Erich thought about it and couldn't stand it any longer! He looked for a place to stop, slowed the car and then pulled off at a dirt road. He had to keep his uniform on if anyone should come by, but he wasn't going to leave Nikki like that, not now! He got out and Nikki looked scared.

"Bitte!" Nikki curled up and leaned over.

"Nikki, stop, bitte. It's me, your love." Erich reached for the cuffs.

Nikki jerked away, "Bitte! I… I don't want to die!" He moved away and Erich pushed the cage to the side to get to him. "Bitte, Bitte! Don't kill me!"

"Stop it! Nikki, it's me! Erich! It's Erich!" He got the keys and got one of the cuffs loose before Nikki jerked his other hand away and kicked at Erich!

"GET AWAY! GET AWAY FROM ME!" He turned and jerked at the door handle on the other side of the car! The door opened as Erich pushed back and Nikki got out, turned and ran to the front of the car! The headlights shined on his back.

Erich ran after him and had no choice but to tackle him! "HALT!" His glasses were knocked from his head and thrown into the grass.

"Don't kill me!" He threw his hands around and Erich got on top of him. They wrestled and Erich was surprised that he was so strong. Nikki swung his hand with the other cuff around and it caught Erich on his face where it cut his forehead!

"I'm not going to kill you! I love you!" Erich forced his hands down. "I'm not going to kill the man that I love!" He held Nikki there and, finally, Nikki turned to look at him.

They breathed so hard from the fight that they might have been runners in the Olympics. "You've got to remember me!"

"It's not possible." Nikki looked away again.

"Stephan told you. He told you that I was coming!" Erich hovered over him for a moment and then slowly brought his face to Nikki's. When Nikki moved his face away, Erich turned it to face him.

"Queer!" Nikki yelled.

"Ja, Ich bin queer." They kissed. For that moment, Nikki was still and his hard breaths seemed to subside. He pulled back and looked at Nikki. "Ich bin queer, Nikki."

The dirt and his tears all made some mud on his face. "Erich," he said.

"Ja, mein Nikki... Ich bin Erich." He kissed him again, "Can you not tell me from this kiss?"

Nikki tried to smile and then saw the cut to the side of Erich's forehead. "I can't believe it."

Erich smiled and then Felix meowed. "That damned cat," Erich sat up, "We've got to go my love." He searched his pockets for the key and found it. Then, he un-locked the other cuff and tossed them into the woods.

"Erich!" He said, sat up and wrapped his arms around Erich so tightly that Erich couldn't breathe! "You came for me?" He was overjoyed, "YOU CAME FOR ME!"

"Ja, Nikki, it's okay. We are okay." He said, though the truth was that they were still quite far from okay. "We must get off the ground my love." He tried to get up, but Nikki wouldn't let go.

"I won't let you go." He interlocked his fingers so that they were a knot and his arms were wrapped around Erich.

"Nein, Nikki, we must get up from the ground." He forced Nikki to let him loose, "just for now, bitte." He said and, finally, Nikki loosened his arms and they got up.

"I'm so happy to see you!" He grabbed Erich again, "I love you, I love you." He held on even harder now and Erich moved with him to the side of the car.

"I love you too, but I must tell you that we have to get out of here or we will go to Sachsenhausen again... and stay." Erich pulled Nikki's arms apart.

Sachsenhausen got Nikki's attention and he let loose, "I'm just so happy to be free, to be with you!" He kissed Erich over and over.

Erich saw the bruises up close, "I know, but for now we must get on the road." He touched the bruises and anger grew in him that Ehrlichmann had hurt Nikki! He got Nikki in the car and tried to close the door.

"Is it true of Stephan?" Nikki held the door.

Erich's happy expression faded, "Ja, he's not coming with us... Felix is." He waited a moment and Nikki let loose of the door, so Erich closed it and got in.

"My glasses!" Nikki yelled and opened the door, but did not step out.

"Damn it all!" Erich got a flashlight from the seat and got out. He went to the front of the car, scanned the ground, "AH!" He saw the metal reflect and they were just there, a few feet or so away. He grabbed them, but the arm was bent. "For now, you'll have to go without."

"Ja," he closed his door. Gently, he put them on.

Erich got in, got the car in gear and they were gone. Felix meowed loudly!

"Your bangs look nice." Nikki smiled, but grimaced as the bruises were still fresh.

"They've had some time to grow so that you would know me better." They sped towards Gramzow.

Prinz-Albrecht Straße, Col. Lippert's driver stopped and opened the door. Col. Lippert got out and went inside to see Gerheim. Maj. Gerheim just closed his door and checked that the lights were off. He went to the main office and saw the lights were still on in the hallway. He looked at his watch and it was after eight. Col. Lippert got to the second floor and saw another man come out of the main offices of Kripo, the investigations unit of the Gestapo. He stopped only for a moment and then turned to go up to the third floor.

"Col. Lippert!" Capt. Ehrlichmann hurriedly came to him, "Colonel!"

Col. Lippert turned and looked him over, "Capt. Ehrlichmann... so late too."

"Ja, just leaving now and very excited about tomorrow." He pulled his jacket on; his hat was in his hand, "you?"

"Maj. Gerheim and I are going to supper late." He looked up at the third floor. He thought, better to wait here.

"Ah, very good," he got his jacket buttoned up. "I can't wait. Jan and I are going to the opening ceremony."

"Jan?"

"Sorry, Capt. Brueder," he got his hat on his head squarely.

"He must be working late too." He looked up the steps and heard boots coming down the hallway.

"Why do you say that sir?" Ehrlichmann ran his hands down his jacket to be sure the wrinkles were smoothed out.

"He was to go to the camp to pick up a prisoner this evening." He looked up the stairs. "Perhaps, I should break Maj. Gerheim's work state." He took a step.

"Can you tell me what prisoner he went to pick up?" Ehrlichmann appeared anxious, but not to leave.

Col. Lippert thought for a moment, "Ech." He then shook his head, "no, ah there are so many. VanEch, Nicholas." He looked at Capt. Ehrlichmann and saw his happy expression fade away into the building's shadows. "Are you well, Captain?"

"Ja," he thought for a moment. "I can imagine that Maj. Gerheim gave permission for this order?"

"He called me." Col. Lippert didn't like to be kept waiting, nor did he like to be questioned. "What is it Captain?"

Ehrlichmann, in that moment, thought the matter through. He could deal with Maj. Gerheim at any point. To continue, he would further incite Col. Lippert. "Nothing, sir, please enjoy your supper." He said, got a cigarette out, turned and went down the stairs. He lit up and then stopped suddenly, "Colonel, please give my regards to Maj. Gerheim."

Col. Lippert nodded at him and had his fill of the entire matter. He heard boots in the hall on the third floor and headed to the stairs, "Fritz!"

Ehrlichmann quickly went downstairs and into the main hall. He got to his car where Johann waited with his other guard, Thomas. "Get in!" They got in the car, "back out and go to the corner!"

Johann didn't ask and drove to the corner where he waited. A few minutes passed and they watched Maj. Gerheim and Col. Lippert come out, get into Col. Lippert's staff car and then leave. "Sir," Johann said.

"Quiet," Ehrlichmann watched the staff car disappear down the straße. "Go back!"

They drove back and got out. "Brueder is it!"

Johann looked at Thomas, "Sir?"

"Brueder is the spy! He has picked up VanEch and they are gone!" He turned and they all went back into SS HQ. "Get me the address for Brueder and family that is proximate to Berlin!"

"Sir, and to notify the Gestapo?" Johann waved at Thomas to go with him.

"Nein! Nein, we will handle this matter." He studied Johann's expression and then they went in.

Nikki was asleep on the back seat with Felix. Though Erich hated the thought of the cat free in the car, he could do nothing and, certainly, would not say no to Nikki. He and Felix eyed each other and Erich made a face at him, but Felix could have cared less. They passed a sign and Gramzow was only a half an hour away.

"Erich," Dr. Scherbit said softly, "Erich?" He didn't touch him and waited a moment as Erich came back to the room.

"Ja," he looked at the lamp and then turned, "Are we at our time?"

"Yes, I'm afraid so."

Erich wiped the sleep from his eyes and sat up. He yawned and looked at Dr. Scherbit who had his jacket and pipe.

"You are so ready to go." He sat up slowly.

"My wife... we have some family tonight." Dr. Scherbit smiled.

Erich got up and got his jacket, his brief and then the smell hit him, "ah." He looked himself over and forgot that he was in a puddle earlier. "I'm filthy." He walked to the door.

Dr. Scherbit was right behind him. "Though I'm very sorry to have stopped you, I'm curious if you made it to Szczecin?"

Erich turned to him, "for that doctor, you will have to wait until next week." He patted the doctor on the shoulder, "good night and best wishes for your evening." They left and Erich grabbed a cab.

The cab stopped on Main Street. Erich walked down the sidewalk to the river walk and then to their flat. There was a mixture of food smells in the air, but there was no mistake that Nikki had made brats, kraut and red cabbage! Erich's mouth watered and he hurried to the door!

"Nikki!" He hung his jacket and went to the dining room. "Nikki!"

"Yes, I'm here." He set his cabbage to the side, so that he could take the brats to the table. "Ah!" He looked at Erich and nearly dropped the brats! "What has happened?"

"Oh, I've fallen on... I'm fine, just dirty." He smiled and hoped that Nikki wouldn't make him bath first.

Nikki shook his head and then gave in, "you will wash your hands, face and up your arms." He set the brats down, then waved his hand in front of his nose, "and put on some cologne!" He went to the kitchen and got the red cabbage.

Erich washed up thoroughly and quickly, then smelled himself. He turned his nose up, but it wasn't that bad after he sprayed some cologne.

They sat down and Nikki said a prayer. Erich was going to go nuts if he didn't eat now! Nikki looked at him, "I see that look, like a starving dog with a bowl full of meat in front of him."

Erich didn't move, but waited, "bitte."

"Ja, okay." That's all it took for Erich to dig in and they ate up. Supper lasted about an hour or so and Erich was so full that he went to his chair in the sitting room and got quite comfortable afterwards. Nikki finished the dishes and came in. He turned on the radio and the jazz music played gently.

"You look happy." He sat down on the love seat.

"I am." He set the rag down.

"Is it nearly over?"

"Ja... yes." He smiled, "and you will go then."

Nikki crossed his arms. "We will see."

Erich thought for a moment and then sighed.

"That was quite loud." Nikki got a rag from the coffee table about Hollywood. "As loud as when we first met."

"There was an attack." He waited for Nikki to look at him.

"An attack... what do you mean?"

Erich opened the can of worms, so it was his duty now to put them back. "About us, I had an attack."

Nikki didn't take his eyes from the rag, "why?" He dipped the rag and looked at Erich, "this matter of blame again?"

"Yes," Erich looked sad and got up. He stood there and looked at a painting of a boy with his grössvater. "I haven't yet been able to let it all go."

Nikki gently laid the rag down on the coffee table, "If... if you had gone back over and were caught... who would come get you?"

Erich was puzzled, "I would not have gone."

"If you had, Erich," Nikki persisted, "If you had gone."

Erich shrugged his shoulders and thought, "I don't know."

"Could I?"

Erich knew that was not a question to answer wrong, "ja, of course."

Nikki made a mad face at him, "Don't be foolish."

"Okay, so no one or maybe Stephan would have helped me." He was frustrated now and walked to the window where he could let his mind drift a little like the river. "What's the point?"

"The King of the Jews," Nikki said.

"Now, I am lost."

"There was a choice and he knew I was going to go back. You were stronger, more able..."

"I don't want to hear this nonsense!" Erich turned and crossed his arms.

They stared at each other and then Nikki got the Hollywood rag, got up and walked to the door.

"Nikki," Erich knew he was in hot water. "I'm sorry."

"You can blame yourself every day and every night, Erich Schmidt." Nikki held the rag at his side, "If you want to believe you are so terrible that you can't see past the impossible, then you believe!" Nikki threw the rag at him. "I'm not going to have this matter again. When I see your face and know you are thinking on the matter, I will leave you to drink it up alone."

"Why are you so mad at me?"

"Because, you refuse to listen to reason, you refuse to listen to me, to something that is greater than us and it is something that I believe." Nikki's face could have heated the room. "He's not just the King of the Jews and he doesn't hate queers."

"So that's what it is about."

"Nein, Erich... nein. It's about you, me and what's happened so many years ago. You, only you could have saved me. Only you could have made this right." Nikki walked over to him and they stood there and looked at each other. "You made it right and, now, we have each other for our lives." Nikki didn't move. "God knew you were stronger and that you would come for me."

Erich ached for him to hold, but waited, "and what of Stephan?"

Nikki huffed, "in all this time with the doctor, you just don't tell a story. You realize that Stephan, at any point, could have told them everything. He made a choice and gave us a chance to get free, truly free... not like the lie that was on the gate at Dachau!"

Erich looked at Nikki and smiled, "I'm... it will be hard for me not to blame myself, because of the pain that you suffered, the death of our freund and that damned cat that we had."

"Now, you are making a joke." Nikki widened his eyes, "you dishonor me, Felix and Stephan when you blame yourself and live with it."

Erich gave in and they hugged. "So, tonight, a little more of it leaves me."

"Then, we will keep after it until all the blame is gone from you." He kissed Erich on the cheek and they stood there and held each other.

"Do you think that Felix watches us?" Erich asked.

"Why? Did you do something to him?" Nikki eyed Erich.

Erich looked away, "I left him on the side of the road when I went to the camp."

Nikki slapped him gently. "Okay, so there is your punishment for that deed." He picked up the rag and went to the love seat. Erich came over and sat down.

"God is right."

"Oh?"

"I am stronger." Erich flexed his bi-cep. "I am a man."

"Ha, don't go too far." Nikki chuckled, held up the rag to block his view of Erich and pretended to read it.

Erich pushed the rag down and they kissed.

"When will you tell Scherbit the rest?" Nikki asked.

"Wednesday," he said.

"Still, to this day, I can't believe it about the sheiße house." Nikki touched Erich's chin, "you were so brave." They kissed again.

CHAPTER 20: SCHEISSE HOUSE, PART II—ERICH, NIKKI & CONRAD

Erich got his work done and did not look forward to this last meeting with Scherbit, though the doctor did make it clear that they would have a follow up to see if therapy helped. Erich talked a majority of the time and Dr. Scherbit felt it was a relief to be able to share the story outside his protected world with Nikki. And by doing so with him, it would break down the matter further so that there was little negative affect on Erich; that's what he hoped.

Erich sat in the waiting room and wondered if the loudmouthed woman was in there. It was quiet for the fifteen minutes or so that Erich waited. Then, Dr. Scherbit opened the door and her husband came out. Erich tried not to laugh to himself, but it was funny that he came after her when he was the one who she beat on verbally.

"Erich," Dr. Scherbit motioned for him to come in.

Erich got his jacket off and saw that the chaise faced the door. "Has he moved it to watch for her?"

"What?" Dr. Scherbit asked while he closed the door. "Oh," he laughed, "no, he's as uncomfortable as you."

Erich thought for a moment and then turned it to face the

clock, "then, I will change."

"I see," Dr. Scherbit sat down, got his pencil and notepad handy. "So, here we are."

Erich sat down and looked at him. "Is there a point of... reality?"

"How do you mean?"

Erich drew his hands over his face, "Where you feel it's done and the blame is gone?"

"Yes, of course." He said, set his notepad down and fiddled with his pencil, "you are close, very close."

"I have a lot of blame from what happened to Nikki and Stephan. I had an attack, anxiety attack." He was uncomfortable about the matter. "Nikki said this is what it's called."

Dr. Scherbit looked at him and knew, "I thought so." He sat up and set his pencil down, "No terrible matter is cured quickly. If you had the plague, how long do you think a person will need to recover with medicine?"

Erich thought on it, "I don't know."

"Months or not at all," he looked at Erich kindly, "you've gone these years with no medicine and survived."

Erich understood and nodded, "I told Nikki that a piece of it had been chipped away from me."

"Good, then to hear that makes me believe you have the medicine and you will be very well." He smiled. "So, today you can chip another piece of it off, a big piece and feel that much better... without that blame."

Erich felt uplifted and, for that second, good feelings got in his heart and soul. "I think I'm ready."

Dr. Scherbit nodded at him. "I'm ready too."

Erich laid back and looked at the lamp's glow once more. The noises of people and the cars fell silent as he focused his mind on the luminescent light that soaked into his eyes and took him from here to there, to Gramzow, Germany, 1936. It was Friday, July thirty-first and late that night.

He turned down the dirt road to the Brueder's home and Nikki sat up. He looked like hell and wiped the dirt, sleep and dried tears from his eyes. "Perhaps, I can take a bath."

Erich looked at him, "of course." His mind drifted and he felt some very light touches of good as they made their way up the driveway and to the side of the house. It was dark there and the moon was only half full with a sky that was crystal clear.

"Will we be safe here?" Nikki asked and looked around. Felix meowed loudly. "He must need to go."

"We will be safe." He thought, "I will tell you everything when we've had some time to get you taken care of. For now, we need to eat, get you cleaned up and prepare for the rest of our mission."

"Mission?" Nikki asked and opened the door.

"Journey," It was a matter of minutes before he had the lamps on, the fireplace lit and the food on the table. There was an oil burner with large grills used to heat a lot of water. Erich found a tub and brought it in, "hope it does not leak." He took his jacket off and brought some things in. "I've brought you a change of clothes."

Nikki nodded at him and looked over his prison uniform and the pink triangle, "danke."

Erich went back to the car, saw the luger and thought about it, then grabbed it and his SS knife. Felix was loose in the yard, but Erich believed that food would bring him back quickly.

He put the tub in the living room, near the fireplace, and brought the hot water in. "We have no soap." Nikki said.

"Let me check the cupboards." Erich went to the kitchen and looked through every single one. He went down to the basement and found a half a bar of soap. He hurried back upstairs where he stopped and saw Nikki with his prison clothes off, nude in front of the fire place. The shadows helped to hide some of the bruises and Erich wiped his eyes as he must stay strong for them. "There was a small bar in the basement." He walked in and Nikki turned to him.

"The water is too hot." He stood there and looked at Erich.

"Yes... I'm sure it's fine by now." He handed the soap to Nikki. They were quiet and stood there for a few moments in silence as the fire gently tossed burning embers into the flute. It had been over a year since they saw each other. It had been close to eleven months since the SS arrested Nikki. Though the bruises were still puffy, they looked like patches of black shadows on Nikki's face. Erich didn't pay any mind to them so as not to upset Nikki. "I should… get out of this uniform."

Nikki wrapped his arms around Erich and they held each other.

Erich was beside himself that they were together; it was surreal. He thought for a moment as he rested his lips on Nikki's forehead, "You are so beautiful." He hummed a song and they moved around. Erich, in his SS uniform, and Nikki, nude, danced around the tub quietly and slowly with the fireplace that burned brightly behind them.

"Veronika?" Nikki asked.

Erich sang, "Veronika, spring is here" they moved slowly back and forth.

Nikki sniffled, wiped his eyes and then rested his head on Erich's chest.

"Nikki, spring is here…" Erich kissed him and they looked at each other, "Nikki, do you want to or not? Outside tis spring." They kissed, "and *then* someone knocks at our door." They turned slowly in front of the fireplace and their shadows danced on the wall across from them. Nikki lifted his head from Erich's chest and looked at him in the firelight.

"I like your version Erich Schmidt." Nikki said as they rocked back and forth.

"For you, I do my best." They smiled and then kissed in a lovely way.

"I want you to sit with me." Nikki said.

"My love, this tub is small."

"Sit with me," Nikki touched Erich's cheek. He stepped over to the tub and the steam rose up as it was still very warm.

Erich took his uniform off and waited as Nikki carefully lowered himself into the tub. He got behind him and sat down now, "ah, it is quite warm."

"Hold me," Nikki leaned back onto him.

Erich wrapped his arms around him and they enjoyed the peace. The time passed and the water cooled. Erich got the soap and gently washed Nikki. As he rinsed him off, he kissed the freshly cleaned places—the nape of his neck, along his ears, his shoulders and Nikki turned so that they kissed each other on the lips. The kiss set fire to what had been kept from them; they found themselves overwhelmed with the surge of emotions that moved through their souls. Their tongues slowly went in and out of each other's mouths, along each other's tongues and their lips panned and surfed as their passion, fraught with impatience, burned as hot as the fireplace.

Nikki rose up to take what he wanted from Erich, though the time that passed made it difficult, it was not impossible, "Ah." He let out an uncomfortable sigh, "Erich," but kept easing himself down onto Erich.

"Perhaps," Erich said and Nikki reached back and put his hand over Erich's mouth.

"Nein," he lowered himself all the way down.

Erich held him tightly and reached around to feel Nikki; he was firm and after all this time, he was very sensitive.

"Ah!" Nikki turned and they kissed passionately as he lifted Nikki up and then held him on the way down, "ja, my love." Nikki bent at the waist and Erich ran his hands up Nikki's back to his neck. Then, Erich rested his hands-on Nikki's shoulders and eased him back and down.

"AH!" Nikki let out, but it was the good feeling of having Erich in him, deep in him, that he cried out.

"You are alright?"

"Ja, please," Nikki did his best to twist and move himself to get Erich where he wanted him. It was difficult with the body aches, but the pleasure overcame the pain.

"Nikki," Erich kissed his neck, his back and then pulled him close, turned his head and kissed his mouth deeply. The fire roared and embers popped and cracked!

"Please, please!" Nikki jumped and shook as he let his

pleasure out! "AH!"

"Ja, my Nikki!" Erich pulled Nikki down to take all of him and trembled! "Ja!" He wrapped his arms around Nikki to hold him. "Nikki,"

"My love," Nikki held his arms up and back so that he touched Erich's face; he felt his cheeks bunch up and tighten, then he smiled, "I love you."

Erich's nerves tingled, jumped and jolted him, "I love you." He sat back so Nikki could sit back on him. They enjoyed what had been taken from them for such a long period of time and stayed in the water where they let the sensations of touch deepen their pleasure. Erich moved his nose around Nikki's neck. Nikki turned and moved his cheek along Erich's cheek, and then he turned his face and went up Erich's face with his chin. Erich moved his hands along Nikki's arms and then went down his thighs. He brought his hands back up the inside of Nikki's thighs, just as Nikki moved his hands back to the inside of Erich's thighs.

They got to each other's genitals and held each other gently. "We must do this more often," Erich said.

"Ja... I've been busy." They tried to laugh, but the reality was still with them.

Erich kissed Nikki again and put his lips right up against Nikki's ear, "forgive me, but..."

"We must go back to reality." Nikki said, turned to him and they kissed. "We're not home yet."

"Meow!" Felix hopped onto the ledge of the living room window and looked at them.

"And there's Felix," Erich said. He edged himself out and up. "There are some preparations we must go over."

Erich took all his SS clothes and put them back in the closet. He kept his long coat and put it with his other things. He changed into plain clothes and looked at his SS knife and the Luger. There was a clip in it and he had another clip that was loaded. He knew he could not take a chance.

Nikki came in and had on some plain clothes. His face was

much clearer but the bruises showed.

"My Nikki, what have they done to you?" He looked over Nikki's bruised face and fought the anger that built up in him.

"Nein," Nikki moved Erich's hand away.

"Nein?"

"You must focus on our escape from this house." He went to the kitchen window. "Are we safe here?" Nikki looked out at the half moon lit yard.

"Ja, this was the home of the man that I impersonated." Erich held up his arms.

"So, to get to *our* home?" Nikki was scared.

They sat down at the table in the kitchen where Erich had set out some sausages and bread with two glasses and a jug of wine. "You've done well for your first meal." Nikki said.

They looked at the fake papers that Erich had from Stephan. Erich looked at Nikki as he tried to chew the sausage. He got his SS Knife and cut the sausage into smaller pieces, "Ehrlichmann?"

Nikki stopped and looked at him, "If you put your mind to him, he will ruin us further."

Erich said nothing else. His knife easily cut the sausage into smaller pieces and then wiped his blade clean.

SS HQ, Ehrlichmann looked at the papers in front of him, "Where is the house?" He threw the papers to the ground, "He can't have gone far!" The phone rang and he grabbed it. "Ja!" He listened and paced as far as the phone line allowed. "So, he has taken VanEch over an hour ago!"

Johann and Thomas stood with some papers in their hands and looked them over as they waited on Ehrlichmann.

"Und sie?" He pressed his fingers into his head, "I should have been called... damn those orders!" He slammed the phone down. "I will not give the command that ruins my career! I will not tell the border guards or the Gestapo!" His Luger and belt were on his desk. He grabbed the belt and put it on. "I... I must arrest them or... kill them!"

"We have looked through the records from Patz." Johann said, "There's no address for Brueder and his parents are dead."

"We know that!" Ehrlichmann's face was red and he paced in and around the desks.

"He was at Patz's flat and then left when we came to search it." Johann finished.

Ehrlichmann thought and the veins on the side of his head looked like worms that crawled in pulses as he burned up with his thoughts, "there is an address somewhere for Brueder!" He looked at the papers on the ground, knelt and went through them.

"Patz, we believe, made their whereabouts unknown." Johann and Ehrlichmann looked up at him. "That's most likely where they went."

"So, Patz thinks he has left us no turn off this road of nothingness!" He stood and drew his Luger, "AH!" Johann and Thomas ducked!

Thomas, normally quiet, spoke up, "What of the Reich directory for the census?"

Johann smacked him on the head, "We've checked."

"Ja, but from the years that they were alive?" Ehrlichmann holstered his Luger. "He couldn't have changed every record!" He roared. "Find them!" They left for the office upstairs.

"They could cross the border before we get to them!" Johann said.

"Nein, they will wait till morning to draw less attention, of this I'm sure." Ehrlichmann kicked at a desk. "Damn it!"

They got to the office with the punch cards, but the door was locked, and then Ehrlichmann kicked it open.

They tossed cards all over the floor and on the desk. Johann looked over it all, "Helga will be upset." They pulled cards from previous years, looked them over and then tossed them to the side.

"To hell with her!" He looked at Thomas who read a yellowish looking card.

"Brueder, Gramzow!" Thomas smiled.

"Be sure of the name!"

"Son, Jan Brueder," Thomas held up the card.

Ehrlichmann rushed over and got the card from him, "This is it."

Johann went to the phone.

"What are you doing?"

"To call for more guards, we…" Johann wasn't pleased with Ehrlichmann.

"Nein!" Ehrlichmann held the card up. "He will make a fool out of me if I don't get him and bring him back myself." They went to the door, "Gramzow is an hour or so. We will go and plan on the way. Get your heavy weapons… if he's not there, I will contact the border guards."

Johann wanted to say more, but kept his tongue silent.

They were down at the straße in minutes with their equipment that included two machine guns, ammo and helmets. "Schnell!" Ehrlichmann shouted!

It was near midnight and Erich walked the grounds again. He looked down the road and it was filled with shadows. The stars were brilliant and shined on them brightly and powerfully. Nikki came out and it was cool, even for July. There was a decent wind that rustled the trees, brush and dust from the road.

"Do you think he will come for us?" He wrapped his arms around himself.

"Stephan destroyed Brueders information." Erich held Nikki. "Chance is in our favor."

They kissed and then looked up at the stars. "There are the heavens," Nikki said.

"So, you believe?"

"In God," Nikki sighed, "ja."

"God does not like queers." Erich said. There were lights that were far off and disappeared in the hills.

"If not, then how is it we are happy?" Nikki smiled.

Erich smiled back and they kissed, "we are happy… no matter what happens."

Ehrlichmann looked over a map with Johann as Thomas drove. "There is the town… this road has to be lined with trees. We will stop at the edge of the town, here." He pointed on the map, "We will walk in the line of trees where the shadows will cover our attack."

"There's a good wind." Johann said, "There will be noise and movement amongst the brush."

Ehrlichmann looked at Johann, "I have been betrayed by this... pig."

Johann nodded, "We will go in and drive them out to you."

Ehrlichmann looked at his Luger, loaded the clip full and put it back in the Luger. "There will be no questions Erich Schmidt." He looked out the window at the passing scenery, "you've had your chance."

It was just after one in the morning when Erich woke after a cat nap and Nikki was fast asleep on the couch. An oil lamp lit part of the living room and it sat on the mantel. They had all their things in the car and were ready to go in the morning. Yes, they took a chance to wait, but to travel at night always drew unwanted questions and checks, because at night the guards had more time on their hands and a desire to have something to do. He went to the kitchen and stood near the corner of the window so he was part of the frame. The view of the backyard, the car and the driveway was good, "nothing." He knew that at some point, he'd have to take another cat nap. He went to the living room and Felix was inside; he sat on the ledge of the window. Erich went to the front door and then leaned over just enough to be at the edge of the window. He looked out and saw the road that led from the house to the village. There were no lights to be seen.

He looked down at Felix whose fixed gaze was on something across the road. Then, Felix growled quietly.

Erich's heart missed a beat. He touched his side, but the Luger and his knife were on the table in the kitchen! "Scheiße," he knelt down. He looked at Felix who, even then, would not break his gaze. Then, Felix jerked his head to the right. He growled harder this time and his tail snapped and jerked around.

Erich stood very slowly and knew that the floor would creak if he made a sudden move. He turned and thought to get to the Luger, now. He looked at the moon light that came through the window and it was clear, only a shadow of Felix. He crossed the living room to the hallway and the wind made some noises against the house, a low whistle or whirr as it rushed over and against the wood siding. He turned back for a moment and saw that Nikki was fast asleep and on his side. When he turned back to the kitchen, a shadow jumped from the tree line to the out building. He couldn't make it out as his eyes adjusted from the moon light in the living room to the darkness. There, on the table, was the Luger, the gun belt and his knife in its sheath.

Felix growled louder in a part meow and woke Nikki.

"Felix, shh," he remained still on the couch.

Erich thought about it. How many would come silent like this? Whoever it was, they did not have many men or they would have brought a truck and barreled right to the front door! He had to get Nikki to safety first and then get his weapons. He walked along the hallway towards the master bedroom and then knelt down. He crawled over to the couch which had its back to the living room window.

A shadow shot across the moonlit floor! Snap! It shot back the other way! It was Felix's tail and he growled deep and hard again. Erich sighed and then crawled quickly to the couch where he put his hand gently over Nikki's mouth, "shh."

Nikki jumped and grabbed Erich's hand, but stopped when he saw the moon light on Erich's face. "What?"

They whispered, "You must go to the basement… quietly."

Just then, Felix leapt to the couch and looked over them, "meow."

Erich mumbled, "You are a filthy cat." Then, he motioned for Nikki to follow him along the floor. Nikki crawled a few feet, but stopped! His glasses were on the coffee table! He turned and looked at the table and they were on the corner. He reached for them and a shadow passed his hand, but it wasn't Felix. His heart beat pushed harder and harder as his hand hovered over the glasses. The shadow was small, but moved to the side and was gone now.

"Nikki," Erich kicked at his hand.

"AH!" Nikki laid still.

"Shh," Erich said and with all the noise now, he thought to get up, turn the lamps up and have a party, "We've made enough noise, bitte." He turned back to the kitchen.

Nikki got his glasses on and then crawled after Erich to the hallway. Finally, they got to the kitchen and Erich had the basement door open. Nikki partially stood and slid around him into the stairwell.

Erich got Nikki's hand and held him for a moment, "make the steps down gently, then go to the corner away from here." He smiled to reassure Nikki, "The path is clear of things, so go there and stay by the brick walls."

Nikki, "ja, and you?"

"I must finish what I started." He pulled Nikki's hand and they kissed. Then, he let loose of him and Nikki slowly went down the steps into the darkness. His wire frame glasses and his eyes were the last Erich saw of him as they faded into the black. There was only a rustling sound from Nikki's feet and hands as he felt his way to the wall and then across the basement to the corner where he got between two large boxes and against the corner of the wall.

Erich closed the door and then turned his attention to the weapons on the table. It was only a few feet, but seemed like a hundred. He crawled to the table and as he reached, he turned his head slightly. He saw through the base of the window that there was a shadow, a lump that popped up and then disappeared by the outbuilding. He had his hand on the knife and planned that they would have to come up the steps, which was an advantage for him. Also, he knew the house and had been through all of it. He put the knife in his pants and to his back. Then, he reached up for the Luger and got his fingers on the handle. He looked at the base of the window again and there was a lump at the window! One of the chairs was in front of him and the cabinets were behind him. The moonlight was overhead, so his body was a black shadow on a dark background. The lump didn't move and then there was no question, it was a man who panned the room and then dipped back down. He got his hand tightly around the Luger and slid it to him. He had seconds to kill the man if he came up the steps.

The gun belt draped over the side of the table and made a clank sound as the belt hook came off the table and hit the leg! He didn't move and had the Luger in hand. He didn't want to shoot anyone as this would lead to a gun fight and he would be one against how many? He thought about a fight with the man, but there was no way it would be just one man. The peace he had when he quit the SA slowly faded from him and he closed his eyes to think about the training and the fights he'd been in.

The SA taught him to fight with knives, guns and his fists. Erich dreaded the thought of using the knife, because there was an inherent connection to another person when you stabbed them. You felt their body grimace; you felt the puncture of the tip of the blade through their clothes and their skin. The worst was to feel a person's life fade from them while they trembled and their blood drip down the blade to the handle onto your hand. He knew these things, because he had done it at the bar and was responsible for one of the deaths of the communist so many years ago. He hated how blood was sticky and became like paste on your skin that soaked into your pores and made you part of your crime.

There was a terrible noise, not loud, but like fingernails on a chalkboard as Erich ground his teeth against each other. He hated that he would have to act, have to use the knife. To use the Luger would draw them right to him and a gun battle or a prolonged gun battle would get them killed. He edged back from the kitchen table and backed up to the wall, which led to the hallway and living room. He thought on the matter of his attackers and it never occurred to him that they might be the neighbors, not at this hour. It never occurred to him that it might be gypsies or thieves, not at this hour and to be so cunning as to go around the out buildings and windows. It had to be the Gestapo or the SS; perhaps Ehrlichmann *had* come for him.

The SS had advanced training, but the Gestapo was polizei and had limited training compared to him. The images of the attacks floated through his mind and he knew that at some point one of them or more would enter. He had to kill one at a time to win. The belt clicked and was locked around him with the Luger in its holster. The knife slid out nicely and he held the point out.

He recalled the drop spots of a person which were spots on the human body that if you stabbed them, the wound would cause death. He recalled the points just beneath the jaw on either side of the neck, the side of the rib cage to collapse the lung, inside the legs and, the one he didn't care for, to slice the throat. He shook his head to rid himself of the anxiety that made his stomach sour and the fear of the job that faced him.

Someone came up the steps to the kitchen as he slid across the floor to the hallway and knelt to be out of their line of sight. Then, he crawled down the hall to the master bedroom. The fire had a distinct glow and it partially lit up the hall and living room as his eyes adjusted to the dim light. Then, there was the distinct sound of the door knob as it turned and "click."

He held the knife tightly and the wind caught the door just as it had when he was there for the first time, "BANG!" The door hit the cabinets! A curse word, then footsteps across the wood floor where a boot bumped the leg on a chair!

Erich studied the hallway where it ended and the opening to the kitchen was. He thought about the man and hoped that he would come up the hallway. Then, he would have him. The man's machine-gun barrel was the first thing that stuck out from the kitchen into the hallway. The man took a step and then waited to set his pace; he was not Gestapo.

Erich edged his arm back a little more to be able to thrust the knife out. He kept his breathing low and peered around the corner as the firelight cast its brightness away from him and towards the other end of the house.

The man was partially exposed now and kept his machine-gun level across the room. He took a step into the living room, then another step and another step. He was just at the edge of the love seat that faced the fireplace and studied the room. His eyes panned the room with his gun wherever he looked. He panned back and aimed it up the hallway to the master bedroom. Then, there was a second set of footsteps that came slowly up to the kitchen. The wind had died down now and there was only a faint sound of a whirr or whistle.

The man at the kitchen door whispered, "Thomas."

Erich knew the man had to come to him at the bedroom so he could strike a fatal blow, but there was no way he could walk up the hallway to him. Then, Felix leapt in front of the man and ran to the master bedroom!

Thomas was halfway across the living room and watched Felix go into the master bedroom. "Ja, klar," he then turned back towards the master bedroom. He took another step and another until he was at the edge of the fireplace and the other man went into the den which adjoined the kitchen.

Erich peered around the edge of the door and his heart nearly jumped out of his chest when he saw the pant leg and boot of the man! He looked up and saw the man's left hand supported the barrel and his right hand was around the pistol stock with his finger in the trigger. The gun was in the way. His partner was at the other end of the hall and then he moved his foot forward now so that he was half way across the door threshold. No matter how it happened, the other man would not shoot until he had a target or would pause before hand, so it was now!

Erich turned the blade upward and thought to stand quickly, put his hand on the body of the gun so he could not turn the gun on Erich and then push him back against the frame of the door.

Erich stood, jammed his hand against the gun and pushed the man back against the door! Then, he thrust the knife into the left side of Thomas's throat! Some blood spat out and onto Erich's cheek, "BANG!" Thomas pulled the trigger and shot a round!

"THOMAS!" The other man yelled and came to the door where he saw Thomas against the frame of the door and a dark figure against Thomas! A second passed as Johann squinted and flashed his light on them, "GET OFF HIM!"

The knife was out and the blood flowed from the vein quickly. Erich grabbed the handle of the machine gun and jerked it from Thomas's hand!

For the life that was left in Thomas, he brought up his hands to stop the flow of blood from his neck! Then, his body trembled and he collapsed to the floor.

Erich had the gun, got behind the wall and quickly put the knife in its sheath. Thomas was dead.

"THOMAS!" Johann squeezed the trigger and littered the end of the hallway with bullets! "TAT, TAT, TAT, TAT, TAT, TAT!" He looked through the smoke, "TAT, TAT, TAT, TAT, TAT!" Bullets tore through the wood work, door frame and hit the back wall of the bedroom! Felix shot under the bed!

Erich moved the machine gun so that the barrel was pointed down the hall and fired, "TAT, TAT, TAT, TAT, TAT!" The bullets hit the wall in the hallway as they worked their way up to the door frame of the kitchen!

"TAT, TAT, TAT, TAT, TAT!" Johan shot back and leapt from the den to the living room and was behind the love seat.

Ehrlichmann pulled his hat down tightly. He waited by the outbuilding and planned to ambush them if they tried to flee. Though he was a trained SS, he was nervous and cowered with his Luger as gun fire flashed in the house!

"TAT, TAT, TAT, TAT, TAT!" Johann shot again and then low crawled across the floor towards the fireplace.

Erich listened and looked at the dust cloud in the hallway. He heard the scraping sounds of a body as it dragged itself across a wood floor. He hoped that Nikki was in the corner as they agreed.

Erich took a breath, stood at the door and slowly stepped over Thomas. He raised the barrel of the machine gun and walked a few feet to the living room. He held the machine gun at eye level and got to the edge of the wall that ended and opened into the living room. He pointed the gun at the body on the floor! Johan rolled to his right and into the couch!

Erich kept calm and leveled the barrel at the yellowish glow of Johann's face. "Wie viele?"

"How many men?" Johann thought for a moment, "It won't matter, you are a dead man."

"As of this moment, I will outlive you." Erich looked at him over the barrel.

Johann slowly got up and had his hand on the pistol grip and finger on the trigger.

Erich nodded at him and then squinted, "You are Ehrlichmann's man."

He smiled, then brought the gun up to shoot Erich!

"TAT, TAT, TAT, TAT, TAT!" The bullets punched little holes all over Johann's body with one that hit his chin and one that hit his shoulder and several that hit his chest. He jerked back a foot or so and then collapsed like a sack of potatoes onto the couch.

"BANG!" Ehrlichmann stood at the kitchen opening and shot Erich with his Luger!

Erich recoiled, turned and shot up the walls by the kitchen! "TAT, TAT, TAT, TAT, TAT!" He dropped behind the chair that faced the couch and stayed there with his gaze on the ceiling.

There was silence and a white haze hung over him and Johann.

Nikki looked up at the boards and wiped his eyes. He looked up the brick wall to the steps and thought to go up, but then what? He knew nothing about weapons and had only been in one fist fight. He covered his mouth and coughed! The dust from all the movement in the living room fell around him like a rain shower. There was a shadow at the corner of the living room by the bedroom and he thought that it was Erich. He fanned the dust away and looked at the shadow as best he could, then whispered to his love. "Erich, you are alive." He leaned over, got on all fours and crawled a short distance so that he was closer to the shadow above him, "You are alive."

"He is dead, Nicholas!" Ehrlichmann shouted from the kitchen and looked at the hallway floor. "And now, I don't have to search this house for you."

"Erich?" Nikki spoke up.

"Ja!" Erich turned over, "TAT, TAT, TAT, TAT, TAT!" He shot up kitchen! The bullets ripped bits of wood, chewed the wall covering, and tore into the door jam. "And I know where you are Conrad!"

Silence followed as each of them thought about their next move. Erich touched his side and he had been shot; the bullet hit him and was inside him or grazed him on the right side of chest. He had no idea how bad, but didn't feel a lot of pain; it burned more than it hurt. He thought about Ehrlichmann and knew he was in the kitchen near the door to the basement, near Nikki.

Conrad looked around the kitchen. The faded glow from the fireplace embers was gone and all that was left was a sliver of light from the oil lamp on the mantel; it was not enough light for him to make out his surroundings. He saw the cupboards, the shelves, and the door that led to the basement or it a pantry door. If he could get to Nikki, he'd have Erich, but if the door only went to the pantry, he knew that Erich would shoot him.

Erich knew that if Conrad got to the basement door and made it down there that he would have Nikki in a bad place. He did not doubt that Conrad would kill Nikki and not care. He aimed down the hall at the blank space between the door to the basement and the edge of the frame to the hallway. Conrad would have to cross that small path to get to Nikki. The thought of ammunition crossed his mind, but Thomas fired one round and he fired, maybe fifteen or twenty more. The magazine for this machine gun was thirty rounds, so he thought.

Nikki looked across the basement at the stairwell and wondered if Ehrlichmann would come down there. He had some protection in the corner and didn't know if they had flashlights. He didn't know what Ehrlichmann would have to do to get to him, so he thought, at some point, he would come for him.

Erich got the gun pointed so that no matter what pain he

felt, he could blast the hall and, most likely, hit Conrad. "Conrad!" He moved a little and tried to get up on his feet. "CONRAD!"

Conrad sat back and thought for a moment. He looked at his Luger and closed his eyes to get them to better adjust to the darkness, he opened them, "Ja, Erich."

"So, you know now." Erich spat the dust from his mouth. "You know."

Conrad got to his feet and edged toward the door, but stopped and looked back at the open kitchen door that led outside; he could flee. He turned his attention back to the hallway and studied the door in front of him, basement or pantry? "Erich Schmidt," he wiped the sweat from his brow and slid closer to the hallway with his Luger's barrel just at the frame of the door. "Why is that queer so important to you?" He lowered himself and edged the barrel of his Luger just past the frame. "Why is it that one queer is so important? Is he a fellow spy and you are here to recover him?"

"Your men are dead." Erich spat, "I make a deal with you."

"What deal does a liar make?" Conrad inched his Luger right to the door jam.

"I am no spy!" He got his breath, but the wound ached and he grimaced. He had to move to ease the pain and then slid toward the living room.

"You are no queer… you can stay as an SS officer." He inched closer and, now, had his Luger turned up the hallway towards Erich. "Kill that queer and free yourself … I know you were in the SA and worked at the Reichstag."

"Ja, so?" Erich cringed again and looked towards the kitchen entry. The oil lamps sliver of yellow glow was enough for him to make out the shiny blued edge of the Luger! "TAT, TAT, TAT!"

Conrad jerked his hand back! The bullets hit just above his hand and blew pieces of wood and debris on him!

Erich slid back behind the chair and his teeth slammed together over the pain, "a deal or your die."

"What deal?" Conrad checked his surroundings again, because he had to get out of the kitchen.

"You give up your weapon." He held the gun steady with his trigger hand and reached around to the wound. "We will leave and you stay here."

Conrad was furious, "As if I was betrayed enough by you!" He punched the wall! "You, a freund, betrayed me for that filthy queer!" He punched the wall again! Why!"

Erich thought for a moment and got his hand back under the barrel of the gun, "I love him."

Conrad gritted his teeth and shook the Luger in a rage, "Queers do not love!" He said. "BANG!" He shot a hole through the basement door. "They do not love; they hump like rabbits at Dachau and that is all they are capable of Erich Schmidt!" He got to his feet. "Filthy vermin!"

"Nein, Conrad. I love Nicholas." Erich edged up into a crouched position with his eyes locked on the little path between the door and the edge of the frame, barely a meter. "If you try to cross Conrad, I *will* kill you."

Nikki looked all over the basement; the door to the kitchen could not be the only way out of here! He looked up along the edges. There had to be a basement door, like a storm cellar door! He was terrified, but stood up and walked toward a sliver of moon light shown through a long seam.

"Queers do not love!" Conrad screamed! He looked at the door and put his weight on one leg. Then, he leapt at the door!

"TAT, TAT!" The gun was out of ammunition!

Conrad crashed through the door, hit the steps, and banged his way down to the dirt floor! His hat flew off into the darkness.

Nikki turned his head away and rammed through the boards! He burst through the storm doors, stumbled, and then fell onto the ground!

Conrad got to his feet, struggled to get his bearings, and then saw the open storm doors. "I come."

"Nikki!" Erich got up, threw the machine gun to the side, and drew his Luger! He rushed to the basement door and stopped at the edge. His chest pain stung him like the tip of a knife jammed into his bare bone! "Ah!"

"BANG!" A bullet hit the ceiling in the kitchen. "C'mon Erich!" Conrad stepped back from the stairwell.

Nikki ran to the out building directly behind the house, "Erich!"

Erich looked out the back window, but knew if he tried to pass Conrad would shoot him and the matter would be over. Now, he felt wet and sticky on his side. He touched the bullet hole on the side of his chest and grimaced!

Conrad looked at the open storm doors and walked over, "You were my freund Erich, but no more." He got to the steps and rushed up!

Erich turned and hurried to the kitchen back door! He stood at the open door and looked at the out building as Conrad came around the corner of the house! Erich aimed at Conrad. "Put it down!"

Conrad aimed his Luger at the out building, perhaps to shoot Nikki.

"I have you, Conrad." Erich struggled to keep his place. "I have you."

"You have me?" Conrad shook his head. "Ha!" He looked at the outbuilding and then at Erich. "To think, after you shot those two boys and such a bad shot... my mind was set that you were Jan Brueder, an SS captain."

"In truth, I am a superior shot." Erich put his foot onto the first step so that he had better footing, "What changed?"

Conrad slowly lowered his Luger, "Lippert."

"You saw him?" Erich aimed precisely at Conrad.

"Ja, he told me you had gone to get your queer." He lowered the gun to his side now and held it there. "I did not want to believe it." He eyed Erich, "I chose to believe that you were a spy."

"You won't make the shot, Conrad." Erich pushed his bangs back. "Better to put it down and take my word."

"The word of a spy?" He said, "Your word is worth nothing." He tightened his grip around the pistol and studied Erich. "I have wounded you."

"I told you, I was never a spy." Erich had some trouble with his aim as the pain flared. The barrel dipped a little and he corrected his aim too much!

Conrad brought his Luger up and, "BANG!" Erich jerked to his right and lost his aim on Conrad.

Nikki yelled! "Nein!" Then, he ran from the out building to Erich!

Conrad took aim at Nikki, "This part I will enjoy most."

"BANG!" Erich shot Conrad in the shoulder and the bullet whipped him to the left, then he fell to the ground.

"Damn you!" Conrad cried out!

Nikki looked at Erich and ran to him!

Erich dipped and fell down the steps to the ground!

"Erich!"

Erich had his gun firmly in hand though.

"Are you alright?" He threw his arms around Erich, "Has he shot you!"

"Stop Nikki, bitte, stop," Erich moved Nikki so that he could see Conrad. "Nein, he only grazed me." He shook his head and looked at Nikki.

Nikki was overjoyed and kissed him as Conrad flailed around. "I love you! I love you!" He kissed Erich all over his face and didn't stop until Erich smiled.

"Nikki, bitte!" He got to his feet, with Nikki's help, and limped over to Conrad. "Don't Nikki," he pointed back for him to stay there. He looked Conrad over and kicked the Luger from Conrad's hand, "get up." Erich holstered his Luger and stood over Conrad. "The matter between us is over."

Conrad held his hand up to Erich for help.

Erich got his hand and pulled him up.

"It's never over!" Conrad punched the side of his Erich face!

Erich recoiled, looked at Conrad, and punched him on the side of his head, then they fought and fell to the ground!

"Erich!" Nikki got closer as the two men punched and kicked one another! He saw Conrad's gun and ran to it. He got it and pointed it at Conrad, but they rolled and turned so that he had the gun aimed at Erich and then Conrad. He quickly lifted the barrel and waited, "Erich!"

Conrad was on top of Erich and threw punch after punch. Erich blocked and then punched! He grabbed Conrad by his neck and jerked him back and off of him! He got on top of him and punched him in the jaw and the side of his head over and over!

"Erich!" Nikki threw the gun down and grabbed Erich! "Stop!" He pulled at Erich, "Stop it, Erich!"

Erich raged! Suddenly, he stopped and turned to him, "Why! Is that not what he did to you... to Stephan!" Drool seeped from his mouth, sweat covered his face, and he huffed like a horse at a race!

"Ja, but I'm not him!" They eyed each other, "and you are not him."

Sweat and blood pooled together in dark shadows on his face as he pushed off of Conrad and got to his feet, then he dropped and laid still.

Conrad wiped his face and looked around to get an idea of which way was up. He rolled onto his side and then fell back on the ground, "to hell with you both."

Erich looked at Nikki, "Our things are in the car?"

Nikki looked at Conrad, "ja, they are."

"Get Felix," He and Nikki eyed each other for a moment to reassure themselves. "Get him, please."

"And what about him?" Nikki turned to Conrad.

"I will take care of him." He sighed relief. "Just get Felix to the car." He looked at Nikki as he waited, "it's got to be nearly fünf uhr morgens."

Conrad tried to get to his feet and fell back down, "hell with you both."

"All right," Nikki went into the house.

Erich watched the windows and the glow from the oil lamp grew brightly. He smiled and knew that they were near to the end. He held his side and spat, "get up."

"You going to tie me up? Leave me?" Conrad stumbled and then got to his feet. They eyed each other, "so you eye me now."

"I was never afraid of you." Erich walked over, grabbed him

by his collar, and put him in an arm bar. "Go!"

Nikki had Felix and stood at the door, "Erich?"

"Get the car started and we need some water and towels to clean up." Erich nodded at Nikki.

Erich took Conrad to the outbuilding.

Nikki went back in the house and got those things, then went to the car and got in. Felix jumped from the front seat to the back, got up on the shelf, and sat at the back window. Nikki wiped the sweat from his brow and looked for them.

Erich forced Conrad past the outbuilding.

"So, will you leave me out with the animals?" Conrad asked and tried to stop Erich by dragging his feet.

"Nein, they would be offended." He grimaced.

"Ja? To hell with you, Erich Schmidt," Conrad looked at a smaller outbuilding just big enough for a couple of people. "You are the enemy." He said angrily and tried to turn, but Erich shoved him along.

Erich hurried him right through the door of the scheiße house! Then, shoved him down onto the seats!

"What is this?" Conrad asked and sniffed the air. His nostril flared!

Erich drew his Luger and aimed it at Conrad. In the moonlight, they studied each other.

Conrad laid partially back across two open holes and there was a musty crap smell. "You've brought me to a scheiße house!" He tried to sit up and Erich punched him in the face! "Ah!" He brought his hands up to his face and jerked back from the pain, "Damn you!"

Erich raised his boot and slammed it on the wood top! The wood cracked! Then, he raised his boot again and slammed it down on the top! "Crack!" A board gave way and Conrad dropped a couple of inches.

"What the hell are you doing!" Conrad tried to sit up, but Erich backhanded him with the butt of the Luger! "Stop it!" He threw his hands up to guard his face!

Erich kicked the sides and then raised his boot up again and slammed it down! "Crack!" The boards gave out and Conrad fell through!

Rage and fury filled Conrad's veins and he screamed, "I'm an officer of the SS!" He stood on the pile of scheiße! "You filthy queer!" Some scheiße splattered around and the warm weather made it wet, slippery! "You've done this to me! To put me in this scheiße!" His boots sunk into the crap and piss when he tried to stand. "You will pay with your life, Erich Schmidt!" The pile of crap gave out under his foot and he fell onto the pile. Crap soaked into his jacket, his trousers, his boots, and his hands! "Damn you!" He flailed around, "Damn you!" He roared! "Damn you, Erich Schmidt!"

Erich pressed his fingers into his eyes to push out the horror of how they tortured and then killed his freund, Stephan. "Was it you who killed Stephan?" Erich held the Luger at his side.

"To hell with him... and you!" Conrad stood and leaned against the side of the scheiße house and held the frame to steady himself. "I'm an officer of the SS!"

"Did you kill him." Erich eyed Conrad and thought to feel sorry for him.

"Nein, first..." He spat and fought to get his balance and then he pointed at Erich, "We beat him! Then, we brought him to a tree and tied him up!" He fell against the side of the dirt wall. "I'm an officer of the SS." The reality of his place pushed back against his arrogance. Then, he looked up at Erich and fought to keep his balance as he nursed his shoulder, "I beat him with my gloves on and then we bent his arms backwards and tied him to a tree." He spat, got his balance, and held his injured shoulder, "Then, he thought to eye me, to challenge me."

"And we know that you don't like to be eyed," Erich leveled the Luger at him.

Conrad looked down and chuckled, "We could have been great freunds." He looked around at the scheiße, "No, I do not like to be challenged in that way." Then, the coolness of the early morning was there among them and their breath warmed the cool air so that they exhaled in white gasps. "I shot him... shot him in the eye."

For a moment, they looked at each other and didn't move or speak. Their warm breaths formed a ghost between them.

"Then, for Stephan, I do as the Jew King says." He pulled the trigger, "BANG!" The bullet tore a chunk of wood from the base of the crap house!

Conrad threw his hands up and yelped! "Ah!"

Gun smoke rose in front of him and it hung there for a moment.

Conrad, shocked and exhausted, dropped to his knees, his upper torso pushed against the dirt wall, and he gasped.

"So, you've come to see that it's over." Tears seeped from his eyes and he nodded at the ghost, the spirit of Stephan. He holstered his pistol and wiped his eyes, "We are going home." Erich sniffled, studied Stephan's face, and then nodded again. "Thank you, thank you for all you sacrificed my freund." His lips trembled. "I promise to keep Felix." He licked his tear-soaked lips and then nodded at his friend.

Nikki stood by the car and trembled, "Erich?"

The wind picked up and Stephan's spirit faded through the cracks in the ceiling. Erich turned and went to the car. He nodded at Nikki.

They hugged. Erich looked at the car and looked at Felix in the back window of the car. "We must get cleaned up."

"I've put the wet towels in the car." Nikki looked him over, "and what about your injury?"

"I've been lucky to be grazed by both shots." He touched his side and jumped, "ah."

"And Ehrlichmann?" Nikki went to look, but Erich got him by the arm.

"This is not for you." He touched his face and Nikki nodded.

They got to the car and Nikki helped him undress. It was another hour before they were cleaned up and Erich's injury bandaged. Now, it was just after six and they were truly ready. Erich believed Conrad was so enraged and embarrassed by the matter that his ego kept anyone else from what they knew;

Conrad had to make the matter right and it cost him the lives of his men.

They were on the road to the border with Poland, "So, you believe that he has not notified the guards at the border?" Nikki asked.

"Nein, I believe we will be fine." Erich smiled at him, "can you look our papers over again?"

"Stephan made us Danish?" Nikki shook his head, "This is the name, Bjorn." Nikki laughed, "I don't know a word of Danish."

"Neither will the guards... at least I hope not." Erich said. "Stephan thought the Olympics were the best time to leave as there would be many people from other countries crossing back and forth."

Nikki pursed his lips, "I miss him."

Erich looked at Nikki, touched his cheek and tried to smile, "me too."

The German border guards were somewhat excited about the Olympics. They talked candidly about Germany and how many medals would go to German athletes. Two guards made faces at Felix while they searched. The guard who looked the car over said that they had seen many Danes and other nationalities for the Olympics; he was ready for the Games to be over. They did make a joke that the Olympics were the other way, but Erich told them that they were just there to help with some preparation for the teams. The guard nodded, lifted the barrier and they passed to the Polish guards who nearly waved them through after they read their papers. The drive to Szczecin was quite simple and they made the ship that took them to Copenhagen. From Copenhagen to Nova Scotia was the easiest for them and they had a time to relax, to think on other things besides the tragedies that happened.

They listened to the radio and clapped when they heard that Jesse Owens won the 200m sprint. The journey home had some unpleasant moments when Nikki woke from a nightmare or Erich checked the doors and then went to the hall to see that it was safe.

From Nova Scotia, they returned to Quebec City and home. Erich sat in his chair and left the curtains closed. Everything felt out of place or disjointed. Erich looked around the room and didn't know what to feel or do. He thought to call the bank and speak to Mr. Lachance about his job, but decided to just sit quietly.

Nikki came to the sitting room and stood by the hallway. He looked better and his bruises were nearly gone; one bruise seemed to want to hang on that was just at the base of his right eye, Johann.

It was late that night and they spent the first day back with just re-familiarizing themselves with their home.

Nikki saw that the curtains were closed and so he opened them.

"I closed them." Erich looked at him.

Nikki hesitated. "How will we have our lives back?" He left them half open.

"I don't know." Nikki walked over, sat on the love seat and looked at Erich.

Erich saw his sullen expression and got up. They sat next to each other and then Erich raised his arms and Nikki leaned over onto him, "Nikki, spring is here."

"Erich?" Dr. Scherbit said.

"Ja, Nikki."

"Erich," Dr. Scherbit walked over and touched Erich's shoulder, "Erich."

Erich jumped! "Ja!" He looked around and saw the clock, then let out a huge sigh, "So, it's you." He wiped the sleep from his eyes.

"Sorry, we are half hour past our time, but I couldn't stop you." He returned to his chair, sat back and put his pipe in his mouth.

"I feel some sense of relief that we no longer bear it alone." Erich sat up and squinted to let his eyes adjust. "Is that true to have that feeling?"

"Yes, the secret is no longer secret." He dipped his head to look over his glasses. "Does Nikki know all of it?"

"Know?" Erich shook off the feeling he had to go back to sleep.

"Know about Conrad," he looked back through his glasses.

Erich smiled and pressed his fingers against his nose, "only that I killed him, but he did not see the body." He put his hands on his sides to push up from the chaise, "you'll have a bill for me?"

"And some thoughts about the future of your therapy," he smiled, "Will Nikki come soon?"

Erich stood up and looked at the doctor, "Ja, but he has a wish for you and your wife to come have supper with us."

Dr. Scherbit smiled and was rather happy about the invitation, "I'd like that."

"Before he sees you," Erich got the chaise lined up, turned the lamp off in the corner of the room and then walked over and got his jacket.

"Of course, I have your number and will speak with my wife." Dr. Scherbit stood, got his briefcase and put his notepad inside it. He walked over, got his jacket and put it on. "You've done so very well, Erich."

"I believe I have forgiven myself... to some degree." He opened the door.

"I believe you have." Dr. Scherbit extended his hand.

Erich looked at him and they shook, but then Erich felt some overwhelming sense of relief and sadness, so he hugged Dr. Scherbit who hesitated and then hugged him back.

After a moment or two, Dr. Scherbit touched Erich's side and they let loose, "I must say here is history."

"History?" Erich raised his eyebrow.

"I've never, till this day, been hugged by a former Nazi." Dr. Scherbit smiled politely.

"For me then, I say that I've never, till this day, hugged a Jew." Erich turned and they went downstairs, then out to the street.

"Good night," Erich nodded at Dr. Scherbit who stood by a cab.

"Gute nacht," Dr. Scherbit said.

Erich got on the main street and hurriedly went to the river walk. He rushed up stairs, but noticed that there was no German food to smell! He got to the top of the stairs, opened their door and went in. He hung his jacket, "Nikki!"

"Yes, I'm here." Nikki was dressed nicely in brown slacks and a cream-colored shirt that looked sharp with his tweed jacket. He had a brown bag about the size of a small case in hand and a clean jacket for Erich. He walked down the hall and stood next to Erich.

Erich looked at it and then Nikki. His smile seemed to fade, but not entirely.

"So, you've said what you wanted and it's done?"

"Yes, it's done." Erich smiled. "Well, we shall follow up next week."

"It's not all done." They hugged. "We have supper out tonight to celebrate, but first," he held up the sack to Erich.

"Ah," he nodded and handed Erich the jacket.

Erich changed jackets and then they kissed. Once they were downstairs, they made their way along the riverfront for a while until there were very few people. They went to the rail and looked at the river that was deep and moved at a leisurely pace. Erich looked around and they had the place to themselves, "all to ourselves."

"Good," Nikki said.

Erich took another look and then reached into the bag. He pulled out something wrapped in cloth and unwrapped it; there, in his hand, was the Luger that Capt. Ehrlichmann gave him the night that they went out to make arrest. He looked it over and put his thumb on the Totenkopf, removed the clip and emptied the bullets from it and the gun. Then, he drew his hand back and threw them in the river, "SPLASH!" The gun, bullets and clip sunk to the bottom in seconds where they went into the mud and would be covered with silt. He gave the cloth to Nikki and reached back in the bag. This time, he pulled out the knife and took the cloth from it. He studied it and felt bad to throw it away as he had a very personal connection to it.

"I know my love." Nikki looked at the river.

Erich took one last look, drew back and threw it! "SPLASH!" It landed a few meters from the Luger and sank as quickly. He seemed sad by this and looked at Nikki who raised his hand and wiped the tears from his eyes. "I feel…"

"You've lost something close to you?"

"It's a part of me that I've throw away." He put the cloth in the bag and they hugged.

"A very bad part," Nikki took his glasses off, the wire framed ones that he had replaced several times, but had yet to change the style. "And I had something similar on the day we met." He drew back and threw them into the river. They seemed to hold for a moment at the surface, but then they sank and were gone. He took out a black framed pair of glasses and put them on.

"This will take some time to get used to." Erich said. They kissed and he folded the bag as they walked away. "Now, the matter *is* over for us." They got near a trash can and Erich went to put the bag in, but Nikki stopped him!

"Wait!" He grabbed the bag and reached inside. He reached in the bag and pulled an envelope out.

"What is it?" Erich studied it and then worked his fingers along the envelopes seal. The flap opened and there was a single piece of hard paper. He got hold of it and lifted it out, "ah." He smiled wide and looked the paper over; it was the ticket for the opening ceremonies of the Berlin Olympics, 1936. "Shall I throw it in the river?"

"Nein!" Nikki thought to grab it from him, but waited.

"I did not realize this made it back." He studied it and threw the paper bag in the trash.

"It did and we did." Erich tucked the ticket back into the envelope and then put it in his jacket pocket. He took Nikki's hand in his and walked back to Main Street where the rest of their lives waited.

MICHAELSLACHANCE

THE END

About the Author:

Michael Lachance writes fiction in romance, religion, mystery, comedy, historical romance, and fantasy.

Satchel of Secrets An ambush in Afghanistan threw Philip out of a career Army job as a combat medic. An angel offers him an alternative, deliver answers to prayers and learn a new way to serve.

It's Such a Big World and Then, It's Not is a story about Marcel, the station chief of Mulhouse Train Station in eastern France, and Vincent, a US special agent on a mission in France.

Polar opposite personalities, Marcel and Vincent feel an odd sense of longing for something more, but they have their lives. So, they part ways, Marcel to the train station, and Vincent to Zurich for a job with his satchel of secrets.

The tables turn and Marcel is the only one who can stop a TGV train to get Vincent's satchel back to him. Will their personalities clash or will they focus on what's important in life and let their hearts speak instead of their mutual dislike?

The Witch and The Roman is about Germania, nine years after Christ is born, Domitius, a Roman legionary, fled the destruction of his legion to a better fighting position only to find that the barbarian ambush had wiped out his brothers.

Grievously injured, he rushed through the swamps and into the hills where he happened upon a hut and fell into the clutches of a witch.

Will the witch betray him to the barbarian horde for a bounty or flee with him to Rome for a better life?

Three Fools for Spies is a story about three friends who go to Europe and get caught up in a race against the Swiss police, United States secret agents, and Russian secret agents in a dangerous game of international espionage.

The Treaty of Versailles, The Power of Love is a story that evolved out of a trip to Poland and a prison camp. This story is about Erich and his love, Nikki. Prior to World War II, Nikki is arrested and imprisoned at a concentration camp. Erich will not let the man he loves die in the camp. In order to save Nikki, Erich must become what he hates most, a Nazi.

The Camera is about a priest, Father Leauvin, who is sent to the front during World War I & takes pictures of the dead & dying. He is torn between his love for Christ & his love for a woman that he met in Paris.

21 Windows is about a family who buys an old farm house in the country.

They discover a painted over window and a room hidden in the house. After they knock a wall out to get into that room, bad things happen.

The Long Short is about two people who survive a plane crash over the Atlantic. She hates him. He hates her. The island is home to treasure and one of them will get what they want no matter who gets hurt. Will it be her or will it be him?

Currently, Michael's working on *The Adventures of Skipper Pete* (YA - four books in the series), *Butch Roberts and The African Adventure* about a gay man who travels to South Africa in search of fun and adventure, but winds up on the run from a rebel army, and *Germanicus* about the return of Rome to Germania after the slaughter of thousands of Romans nine years after Christ's birth.

To connect with Michael, please visit

Website: www.skipperpete.com

YouTube: Skipper Pete Books & Skipper Pete Travel

Please join him on Goodreads where he blogs about novels, pre-orders, and Q & A.

Michael's books are available as eBooks, hardcover, and paperback at all major book sellers.

www.ingramcontent.com/pod-product-compliance
Lightning Source LLC
Chambersburg PA
CBHW022145170626
46807CB00005B/2088